THE FATHERS

JOHN NIVEN

THE
FATHERS

CANONGATE

First published in Great Britain, the USA and Canada in 2025
by Canongate Books Ltd, 14 High Street, Edinburgh EH1 1TE

Distributed in the USA by Publishers Group West
and in Canada by Publishers Group Canada

canongate.co.uk

1

British Library Cataloguing-in-Publication Data
A catalogue record for this book is available on
request from the British Library

ISBN 978 1 83726 051 5

Typeset in Bembo by Palimpsest Book Production Ltd,
Falkirk, Stirlingshire

Printed and bound by CPI Group (UK) Ltd, Croydon CR0 4YY

The manufacturer's authorised representative in the EU for product
safety is Authorised Rep Compliance Ltd, 71 Lower Baggot Street,
Dublin D02 P593 Ireland (arccompliance.com)

MIX
Paper | Supporting
responsible forestry
FSC® C013604

To Dave and Shona

PART ONE

ONE

'IT'S A BOY!'

Finally, after thirty hours, it was over. And thank God, Dan Chambers thought. He'd begun to wonder just how much pain and abuse the human body, his wife's body, could take. He was trembling, his right hand still tightly clutching Grace's left. One of the guys (Jack? Ally?) had told him the process would be like Orwell's description of warfare: endless stretches of boredom punctuated by terror. Boy, he got that right. They were doing stuff down there, the professionals, talking to each other, conferring. It reminded him of when he'd owned the Porsche, when something went wrong, the mechanics murmuring in hushed tones, hunched over the open bonnet while he stood there, useless, hoping for good news. He didn't dare look down properly, but he stole a glance: a streak of ruby blood on her thigh. Hands in bloodstained surgical gloves taking something out, a dark mop of curls and then the sound of crying filling the room, almost comic in its feebleness. A weak, bleating lamb. Dr MacSween held him up, his hands circling the ribcage, the tiny thing drenched in gore, writhing, the pale yellowish tendril still connecting it to the host. (Dan noted the terminology of the genre they were in: it was horror. Pure horror. It was a John Carpenter film. Cronenberg.)

The baby opened one eye slowly and seemed to look directly at him.

Dan met the eye of his firstborn son and, unexpectedly, he saw the face of his long-dead grandmother staring back. The genes, doing their gene thing, encoding, carrying on. And he promptly did that other thing one of the boys (maybe Bob?) had told him might happen: he burst into tears. He felt Grace tugging his hand and looked down. She was smiling, woozy, so pale as to be translucent. 'A boy . . .' he repeated in wonder. Almost alone among their friends these days, they hadn't wanted to know. The doctor was approaching, coming around his splayed, wrecked wife, holding what looked to be a howling pizza in front of him. 'Would you like to hold him?' Grace nodded weakly and MacSween placed the baby gently on her chest, the face caked in blood and what looked to be dried milk. (Ash the android – *'You have my sympathies.'*) The crying was subsiding into a kind of mewling. Dan reached out and held the little fist resting above Grace's heart, like he was shaking hands.

'Tom,' Grace said.

'Hello, son,' Dan said through tears, trying the word out for the first time. The ordinary miracle – two people go into a room and three come out.

An hour and a blood transfusion later, five-thirty in the morning, and mother and baby (who had been confirmed to be in possession of ten fingers, ten toes, a penis, testes, eyes, tongue and anus) were both sleeping as Dan went bounding down the concrete stairwell, his overcoat and scarf over one arm while he dialled with the other hand.

She answered on the second ring, her voice already, always, anxious. 'Son?'

4

'It's a boy! A wee boy, mum! Thomas. Tom.' They'd long agreed it was a good, solid name. You could always depend on a Tom.

'Aww, son. A boy!' She started crying too, which set Dan off again. They got through it quickly: six pounds, seven ounces, mum had lost a bit of blood, she was fine now, sleeping, they'd be keeping them in until tomorrow. She could come up later today. He'd pick her up at Hillhead tube station. 'Ah'm that pleased for you both. Ah know all what ye've been through.' Then, sitting on a plastic chair in reception, he had the same – although more formal, tearless – conversation with his father-in-law. (His mother-in-law was still asleep.) 'Very good,' old Ed said. 'Congratulations to both of you. We'll see you this afternoon.'

Ah know all what ye've been through.

Five years it had taken them to get here. Five years, six rounds of IVF and just north of thirty grand. They had sat in the consulting rooms of private hospitals and been told that the most common causes of infertility include poor-quality semen, irregular ovulation, blocked or damaged fallopian tubes and endometriosis. Grace was no stranger to the speculum and the stirrups. Dan, the white cubicle and the sample cup. With the polite box containing heavily thumbed copies of *Men Only*, *Penthouse* and *Razzle*. (The fertility industry being one of the last bastions of physical pornography, seemingly unaware that humanity's entire store of depravity now existed on your phone, sleeplessly available.)

The things he'd never told Grace . . .

The first time through the process, he'd worried about a child conceived in such a manner, whose life had begun with the joyless handjob in the windowless boxroom, with his ear

5

cocked for the squeak of the rubber soles of the nurse outside the door. He'd found himself thinking of Gloucester's words about the bastard son Edmund in *King Lear*: *'there was good sport at his making.'* What kind of child would you get without good sport? Might they be joyless? Lacking in, well, spunk? He knew Grace wouldn't be listening to all this rubbish about good sport. They were going to get this thing done. So, off they went, round after round after round. But, in the end, it wasn't any of these things. Not semen nor tubes nor hostile womb nor disease. After lengthy and expensive testing, the experts concluded there was no definitive 'why'. It wasn't his or Grace's fault. It was simply 'unexplained infertility'. Well, Dan had thought, as he frowned into the comically long printout of the bill, page after perforated page concertina-ing towards the floor, my fucking mum could have told you that with a cheery 'ach, son – whit's fur ye willnae go by ye'. Ultimately it seemed that fertility, like Hollywood, was a 'no one knows anything' business. After the failure of round three they'd sat in the tastefully decorated therapist's room on the ground floor of a Victorian building on Park Circus (the teak box with the Kleenex periodically reached for by Grace) and listened to a woman telling them how infertility could have a devastating impact on your emotional and psychological health. How it could lead to stress, grief, depression and a loss of self-confidence and self-esteem. How your relationship with your partner could become strained. How you might avoid socialising with friends or family members with children. Again, 'no shit', Dan thought as he settled her (not inconsiderable) invoice by bank transfer, reflecting on the argument he and Grace had just had, on how stressed out and depressed he was, on how little confidence he had, on how they hadn't seen some of their friends for *months*.

As things had got darker and darker through the failures of round three and four, they had retreated into themselves, recoiling from everyone around them. Gradually Dan had come to hate anyone who managed 'the most natural thing in the world' with complete ease, seemingly without planning, preparation or any thought whatsoever. The smugness with which your friends would announce 'Hey! *We're* pregnant,' made him want to turn and walk away, or just tell them to go and fuck themselves. Dan remembered standing with Jack and Bob at a party, both of them knocking back the whiskies while they bragged about the ease – literally within hours of making the decision to start a family – with which their partners had been knocked up. Dan had stood there, clutching his tumbler of orange juice with a rictus grin on his face, all the while dreaming about taking them both out back and standing on their fucking heads. At that point, on medical advice, he hadn't drunk alcohol for months. (Sperm motility issues.) He ran five miles every morning. He meditated. He took complex cocktails of vitamins and had embraced a caffeine-free, low-salt, no-sugar organic diet. They both did. He'd read that seeds and nuts were helpful for fertility and duly began stacking Grace's lunchbox with them every day. What few (and childless, of course) friends they did see called them 'Lord and Lady White Adder'. And the upshot of all this – of the failure of round four with another negative pregnancy test, being told again that their inability to conceive continued to be 'unexplained' – gradually came to be a near-constant state of rage. There came a point where they could barely walk down Byres Road together, for fear of seeing some toothless missing link pushing a pram, while here they were, with their degrees, their health shakes, their fabulous media careers – childless. Barren. Surely, they were the best, the most deserving parents imaginable! Dan remembered one lunchtime, having just heard what felt like the tenth pregnancy announcement from one of their friends in so many weeks, when he'd gone for a walk to calm down and found himself face-to-face with a pair of chain-smoking, morbidly obese, additive-fuelled halfwits waddling along in their shell suits trailing their *three* children, and no doubt another on the way before he even had time to pop into Peckham's for a green juice to wash down his organic seed trail-mix. He'd had to sprint up University Avenue, lock himself in a toilet in the Boyd Orr building and scream into his rolled-up jacket for two minutes.

And now he'd never have to tell her any of this. Because it was all over. Dan whooped again, his voice echoing up the concrete stairwell. *A boy! A son!*

Having sent WhatsApp messages to the boys and to their pre-agreed immediate circle of friends and family, Dan pulled on his thick overcoat and went out through the pneumatic hiss and crank of the automatic doors into the frosty January morning, the air so fresh and cold that all you could do was sip at it. All around the great hospital, Glasgow lay silent, still sleeping. He looked up into the night sky over Govan and laughed with joy.

'Ye awright there, pal?' a voice said.

Dan turned.

A glowing ember, an orange pinprick of light, emerged from the darkness. The ember moved south, going from somewhere just above Dan's head height to down near his waist as the cigarette went from mouth to hip. And now the smoker stepped into the pool of light cast by the glass doors. The guy was about Dan's age – late forties? – but there the similarities ended. His face was lean and craggy, with a yellowish tint to it. There was a scar across the bridge of the nose. The hair was black streaked with silver, cut short, with a row of curls across the fringe, Roman emperor-style. But it was the eyes that set this face off – small, dark marbles, slightly hooded, flicking from side to side as he approached, their natural setting seeming to be one of vigilance, if not suspicion. He was dressed differently to Dan too. No deference to the biting Scottish winter here. No sweater nor overcoat nor scarf nor boots. Just a thin, navy, long-sleeved top and grey jogging bottoms, terminating in a pair of trainers, gleaming white and box-fresh. He was just over six foot, tall indeed for this part of the world.

'I, yeah,' Dan said, 'I . . . just . . . I'm a dad!'

'Aye?' the man said. 'Boy or girl?' The accent rough, hard.

'A wee boy,' Dan replied, beaming. 'Tom.'

'Magic. Congratulations, wee man. Me an aw.'

'Really?' Dan said. He laughed. This guy seemed so calm. 'Well, congratulations to you too! You got a name yet?'

'Ach, Cayden or Jayden. She's no sure. Still, wi' a wee boy you've only the wan cock tae worry aboot, eh?'

'Er, yeah,' Dan said. He held out his hand. 'Dan.'

'Jada.' He looked at Dan's hand suspiciously for a moment before he brought his own up slowly. His handshake was as brief as possible, as though shaking hands was something shameful, immoral, or just weird. As they shook, Jada noticed the stainless-steel bracelet of Dan's watch, glinting in the milky light. *Rolex, aye. Sub or a GMT. Grand and a half, maybe two, fae Big Malky depending oan the model.* Jada was also performing the calculation he always made upon meeting a stranger: if they had to fight, would he triumph? In this case the answer was yes, comfortably. Not that it was phrased like this in Jada's head, where the solution was more practical: *boot tae the Rab Haws, shove him doon on the floor, put the leather intae his fucking dome.* But this was all automatic. Perfunctory. For Jada detected no threat here. If the stranger had been a woman, then Jada's calculation would have run more along the lines of can I get up this, and how quickly?

'This yer first, Dan?' Jada jerked his head towards the maternity unit behind them, its windows glowing yellow in the chill darkness.

'Yeah. Uh, aye.' Dan, roughing his accent up a little bit. 'You?'

'Away tae fuck. Naw. Been here a few times, know whit Ah mean?' He took a last drag on the cigarette, drawing it down, his face screwing up, the fire disappearing right inside the filter. Dan wondered if he might in fact simply swallow the entire thing. In his turn, Jada was wondering why this ancient wank was only just having his first wean when he should be well into the grandkids by now. Firing blanks? A Jaffa? Bent? Something was up.

'Right. Aye,' Dan said. 'How many kids is this for you?'

'*Pwwwhhh . . .*' Jada blew his cheeks out, as though trying to calculate something monstrous, something requiring a super-computer. A team of experts. 'Five?' Incredibly, he was already producing a pack of cigarettes from the pocket of his jogging bottoms and taking out a fresh one. 'Naw.' He stopped himself, thinking, tapping the end of the cigarette on the box. 'Six.' He thought for a moment longer, seemingly unsure, before saying, more firmly, 'Aye, six.' He lit up, inhaled deeply, then exhaled, the smoke pluming from his nostrils as he added, 'Ma elephant's trunk's fucking radioactive, so it is, pal.'

Aye, the producer of the radioactive semen reflected with

10

some pride, he was pretty fucking far from firing blanks. Jada Hamilton? The Pumpatron? Mr Positions? A fucking *Jaffa?* That'll be shining bright. As was known, all Jada had to do was look at some wee bird and she was up the duff. And, as was known, Jada almost always did more than just look. (No any more though. Watching his son being born a few hours ago, he had decided that was it − he was gaunnae make a go of it wi' Nicola and the wee man.) And his position on male contraceptive responsibility had always been unwavering, arrived at in his early teens, after his dad told him, 'Ye don't wear yer wellies in the fucken bath, wee boy.' Jada employed the time-honoured solution of getting off at Paisley. Although, too often, he had remained on the train − teeth gritted, some girl's ankles cradling his ears − until much, much too close to Glasgow Central. The final destination. So, yes, now and then in the three-plus decades that had followed, Jada had found occasions to doubt his father's wisdom. Well, at least six occasions to be precise.

'Wow,' Dan said, his mind spiralling, trying to calculate the incredible cost, the awesome responsibility of this amount of parenthood.

'That Ah know aboot anyway. Know whit Ah mean! There's a few weans running aboot this town wi' ma coupon.' Jada laughed for the first time, showing Dan a mouthful of ruined dentistry, of mixed nuts and raisins wreathed in blue smoke.

Dan laughed along, wondering if he was joking. 'Wow. That . . . that's amazing. Your wife−'

'No married.'

'Sorry. Ah, girlfriend, she must be used to the whole−'

'Eh? Naw, naw, it's her first.'

'Oh. So you've been−'

'Aye. Six weans. Six maws.'

What could you say to this? 'Wow,' Dan said again, trying to wring fresh wonder out of those three letters as he pondered what would follow this statement in his world. If one of their friends casually revealed – over aperitifs, over dinner – that they had fathered six children by six different women. *My God! Are you insane?* Or *Jesus Christ!* But looking at Jada, in his thin sportswear, tugging happily on his fresh fag, Dan got the impression that the cost of child-rearing wasn't a major concern here.

'Been a busy boy, eh?' Dan said.

'Fuck, aye, pal,' Jada conceded graciously. His hand, heavy with three gold rings, clapped Dan on the shoulder as Jada came close to intone some more heavy wisdom, another nugget that had been gifted to Jada by his father. 'See, Dan, you've goat tae get that dirty water oot yer baws, or it rots yer fucking brain.'

Dan laughed along heartily, keen to assure Jada that he fully understood the pressures of the male libido. A pneumatic hiss behind them, and two women came out of the hospital, what looked to be a mother and daughter, the mum in her forties, the pregnant daughter in her early twenties. Dan smiled politely and nodded.

'Morning, ladies,' Jada said. 'Long tae go?'

'Another month!' the mother said, nodding towards the girl. 'Her first. Taking forever, so it is.'

'Aye. Been there. Well, best o' luck tae her. Cheerio!'

Jada waved airily with his fag as they walked off. Dan continued smiling politely. They'd nearly gone fully private but, him and Grace, they were socialists at heart, so a private room here, at the Queen Elizabeth on Glasgow's Southside, had been the compromise. And it was good. Fine. All human life was here.

'Cheerio!' the woman said.

As they walked off Jada stared after them with some hunger. 'Oof,' he said, lowering his voice a notch and nudging Dan in the ribs. 'Fuck sake. The erse oan the wee yin? Two boiled eggs in a fucking hanky. Ye'd ride that until the fucking wean pushed ye oot, eh?'

Dan laughed, weakly this time, it had to be said. 'Ah, yeah . . .'

Perhaps sensing his reticence here, Jada went on with, 'You mair o' a tit man than an erse man, then, Dan?'

'Umm . . .' Not that he often encountered this question these days, but Dan had always struggled with it. It seemed to him that the ability to parcel up the female anatomy into the pieces that pleased you most was one notch away from the thinking of the average serial killer. But he sensed this argument wouldn't fly with his current interlocutor. So he just said, 'Well, uh, you know, Jada, I . . .'

Jada simply made a hawking sound in his throat and launched an enormous mouthful of phlegm into the bushes beside them. 'Right!' he said brightly. 'Ah better get back up there. Cannae be standing aboot here aw day, clawing ma fucking beads. Nice to meet ye, Dan. See ye roon, pal.'

Another clap on the back, and Jada strode off into the warmth and light of the hospital, shoulders pumping. The walk of Jada Hamilton: as if he was asking the very world if it wanted some. To come ahead. Square go. Absolutely extraordinary. *Clawing ma fucking beads?* Jada had long disappeared into the lift across the reception area by the time Dan had worked out that this most likely meant 'scratching my balls'. Incredible. He got his phone out and opened the Notes app. Choice dialogue, to be sure, although it was unlikely any of it could ever make its way onto a family show like Dan's. Still, it would be worth sharing with Jack, who collected ned patter in the same way some people collected wine or art. Just as he began typing, the pinging and vibrating began as text message after text message began arriving, all the congratulations. Then one from Grace: *Can you pop back up? Need some stuff from home x.*

Dan contented himself with recording just the one Jadaism. Which was how he found himself standing outside the Queen Elizabeth Hospital on a frozen January morning tapping the legend 'ye'd ride that until the fucking wean pushed ye oot' into his phone.

Grace lay on her side on the very edge of the bed. She reached out and traced a finger up and down the wall of the cot. Behind the Perspex, beneath her finger, their son slept. Exhausted, woozy from the drugs, the gas and air, she felt herself drifting in and out of sleep, then snapping awake she would feel the shiver of joy that this was real, that it had happened and there he was – all six pounds and five ounces of him.

The things she had never told Dan . . .

One night, very early on, when they were still trying to get pregnant 'naturally', but it seemed to be taking some time, she'd thought about writing 'ABANDON HOPE ALL YE WHO ENTER HERE' on a Post-It note and sticking it on her belly just above the line of her pubic hair. She thought it would make Dan laugh. Ease the pressure and unease they were both beginning to feel back then. (All the literature she was reading was telling her that 'pressure and unease' were not helping the situation.) But she didn't do it. And that had been back when they were still able to laugh about fertility-related things . . .

Fast-forward a few months, and during the beginning of the IVF nightmare, she'd been told that although, yes, one of her

14

fallopian tubes was twisted, they were still able to get dye through it. Which meant that, technically, it should have been possible for her to get pregnant naturally. *My fault, then,* she thought. The first time through they had a setback right away as, thanks to the hormone injections she'd been having to stimulate egg development, they'd collected twenty-one eggs: a potential sign of ovarian hyperstimulation syndrome which can be life-threatening. And then the fertilisation rate was low, yielding just three viable embryos. Which all failed. *I failed,* she thought.

During the next round, the decision was made to go with intracytoplasmic sperm injection to make sure they had a higher fertilisation rate. This did provide more embryos, but none of these succeeded either. Around this time one or other consultant explained to her that the body's response to IVF drugs was a 'very tricky thing' to predict and they were very much adopting a 'suck it and see' approach. Somewhere around the third failed attempt − her head swimming now in acronyms − she'd got the phone call from her cousin Megan to tell her that she was pregnant. They'd just had the twelve-week scan and they were letting everyone know. Grace congratulated her, hung up the phone, and thought about driving over there and firebombing their house. In the wake of the failure of round four there had been Dan's mum's attempt to make her feel better by saying, 'Ach hen, I know it'll happen if you want it enough.' Ah! Grace had thought − as she restrained herself from punching the stupid old boot in the face with her bunched car keys − so that's my problem! I just don't *want* it enough. And then there were all the nuts and bloody seeds Dan insisted on putting in her lunchbox every day. She *hated* fucking seeds. So, somewhere around the fifth failed attempt, Grace started coming up with her own 'suck it and see' ideas. Ideas involving a high bridge. Or the sea. A length of rope. A toaster and a bathtub. A fistful of pills and a razor blade. She couldn't escape the thought that, due to some biological failing on her part, Dan was doomed to be childless too. Well, she reasoned, if I'm not around, he might eventually be able to meet someone he can have a baby with. Two things stopped her. Firstly, and most powerfully, the thought of Dan having to cope with her suicide on top of everything else and, secondly and more faintly, her childhood and the tug of Catholicism that never quite leaves you. While Grace had not been to chapel in many, many years, there it lurked, hardwired somewhere inside her, the idea that life was God's to take and God's alone. She would never have articulated this sentiment among their crowd of university educated, met lib elite, West End pals, but there it was nonetheless. *Give me the child until seven* and all that guff.

Suicide was off the menu. So she laboured on. And then, just when all hope really had been abandoned, there had been the outcome of attempt number six: his tiny nostrils flaring now as he slept soundly across from her. And here was Dan, coming back in the door, beaming. She smiled back at him woozily.

TWO

'GET IT ROUND YE THEN, YA FUCKEN WANK! COME
AHEAD!'

Jada angrily stabbed the button to end the call. 'Fuck sake!'
No even in the door five minutes and hassle already. Some
folk. I mean . . . ye buy an ounce o' grass aff some bloke ye
barely know in a car park and it turns out tae be just floor
scrapings that widnae get ye aff yer nut if ye smoked fifteen
ounces o' it, and then whit? Yer fucking *surprised*? Whit did the
wank expect? And how the fuck had he got Jada's number?
This was the problem wi' swindling folk, Jada reflected, not for
the first time, as he blocked the guy's number. Sometimes they
didn't just wear it and go away. Chalk it up tae experience an
aw that. Naw. Sometimes they kept coming back, trying to get
a fucking refund. Or store credit or something. Whit the fuck
did they think this was? Fucking Argos? Jada had heard an
expression once, some salesman in the pub, talking about how
ye don't sell a guy one car and rip him off, ye sell him five
cars over his lifetime. Good service. Repeat business. Aye, right.
Safe to say Jada didn't get too much of that.

Fucking starving, but.

He walked from the lounge through to the kitchen – a
journey of just five paces that involved stepping over an

overflowing carrier bag of empty lager cans, a plate heaped with the remains of a Chinese takeaway, the corpse of a busted Xbox and the sleeping form of Bishop, his greyhound – and opened the fridge. Immediately, as the smell assaulted his nostrils, Jada conceded that this had been a mistake. There will have been refrigerators in human history that have contained a sadder inventory – the serial killer's keepsakes, the redneck's stillbirth, perhaps – but the list would be short. The main source of the smell seemed to be a crumpled tinfoil container of three-day-old chicken tikka. This represented the most edible of Jada's victuals. A piece of cheese of indeterminate origin lay there on the shelf in the doorframe, its edges a grey-green warning colour. And he didn't need to pick up the half-empty litre of milk next to the cheese to know that its consistency was milkshake-on-the-road-to-cottage-cheese. On a wild impulse of irrational hope – and holding his nose now – he tugged open the salad crisper. A head of lettuce that Nicola must have bought lay there, its leaves completely white, the chlorophyll they once contained now forming the green puddle gluing it to the floor of its plastic tomb. 'FUCK SAKE, MAN!' Jada yelled to the very walls. He stood there in the narrow galley kitchen, hands on hips, nostrils flaring, and balefully surveyed his property, as though the flat itself might have been responsible for his foodless plight, rather than the fact that Nicola had been in hospital for two weeks now, mad wi' the fucking pre-eclampsia an aw that. He could see through the living room and down the short hallway to the two bedrooms at the end, the bathroom halfway along. A little over 800 square feet of living space up here on the tenth floor of the brutalist 60s block in Partick. The flat was so small that Jada could just about open the front door with an angled trainer dangled off

18

the end of the couch. The council paid the (hugely inflated) rent directly to the landlord, who then paid a goodly chunk of it directly back to Jada. It was an arrangement that had held for the last eighteen months, not long after Jada moved in and invited Mr Ravinder the landlord to his housewarming party, where he proceeded to give him: a) three Es (the decent stuff, not the dog-worming tablets Jada sometimes had one of his boys knock out downtown on the weekends) and b) a turn at wee Senga. Senga got a good video of the action on her phone, which she then, as arranged, forwarded to Jada, who then forwarded it to Mr Ravinder, along with a screengrab of Senga's (faked) birth certificate, a cursory glance at which showed you that her sixteenth birthday was still a few months in the future. When it came to negotiating Jada firmly believed in the philosophy that a smile alone would only get you so far. A smile backed up with the very real threat of serious time on the sex offenders' wing at Barlinnie was a beast of a different order. *Fuck it*, Jada reasoned, slamming the fridge door shut. He could grab a bag of crisps or something down the Flaps, where he was due to meet the Shite and his pal from the airport. It could be big, this thing.

If the Shite was even half right, it could be big. A deep trough. Maybe a long runner. And Jada wanted that, God did he want that. He worked hard. Never stopped. But that was the thing with swindling and cheating and thieving – it was time-consuming. And he was no spring chicken any more. Getting towards time to kick back and take his foot off the gas a wee bit. Enjoy life. Enjoy . . . what exactly? The horses and the dugs? Mmm. Maybe. But if he was being completely honest, he'd have to confess that the horses and the dugs were part of the reason he was constantly having to swindle, cheat and thieve. Maybe take up something new. Fishing or some fucking thing. What did ye see aw these auld, retired spunkers doing on telly? Going for walks and pish like that? Naw, face it, Jada was a grafter at heart. Needed the action. As he prepared to leave the flat, just as he was about to pull the front door open, the doorbell rang. Jada opened it to see Big Katrina from down the hall standing there in her pyjamas and dressing gown.

'Hiya!' she said brightly. 'Any news?'

'Wee boy,' Jada said. 'Both fine, so they are.'

'Aww, magic,' said Katrina. 'When are they getting hame?'

'Couple o' days, hen,' Jada said. 'The pre-eclampsia an aw that.'

'Aye. Ah wiz the same masel wi' Hayden.'

Katrina leaned on the open doorframe and pushed a strand of her brown hair behind her ear. 'So,' she said, 'whit ye up tae, then?'

Jada thought for a moment. He had always been culpably weak in such matters. And he had promised himself a new beginning with Nicola and the wee man. He had to be strong. 'Come on, then,' he said, glancing down the passageway as he ushered Katrina inside and pointed her towards the bedroom. Yes, he would remain true to this morning's solemn vow. Gobbles only.

Twenty minutes later, and a cheer went up as Jada shouldered his way into the saloon bar of the Flaps.

The blighted pub lay on the hinterland between Partick and Whiteinch and was called Fanny Bryce's. The etymology had gone something like: Fanny Bryce's = Fanny's = the Fanny, and then finally, possibly via things like the Nan and the Fud, the Flaps. Jada's warm welcome was not unusual, as the regulars

20

often had cause to celebrate one or other of his triumphs: victory in a brawl in the street outside, the liberation of a box of goods – socks, scarves or handbags – intended for the shelves of Frasers. Perhaps an early release date.

But there was an even warmer edge to his welcome today from the half-dozen regulars whose lifestyles meant they were free to fortify themselves with a pre-lunch pint.

'BIG MAN! A wee boy, is it?' said Wee Sandy the barman.

'Eh?' Jada said. 'How the fuck did ye—'

'Fat Rab's wee niece's pal's maw is a trainee nurse up the Queen Elizabeth.' With a nod Sandy indicated the ruin of Fat Rab, slumped by the pumps. 'She knows your Nicola fae school.' *Your Nicola.* In Jada's world, as in the world of the Minsk oligarch or the Beverly Hills super-producer, it was in no way unusual or worthy of comment that a man in his late forties should have a nineteen-year-old girlfriend.

'Aye?' Jada said. 'She's right enough. Wee boy!'

'Aww, congratulations, big man.' Sandy extended a hand over the bar, Jada shook it and all the others proffered. Now he saw the Shite, up in the corner, with Billy Campbell.

Jada raised a finger to the Shite in give-me-a-minute fashion. 'Gie everyone wan oan me, Sandy.' A flicker of apprehension crossed Sandy's face. It was caught and powerfully stared down by Jada, his eyes boring into Sandy's, telling him that this was neither the time nor the place to be questioning the extent of Jada's current bar tab. Sandy felt he was being unfairly maligned here, as surely the time (just as Jada was ordering a large round) and the place (the very pub he owed money to) were both fair game.

Ach, no worth the bother, Sandy thought as he started pulling the pints and sticking the short glasses under the amber bulb of the whisky optic to pour the doubles that were instantly being ordered. *Leave it tae Big Sandy.* Big Sandy: Sandy's larger, elder brother, who played bad cop around here.

Jada took his pint and three of the whiskies – daintily, thumb, index and middle finger linking the glasses, pinkie raised – and made his way to the far corner of the pub, where the Shite was awaiting the approach of his benefactor and sometime employer. 'Congratulations, sir,' the Shite said, taking one of the whiskies as Jada handed the other to Billy. They clinked glasses and knocked them back. Jada took a moment while the hard burn of the 100 Pipers (fifty quid a case) made its way through his larynx to appreciate the Shite's face anew. Certainly, God had created uglier faces – a couple of them in Jada's peripheral vision even now – but it was doubtful He'd fashioned many more devious, more dissembling, more *bent* than the one Jada now contemplated. He always looked like he was doing some calculation, doing some criminal mental arithmetic.

'Nice tae have a wee boy, eh?' Billy said.

'Aye. He's a wee outlaw an aw. The eyes, man.'

'Another bloody mouth tae feed, eh?' The Shite laughed.

'Aye,' Jada sighed ruefully, shaking his head. 'Ach, well. White man's burden, eh, boys?' In truth, as Jada's involvement in feeding any of the six children he'd fathered so far was minimal, to say the least, this was at best a performative statement. But the moment provided him with a graceful segue into the business at hand. Lowering his voice, Jada said, 'Speaking o' mouths tae feed, whit ye saying then, Billy?' Billy Campbell was the big brother of their old pal Simple Tam Campbell (RIP). Billy was a few years older than Jada, in his early fifties, overweight and over-fond of the bevvy and the pies. His gut dangled over his belt, his shirt pulled taut, his tie riding halfway up his belly. What Billy was saying was this . . .

'Right, so, after many years of diligent service at Prestwick Airport I will be receiving a promotion. I am going to be Deputy Head of Security in charge of the International Freight Transit Area.'

'Congratulations. Whit does that mean, like?'

'Goods going from country to country. What it really means, but, is an open invitation to *pruch*.' (*Scots vernacular (noun): goods or benefits received at work in addition to pay.*)

'Good for you,' Jada said, wishing the fat bastard would get to the point.

The Shite sensed Jada's restlessness. 'Go on, tell him, Billy,' he said.

'Aye. So here's the thing. Ah need the right partner, someone who can get the stuff away and get it fenced.'

'Whit kind o' stuff are we talking about?' Jada asked, his voice just above a whisper as he cast a quick glance around them.

'Fuck. Everything you can think o' comes through there,' Billy was saying. 'Tellies, video games, fridges – you name it. But the easiest gear tae get away is aw the military stuff.'

'Military stuff?' Jada said. 'Whit, like fucking rockets? Fuck dae ye think Ah am, Billy? Fucking arms dealer?'

'Naw, naw. Ah mean shite like tents, boots, flasks and water bottles, canteens, jumpers, aw that kinda stuff. See wi' aw that pish going oan in Ukraine the now there's hunners o' that shite passing through. British stuff, American stuff. French. These massive big transport planes come in – fucking Hercules, Antonovs – aw packed tae the gunnels. They open the tailgates and it's like yon warehouse in *Raiders o' the Lost* fucking *Ark*,

23

man. And 'cause it's aw government, right, it's aw over the place. Paperwork's aw tae fuck half the time, no fucker knows if it's meant tae be fifty crates o' this or eighty crates o' that. And no one really gives a fuck, 'cause it's aw the taxpayers' money, right? Muggins here. Us lot.' Jada and the Shite both nodded solemnly, even sorrowfully, at this, despite neither of them having knowingly paid tax in their entire lives.

'Whit aboot cameras? CCTV?' Jada said.

'Fuck all. They unload it aw way out on the runways, straight intae the vans and then intae hangars and then oantae wherever. Pilots just stay in the cockpit huving a wee nap. Ah just need a couple of boys tae help wi' the unloading.'

'Ye got a couple of boys in mind out there?'

'Big Boab and Chas. Ah'll need tae sort them out obviously.'

'Aye. Course.'

'So Ah'm thinking,' Billy leaned in even closer, 'Ah get Boab and Chas tae load up one o' oor vans wi' a few crates o' whatever looks good. They drive it aff site, Ah'm the Gatekeeper, Ah wave them through, and they meet you wherever. Gordon' – he indicated the Shite, who enjoyed the rare pleasure of hearing his given Christian name being used – 'says ye know a guy who could, y'know . . .'

'Aye. Mibbe,' Jada said. 'Specialised area an aw that, but, aye, Ah might . . .' He was thinking about Dom's garage over in Royston. Bit o' a drive fae the airport, but big enough. Have tae backhander him an aw, mind. And then onto the Gypsy down in Carlisle. He was bound to know somebody that knew somebody that was intae this kind o' shite. 'But remember, Billy,' Jada leaned in. 'See wi', uh, specialised kit like that, it's a buyers' market. Ah'll probably be lucky tae get something like thirty pence oan the pound.'

'Aye, course, course,' Billy nodded, way out of his depth here. 'End o' the day, it's aw profit, eh, boys? Victimless fucking crime an aw.' Naturally, Billy fully expected to be cheated by Jada, just as Jada would be cheated by the Gypsy, just as these two bams Big Boab and Chas would undoubtedly be cheated by Billy. 'Got tae be done right, Jada,' Billy said, with all the gravity he could muster. 'This is ma retirement we're talking about here.'

Jada took a pull on his pint. 'When ye looking tae retire?'

'Ma fifty-fifth. Get oot early. Play a bit o' golf. Get over tae Spain in the winter an aw that. Only four years away . . .'

'Is that right?' Jada said. 'Ah never thought ye were even fifty yet, big man.' Fat bastard. The state o' him. Be lucky if he made it another four years. 'Here's the fucking script, then. It's like that joke – the auld bull and the young bull looking at aw the cows.'

The Shite and Billy looked at him blankly.

'Ye no know that one? Right, there's an auld bull and a young bull, and they're looking at a field o' cows. And the young bull says, "Ho, auld yin, let's fucking run doon and pump wan o' those cows."'

'Pumping a cow,' the Shite chuckled.

'And the auld bull says, "Naw, wee man. Let's *walk* doon there and pump the fucking lot o' them."' Jada drained his pint with a flourish. And found himself looking into a pair of blank faces. Fuck sake. Dense bastards.

'It's a fucking, whit dae ye call it . . .' Jada was reaching for 'metaphor' or 'analogy', but these terms were unavailable to him. 'Whit Ah'm saying is, we milk this. Take our time.'

Billy's pisshole eyes glimmered. 'Aye. Makes sense, Jada.'

'Ah telt ye, Billy,' the Shite said. 'Telt ye the big man wid huv a plan.' Feeling triumphant, Jada signalled to Sandy for a celebratory round.

'Aye, thing is, but . . .' Billy said. Here we fucking go, Jada thought. 'If Ah bring ye in oan this, Jada, Ah want a guaranteed minimum. Ah don't want tae hear any shite like "oh, we couldnae shift it this month." Ah get two grand a month, minimum, every month, whatever happens at your end.' Billy folded his arms.

They sat for a moment, the Shite looking back and forth between them like a tennis umpire. Jada considered. Did Billy know anyone serious? Obviously, he fucking didn't. If he knew anyone serious, then he wouldn't be sitting here talking to Jada and the Shite. So it was easy enough, really. If anything went tits up, and Billy came the hardman, Jada would just have to kick fuck out of the fat bastard. Jada extended his hand. 'Fair enough, Billy. Let me make some enquiries, then.' He knew the Gypsy was up here next week on some bit of business. Have a chat then. See what he thought. They shook hands as Sandy arrived with three fresh pints on a tray. 'Here you go, boys.'

'Cheers, Sandy,' Jada said. 'Bring us three double whiskies an aw. And huv wan yersel. Stick it oan ma tab, eh?'

This fucking . . .

'Aye. Thanks, Jada,' Sandy said. 'Cheers.'

'So when dae ye start this new job?' Jada asked, turning back to Billy.

'No for a bit. The summer.'

'Awright, then. Gives me time tae huv a coupla wee conversations with ma . . . connections' – aye, that sounded good – 'and I'll let ye know if it's a goer.'

'Fair enough,' Billy said.

Jada raised his glass. 'Boys? Cheers!' They all drank. Then Jada remembered something. 'FUCK SAKE!'

'Something wrang?' the Shite asked.

'Ach, naw,' Jada said. 'Jist something Ah meant tae dae.'

Clean T-shirt, comfy jammie bottoms, Lucozade.

Ach, fuck it. She could manage until the night.

THREE

Dan drove home (*clean nightie, underwear, hairbrush, cleanser and moisturiser, fruit, laptop*), enjoying the bright winter day and the exhilaration of *I have a son!* He pointed the Tesla down the dip and slid into the Clyde Tunnel, the near-total silence replaced with the sizzle of tyres rebounding off the tiled walls of the tube. As ever, the thought of the millions of tons of river water all around him. He felt empathy with his just-born son down here, a bubble inside a tube surrounded by fluid.

He came up out of the tunnel, past the Arnold Clark garage, its sign glowing banana-yellow, and made a right, heading east along Dumbarton Road, the traffic beginning to thicken now as he approached the West End.

I have a son! This morning he even found the interminable wait at the traffic lights on the corner of Dumbarton Road and Byres Road pleasurable. He was accepting of the − internationally recognised − fact that Glasgow traffic lights spent three times longer on red than any other traffic lights in the world. *Not a problem*, Dan thought to himself as the crimson ball fell into the amber one and then into the green one. He turned left and headed up Byres Road into Hillhead, the traffic heavier as he came towards University Avenue, glancing over to his left, peering into the Formica interior of the University

Café, unchanged since he was a student here thirty-odd years ago, one of those places he never went to any more, but that he liked to make sure was still there.

Each round of IVF had meant three attempts, three embryos. After eight misses, the aftermath of each one escalating in heartbreak and despair, it had been on the final attempt of the final round that they'd gone into the consulting room for what they'd agreed would be the final time. They held hands tightly, the adoption paperwork already in Grace's bag, ready to begin that afternoon. But, as soon as they walked in and Dan noticed that Dr Goldberg was fighting the hint of a smile, he'd known – *known* – before they sat down that they were about to hear different news. 'Well,' Goldberg said. 'Congratulations. You're pregnant.' Grace burst into tears. Dan felt soaring, joyous relief. For about three seconds.

Then the Terror crept in.

And it didn't just creep in. It *flooded* in. It moved in. It unpacked its things and put its feet up and made it very clear it was going to be here for the duration. The Terror was of the fragility of the thing Grace was carrying inside her. To Dan – a cautious man by nature – it wasn't a sac with a thick membrane containing a growing embryo protected by fluid. No, it was more like she was incubating a crystal bauble more delicate than any Christmas tree decoration. A gossamer-thin bauble that might be shattered by a strong breeze. A priceless china vase whose walls were thinner than a credit card. Dan feared Grace dealing with stairs of any kind. He feared her sitting down too heavily. Getting up abruptly. Sneezing too violently. Moving too fast. Walking to the shops. Driving. Eating too quickly. Laughing too hard. Spicy food. On one occasion he had to be restrained from calling an ambulance after Grace had unleashed a particularly enthusiastic fart that he felt must surely have dislodged the foetus. Well, after a couple of months of this he found himself back in the ground-floor room on Park Circus, alone this time. The therapist posited that his behaviour might be due to a loss of control: his part in this was over and Grace had to carry the baby alone. It seemed to her that 'control is very important to you in your work' but he had to accept that some things lay beyond it. Sensible precautions were fine (he knew that – he'd already spent thousands turning the house into what basically resembled a huge bouncy castle), but all the worrying in the world could not affect what was, or was not, going to happen in his wife's womb. *I get that*, he thought, as he gritted the path and the front steps just one more time, as he practised the drive to A&E again, and as he supervised the carpenter drilling holes for yet another handrail in the bathroom.

At University Avenue he turned left onto Highburgh Road, followed it round as it became Hyndland Road, and then he was turning right into their crescent. The streetlamps glowed, sixteen white orbs on cast-iron posts, two of them standing sentinel on either side of the front steps of each of the eight wide Victorian townhouses that formed his street.

Back in the early 90s, when Dan first came to Glasgow as a student, most of these four-storey houses – formerly owned by the magnates, by Glasgow's Barons of sugar, tobacco, cotton and slaves – had long been divided into flats and then sub-divided further into bedsits. The only single-occupancy home had been the one at the end of the terrace belonging to Frazer and his wife, who had been there since the late 60s. The doorbell matrixes of all the other houses resembled the grids of Soviet-era telephone exchanges. There were cheese plants and lava lamps in the windows and skew-whiff Blu Tacked posters on the walls: *Betty Blue*, *Meat Is Murder*, *Stop the Poll Tax*. Gradually, over the last twenty years or so, the reverse process had taken place, and the buildings had slowly returned to their originally intended use: as huge-scale family homes for Glasgow's new magnates, the Barons of Arts, Entertainment and the Media. They had an STV newsreader, a children's TV star, a senior BBC power couple, an actor and two comedians. (No footballers. An estate agent had explained to Dan that they increasingly tended to shun older properties, preferring to build their temples of steel and marble from scratch.) Frazer lived on in the end house, a teetering nonagenarian widower now, but still a formidable presence who was all too aware of his next-door neighbour's (one of the comedians) designs on buying his property the minute he was cold in the ground and knocking through to create a superhome. It gave the good doctor some comfort to know what everyone on the street knew (because he never missed an opportunity to tell them) – that he'd paid just £2,800 for the house back in 1968.

Dan managed to snag a parking space almost in front of the house, hopped out (and it *was* a hop this morning – *I have a son*.) and fairly bounded up the four broad steps to the front door of the house that *McCallister* built. He punched the keycode in – opening the door and disabling the alarm at the same time – and stepped out of the cold and into a controlled perma-temperature of 20 degrees. He stood on the polished herringbone oak floor that covered an entrance hall the length and width of approximately half a tennis court. The *Close Encounters* mothership of the chandelier loomed somewhere above his head. Throwing his overcoat on the rack in the corner and singing out, 'Home again, home again, yakkity-yak,' he

31

resumed bounding, heading upstairs to fetch Grace's things. In the bedroom – vast, three floor-to-ceiling windows overlooking the communal gardens – as he packed the holdall, he saw his phone, which he'd turned back on and thrown on the bed, was lighting up as many, many messages of congratulations came in from friends and family, the closest of whom knew exactly what they'd been through to get to this morning. A few missed calls from the very closest friends and then . . .

No fewer than *four* missed calls from Gregor. Then two missed calls from Debbie, who ran Cheviot, Dan's production company, who made *McCallister*. Oh yeah, Gregor had read the script all right. No doubt about that. Dan really didn't want the aggravation today, but some unreturned calls had a habit of niggling and eating away at the mind worse than if you just dealt with them. It'd be easier to deal with Debbie on no sleep than with Gregor.

Two rings, then: 'Dan! Oh, congratulations. A boy! I'm so happy for you.'

'Aye, thanks, Deb.'

'How long was the–'

'Och, thirty hours? A wee bit more.'

'Oh my God. Grace must be shattered.'

'Not half. Hey, look, I haven't got long, but I saw a few missed calls from Gregor.'

'Oh God. Look, I'm so sorry, but, it's – ha ha, you know, Gregor got the new scripts and–'

'About what I imagined?'

'Yep. Possibly worse. I didn't want to bother you with it today, Dan. But–'

'I know. Look, tell him . . . tell him about the baby, OK? Even he should get that. Tell him about the baby and that, ah,

32

I'll call him later? Grace's mum and dad are going to be here soon so I'll have a bit more time, all right?'

'Sure. And sorry again. He's such a fucking . . .'

'Actor?'

'Aye. Something beginning with "A", right enough. Thanks, Dan. And congratulations again. I'm so happy for both of you. Give my love to Grace.'

'Will do. Bye, Debs.'

Gregor. Even the birth of someone's kid . . .

Fucking *McCallister*. Where to begin? A long, long time ago, in a Glasgow far, far away, an aspiring writer fresh out of university called Dan Chambers pitched BBC Scotland an idea for a show about a rough-hewn, dry, laconic Glasgow detective who found himself put out to pasture, forced into semi-retirement in the Highlands, where his life of malt whiskies, beach walks and comic interactions with the native sheep-shaggers was punctuated by a murder rate that would have stunned war-torn Africa, or 70s New York, let alone the picturesque stretch of Sutherland coastline where the show would take place. '*Morse* meets *Local Hero* meets *Taggart*' was the one-liner. Unusually, for Dan was young and green, they commissioned a pilot script. And then the pilot episode. The stage star Gregor Wappler, fresh from his triumph in *Coriolanus* at the Old Vic, was cast as the titular Detective Sergeant Colin McCallister. Even more incredibly, the BBC *liked* the pilot and green-lit the first season. More unlikely still, the public liked McCallister. Liked him? They loved the hard-bitten shit with a heart of gold. And now here they were a little over two decades later – one of Scotland's most beloved and longest-running shows.

Twenty-two years on, and Dan was still writing *McCallister*, and Gregor – nearly sixty now – was still playing McCallister. They both owed the laconic old tosspot a lot – for he had made them both rich – and they both hated him for taking them away from their true callings: all the novels and films Dan had never written. All the Hamlets and Macbeths Gregor hadn't played over the years. All the Lears and Willy Lomans he wasn't playing now. In recent years, Dan had stepped back a little from the day-to-day. He was showrunner and executive producer. A roomful of bright young twenty- and thirty-somethings did most of the actual writing, with Dan weighing in on big story calls and getting wheeled out when there was a crisis. Usually involving Gregor. Usually happening when there was a major event, like when the scripts for a new season were delivered. As the scripts for season 22 had just been. Where there was indeed a major event.

The death of McCallister. And the end of *McCallister*.

It was time. It was way past time. Christ, Dan didn't need the money any more. And he was mindful of the fact that fifty was looming on the horizon and, lurking behind that milestone age, all those unwritten novels and films. From time to time, Dan would find himself settling down in the book-lined study he'd built for himself in the basement, putting his feet up on the antique, green-leather-inlaid partner's desk he'd bought at auction, settling back in the creaking wooden captain's chair, and . . . just staring at the blinking cursor on the screen of his monitor for a long, long time, where 'UNTITLED' by Dan Chambers lay waiting for him. It was *McCallister*'s fault, of course. As long as *McCallister* existed, Dan would never write a word of anything else. So *McCallister* would have to go. And now, with the birth of his son, it all felt doubly right, the death of his albatross coinciding with the arrival of new life. Physical birth prefiguring the creative rebirth Dan would soon find himself enjoying. Not that Gregor would see it like that. He should – God knows he'd complained about it often enough – but actors were funny creatures. And, unlike Dan, Gregor *did* need the money. Gregor with his four divorces, three houses and his eight children, five of whom were still at school. Hence those four missed calls, Gregor having undoubtedly just read the final episode this morning. But supporting the extended family of a priapic madman was no reason to keep doing something. They'd start shooting the ten episodes in the summer. Wrap in the early autumn. Into post and editing, and then the first episode would drop in the spring. Ten weeks later, it would be done. A couple of years from now *McCallister* would be part of his past, and the unwritten novel – and his son – would be his future.

He finished the packing.

FOUR

'Is that aw the fucking thanks Ah get? Fuck sake!'

On the public ward, with the curtain pulled around the bed, Jada: indignant. The presents he'd hastily grabbed at the wee shop down in the foyer of the hospital – the box of Dairy Milk, the half-litre bottle of Irn-Bru and the latest issue of Nicola's mum's beloved *Time For You!* magazine (*'I married my daughter's rapist!'*) – all lay unloved on the bed.

'Ah telt ye, Jada, Ah need ma claithes! Ma toothbrush. No aw this stuff.' Wee Nicola folded her arms huffily across her chest.

'Ah said Ah'm sorry! Fuck sake! Ah hud business tae sort!'

'Aye,' she snorted. 'Some business. Ye reek like a bloody brewery, so ye dae.'

'Don't go oan at him, hen,' Nicola's mother, Wee Kirsty, interjected, coming to Jada's defence. 'Ah'll pop along the road tae the shops, get ye a toothbrush and whatnot.'

'He was meant tae get them, maw!'

'Aye, well.'

'Ye sure, Kirsty?' Jada said.

'No take me long. You two sit and have a wee catch-up.'

'Cheers, doll,' Jada said, eagerly sliding onto the seat Kirsty was vacating.

Whit a fucking midden, Jada found he had time to reflect as he cast a glance over Kirsty as she bent down to collect her bag and coat. The giant, shapeless ruin of the arse in the grey joggy bottoms, like ten litres of porridge poured into a binbag, an arse that Jada had, in fact, pounded back in the mists of time, back when Nicola was just a wee girl. Aye, Kirsty wasn't looking great for thirty-five. *Check the maw before ye go riding the daughter.* Another aphorism his father had given him. He tuned out Nicola's nagging (even now she was saying something like 'honestly, Jada, it's like yer no even listening tae me half the time') and looked at the wee man – wee Jayden, or Cayden – fast asleep. The boy was Jada's third – hopefully final – son and he found himself pondering briefly on Jayden's two elder brothers. His eldest son, Lee, would be, what? About twenty-four or twenty-five now? His whereabouts were uncertain. Last Jada heard he was working abroad, as a roofer in Portugal or some place. But that was a while back. The next in line, Rory, was twenty-one soon and his whereabouts for the next twelve to sixteen months were very certain: HMP Barlinnie. Two of the girls had stayed closer to home: Britney and Taylor both just a couple of streets away, both with weans o' their own now, and wee Britney about tae become a grandmother at the age of thirty! Taylor, his youngest daughter, was still living at home wi' her maw, with what's-her-name. Whit was Taylor's maw's fucking name again? Fuck sake. The memory oan him.

His eldest daughter, Rhiannon, well, they weren't talking any more. Her choice. Fuck it. Anyway, wee man, Jada thought, gazing at Jayden/Cayden, it's going to be different this time. Make a go of it wi' yer wee maw here. No like aw they other times. And this time, he really believed he could do it. Look at the episode with that Katrina earlier. Or a couple of weeks back, for instance, just before Nicola went into hospital. He'd popped out to the PriceBeaster to get her some of that ice-cream she liked. He'd forsaken the Flaps and stuck his head into the Nightmare for a swift pint on his way there and, what with one thing and another, it wound up being three or four pints and Big Maggie Brennan was in there. Tall, skinny bird wi' massive paps. Fucking pair o' Spacehoppers strapped tae a pogo stick. She'd always had a thing for Jada. Anyway, Hammy Reid had pushed in front of Jada at the bar, so Jada had told him to get to fuck, and Hammy turned round and gave it the whole 'whit did ye jist say, ya wank?', so Jada glassed him – nothing major, just a fast rap up the side o' the head wi' a pint pot – and then, after Hammy had been helped back to his feet ('boy's awright, boy's awright') Maggie was all up in his ear giving it the whole 'come oan back tae ma bit' patter. Well, it was like a nature programme in the Nightmare, eh? Alpha sorts out the Beta, and the females are all desperate for the message. But Jada told her, straight up, 'Naw.' Wi' wee Nicola up the road up the fucking duff? 'No way, hen.'

'Fuck sake, Jada,' Maggie laughed. 'You've changed.'

And he had. No way was he going back to some slapper's flat for the night while his own bird was back home wi' Jada's wean in her. Instead, he let Maggie sook him off round the back. After he'd finished – Maggie kneeling between the crates of empties, blinking, coupon like a painter's radio – Jada had zipped up and headed straight home. Obviously, he'd forgotten the fucking ice-cream. But still. Dignity. Restraint. The new watchwords. *Gobbles only*.

Jada watched his sleeping baby son. The furrowed brow, like he was working out some complicated problem. The fat, bunched fingers. The wide brow. Aye, that brow would see a few bawbags' noses before it was done and no fucking mistake. He felt Nicola take his hand.

'He's a good boy, eh?' she whispered.

'Aye,' Jada said. 'He's no that good, but.' He smiled as he felt himself drifting off, the warm fug of the hospital enveloping him. And then, and it felt like only seconds later, wee Nicola was banging his leg.

'JADA!' she hissed again. 'Fuck sake!'

Jada snapped awake, terminating his insane snoring, to see Dr Singh standing there patiently, a slight smile on his lips.

'The doctor's here!' Nicola turned to Singh, a young man in his late twenties, and said, 'Ah'm sorry, doctor.'

'That's fine,' Singh said. 'It's a tiring business, eh?' He looked at Jada. 'Becoming a parent?'

'Ah. Aye, right enough,' Jada agreed.

'And how are you feeling, Miss . . . McGovern?'

'No bad. Bit sair, but.'

'Of course. You'll have to take it easy for a bit. Get . . .' He looked at Jada until Jada realised he was asking for his name.

'Jada.'

'Ah, Jada . . .' The strange, gangsterish nickname sounded odd in the doctor's mouth, as if a high-court judge had just been forced to say 'Mr MacFisto' or 'Dr Octagon'. ' . . . to help out around the house.'

Jada looked at Nicola as if the doctor had just suggested Jada spend the evening down the docks in full drag.

'Ma maw's gonna be coming over and helping me oot,' she said.

Order restored, Jada began scrolling on his phone: pictures of supercars on Instagram.

'Ah. Very good.' The doctor made a note.

39

'When am Ah getting oot, then, doctor?'

'I'm hoping you can go home tomorrow morning.'

'Aww, magic.'

'Now you spoke to the midwife about the post-natal care schedule for you and, uh, Jayden?'

'Cayden.'

'Pardon me. Cayden.'

'Aye.'

'OK, then. Good. I'll leave you with this for now.' He handed Nicola a leaflet. 'See you later.' The doctor departed.

His suspicions from reading Nicola's chart — pre-eclampsia, high blood pressure, poor skin, teeth and bones, underweight — had been confirmed by the evidence around the bed: the pack of fags and lighter by the bottle of full-fat Irn-Bru. The catering pack of crisps and the giant Toblerone. And, to an extent, by the glowering, snoring shape in the tracksuit. Yes, safe to say they'd be seeing plenty of Nicola and Cayden/Jayden in the future.

'Fuck sake. Snoring yer heid aff in front o' him.'

'Ach, gies peace.'

Nicola opened the leaflet and began to read slowly, her lips softly moving. Under the section headed 'GOING HOME WITH BABY', there was a sub-section titled 'BABY'S HEALTH' and then, beneath that, 'SMOKING'. Nicola read on for bit.

Jada scrolled: *Ferrari, Lambo, Porsche* . . .

'Says here we shouldnae smoke roon the wean, Jada.'

'Aye, well, no gaunnae smoke right in his coupon, are we?'

Audi R8, Maserati . . .

'Naw, it says we shouldnae smoke in the hoose.'

'Aye, in another room, but.'

Aston Martin, Beamer . . .

'Naw, it says here, *second-hand smoke is harmful for you and your baby.*' Nicola read on haltingly. '*Chem . . . chemicals linger in the air and can still be in the room 5 hours later. Opening windows or smoking in another room or out of a window won't help.*'

'Gies peace wi' aw that shite, Nicola.'

'*When your baby is born and you bring them home, ask anyone who cares for them to smoke outside or to stop completely.*'

'DON'T TALK PISH! OOTSIDE? FUCKING JANUARY FUR FUCK SAKE!'

The baby woke with a start, crying.

'Shh. Fuck sake! Ye've woke the wean. You should read this.' She picked up the baby and cradled him with her left arm, soothing him.

'Away tae fuck. Ah've enough fucking pish tae listen tae! Look, Nicola, Ah've hud a few weans, right? Smoked aw ma days and they're aw fine, eh?'

Nicola paused to consider this. The proposition that Jada's kids were 'aw fine' was certainly open to debate. But she chose not to pursue this. She turned the page with her thumb and read on as Jada stood up and stretched.

'Anyway, aw this shite's no gaunnae put food oan the table, is it? Ah need tae get back tae work.'

'Mind and make sure ye put the wean's cot up before ye come and get us the morrow.'

'Aye, aye.'

Nicola's eye had moved on to a section of the leaflet titled 'RETURNING TO INTIMACY': *Sex may be difficult or painful after giving birth. If you don't feel like sex, you can find other ways of being intimate: try lots of warm, physical contact that doesn't have to lead to sex.*

41

This was obviously not a sentence – or indeed a concept – to much trouble Jada with. She modulated it. 'Jada? Says here we huv tae be . . . careful for a wee while. In bed, like?'

Jada picked up on her euphemism and tact. He respected it. Mentally, he thanked her for it. He tenderly cupped her face. 'Don't worry, doll. No ma first rodeo. Jist means yer dung funnel's gaunnae take a pounding fur a wee while.' He turned to Cayden/Jayden – 'See ye later, pal' – ruffled the baby's hair and left.

Nicola watched him go, shouldering his way across the ward with that swagger he had, his nightmarish promise of vigorous anal sex ringing in her ears.

Nicola sighed as she pulled the sheets up under her chin and looked across the ward. There was a young girl in the bed to the right of her. Her partner – husband, boyfriend, whatever – was holding her hand and looking into her eyes as they talked, and Nicola found herself drifting back in time, thinking back to when she had been one of the Clydebank Young Team. Not a care in the world, her days spent patrolling the estate with the CYT – bamming folk up, the odd rammy with a rival crew – her nights a bonfire of wild abandon, of drinking and partying and speed and jellies and hash and Bucky, a mad, wonderful parade that she thought would never end. And then it had. She'd met Jada just before her seventeenth birthday, after her pal Annette pointed him out to her across the crowded, smoky living room at that party in Clydebank, in wee Bernie McCluskey's house. His maw and da were in Lanzarote and he had an empty. She'd known who Jada was, of course. His reputation preceded him. But in the flesh? God, he'd looked like a film star. Aye, he was much older than anyone else at the party, old enough tae be her da in fact, but he was in some

42

shape, slim and muscled in his box-fresh trainers, with the gold chain around his neck and the massive TAG dangling loose on his wrist as he stood there, topping up his Jack and Coke from his own bottle and watching the lassies aw dancing away tae the hardcore tunes.

After much urging from Annette – 'go and talk tae him, Ah dare ye, Ah fucken double dare, so Ah dae, ya wee hoor' – she'd finally plucked up the courage, sidled up to him and whispered, cheeky and seductive, 'Gies a wee belt o' yer JD, then, big man.' She remembered the way Jada had looked down, towering more than a foot taller than her, an amused smile on his face for a moment before he'd poured a slug into her plastic cup. (Jada had in fact been trying to place her, her face looked that familiar. It had been a few weeks into their relationship when he realised Nicola's mum was Wee Kirsty, who he'd rattled over the bins behind the bowling club, years back, at Kenny Brown's twenty-first.) After a bit Nicola had leaned into his ear and whispered, 'Me and ma pal are after some ectoids, so we are.'

He'd raised an eyebrow before smoothly coming back with the first words he ever spoke to her: 'You trying tae get me the fucken jail, doll?' He did not mean the drugs.

'Away tae fuck,' Nicola had said, mock-outraged, before adding, coquettishly, 'Ah'll be seventeen next month.'

'Is that right?' Jada said, reaching into his right-hand pocket.

He'd told her later, romantic fool that he was, that he'd liked her that much that, without even thinking about it, he'd gone for his right-hand pocket, where he kept the good Es, the quality biscuits that were for mates and top birds. Not the left-hand one, where he kept the dog-worming tablets reserved for fannies, shavers and mad gouchers.

True love, man, right off the bat.

The night that followed was the most exciting and romantic whirlwind of her young life. She could still remember all the songs they'd danced to, all the old classics – 'Mentalizer' by 303 Terrorists feat. MC Doughnut, 'Frequency Meltdown' by The AssBoys, 'In The Lair Of Bass' by TFM – and how she'd noticed he was some mover for his age. Then the moment of chivalry when Jada stuck the nut in some wee fanny who was bamming her up. And then – so high on MDMA and bourbon – the moment in wee Bernie's maw and da's bedroom when Jada had finally penetrated her. The way he'd sighed *'fucking magic, doll'* as he entered. Then the many complex and varied situs he seemed to require: doggie-style and reverse cowgirl naturally, but also the piledriver, the corkscrew, the wheelbarrow, the butter churner and one that involved her sucking on his penis upside down while Jada held her by the ankles, an arrangement he called the Alabama Meatballs, and many other even more outré combinations that, like distant stars whose pewter light has not yet reached us, were still to be named. When Nicola had finally worked up the courage to tell her mum of their blossoming love, she'd snorted into her glass of MD 20/20 and muttered, 'Jada Hamilton? Mr Bloody Positions?' An awkward moment between mother and daughter, to be sure. Nicola might have thought to ask her father's views, but which one? There was only a bunch of uncles who, after an interval of a few weeks or months, she would be instructed to call dad.

There had been Uncle Gary, who was nice and had been around a lot when she was wee. He'd played her songs on his guitar! 'Postman Pat' had been a favourite, Nicola loving to watch the way his fingers squeaked up and down the nylon strings. Sometimes, late at night, she'd hear him singing sadder songs to himself, in the kitchen below her bedroom. Things about being lonesome and cheating. Maybe Uncle Gary was sad because he wasn't very well – there were his wee brown medicine bottles she'd started to find in the rubbish bin. Gary had vanished when she was six or seven and was rarely seen around the estate after that, though occasionally you'd spot him begging/busking outside the Co-op. The tattered blanket, the greasy lining of the cap with two or three coins in it, the thin brindle greyhound and, most heartbreakingly, the cheap Spanish guitar that used to thrill Nicola so, now tuneless, cracked and reduced to two strings. Nicola felt bad for him, but her mum always hurried them away, saying he was a 'waste o' space'. Then there was Uncle Tony, who'd kind of replaced Uncle Gary and was less nice, who'd just sit there and pound the Bucky and watch the racing and who'd belted her in the face that time because the 3.10 from Newmarket was starting and she'd lost the remote control for the telly when she was watching CBeebies. He'd lasted a few years – oh, they were well into the 'dad' stage – before he too vanished. Away to 'work on the rigs' her mum said. And then, in more recent memory, just as she was entering her teens, there had been Uncle Tam, who'd started coming around when she was twelve. Like Tony with the racing, Tam was always on his laptop, which he'd shut suddenly whenever you approached. Soon enough, he'd taken to coming into her bedroom late at night – when her mum was snoring on the couch downstairs, having overdone it on the MD and the jellies – and showing her weird videos on his phone. (Some of these videos featured the kind of stuff that Nicola believed only existed onscreen until she met Jada.) Then Uncle Tam began suggesting certain . . . re-enactments. Then, suddenly, he too disappeared, vanishing into the back of the police car that had pulled up in front of the house, along with

45

his laptop and phone, both thoughtfully carried for him by one of the rubber-gloved officers while her mum cried and shouted abuse after him. So, no, asking her dad wasn't a possibility as Nicola had no idea who he was.

Anyway – savage bouts of cystitis aside – it was safe to say that the summer weeks with Jada following wee Bernie's party were by far the happiest of her young life. Within two months, Nicola was pregnant. All her wild, wild nights were behind her now. And probably about time too, she thought as she fondly watched Jayden/Cayden sleeping.

After all, she'd be twenty soon.

FIVE

'Dan!' His father-in-law, Ed, was in the doorway of the private room as Dan came in with Grace's stuff in her Mulberry satchel. Behind Ed he could see his mother-in-law Clare sitting by the bed, holding the hand of a still wan but smiling Grace. And, beside her, the tiny, plastic, blanket-stuffed crib, the crown of dark hair just visible. 'Congratulations!' Ed said as they embraced, him in his golf sweater and tan slacks, with his full head of white hair.

'Aye, thanks, Ed. You're an old hand at this now, eh?' This being their fourth grandchild. Grace, their eldest, having been the last of their children to bear fruit.

'Aww, he's just adorable, Dan,' Clare offered, standing to embrace him. 'He's the absolute spit of you.'

'You think? Hi, Clare.'

'Oh, goodness, yes.'

Dan moved around to the bed, setting the bag down on the floor. Everything she had asked for plus a bottle of one of those juices she favoured from Roots & Fruits on Great Western Road, the green stuff that cost more than wine and tasted like cut grass. He kissed his wife's proffered cheek and leaned over the crib. 'Is he still–'

'Not a peep,' Grace said.

'Have they said if you're getting out tonight?'

'In the morning,' Grace said. 'They just want to make sure . . .
you know . . .'

Dan nodded. There had been an incredible amount of blood.

'Tiring business, being born,' Ed said, nodding to his
grandson.

'That's all they do at first,' Clare added. 'You'll know he's
here soon, right enough – don't you worry about that.'

'Oh, here you go.' Dan took out the juice and handed it
over.

'Ooh, yummy,' Grace said, smiling to herself as she watched
Dan watching the baby, transfixed. The teeny fists were bunched
on either side of his head, the prawns of the fingers clenched
tightly into the palms, his nostrils widening rhythmically. Already,
just hours after birth, he looked completely different.

Every day I look in a different face, Dan thought.

'Here, sit down, son,' Ed was saying, clearing his own coat
off the only other free chair in the room.

'No, you're fine, Ed.'

'Come on now, you look shattered.'

'Well . . .' He *was* shattered. He sank into the padded vinyl
chair and realised that – with the completion of this latest
errand – this was the first moment in the last forty-eight hours,
since the labour began, when nothing was being asked of him.
Not that much had been asked of him compared to what Grace
had been through, of course. He could feel the adrenaline
leaving him now as he sank further down into the chair, tuning
out the pleasant, comforting chatter of his wife and his mother-
in-law as they talked on about food.

' . . . there's a couple of lasagnes, a shepherd's pie and a pasta
bake thing in the cool box in the boot. I'll give them to Dan
before we leave.'

'We're not helpless, Mum.'

'You'll have your hands full for the first few days . . .'

Ed over by the window, tuning this out himself as he leafed through the *Herald*. They were decent sorts, his in-laws, maybe a wee bit 'up themselves' as Dan's mum would likely have put it. Ed had been a lawyer, like his daughter. Commercial property deals mostly. Retired now. Dan sometimes wondered if they would have approved of Grace marrying him if they'd met just a few years earlier, when Dan was a struggling writer without a hit show to his name. Grace was thirty-eight, almost a decade younger than Dan, and they'd met, what, nearly fifteen years ago, when she was working as a junior lawyer at Dunbar, McKillop & Parks. It had been during the contract negotiations over Dan renewing his deal for *McCallister*. By the time they were married, four years later, Grace was already running Dan's production company, overseeing all the stuff Dan was useless at: deals, budgeting, scheduling, hiring and firing. Pretty much everything bar the writing.

But thirty-eight. Boy, they'd cut it fine. Grace's younger sisters, Pamela and Maria, were already mothers and married, respectively, to Ross, a chartered accountant from Edinburgh, and Graham, another Glasgow lawyer (commercial property), both more obvious fits for posh girls from Bearsden than Dan had been. Still, Dan was welcome now, an exotic 'creative' amid all the number crunchers and briefs. A talking point at family gatherings. (*'So do you make up everything they say?' 'What's that Gregor Wappler like?' 'Do you get paid every time it's on the telly?'*) He reached out and held Grace's hand as she talked on to her mum, not taking his eyes off the sleeping bundle in the cot at Grace's elbow. It was incredible: the desire to protect and nurture unfathomable. Primeval.

'Some weather,' Ed said, looking out across grey, icy southern Glasgow.

'It is that . . .' Dan yawned.

'You'll be OK tonight, won't you?' Grace said.

'Of course,' Dan said. 'The boys are keen to wet the head, obviously.'

'Hey,' she replied, mock-indignant, 'no parties just because you've got an empty!'

'Does a young man good to cut loose once in a while,' Dan said.

'Don't you be cutting too loose,' Clare said.

'He's joking, mum,' Grace said. 'I think.' She had no fears there. Dan was the ultimate lightweight. One-Can Dan indeed.

'Well, then. Anyway, when it comes to his bottle . . .' Clare went on, micromanaging. The soft chair, the warmth of the hospital, the soothing yammer of his mother-in-law – *make sure and just test it on your wrist, darling . . . three or four minutes in hot water . . . don't get frustrated if he won't latch on right away . . . Pam had a terrible time . . . you know Pam . . . wouldn't listen* – all did their thing and Dan was soon drifting off, feeling his mind snapping hungrily at bits of random nonsense, and then the voices in the room faded further and further away and he sank gratefully into a deep doze.

SIX

Thoroughly refreshed by his nap, Dan left the ward at six o'clock as mum and baby settled in for the night. He'd earlier transferred the cool box of frozen homemade meals from the boot of his in-laws' BMW 5 series to the Tesla. Now he had an hour before he was meeting the boys in Tennent's. Pop home, drop the car, quick shower and change. Fuck – Gregor! He was typing a message in reply to Gregor's most recent voicemail (30 per cent congratulations, 70 per cent call me as soon as you can to talk about this fucking script) and waiting for the lift doors to close when he heard a voice yell with some urgency, 'Haud the fucking door!' Startled, Dan panicked a little, jabbing blindly and hitting the 'close doors' button by accident. A further 'Fuck sake!' and then, just as Dan hit the correct button, a fist weighted with two chunky gold rings appeared between the closing doors, sending them creaking back.

'Sorry–' Dan began, and then Jada was shouldering his way into the lift. 'Wrong button!'

'Aye, nae bother, pal. That you aff fur the night?'

'Aye.' Dan scrabbled for the guy's name. Jesus, it was only this morning. Felt like a lifetime ago. 'How . . . how's the wee man?'

'Brand new. Sleeping away, so he is.'

'Aye, ours too.'

They descended. A beat, then both speaking at once: 'So, are–' They both laughed, then Dan, 'You first.'

'Are ye off out tae wet the wean's head?'

'As a matter of fact, I am. Meeting some pals.'

'Very good,' Jada said. 'Where youse going?'

'Tennent's.'

'That right?' Fucking students, Jada thought. He was barred from Tennent's. A simple misunderstanding that had escalated into a gantry papping, Jada launching a stool into the optics with a cry of 'GET IT ROUND YE, YA FUCKING BENDERS.'

'Where you off to?' Dan asked as they reached the ground floor.

'Same as yerself, Dan. Couple of pints wi' the boys. Down Dumbarton Road.'

Shit, he'd remembered his name. Why couldn't Dan . . .? Began with a 'J', he thought. They stepped out into the cold night air of the car park.

'Just gaunnae jump the bus,' Jada said. 'Motor's in the garage.'

The tangled motoring arrangements of Jada Hamilton. Jada cycled through perhaps half a dozen vehicles every year. Depending on where he was in the feast-or-famine cycle that seemed to be an essential feature of his chosen profession, he might either be driving a powerful used Audi or a feeble, whining Nissan Micra. Or indeed, and as was the case at the moment, nothing at all, his last car – a fifteen-year-old Mercedes estate – having been sold just a few weeks ago to cover his outstanding debt to the unlicensed bookmaker Tony 'Darkside' Meehan.

They were going the same way, Dan realised. It was freezing. 'Look, uh, I'm really sorry,' he said. 'I've forgotten your name.'

'Jada.'

'Jada, aye. Look, uh, do you want a lift? I'm going that way.'

A moment. Jada considering. 'Ye sure?'

Dark, wintry Govan slid silently by. It was trying to snow again, tiny flecks blowing through the orange balls cast by the street-lamps, the interior of the car softly lit by the computer screen set in the dash.

Jada looked around, appraising. 'Tesla, eh?'

'Yeah, I know,' Dan said, shaking his head. He'd been touched by the way Jada had watched him start the car, fascinated by the keyless procedure, the car unlocking simply by responding to Dan's phone as they approached it, then the tapping of the four-digit code into the touchscreen. 'I keep thinking we should sell it. At this point it's like driving a MAGA cap on wheels, right?'

Jada looked at him as if he'd said 'Bumbellybuttonfeet'.

'But,' Dan went on, 'it just drives so well.'

'Aye. They're hard to fucking' – Jada just stopped himself saying 'steal' – 'beat. Hard to fucking beat.'

A *whumf* as they entered the Clyde Tunnel, the light bright, flooding the car. Dan noticed the frayed cuffs of Jada's grey jogging bottoms, the thin hoodie he was wearing. Had to be minus 3 out. 'So, Jada, you got any tips for me?'

'Tips? The horses, like?'

'No, no – fatherhood. It's not your first rodeo, you said, eh?'

'Right. Tips, wi' the weans?' Jada thought, What the fuck? 'Er, well, Ah'm maybe no the best person to ask, like, Dan. I'm kinda old school, know what Ah mean? Like, hands-aff type?

53

Jist let them fucking get oan wi' it. Wipe their ain arses as soon as they're old enough?'

'Right, right,' Dan said. 'Wipe their own arses.' He repeated this as though it was a maxim handed down from Dr Benjamin Spock himself.

Silence. After a moment Jada coughed and broke it. 'So where do you live yourself, Dan?'

'Hyndland.'

'Oh aye. I've a couple o' mates up there. Whereabouts?'

'Park Crescent?'

'Aye? Nice. Very nice. Obviously daeing well for yersel, living up there and driving a motor like this. Whit kinda business ye in, Dan, if ye don't mind me asking, like?'

Here we go, Dan thought. Very often, when this came up in casual conversation, with the cab driver, the barman, he would lie. Go generic. 'Computers,' he'd say. Or 'management'. For whatever reason – tiredness, an urge to impress – he decided to be straight with Jada. 'Well, you know *McCallister*? The detective show?'

'Aye. Course.'

'I write it.' He'd never say, 'I created it.' Too pompous.

Jada's eyes going sideways to look at him. Then, 'Away tae fuck.' Jada said this simply and without malice.

'I do. Swear to God,' Dan laughed.

'Is that right?' Jada looked at him with fresh interest.

'Yep. Twenty bloody years now.'

A silence as Jada absorbed this news. 'So dae ye write, like, the stories? Aw whit they're gaunnae dae and that?'

'Yeah. And the dialogue.' Another 'bumbellybuttonfeet' look from Jada. 'You know, the words they say.'

'Aye?' Jada said. 'Somebody writes aw that?'

'Yeah.'

'Ah always thought they actors just made it up as they went along.'

'Ah, no, not usually.' Though who could forget Gregor's passion for improvisation in the early days?

'And ye get good money for that, aye?'

'Yeah, it's not bad.'

'Go oan yersel, pal.'

A sonic pop, the ambient noise changing as they emerged from the tunnel and out into Whiteinch. They passed Victoria Park on their left, and Jada fleetingly remembered taking Big Sonia McPherson from behind in some bushes in there in his late teens. There was also the time over by the pond when him and Panda had taken on five of the Scotstoun Young Team and leathered the fucking lot of them. Jada's personal topography of Glasgow was overlaid with a grid referencing many, many fucks and fights. 'And what line of work are you in yourself, Jada?' Dan was asking now, the name still feeling ludicrous in his mouth.

'Ach, a bit o' this, bit o' that,' Jada said. 'Here, whit's yer man like?'

'Sorry?'

'Yer man that's McCallister?'

'Gregor?' Fuck. Still had to call him back. Do it after he dropped Jada. 'Oh, nice guy.' Dan's standard answer.

'Aye? Ah heard he was a total fud, like.'

'Really?' Dan's interest perked up at this. It was always pleasing to come across stray stories of Gregor behaving badly.

'Aye. My pal Hughie, right, his brother's pal's oan the taxis and he said he hud him in his motor wan time, in fae the airport, and he said he was aw pure up himself.'

'Is that right?'

'Aye. Fucked him oan the tip an aw.'

'Mmm-hmm. I'll have to pull him up on that.'

'Are youse pals, like?'

'More colleagues.'

'Oh aye. So he is a total fud, then?'

Dan laughed. They were coming along Dumbarton Road now, heading east. 'Just up here's fine, cheers, wee man. Appreciate it.' Dan pulled over, up on the pavement in front of a row of shops. 'Who ye aw meeting in Tennent's, then?'

'Oh, just some pals. Boys I went to uni with.' Dan extended his hand. 'Well, good luck with the wee one. When are you getting him home?'

'Ach, doctor says it'll be a few days yet. Nicola's still bad wi' the high blood pressure an aw that. Jist couldnae get aff the fags. She cut doon, so she did. But it's hard, eh.'

'Uh, yeah.' Jesus.

'When's your boy getting oot?'

Made it sound like prison. 'Tomorrow morning.'

'Right, well, see ye roon then, Dan.'

'Yeah. Sure. Take care, Jada.'

The heavy clunk of the door.

Dan drove off, casting a glance in the rear-view mirror, seeing the tall, slim figure hurrying across the road, dodging cars, towards the light of some dismal pub. And Dan Chambers thought all the usual things someone of his education, income and class would think.

Six kids from six women.

Smoking while she's pregnant.

Jesus − what chance did that poor kid have in life?

But he also thought it must be liberating to some degree.

The pleasures of the unexamined life and all that. Dan had read somewhere that the lower classes – as a good socialist he hesitated to even think in these terms – and the upper classes had all the fun. All the fucking and fighting without a care in the world and never a worry about money because there was a surfeit of it in one case and none of it at all in the other. Father a bunch of illegitimate kids? Fuck it, someone will sort it out, either the state or the centuries-deep pockets of your family. Yes, it must be nice, freeing, to not be poleaxed by all the usual middle-class handicaps and foibles.

Jada, in his turn, lit a Piccadilly in front of the Flaps, the tiny crystals of snow stinging as they landed on his face and forehead, and drew heavily on the rough fag as he watched Dan's tail-lights disappear towards Byres Road and made his own judgements and calculations . . .

Park Crescent
LD70 KVH
3376

He dialled Tony. 'Tony? Wee job fur ye the night.' Jada listened, letting Tony say his piece, his 'fuck sake's and his 'it's freezing's and whatever. Then he retorted: 'Listen, ya wee ginger prick. Ah don't gie a fuck if it's fucking snowing. Get yer arse oot o' that bed and do as yer telt. There's fifty bar in it fur ye. Another hunner if ye get it done . . . Aye, thought that'd get ye moving. Meet me in the Flaps. Soon as.'

Jada hung up and pushed through the doors into the warmth of the pub.

SEVEN

A mile and a half northeast of the Flaps.

Tennent's Bar, Byres Road.

Four pints were raised.

'That's your life over, then!' from Ally. (Medicine.)

'Cheers pal, really happy for you,' from Jack. (Law.)

'Ah, how much was it for the kitty?' from Bob. (Sociology.)

'Thanks, lads,' said Dan. (English Lit.)

Jack's sincere 'really happy for you', and the brief, direct eye contact he made as he said it, belied the fact that Jack was the only one Dan had breathed a word to about their IVF struggles, when they'd been pissed, a couple of years back. He'd obviously never brought it up with the whole group. (Well, you didn't want the lads thinking that your spunk was all fucked up. You didn't want that kind of talk doing the rounds, did you? *Heard about Dan Chambers? Yeah, he's a fucking Jaffa, mate.*)

The four pints clunked together and, with a hearty 'TO TOM!', they all drank. Nearly thirty years since the four of them first sat down around a table in this pub. The cross-section of their varying degrees testament to how they had met – in halls, first year. Second year, they'd all shared a flat, a subhuman toilet of a basement down on Ashley Street near Charing Cross, with slugs on the carpets and damp climbing the walls.

Now, a quarter of a century later, here they all were. Men in the second half of their forties having replaced the children who nervously clutched their pint tumblers in here, still astonished they were being served without ID being checked. Dan looked from face to face: Ally, with just a fine sheen of silver fuzz on his bald head, Jack, whose thick ginger hair was now grey and frizzy, and Bob, who had somehow contrived to double his body weight. You looked in the bathroom mirror sometimes and you couldn't believe it, they all agreed. Once upon a time they would all have been wearing band T-shirts. Now Jack, Ally and Dan had segued into the uniform of the comfortably-off middle-aged man: dress shirts, cashmere sweaters in black and navy. Brogues. Only Bob remained true to the old ways, in his battered trainers and tattered Fall T-shirt.

'The last man into the club,' said Ally. Most of the guys had been married a long time, with kids in their teens, or early twenties in Ally's case.

'It's something when the bugger comes out, eh?' said Jack.

'Jesus, not half,' Dan replied, blowing his cheeks out at the memory of the howling slab of raw beef spattering onto the delivery table.

'You looked?' said Bob, incredulous.

'Didn't you?' said Dan.

'Fuck that,' said Bob.

'Unbelievable,' said Ally. 'Not watching the birth of your own kid?' Ally was a consultant cardiologist, mainly in private practice, at Ross Hall Hospital over in Braehead.

'How's Grace doing?' Jack asked. Jack had worked with Grace's dad back in the day, not long after graduation. He was in criminal law now, with his own large practice down in the Saltmarket. Business was booming, and Jack's clients provided the lads with an endless supply of anecdotes and mad ned patter.

'Fine, fine,' Dan said. 'Fucking hell. Better than I would be if I'd been through . . .' He searched for the words. What was the equivalent experience?

'Pushing a four-kilo bag of flour out your arse?' said Ally. 'Exactly.'

'Bob's arse could probably handle it though,' said Jack.

'Ah, you using the whole fist, doc?' said Bob, unoffended.

Bob's job — or jobs — were largely a mystery to them. He'd somehow contrived to arrive in middle age without ever having had anything close to resembling proper employment. He ran a wide range of enterprises, from a man-with-van set-up to a DJ booking agency, writing occasional reviews for what remained of the music press and giving guitar lessons. These various activities all had only one thing in common: none of them seemed to make Bob any money.

'Feels like a big responsibility, doesn't it?' Dan said.

Ally snorted. 'With one? One's nothing, pal.'

The conservative of the gang, Ally had married the most old-school girl of all of them. Sinéad, a staunch Catholic from a family of seven, had wanted seven children too, but Ally had drawn the line at five. Their house, when the kids were younger, resembled a battlefield in the final stages of a bitterly fought civil war. 'HOW DO YOU STAND IT?' Dan had once asked Ally during a visit, standing in the kitchen after the golf, with their bowls of white wine, having to yell over the whooping, screaming and crying. 'I don't hear ninety per cent of what you're hearing,' Ally replied. 'I mean, if someone breaks a limb or something, I might respond.' In truth, Ally had it pretty good. Sinéad did it all.

Jack had it pretty good too. He was on his second wife, the lovely Marianne, who did something complicated in public relations for a chemical company. He was on his second batch of children, with the two from his first marriage now entering their teens and his youngest two, aged five and seven, now at school. Jack and Marianne employed a housekeeper and a full-time nanny and, like Ally and (until recently anyway) Dan, Jack pretty much got to do whatever he wanted to. A wee trip up to Gleneagles for eighteen holes? No problem. A week in Spain with the lads? Sure. Dinner at the Ivy on Saturday? I'm in. Bob, meanwhile, *never* got to do what he wanted. In fact, it was something of a coup that he was even allowed to be here, drinking in the pub on a school night . . .

The pitiful revenue streams of Bob Industries meant that his wife – the ever-complaining Jennifer, a university lecturer – was the main breadwinner. And he who pays the piper . . . She didn't have Bob on a short leash so much as there was no leash – just a gun in his mouth. Whenever a trip or an activity was mooted, Bob would utter the dread words, 'Ah, I'll talk to Jen.' And negotiations would begin. For their annual summer golf trip – a trip that the four of them had been taking for over twenty years now – Bob would begin discussions the autumn before. Any expense beyond the humblest hotel, the cheapest dinner, the most basic golf course, would cause Bob to rend what remained of his hair and gnash his teeth in despair. After two decades of this, they had come to an understanding: everyone else just paid for him. Unlike the others, scattered across the West End, Bob and family lived in a cramped three-bedroom flat on the Southside. When he wasn't working one of his five or six jobs, Bob functioned as a sort of house husband-cum-nanny to their two daughters. Given that the girls were now aged seventeen and nineteen, he seemed to spend an incredible proportion of his life driving them to and from events, classes and parties. And yet here was the thing: despite all this, despite the gun-in-mouth deal and being church-mouse poor, Bob and Jennifer had been together longer than any other couple they knew, with their *thirtieth* anniversary looming on the horizon in a couple of years. *Something* had to be going right.

Perhaps, the boys had often speculated, the sex was off the scale. An anything-goes hell pact of leather, implements, teabag-ging and pegging. Granted, this seemed unlikely given Jennifer's habitually cassock-shrouded, bespectacled, perma-frowning appearance, but there was more on heaven and earth than was dreamed of in our philosophy and all that.

'So,' Dan said to Ally, 'you got any parenting advice for me?'

'Parenting advice?' Ally said. 'Do you know what parenting is like, Dan?' He didn't wait for an answer. 'It's like putting the cover on a double duvet – no fucker ever knows what they're doing. You just muddle through and eventually it works out one way or another.'

Across from them, Jack was already draining his pint. 'Come on, let's get the boy a bottle of champagne,' he said, clapping his hands together.

'Now you're talking,' said Ally.

'Fuck sake,' said Bob instantly.

'You're OK, Bob,' Jack said. 'On me.'

'Ah, cheers then,' Bob said.

The champagne went down in one round. Then another bottle. Then they were working their way through the malt whiskies list and from there it was a short hop into 'mind the time?' *Mind the time Bob shat himself in the queue to get into the*

QM? *Mind the time Ally spewed up all over Professor Drummond at the medics' cheese and wine? Mind the time Jack wiped his arse with nettles on the camping trip?*

Dan's head was swimming, blissed out on booze and exhaustion as he luxuriated in the soothing babble of these voices he'd been hearing since he was eighteen years old.

BANG! A pint pot went clattering across their table, knocking over several empty glasses.

'Jesus!' Bob yelled.

'Easy there,' said Jack.

A small, very drunk, red-haired kid leaned in over Dan, trying to wipe up the mess. 'Christ, Ah'm sorry, lads! Fuck sake! Really sorry! Jist slipped oot ma hand. Ah'll get youse a round!'

'You're OK, son,' Ally said. 'They were empty.'

'Are youse sure, boys? Ah'm no even steaming, honest!'

'Aye, aye, accidents happen,' Jack said. The kid was on his knees next to Dan now, scooping up pieces of glass even as Findlay the barman approached with the dustpan and brush and the cloth thrown over his shoulder. 'Mind you don't cut yourself,' Jack said. 'Here, leave it to the professionals.'

'Aye, awright, cheers, lads.' The kid staggered off towards the toilets as the barman started mopping the table.

'Everyone OK?' Findlay asked.

'Fine, Fin,' said Jack, getting up. 'Right, lads, the Highland Park next? Doubles?'

'Oof,' Bob said. 'Just a single for me. Early start. Got to drop Emily at school before—'

'Christ, Bob. She's sixteen,' Ally said. 'Can she not walk?'

'Seventeen,' Bob corrected. 'And no, it's too far.'

'Bus?' Ally suggested.

'Ach, it's complicated.' Everything with Bob's familial arrangements was incredibly complicated.

Jack gave up, headed for the bar. Got him a double anyway.

'Really sorry about that again, so Ah am.' Dan turned. The ginger kid was there again, squatting down behind his chair.

'Honestly,' Dan said. 'Don't even worry about it.'

'Are youse celebrating something, boys?' the kid asked, nodding at the empty champagne bottle upside down in the ice bucket.

'Your man there,' Ally said, indicating Dan, 'just became a dad.'

'Is that right? Go on yersel. Whit did ye have?'

'Wee boy,' Dan said, still glowing when he said it.

'Ah, brilliant. Can I no get ye a pint or something?'

'Honestly, son, you're fine.'

'Right, Ah'll leave youse be. Have a good night, lads.'

'Cheers, son.'

The kid stumbled off towards the door.

'Nice lad,' Ally said.

Tony walked out of the side door of Tennent's onto Highburgh Road, now completely sober. He saw Jada's fag end glowing in the dark across the road, and hurried over. 'Here ye go,' Tony said. 'Slipped the wallet back in his jacket. Clueless bunch o' fannies, right enough.'

'Good boy,' Jada said, handing over five twenty-pound notes.

Tony stuffed them in the front pocket of his jeans. 'A wee bonus, eh? When ye get it shifted?'

'Away tae fuck, Tony,' Jada said. Wee chancer. Good pocket man though. Gentle touch.

Tony nodded, spat and crossed Byres Road. Jada slipped the card into his inside pocket and walked off the other way.

He put his ear buds in and pressed 'play' on his phone. Jada was old school – still a CD man at heart – but Nicola had been helping him gradually put stuff on his phone. This was one of his favourite gabba playlists, *DJ Multiple Offender Live In Rotterdam '91*, the classic 'We Will Dominate' by Kasparov feat. MC Raw gradually giving way to Nasenbluten's monstrous banger, 'Cunt Face'. Fucken magic.

Jada cranked up the volume and strolled off towards Hyndland.

EIGHT

Dan's bladder woke him around 6.30am. Standing in their en-suite, his palms and forehead flat against the cool marble, his bare feet tingling with the underfloor heating, he listened to the steady drill of his urine while he ran a damage assessment: head a little fuzzy, legs aching slightly, mouth dry. But it didn't feel like it'd take much more than a couple of litres of water, a couple more hours' sleep, Nurofen and some eggs to get over this. Thank God he'd come home at closing time and declined the offer to go back to Jack's, where Jack and Ally were going to break out the Cubans and a thirty-year-old Glenfarclas. (Having missed the last underground, Bob had been outlining the hellish multi-bus trip he would have to make back to the Southside until the Uber Jack had called for him whispered up to the kerb.) Dan drank a couple of glasses of tap water at the sink and scooted back between the sheets. Where, obviously, he couldn't get back to sleep. Fuck it – he'd rock up early at the hospital. Max Brownie points. He texted Grace: *How went the night? Did you get much sleep? Wee man OK? xx.*

Instant typing, those three ominous dots scrolling across, then: *Not much. Shattered. And starving. x.*

I'll be there shortly. Shall I bring you a bacon roll or something?

That'd be lovely x.

He showered, coffee'd and pain-reliefed in fifteen minutes. He checked the fridge and hit the pavement at 7.30am. Just as the sun was coming up. The morning was chilly but dry and looking like being one of those fabulous Glasgow winter days – sharp and crystalline. Whistling, he strolled towards the car.

And stopped whistling.

What the . . .?

Had he moved it? Was he *that* pissed last night? Did he park it further along? A flash of panic igniting now as he fumbled for his phone and clicked on the Tesla app. Into 'Location'. A moment while it refreshed and then, rather than the map showing him where his car was, just a black screen and the words 'LOCATION SERVICES DISABLED'.

Eh?

It took a few minutes and a call to Tesla customer services for Dan to properly assimilate it. *Stolen?* How the fuck do you steal a Tesla? 'FUCK SAKE!' Dan yelled to the silent row of giant Victorian houses. He clicked on Uber.

Just as Dan was getting into the black Mercedes and calling the police, Jada – exhausted, unshaven – was counting his money in the garage in Royston. It'd been quite the night. You had to move fast on Teslas.

After flashing Dan's keycard at the door and tapping the 3376 code into the onscreen keypad (the daft bastard hadn't even tried to hide it) he'd got it straight over here to Crazy Dominic. Dom had instantly disabled the tracking device and then got his boys to work: Dan's Model X was already stripped right down to its constituent pieces which would be sold off

67

for parts. It was a brilliant operation. The only downside was that you realised just a fraction of the vehicle's value: Dan's seventy-grand car would be worth around fifteen in resaleable bits. Which was why Jada was holding an oil-stained brown envelope with just three grand in it. How he pined for the old times, before GPS and tracking devices up the arse. New plates, respray, bosh. Few of those, and you had a good year. Fucking technology. Fucking Elon. Tough to make an honest living these days.

'Nice wee score there, big man,' Dom said, coming over and lighting a fag while, behind him, the cream leather seats were being spannered out of the demolished Tesla.

'Aye,' Jada sighed, already running through the mental arithmetic: a grand to the bookies, nearly a thousand in back rent, some shite still to buy for the new wean, tab at the Flaps . . .

'Oh, congratulations by the way.'

'Eh?' It took Jada a moment. 'Oh aye. Cheers, Dom.'

'Wee boy Ah heard?'

'Aye. Jayden. Or Cayden. She's no sure yet.'

'Well, another mouth tae feed. Gives a man an incentive tae work, eh?' Dom nodded towards the Tesla, its skeleton gradually being revealed. 'Keep 'em coming, pal.'

'Whit dae ye want to do wi' aw this, boss?' One of Dom's mechanics was coming towards them with a carrier bag he'd lifted out of the car boot. He produced a green felt dinosaur, getting an oily thumb print on it. Dom and Jada peered into the bag – a pop-up book called *Wally Has a Bath* and a wee Babygro from somewhere called Petit Bateau that seemed to have cost some mug an incredible fifty fucking quid. The tag still on.

Dom took the bag, popped the dinosaur back in and handed

it all to Jada. 'Here you go, J. Wee bonus ball, eh? Some timing!'

'Nice one,' Jada said, taking the bag of baby gifts.

'Stolen?' Grace said. She put her phone down. She'd been replying to texts from all the girls, from Becky and Rose and Sarah and Yvonne: *YAYY! . . . CONGRATULATIONS! . . . WELCOME TO THE CLUB!* and so forth.

'Yep.' Dan was walking around the room, cradling Thomas. The baby was holding on to Dan's index finger, its five tiny digits wrapped around his one with surprising strength. Tom appeared to be imperiously taking in the room as they walked their circuit, but Dan knew he couldn't see more than a few feet yet.

'I had no idea you could steal a Tesla,' Grace went on.

'Apparently there's some device they use, some kind of a radio-frequency thing?'

It had been quite the time for Dan, on the phone in the back of the Uber. 'Yes, Mr Chambers,' the policeman had assured him. 'They can use a radio-frequency device to hijack the code from your card. We're seeing more and more of it. They need to get quite close to your keycard to do it, though. Has anyone had access to it recently?'

'No. Definitely not. I never use it. I use the phone. The card's right here in my . . .' As Dan was saying this he was rifling through his wallet. He'd dumped all his cards onto the back seat of the Uber: debit card, credit cards, BA Exec Club card. It took a few seconds to realise that the keycard was, of course, gone. 'Shit.'

'Sir?'

'It's gone. My Tesla card.'

'Ah,' the policeman said. 'Is it possible that—'

The ginger kid. In the pub last night. Bending down behind his chair. 'Yes,' Dan said. 'I think someone might have picked my pocket.'

'Right. I'm afraid I'll need you to come into the station and fill out a report.'

'Sure. It's just, well, my wife and I just had a baby yesterday—'

'Congratulations.'

'Yes, thank you. So maybe later this afternoon?'

'The sooner the better, sir. Obviously you won't be able to proceed with your insurance claim until you have a police report number from us and I can't give you that until—'

'Yes, I understand, officer. Thank you.'

Dan hung up. Fuck it – they had gold-plated insurance. Go and hire a car later and sort out claiming it back down the line. Or, better yet, get someone at the office to do it. He was in the process of dialling Debbie to put this in motion when his phone came alive in his hands, the dread word 'GIELGUD' lighting up the screen. Fuck! How could he have forgotten? No way to blank it now. He clicked the green phone symbol. 'Gregor!' he tried to sound delighted. 'I'm so sorry I haven't call—'

'Nonsense, nonsense, my boy.' The soft, silky purr, familiar to millions of viewers from uttering one of McCallister's catchphrases: the deadpan 'Well, this'll need a lick of paint' upon viewing the blood-spattered walls of the triple murder. The laconic 'Rough night, pal?' when being shown the mutilated corpse upon the mortuary slab. (Both of these usually accompanied by some or other hapless junior detective dry-heaving in the background.) 'And congratulations!' Gregor went on. 'Welcome to the club, finally!'

70

'Thank you.'

'All went well, I trust?'

'All good. Quite the experience though.'

'Isn't it just? *When we are born, we cry that we are come to this great stage of fools . . .'* The mad old ham was making with the Shakespeare.

'Quite,' Dan said, waiting for him to get to it.

'And mum's doing well?'

'Fine, Gregor, fine.'

'And yourself?'

'Good. Though I had my bloody car nicked this morning.'

'Grand, grand.' Not even listening any more. 'Now, Dan, I expect you know why I'm calling.'

'I've a fair idea, Gregor.'

'It's just . . . Dan, it's so . . . abrupt.'

'It is.'

'And violent.'

'True, but—'

'I don't see the need for it in all honesty. I — we — always thought that, after all he's been through, the old bugger would get the chance to, you know, walk off into the sunset, so to speak.'

Aye, with the door open for him to walk back in from the sunset, Dan thought. Not a chance. But all he said was, 'I understand it must have been a shock, Gregor. Reading the pages.'

'A shock? That's putting it mildly. If you look at episode ten, page forty-two. Do you have the script in front of you, Dan?'

'Well, no, Gregor. I'm in the back of a taxi going to the hospital to see my—'

'No matter. So about halfway down, "The man turns around . . ."'

Even without the script in front of him, Dan knew very well what happened halfway down page forty-two of episode ten, the final episode of the final season of *McCallister*. During a routine traffic stop (McCallister having been busted back into uniform at the end of the previous season: a punishment for his savage rule-breaking in pursuit of an unrepentant paedophile) McCallister sticks his head into a car he does not know belongs to an armed robber on the run and is blasted in the chest with a 12-gauge shotgun. He dies by the lochside road, a faint smile playing on his face as he watches a golden eagle circling high above him.

'No, no, no. We can't end it this way, Dan.'

'But, Gregor . . .' Dan wearily went through his rehearsed arguments. It was shocking. Unexpected and total. After a career spent dealing with the results of violence, did it not make sense that this man's life be ended by an act of senseless random violence? It was like *Electra Glide in Blue*. Or *Easy Rider*. Or Omar in *The Wire*. Admittedly these were all reference points that would mean absolutely nothing to the average *McCallister* viewer − sat there with their bag of boiled sweets and tartan blanket over their knees − but even so. Dan *wanted* to shock them. To stun them. To deny the ancient, *Daily Mail*-reading bastards the joy of seeing McCallister solve his final case, then his retirement party, then the old spunker sailing happily off up Loch Eribol in his stupid wee fucking boat. Besides − because of the hard negotiations that had led to Dan agreeing to do season ten − he had final cut. Dying on a soft bed of summer heather with a smile on his face? Gregor should have seen what Dan *wanted* to do: McCallister's

72

dismembered corpse being forced roughly into a weighted oil-drum, the severed legs being jammed in beside the astonished, decapitated head, following a marathon of torture and depravity that would have strained the credulity of John Wayne Gacy. All of it was designed to ensure Dan's fundamental point, the one that, even now, Gregor was attempting to subvert: *that the only way Detective Sergeant Colin McCallister was ever coming back was as a fucking zombie.*

'Maybe,' Gregor was musing, 'if he was wearing a bulletproof vest. Because it's a hell of a world out there, Dan, it really is. Then he . . .'

They were pulling into the car park now, the dark edifice of the huge structure looming above them. 'Gregor, sorry, sorry, but I'm just heading into the hospital now. I'll have to call you back. But–'

' . . . perhaps it stops his heart, but later . . .'

'There's a read-through scheduled for next week. Why don't–'

'So, hear me out, with what's left of his strength, he–'

'Gregor!'

'Mmm?' The modern-day Robert Towne stopped spitballing. 'Why don't you and I meet for lunch before that?'

'Well, I think we have to, Dan. Because–'

'Great. I'll have Debbie set it up.'

'I really can't sign off on–'

'Fantastic. Bye, Gregor.' *Can't sign off on?* What planet was the old madman living on?

'Well, this is all a bit of a pain in the arse, eh?' Grace was saying now. 'Here, give him over. He needs feeding.'

'Och, it is what it is,' Dan said, taking one last, deep sniff of the wonderful baby aroma before handing the gurgling bundle across the bed. 'Life in the big city, eh? Anyway, have you heard if you're getting out today?'

'Not yet. Please God though. Hey, aren't you picking your mum up at the station later? How are you going to manage without the car?'

'I got the office to book a hire car. We'll get the insurance to sort it all out down the road. Sorry about your food and coffee though. I'll go and see what I can rustle up from the café, eh?'

A knock at the door.

Dr Singh appeared. 'Morning!' he said cheerily. They chorused the same back. 'And how are mum and baby doing today?'

'Oof,' Grace said, levering herself up on the pillows. 'Bit better, I think.'

'Good. How are those stitches feeling?'

Grace made a face.

'Bit uncomfortable? They will be, I'm afraid. Is he feeding OK? Latching on?'

'God, yes.' Grace put a hand over her aching, tender right breast.

'Great. In which case, I think you go home today.'

'Oh, fantastic!'

'Probably be later this afternoon before we can get you discharged. And you'll need to take it easy for a few days. Let dad do the heavy lifting.'

'Aye, aye, captain,' Dan said, doing a little salute.

'I'll just leave, uh, this with you.' A little shamefully, Dr Singh slid a leaflet onto the side table. Dan could see the title – 'READY, STEADY, BABY!' Evidently an idiot's guide to not killing your kid within five minutes of leaving the hospital.

'See you later.' Singh left the leaflet, but he knew they wouldn't need it, this pair. He'd seen the brimming basket of fresh fruit next to the bed. The bottles of mineral water and green juices and whatnot. Grace's jewellery on her bedside table – a little pile of gold and platinum with a stainless-steel men's Rolex sitting atop it. The thick, expensive overcoats hanging on the back of the door. He'd practically felt the middle-class reek of research and can-do steaming from Dan and Grace. In an instant Singh pictured little Tom's life spooling out in front of him, like train track being laid down: the nannies and the private school and the tutors and the leather seats of powerful 4x4s and France or Italy in the summer, the Caribbean or Thailand in winter, and good shoes and fish and fresh vegetables and university and all points north.

'Right, then,' Dan said. 'What do you fancy?'

'See if they have a plain yoghurt? I've plenty of fruit here, but maybe bring up a knife? I think they took the last one away. Oh, is it Saturday? Do you think they'll have the *FT*?'

'They will *not* have the *FT*, Grace. I'll be amazed if they even have the fucking *Guardian*.'

He closed the door to the private room behind him – the Renaissance-painting image of mother feeding baby caught golden in the corner of his eye, making his heart sprout wings and flutter up towards his throat – and strolled through the main maternity ward towards the lifts. Dan took in the teenage mothers and thirty-something grandmothers and the occasional sullen, head-to-toe-in-grey-sweats fathers sitting by the mewling infants in their plastic mangers, and he paused, just for a fraction of a second, to check his privilege, a world where having your car stolen was just a 'bit of a pain in the arse'. Where things could be instantly rectified with the snap of a credit card being laid down. Get someone in the office on it. Press the button and the machine will respond. Dan walked on, whistling, towards coffee and bacon rolls, his hangover almost entirely lifted and gone. He walked past a bed with curtains drawn around it and almost flinched from the deafening racket that was band-sawing from behind them. It sounded like a seal with sleep apnoea breathing through a PA system. Dan walked on.

Behind the curtain, Nicola continued her packing and glanced sulkily at the snoring form of Jada, collapsed in the chair by the bed, reeking of drink and weed. Cayden/Jayden was sleeping too. But he'd the right. Just a baby. Bloody Jada. 'Been busy,' he'd said. 'Working.'

'Working,' Nicola sulkily repeated as she stuffed her clothes into a plastic bag.

But he had been. Unbeknown to Nicola, the previous night, and all morning, Jada had worked like a man possessed. Or, rather than that cliché, more accurate to say he'd worked like a man *in* possession. For, after he'd popped into the Flaps and paid off his bar tab, which obviously involved a couple of celebratory pints, after he'd visited Fergus out in Whiteinch and paid off his gambling debts (*'ye cut it fine there, big man'*) and after he'd got his TAG Heuer out of the pawnshop, he'd taken the remaining cash from the Tesla windfall and bought a half-ounce of smack from Paedo Boyle over in Maryhill. He shot home where he got busy with the scales and the playing cards as he cut the – already heavily cut – smack with baking powder to turn fourteen grams into twenty-eight. Triple his money. Easy. Well, not *that* easy. For he spent the remainder of the morning trudging around dropping off: ten grams with wee Malky, five with the Poof, five with the

Coupon and five with Big Sean. All on a sale-or-return basis. But they'd shift them, no bother. If they were going to cut it further, no skin off Jada's nose. It widnae be Jada looking down the Stanley knife of some bampot junkie after he'd turned over his sixty shitters and got about as aff his nut as half a Valium. And those boys knew better than to hold out on him. The Poof had tried it on once, claiming he'd been mugged, aw Jada's smack taken aff him. He *definitely* looked like he'd been mugged after Jada got through wi' him: twenty rapid to the fucking dome and a good few boots in the Rab Haws to drive the point home. Next boy that went tae sook oan the Poof's plums would get a fright, right enough. Aye, a week tops and the cash would roll back in. Like all good businessmen Jada understood the speculate-to-accumulate deal. He kept a gram back for him and Nicola. She mainly just smoked it, but she'd let Jada shoot her up now and then. Maybe they'd have a wee party when she was back on her feet in a couple of weeks. Jada was blessed in his constitution to be that rarest of creatures – an occasional heroin user. He loathed junkies. You had to have self-discipline. Willpower. They would have the odd blowout when they knew they had a day or two to recover after. Just a wee dig now and then. That was fine. Skagged oot o' your fucking baws from dawn till dusk 24/7? Get tae fuck. You had to give it to heroin though – like they said, it was like Jesus pumping his load up ye. Having covered many miles by bus, tube and taxi – between Whiteinch, Maryhill and Anderston, going as far south as Cardonald and as far north as Milton – Jada had finally flopped onto the sofa thoroughly exhausted. He was looking forward to sparking up the joint he was holding – the one he'd laced lightly with a sprinkling of the milk chocolate-coloured heroin – and uncapping the half-bottle of Bucky he had chilling in the fridge door. There was the nagging feeling he'd forgotten something though. His phone started buzzing again in his pocket – he'd been ignoring it for the last couple of hours. He didn't recognise the number, answered anyway.

'Aye?' Jada said cautiously, gruffly, trying to disguise his voice in case officialdom – the Social Security, the polis, whatever – had tracked him down.

'Jada!' Desperation, almost tears, in her voice. 'Are ye no coming tae get us?'

Fuck! Nicola and the wean! He'd totally forgotten. 'Aye, doll! Oan ma way. Be there in ten.'

'They said we could go ages ago! They need the bed ba–'

'Traffic. Got tae go.'

He hung up and sprang into action. Which is to say he put some tunes on (*Chanks And Fucker Live At The Arches*) and lit the joint. Whit were they gaunnae dae? Kick the two o' them intae the street? Fucking NHS. His taxes that paid for aw that shite. Well, aye, OK, obviously not Jada's taxes. But still. He inhaled deeply and, for the first time that day, felt a blissful wave of peace wash over him. It lasted all of a few seconds until he turned his head to the right and looked through the open doorway into the spare bedroom. 'FUCK SAKE!' Jada exclaimed as he gazed upon the components of the baby's cot, still resolutely unassembled. Fuck it. Dae it later. And then, when he got here, she wiznae even packed!

'Come on, hen,' Nicola's mum said, looking up from her magazine. (*'Strangers tried to burn Sharon and her kids alive! Who put them up to it will shock you!'*) 'He's always busy.'

Nicola snorted. 'Aye, right. He . . .' She lowered her voice so as not to disturb the slumbering Jada. 'Ye know what he said to me the other day?' Nicola told her about his proposed 'return to intimacy'. Wee Kirsty sighed. This was obviously far from the ideal time to tell her daughter about the trauma her own dung funnel had once suffered at the hands of Jada Hamilton. 'Well, hen,' she said, 'at the end o' the day, ye've got tae give yer man his rights.'

'Rights?' Nicola hissed. 'We're no even married!'

Wee Kirsty shrugged, as if to say this was a mere technicality, and went back to her magazine. Ach, what had Nicola expected from her mum in the realm of relationship advice? Given her own track record and all. A round-up of bloody junkies, alkies and sex cases. Jada's snores filled the cubicle again. Nicola looked at him huffily. 'Aye. *Working*.'

NINE

The three of them lay in bed. Late afternoon. The Glasgow rain was driving at the window panes of the bedroom that overlooked the communal gardens. Dan had Tom balanced in the cradle made by his thighs, the baby quiet as his dark brown eyes moved over the ceiling, taking in the spots of light that danced around as the sunshine broke through now and then and glanced off the glass chandelier that hung fifteen feet above them. They were leafing through the Sunday supplements – food, money, travel, houses. Dan was feeling *flungi* – a family word that meant warm and snug in bed as the elements did their thing outside.

He reflected on the first month of parenthood from the vantage point of having survived it. It had been unreal. Surreal. Firstly, there had been the sensation he'd felt as they'd brought Tom home. It had been difficult to name, this feeling, but it had reminded him most of when he'd passed his driving test – first time around, at the age of seventeen – and his dad had handed him the keys to the family car. Alone at the wheel for the first time, with no instructor or father to take over the controls if something went wrong, Dan had burst out laughing at the ludicrousness of it. The fools! Who on earth thought this was a good idea? He really didn't know what he was doing.

He could kill someone. And very nearly did: a friend's mother had seen him approaching – hands gripping the wheel at the ten-to-two position, a furious scowl of concentration on his face – and had started waving excitedly at him in recognition of the fact that he must have passed his test. In attempting to return the wave, Dan nearly mounted the pavement and ran her over. And so it was when he carried Tom over the threshold and sat him down in his tiny car seat in the hallway. Why had they been allowed to do this? They'd been given responsibility for an actual human life. No doctors or midwives here. What were they thinking? This feeling lasted several days.

Most of the time he and Grace just lay in their bed, on either side of the sleeping or gurgling bundle, scarcely able to believe their luck. When Tom cried it was soft and quiet and quickly resolved when Grace drew him to her and his mouth found her nipple. The gasp of pain this sometimes drew from her, the intensity of concentration on the baby's face as he sucked, like Dan at that steering wheel all those years ago. Tom would occasionally sneeze. The first time, the expression on his face was such a perfect encapsulation of *what the fuck just happened?* that they both rolled around laughing for a good ten minutes. At night he slept beside them in the Moses basket, waking every few hours, mewling. Grace would slide him onto the bed and feed him on her side, sometimes even managing to doze as she did so.

No, Tom was no problem at all. However, all around them in the great house, you sensed the constant activity of the in-laws. Dan's mum was staying for a week and Ed and Clare drove over every day. Anna came every other day, only to find that most of her usual tasks had been taken care of by Margaret and Clare, the two grandmothers having engaged in a death match to see which of them was Queen of Housework. Grace and Dan lay there listening as, every minute or two, it seemed, from downstairs there came the distant sound of a hoover being run again, the clank and rattle of yet another load being taken out of the dishwasher. Every fifteen minutes or so the doorbell would ring as another delivery for the baby came from Amazon: bath toys, clothes, bottles, sterilising kits, dishes and cups in bamboo, Bakelite and other exotic materials, teething rings, little sleeping bags. Gifts from colleagues and friends arrived: flowers for mum, bottles of champagne, cashmere blankets and designer babywear.

'Ooh. Recipe for sriracha salmon here,' Dan said.

'Mmm.'

'Jesus, I could really go for something like that tonight.'

They had been living for a week now on meat and two veg. Mash. Spag bol and shepherd's pie. Old people's food.

'Good idea,' Grace said.

'Well, you say that. My mum doesn't "take the fish" and your folks don't do spicy.'

'There's plenty they can eat.'

'True enough. Bugger it. I'll make us the salmon thing. Yes, Tom. Daddy will. Daddy will make the fish. Oh, have we got any salmon?' Dan looked out the window at the sheeting rain.

'Don't think so.' Grace looked at the rain too. 'You could go to Waitrose.'

He could. Park in the car park, covered. However . . . 'They'll only have farmed.'

'We could survive it this once, Dan.'

'Oh, come on. That's—'

'If you're going to the fishmongers, you'll need a brolly, babe,' Grace said, cutting off Dan's farmed-salmon riff. The damage it was doing to the rivers and seas, the incredible amount of waste produced by millions of fish crammed into small areas, the lesions and sores and infections.

Dan looked again at the rain. 'Ach, it's not that bad.'

'I admire a man who stands by his principles,' Grace said. 'Here, give him here. Time for his nap.' She gently took Tom from him and headed off down the hall. After Grace turned the corner, Dan turned his attention to the monitor by the bedside, where Grace and Tom were almost immediately reproduced on the screen as they entered the nursery. He watched her smooth his hair and murmur to him before he glanced at the bottom right-hand corner of the monitor screen, where a digital readout gave the time and temperature. Seventeen degrees! How had it got so low! Those old bastards downstairs – forever at the thermostat in the hall. In their crazed, pensioner minds anything over eighteen was equivalent to just tossing handfuls of fifty-pound notes into the log burner every five minutes. Dan grabbed his mobile with some urgency and clicked on the Hive app just as Grace walked back in. She sighed and said, 'What are you doing, Dan?' in the tone of HAL the computer.

'The oldies have been buggering about with the heating again. It's February! It's seventeen degrees in his room!'

'Jesus, so what?'

'Nineteen to twenty-two degrees!' Dan said, parroting again the ideal temperature range for a baby's room, the one he'd settled upon after reading many, many articles on the subject, after he'd scrolled his way through many warm debates on the subject on Mumsnet. (Not a complete waste of time: one argument had been resolved with YummyMummy1978 responding to Winelover's accusation that she was talking 'utter b****cks' by threatening to 'punch her in the tits'.)

'Dan,' Grace said, getting back into bed, 'we need to keep you the fuck off Mumsnet. Tell me, what exactly do you think is going to happen to him if his room is one degree below the ideal temperature? Hmm? Do you really think he's going to freeze in his little sleeping bag?'

'No, but—'

'It's a non-problem, isn't it?'

'It's not a problem to keep the room at the right temperature either, is it?'

'What if other parts of the house get too hot?'

'Then they can take their fucking jumpers off!'

'Next thing,' Grace said, picking up her paper and resuming reading, 'you're going to do is go in there and turn his radiator up to max. Then, later, his room will be too hot and you'll be running around like a madman turning the heating back off again.' Something like this had already happened, twice, in the last week. 'So just leave it. He's fine.' Dan looked at his wife, supine on the bed, licking her thumb as she turned the page. He envied it, her penetrating sanity. 'If you want to do something useful,' Grace continued, 'pop down to Byres Road and get the salmon.'

'Right. Fine. If he freezes to death—'

'And please don't go down there banging on about the bloody thermostat. They'll all just deny it.'

Dan entered the kitchen, a little bigger than a squash court, with a similar sense of height, of elevation. And of equally blinding brightness. For, along with their fondness for Arctic temperatures, the grandparents shared a similar taste in lighting concepts, concepts more suited to, say, an operating theatre than a family home. Ed was sat at the table reading his *Daily Mail* under the glare of the big light. Dan's mum was washing up at the sink, while Clare, not to be outdone, was sorting through a basket of laundry. Dan could see the bulky form of Anna, their feisty Bulgarian cleaner, down in the utility room off the far end of the kitchen, stuffing a load of sheets into the machine, her usual kitchen tasks having been appropriated by the new grandmothers.

'Guys,' Dan said, holding his hands up in front of him like a politician urging a baying crowd for silence, 'can we please stop fiddling with the thermostat?'

'Eh?' Ed said.

'The temperature. It's far too cold in Tom's room.'

'I've not touched the thermostat,' his mum said.

'Me neither,' said Clare.

'Right. Fine.' What was the fucking point? Like children. Like toddlers. He grabbed his coat, scarf and the big golf umbrella from the rack in corner. 'I'm just off to the shops if anyone wants anything.'

'What are ye needing, son?' his mum said.

'We quite fancied salmon tonight.'

'*Salmon*?' Dan's mum echoed, doing a very good job of making 'salmon' sound like 'shite', or 'broken glass' or 'syphilis'.

'Ye sure you're wanting to go out in that, son?' Ed nodded towards the rain lashing the kitchen window.

'Fancy a wee walk, actually.'

'And there's that much food in the fridge to use up,' Dan's mum went on with some exasperation, gesturing towards the vast chromed Sub-Zero. 'Use up' – the way Dan's mum habitually referred to food, as though it was some surplus stock that just had to be got through as fast as possible. For her own part, she lived on toast, instant coffee and baked potatoes and thought that, just as setting the central heating to anything over eighteen degrees was strictly for sick, twisted billionaires, any meal involving more than three ingredients was the kind of wild indulgence enjoyed by sheiks or tsars.

'But I've already defrosted a cottage pie!' Clare said, finding herself in unusual agreement with Margaret.

Dan faced down this unholy alliance. 'OK, how about this – and stay with me here – but how about you three have the cottage pie and we'll have the salmon?'

'Och for goodness' sake! Cooking *two* meals?' Clare said.

'Clare, it's no bother.' Dan was looking for his keys now. It was another ritual that began whenever the in-laws came to stay. Dan had three places where he put his essentials of keys, wallet, phone: hall table, mantelpiece in the living room, or, sometimes, on the island in the kitchen. For some reason, none of these places was ever deemed 'tidy' enough by Clare. Subsequently, and without consultation, they always had to be moved. 'Has anyone seen my keys?' Dan said, trying very hard to keep his tone of voice neutral, trying to keep the strain of exasperation out of it.

'Oh, they're in the bowl by the door,' Clare said, her own tone of voice suggesting that anyone who thought to keep their keys elsewhere was clearly a child molester.

'See you in a bit,' Dan said.

Grace heard the front door close. She turned over on her side and watched the rain streaming down the glass. It was about the only thing she disliked about living on the west coast of Scotland. In the mornings in the summer, they'd lie in bed with their early morning tea and watch the weather on break-fast news, looking at places like Maidenhead, London and, say, High Wycombe, all with huge sun stickers over them as they basked in temperatures of twenty-five degrees. Then you'd look out of the bedroom window and see, well, pretty much what she was seeing now in February. Just over a year ago, when all looked lost, they had been talking seriously about a move down south. *McCallister* was going to be over, gone from their lives. Dan was going to be working on his novel. There was nothing tying them to the city bar their parents, who were all still young and healthy enough to jump on a plane or a train when they wanted to visit. Grace had found herself losing hours going down property wormholes on Rightmove. North London. Maybe Crouch End or Highgate. Or just outside the city. Buckinghamshire or Surrey. But, Jesus, your Glasgow money didn't get you far. They had no mortgage, but they'd have to dig into savings. While she was doing all of this, she was telling herself that it would be nice just to feel the sun on their faces for more of the year. But she knew in her heart that wasn't quite it. She knew she just wanted to get further away from everyone they knew. From their failure. From the phone ringing and then having to say, 'Oh! Congratulations!' while every atom of her being was screaming 'FUCK YOU!' The idea of living somewhere remote, out in the Home Counties, somewhere she wouldn't have to see all those happy mothers pushing babies in fucking strollers on her way to the shops. And then, as soon as she got pregnant (well, as soon as they were safely into the second trimester), all these feelings just vanished and she had no inclination to leave the city whatsoever. She loved living in Glasgow. She yawned, spreading a leg onto the cool patch of the sheets and then wincing a little. The rawness of the stitches. Salmon. Dan battling his way up Byres Road right now because of his one-man crusade against the farmed-fish industry. Bless him. It had been an early misgiving about Dan – was he too nice, too right-on? As a student he'd had his crusades, his enthusiasms. But she'd found he was always able to laugh at himself. And, as they got further into their twenties, she'd watched as some of her friends – Sarah, Becky – had gone down the bad boy route. And then the inevitable discovery of the heart-breaking text messages. The 'quiet pint' with their mates that turned into a two-day coke bender. This was the problem with the bad boys. They were *bad*. God, that rain was getting harder. All for a bit of salmon. Wild salmon, they went through a lot to have their young too. Swimming upstream against frothing torrents. That was what the last few years had felt like to Grace. And now here they were – safely upstream. Wallowing in a cool, calm pool.

She couldn't help herself. She got up, crept down the hallway and stood in the doorway. The lilac walls of the nursery and the sleeping bundle, his chest gently rising and falling. Grace didn't know how long she'd been standing there when she heard a creak on the stairs and turned to see her mum just reaching the half-landing below her, a steaming mug in her hand. 'Everything OK?' she asked.

'Fine, fine,' Grace whispered, stepping back and gently half-closing the door.

'Brought you a wee cuppa.' Grace took the mug, half-filled as always, her mum always seeming to think a full mug of tea was just too extravagant. 'He's off his head going out in this,' she said, tilting her head up towards the rain drumming on the huge skylight far above them, at the very apex of the townhouse. 'Is the wee one all right?'

'Aye. Sleeping away.' Grace smiled.

Her mum edged past her and peeped into Tom's room. She smiled as she gazed at Tom and said, 'You're blessed.'

'Mmm.'

'I told you God would listen.' Grace's mum was devout, and Grace knew she was quietly disappointed Grace didn't fully share her faith. 'Och, the prayers I said for you both . . .'

Grace kissed the top of her head. The mum smell, as familiar to her as her own. 'Well, looks like He was listening, mum. I'm away for a wee nap.'

A ten-minute walk east, the north wind cutting sideways across the wet pavements of Hyndland, the rain patterning off the navy canopy above him. The sky above the sooty tower of the university, the point he was heading towards, was black and swirling alarmingly. He turned left when he hit Byres Road, the wind keening straight into him now. He tilted the umbrella in front of him. Not yet four o'clock and already the streetlights coming on. Normally, of course, they'd have just got back from holiday. Every January for the last ten years they'd decamped to the Caribbean, to Antigua, leaving right after New Year for four weeks, breaking the back of the hellish, endless Scottish winter. There'd been a group of them who'd started the winter holiday together: Ally and Sinéad. Grace's friend Abby and her husband Finn. Gregor and wife number three (or was it four?) even came one year. But, in truth, in recent years, it hadn't been as much fun as it had been early on. Couples had begun to drop off because of the children. *'Ach, we'd need to be back for school starting. Hardly seems worth it.'* As the rounds of IVF had continued (another session in the consultant's room, Grace weeping on Dan's shoulder), he'd begun to foresee a future where it was just the two of them on the beach, childless and free. Free to do whatever they wanted: water-ski, get drunk on Piña Coladas in the afternoon, go to fancy restaurants without worrying about toddlers smashing the place up. Free, free, free. And then he'd look up from his book, to catch his wife in profile, her sunglasses hiding her damp eyes, damp from gazing across the beach to the surf line, where the children ran and played. 'I don't know what they do all day,' Jack had said to him once, a long time ago, before he knew what Dan and Grace were going through, 'the childless.'

And now, only a week in, Dan knew what he meant. The little bundle at home, waiting for him now. The best gift ever, endlessly available. What *did* he do with all his time before? And the shiver of relief, of joy, that went through him – even here, on damp, freezing Byres Road in the jaws of February – when he remembered that they wouldn't now be that couple.

Into the warm glare of the white-tiled fish shop, bright as a room lit by their parents. There was a queue of well-heeled West Enders, with all the bounty of Scotland's seas laid in front of them on the iced marble slab: the barnacled oil-black pods of the mussels, the tiger-striped mackerel, the intense blue of their backs proof enough of God, a whole plaice the size of a tennis racket, its spots as crimson as blood spatters, the lopsided snarl of a huge, luckless monkfish, bigger than Tom. And there, at the back, a gleaming wild salmon, about a seven-pounder, its eye still dark, the crushed ice packed into its gills stained a soft red from its blood.

'Afternoon, Dan, what are you after?' Craig, the owner.

'Hi, Craig. Got any wild salmon in?'

'Yer in luck, sir. Couple back there. Speyside.'

'Fantastic. Reckon you can gut and prep one for me.'

'No bother. Few ahead of ye though. Gonna be about half an hour if that's OK?'

He looked out of the window, at the rain that was starting

to tip sideways now. Thirty minutes? A quick half in the wee bar of the Chip? Or maybe a glass of Chablis and half a dozen oysters? Why not? Nearly five o'clock. By the time he got home it'd be a reasonable enough time to open some wine and begin the gentle numbing he needed to get through dinner with the oldies. 'Aye, no bother, Craig. I'll pop back then.'

Dan sat by the window of the Ubiquitous Chip, looking out onto the cobbles of Ashton Lane, three of the six oysters and half a large glass of Chablis inside him. He watched the students hurrying back and forth and remembered the businesses of yesteryear that lined this lane when he was their age: the impossible hipness of the Cul De Sac bar on the corner, the fear of the knockback from the bouncers as you approached the door on a Friday night. The stout bottles of strong, exotic Fürstenberg lager they sold. The 'festive Fürsties' at Christmas, the label all snowy and jolly. The Grosvenor across the cobbles. Some kind of vodka bar now, but back then a proper old-school Glasgow café: basic cheeseburgers, a slice of pizza with a fried egg on top, a 'Grovcoff' ice-cream (vanilla with a sprinkling of instant coffee. 'Reeks of his own invention, eh?' Jack had said, the first time they went there). He felt himself growing expansive, poetic even, as the wine tumbled through his veins, getting to work on his empty stomach, as he watched the darkness falling. Many of the students were looking at their phones as they walked, the bright screens lighting up the thin, colourful nylon of their umbrellas, reds and greens and yellows, glowing like lanterns.

Of course, the students were different from back in his day. Today, some of the girls looked like boys and some of the boys looked like girls: the spindly-legged one in the mini-skirt, teetering heels and bob, with the Adam's apple like a fist and thick five o'clock shadow. The huge broad-shouldered bruiser with short hair plastered to her skull and heaving tits strapped down. Dan recalled that Ally's seventeen-year-old daughter had recently told him that out of her ten closest friends, two were bisexual, three were gay, one was non-binary and two were transitioning. Eight out of ten, then. When Dan was seventeen, they had Poofy Colin – the one gay guy in the whole school of nine hundred. Did this simply represent the way it was really meant to be? Was human sexuality always this diffuse and polyamorous but had never had the courage to speak its many names so loudly? Or did it just represent another escalation in the never-ending rebel war youth wages on age. Dan remembered an incident from his own teens, when his father had wandered into the living room where Dan and his mates were watching a video of the New York Dolls. His dad had stared slack-jawed at the screen for a few seconds, numb at the sight of David Johansen and Johnny Thunders slathered in make-up and women's blouses as they tottered on stack heels, caterwauling about their Jet Boy. Eventually dad – born in 1938 – had managed a stunned 'Jesus Christ' before he backed out of the room, terrified and appalled. The boys had laughed, and Dan remembered thinking something like, *wow, what are our kids gonna have to do to shock us?* Here it was, then. *Dad, I'm a bloke.* Or *Dad, I'm a bird.* Because you couldn't really do much with the traditional tools of rebellion these days, could you? Bands? No one cared. Your dad liked the New York Dolls. Tattoos? Yeah, right. *Everyone* has tattoos. Your gran has a tattoo. Haircuts? No chance. Everyone has a mad haircut now. When Dan was at university there was one barber in the West End. Now every other shop was a barber, all queued out of the door from dawn to dusk as the kids obtained and maintained their elaborate premiership-footballer-inspired rugs. The day was fast approaching, Dan reflected, when the High Court judge would saunter into the chamber with 'love' and 'hate' tattooed upon the knuckles of his/her/their hands and the dotted 'CUT HERE' line inked around his/her/their throat. Pausing only to smooth out a full Mohican, he/she/they would rap the gavel to bring the court to order. No, it seemed that for true rebellion these days you really did have to go with *I'm getting my cock chopped off.* Or *I'm having a cock grafted on.* And forget Ally's daughter's friends, there was Bob's nephew, Gordon. Gordon was a Furrie: only fully comfortable when dressed as a cat. Or there was Andy, the eighteen-year-old cousin of Debbie from the office. Andy was now Andrea, having been taking the pills and growing breasts since he – she! – was fifteen. He – she! – was scheduled to have his – her! – penis removed this summer. She was now in a relationship with James, who used to be Janet, who had also been taking the pills since she – he! – was sixteen. The operation to remove her – his! – breasts and turn her – his! – vagina into a penis was scheduled for September. At which point, surely, someone was finally getting pumped. It seemed a hard, circuitous road though. And Dan found himself wondering what might be afoot when Tom was that age, about fifteen years from now. Maybe everyone would be having everything removed by then, just a nation of Action Man groins, dressed up as animals in, say, full Nazi uniform, cybersexing each other in the Metaverse. *There are more things in heaven and earth than are dreamt of in our philosophy.* True, Will, true. There was more right now on Ashton fucking Lane than had ever been dreamt of in Dan's dad's philosophy. Ach, what do I know? Dan thought. God love you all. He raised his glass and toasted them through the window, out there in the rain on the cobbles, the young, the old, the bi, the queer, the non-binary, the fully binary, the transitioning, the Furries, the he/she/they/whatever. Good luck to you all, friends. Forget about us, the ancient and the uncomprehending. Get out there and do your thing. Make sure someone gets pumped, however you get there. I salute you all with fine French wine.

He slipped out of this reverie as he realised someone was standing right in front of the window, blocking his view. A big guy, thin and tall and woefully underdressed for the weather, was trying to light a cigarette in the rain, trying to make a kind of tent for himself by holding his tracksuit top out, the spark of the lighter strobing within. He gave up after a few tries and looked into the Chip. Directly at Dan. It was the guy from the hospital last week. He'd given him a lift. His son, born the same time as Tom. J something. James? No, odder. A nickname. *Jada!* Dan smiled and raised a hand. Jada squinted, then recognition came over him too. Looking at him in the rain, there seemed only one gesture to make. Dan beckoned, indicating the empty seat next to him. Jada seemed to think for a moment. He glanced up and down the rainy lane, then nodded and vanished left. A second later, he was coming through the door, soaking wet, one hand brushing rainwater from his face as he lowered himself into the empty seat with a gruff 'awright?'

'Jada, isn't it? It's Dan. From—'

'Aye. Ah remember.' Jada chanced his arm. 'The Tesla man.'

'Ha! Not any more.'

'Eh?'

'Nicked.'

'Yer joking? Ah thought ye couldnae nick them.'

'Me too. Anyway, fancy one of these?'

'Whit is it?'

94

'Oysters!'

'Nae fucking danger.'

Dan laughed. 'Acquired taste, right enough. Can I get you a drink, then?'

'Naw, yer awright, Dan, Ah'll get them.'

'Not at all. I've got a tab open. What'll it be?'

'Er, wee pint o' heavy, then.'

Dan drained the splash of wine he had left and headed for the bar. The guy didnae even seem bothered, Jada reflected. Victimless fucking crime, right enough. Dan got another glass of Chablis and Jada's pint and came back. 'Here you go. Well, to the boys, then. To Tom and . . .?'

'Cayden. Or Jayden.' They clinked glasses, Dan's dainty stemmed bulb nearly breaking against Jada's pint tumbler, like a ballerina bouncing off a gorilla. Jada drained close to half of it in one gulp. 'Aye. Nicola's been up and doon on the fucking names like a hoor's fucking drawers, so she has.'

'Right. So . . . you don't get too involved in that stuff?'

'Ach, ye know fine whit it's like, Dan. Best tae let the birds dae whit makes them happy wi' aw that shite.'

'Yeah. When Somerset Maugham's wife gave birth he was in India and he wrote to her saying, "Have you had your child yet and what have you named it?"'

Jada took another swallow of dark beer, looking over Dan's shoulder. 'Aye? Boy didnae give a fuck, eh? Pal o' yours?'

'No, no. He's . . . well, was . . . a wri–'

'Ho, seen the fucking erse oan that?'

'The er–' Dan followed Jada's gaze across to where two women – early thirties, business suits – were sharing a bottle of champagne with two business-suited men. Maybe their husbands or boyfriends, maybe simply colleagues. Whatever they were, it made no difference to Jada, who continued to periodically stare at one of the women's rumps.

'Ye could sit yer fucking pint oan that,' Jada elaborated. 'Decent set o' fucking bazongas an aw.'

What to say to all this? 'Yeah.'

'Always hoaching wi' class fanny in here, but, eh Dan?' Jada gave him a wink, as if to indicate that Jada was onto him. That the only possible reason Dan would be in here on his own at half four in the afternoon was so that he could cruise 'class fanny'.

'Ha! Yeah. Well, no, the thing is, I had a few minutes to kill. I'm just picking up some' – *don't say 'salmon', you'll sound like a dick. Already nearly fucked it with the whole Somerset Maugham thing. What were you thinking there, genius?* – 'eh, picking up some messages.' 'Messages'. Nice. Old school.

Jada only had a few inches of beer left. He had drunk the pint astonishingly quickly. 'Ye fur another?' He indicated Dan's almost untouched white wine.

'Ah, no, no. Got to run in a minute. I–'

'Come tae fuck, Dan. Huv tae stand ma roon.'

'Honestly. No bother.'

'Oof, fuck sake.' This was Jada. Regarding the arse again.

Finally Dan heard it from behind him, one of the women saying, loudly and clearly in their direction, 'Can I help you?' Dan turned. She was staring at Jada, clearly having had quite enough.

Jada, unperturbed, met her gaze. 'Yer awright, doll,' he said coolly. 'I'm just having a wee swatch at yer erse.'

Dan closed his eyes.

Almost immediately one of the guys was over, standing above them.

'I'm sorry . . .' Dan began.

'What's your problem?' the guy said to Jada, ignoring Dan. And he wasn't nothing, this guy. Edinburgh, maybe Borders, accent, suit with no tie. Dan was guessing finance or law. And he looked like he'd played some rugby, this lad. Broad shoulders, ruddy pink cheeks. 'Apologise to the lady.' Yes, Borders accent, so rugby a high possibility. Jada ignored the guy for a second, taking a swallow of his pint while Dan spluttered, 'We're just leaving!' But now Jada was setting his glass down. He looked up at the guy and said, 'Whit ye saying, ya fucking prick?' He said this softly, even equably.

'Just leave it, Malcolm!' the other guy at the bar shouted.

Dan felt sweat breaking out on his forehead. Yes. This was an unusual business to be unfolding in the Ubiquitous Chip.

'Ye should listen to yer pal there, Malky,' Jada said.

Malcolm (for this fellow had surely never been called 'Malky' unironically in his life) leaned down and hissed, 'I think you should listen to your friend and leave.'

Jada nodded, thinking. Then held his hands up, palms towards Malcolm, and said, 'OK. OK.' He stood up. And now Dan saw that Malcolm fairly towered over Jada. Had a good four or five inches on him. Got to defuse this, Dan was thinking. Stop it escalating. He reached for his wallet. Offer to pay their drinks. Then, abruptly, things escalated.

'Look,' Jada said.

Then he booted Malcolm full force in the balls.

Jada had never understood the bad press the sucker punch got. The only fights worth being in were the ones begun – and ended – by a sucker punch. Square goes were for tourists. Idiots in the pub, circling each other and giving it aw that Marquis o' Queensberry pish. Stand there waiting for some fud tae hit ye? Aye, smoke ma dobber. If the fight wasn't over before the other guy knew it had begun, it wasn't worth having. The element of surprise x astonishing force = victory was what Jada had grown up with. In Jada's world Sun Tzu's famous aphorism would have been paraphrased as: 'If your opponent is of equal strength, fire a boot intae his Rab Haws and ten rapid intae his dome and all before the fud's taken his watch and rings aff.'

For Dan, it was a strange moment. For it was an expression that, like any Scotsman, he had heard all his life.

'I'll boot your baws.'

'He took a boot to the baws.'

'Got his baws booted.'

But he had never actually witnessed it. Oh, he'd seen people *try* to do it: the odd attempt at putting the knee into the nuts during a playground fight, a couple of neds flailing blindly at each other in the street, or in one of the rougher pubs they used to slum it in back in their student days, the Sarry Heid, Bar 82. But he'd never actually seen the art form in its purest expression, so to speak. Firstly, he realised why all those other attempts at ball-booting had been just that, for they were all attempts at making connection with a moving target. In this case, Jada's target was completely stationary. And then, and always impressive to witness, there was the ease with which the professional makes anything – from the crisp golf swing that splits the fairway to the 50-yard free kick that curls sweetly into the corner of the net – appear effortless. Jada just said, 'Look,' placed his left hand on Malcolm's right shoulder, took a half-step back and whipped his right foot up with astonishing speed, force and accuracy. For a second, Dan was reminded of Alan Clark's famous diary entry about shooting the heron, how the great bird just seemed to 'absorb' the shot. Malcolm didn't crumple the instant Jada's foot (clad as ever in a box-fresh white trainer) smashed into his testicles. It seemed to take a fraction of a second for him to assimilate the enormity of the blow. And then his knees buckled and he started to crumple to the ground. He was trying to say something as he went, something like 'oh my what' or 'off my you'. Perhaps 'ahh more no'. To add insult to injury (and Dan, trying now to calibrate the extent of the actual injury, found he was picturing the two baked potatoes they'd left in the embers for far too long one bonfire night: two shrivelled, smoking black plums when they took them out of the tinfoil), Jada still had a grip on his shoulder and was using it to help him, to guide Malcolm gently down onto the floor of the pub, as if saying, 'Come on. It's OK. It's all over now. Just rest here.' Jada's manner was calm and relaxed, as though he were dealing with a minor inconvenience, a sommelier having brought the wrong vintage perhaps, and Dan remembered a truism about violence – to get good at it, you had to do an awful lot of it.

Malcolm's pal had got up off his bar stool. Jada looked at him evenly. He stayed put. Malcolm himself was now making a hissing sound from the floor, like steam escaping from a small nick in a pipe. His face was the colour of an aubergine and saliva bubbled at his lips like champagne.

Jada drained his pint, burped heartily, and said, 'See ye roon, Dan.' With that, he stepped over Malcolm and was gone.

It was another half-hour before Dan left the pub. As well as heavily tipping the staff and insisting on settling the bar tab of Malcolm and his friends – 'the least I can do' – he also felt it necessary to give everyone a lengthy apology and an explanation of how he didn't really know Jada, and an assurance he would never be found in here in his company again. Walking back towards the fishmonger's, Dan was trembling as his own adrenaline left him. Jesus Christ. Wait till he told the boys about this.

TEN

Jada walked through the students – thinking, reflexively, *fucking weirdos* – and around the corner onto Byres Road, where he ducked into Curlers. His eyes took a moment to adjust to the gloom of the low-ceilinged pub. The icy trickle of rainwater making its way down his spine pooled in the small of his back. Then he saw him, at the far end of the bar, raising a hand in greeting.

Jada strolled over. 'Awright, pal?' The place was quiet, just him and the Gypsy at the bar and a wee gang of bams on the piss in the far corner. Just boys.

'Afternoon,' the Gypsy said in his West Country burr, the word coming out as something like 'Arrrfterrnewun'.

'Happy new year,' Jada added.

'You Jocks say that until bloody Easter!' They shook hands, Jada being reminded of the man's powerful grip. The Gypsy was not a big man, maybe five foot seven, but his chest was like a small fridge – utterly solid. Squat and powerful. Low centre of gravity. Very thick, very black hair. Almost an afro. Small, fast eyes that missed nothing. Even the seasoned brawler, like Jada, would look at the Gypsy and most definitely have second and third thoughts about taking him on. He was wearing what he always wore, winter or summer, rain or shine: an olive-green army jumper dotted with oil stains, greasy jeans and battered, steel toecap work boots.

While he was worth a great deal of money, to look at him you'd have thought the Gypsy earned a crust going door to door selling pots and pans and sharpening knives, as his forefathers had. The leathery, chestnut-coloured face was ageless. He could have been anything between forty and sixty.

'What yew drinking then, Jada?'

'Er . . .' He took in the Gypsy's pint of Coke, remembered he didn't drink. Follow suit? Be aw that businesslike way? Nah, fuck that. It was gone five. 'Pint o' heavy, please.'

The Gypsy placed the order and turned back. 'I 'ears congratulations is in order.'

'Aye, cheers.'

'A boy an all, I hears.'

'Aye. Wee boy. Cay . . . naw, Jayden.'

'You're blessed true enough, Jada. Boys – ye put 'em out and they comes back 'ome. Girls? Ye gotta go out looking for 'em. Especially once the rooting starts, eh?' He laughed as he nudged Jada. And the man knew of what he spoke – the Gypsy had at least fourteen children. No one really knew for sure. Jada's pint arrived. 'Anyways – cheers, Jada. 'ere's to the boy.'

They clinked glasses.

'How's yer trip up been?' Jada asked.

'Good enough. Heading back down home tonight.'

'And the family?'

'All sound, mate. Now what can the old Gyp-Gyp do for ye?' The Gypsy was indicating that time was money and that the small talk was now over. Jada nodded to a table in the corner and they headed over and settled in. Jada had chosen Curlers deliberately for their meeting. Neutral ground. No way did he want the Gypsy – his primary fence – in the Flaps, where he'd be exposed to all manner of bams and fuds who knew a bit about Jada's business. The last thing he wanted was the Shite or whoever getting wind of what kind of deal Jada cut for himself. Jada laid it all down: army surplus kit, sleeping bags, tents, boots, flasks and water bottles, canteens, jumpers and all that shite. The Gypsy sat back in the corner, nodding, thinking, his hand scratching his silvery stubble. Finally . . . 'Aye, 'appen I might be able to do something with that type o' stuff, Jada, 'appen I might.'

'Magic.'

'Let me make a few enquiries . . .'

'No starting for a while, like. Ah'm getting things aw . . . in place and that. So maybe the summer? But once we get going, should be regular, know whit Ah mean? Wee shipment once every month.'

'Arr. Regular is good. So, tell you what, I'll make me enquiries, let you know, and we'll go from there, eh?'

'Aye, man. Ideal.'

The Gypsy was getting up now, his Coke half-drunk. He leaned on the table and lowered his voice. 'Remember now, the usual terms of business. You gets paid when the Gypsy gets paid, and if old John Law comes sniffing around, you never met the Gypsy, did ye?'

'Fucking course not.'

'Grand. I'll see ye, Jada. And good luck wi' the wee one.'

'Aye. Cheers. Safe drive home.'

Home for the Gypsy, his farm near Carlisle. Jada watched him head out into the drizzle. He took his empty pint pot to the counter and signalled for the barman to refill it. He really should be getting home, he'd promised Nicola he wouldn't be long, but, hey, he was out grafting. What was it she'd asked him to get? Jada took a deep draught of his heavy and thought, staring into the treacle eddies of the dark beer. *Get the stuff oot o' Prestwick, over tae Royston, switch vans, doon the M74 tae the Gypsy, bosh. Eat. Sleep. Repeat.* Aye, sound enough. Prison lurking at every step though. Fuck. Imagine that again. Jada thought of the boy, his son, and pushed the thought away. I mean, that rich cunt round the corner, wi' his fucking wine and oysters and no a care in the fucking world, what was so different about me and him? What kind o' world was it when aw ye hud tae dae tae get Teslas and massive houses in Hyndland up the erse wiz tae think up some pish about some weegie detective up among the sheep shaggers? Meanwhile, there were guys like Jada knocking their pans in aw day long getting fuck all. He looked up and caught his reflection in the mirror behind the bar and, unexpectedly, two and a half drinks in, the philosopher in Jada emerged. What would they say about him when he was gone? Like, imagine something like on that auld programme where the cunt comes oot wi' the red book and surprises ye and then they drag out every fucker ye've ever known? Jada Hamilton. Cheat. Conman. Benefit fraud. Thief. Drug dealer. Who'd be on that show? Jada saw only terrible faces from his past. He saw his dad, his headmaster, his first boss Mr Penders, all of them telling him the same thing: yer a useless wank and ye'll never amount tae anything. Ach, fuck the lot o' them. He had people – wee Nicola and the boy, Jayden/Cayden – who were waiting at home for him right now. Suddenly he felt a powerful urge to be there, to bask in their love. One for the road first though, obviously.

★   ★   ★

'Ye said ye widnae be long!'

'Ah hud fucking business!' Wee Nicola continued to look at him expectantly, the baby in her arms. All around them sprawled the mess of the tiny lounge of the flat, the carpet barely visible beneath clothes, plates, cups, magazines, toys and the like. 'Whit is it?' Jada said, looking around him, trying to see whatever she was looking for.

'Ah asked ye tae get something fur oor tea!'

Fuck! That was it! 'Oh aye, fuck,' Jada said. 'Look, nae bother. Ah'll run doon the chippy.'

'Naw, Jada. Ah telt ye, Ah need something wi' vegetables.'

'Wi' fucking whit?'

'Vegetables! That nurse at the hospital said.'

'Chips are fucking vegetables!'

'Naw! Fresh vegetables, she said!'

Fuck sake, Jada thought. Whit wiz he dealing with here? Aw this health food shite. 'Fucking mushy peas, then?' Jada suggested.

'Fuck sake,' Nicola said, stomping away with the wee man.

Not the glowing welcome he'd been looking for. Jada looked around at the mess. She'd never been much of a homemaker even before the baby, but things had deteriorated over the past week and no mistake. Took him fifteen minutes to find the Sky remote the other day. What could be done? He'd talk to her about getting her maw around, to help clear up. Nicola came stomping back in without the baby – aw the wee man did was sleep – but clutching a leaflet. 'Here,' she said. 'Ye need to read this.' Jada took it from her. A photo of a woman – quite fit – cradling a wee baby, looking at him aw affectionate and that. All around her were photos of plates o' food: broccoli and cauliflower and hunners o' other stuff that Jada didn't recognise. Words swam around it all. 'Aye, aye,' Jada said, throwing it onto

105

the side table. 'When Ah've got time. Look, tell ye whit, Ah'll go tae the Chinky. Get ye vegetables in black bean sauce or something, OK?'

'Aye, awright.' Still huffy, arms folded.

'How's the wee man been?'

'Fine. Gaunnae just get the Chinky and come straight back, but, Jada? Ah'm starving. Don't go tae the Flaps.'

'Aye! Course!'

Jada placed the order in the Chinese takeaway on the corner: vegetables in black bean sauce for Nicola, beef Chow Mein, chips and curry sauce and a couple of spring rolls for him. 'Some prawn crackers an aw, pal.'

'Fifteen minutes,' the wee guy told him.

Jada crossed the road and headed into the Flaps.

ELEVEN

'He's just wounded.'

'No.'

'Left for dead then, but we don't actually see him—'

'Gregor, no.'

'How about he, uh, has a brother? An identical—'

'Jesus Christ.'

Dan was tired. Tom had woken every twenty minutes last night, howling for more and more milk. He suppressed a jaw-cracking yawn as he listened to Gregor Kübler-Rossing it. Having spent the last few weeks in denial, he was now firmly into stage two: bargaining. They were in the Ivy, the restaurant that, since the pandemic, had replaced Rogano around the corner as the locus of Dan's annual script-bartering sessions with Gregor. For two decades now their negotiations over storylines, screentime, close-ups and dialogue had taken place among heavy silverware, heavy wines and heavy tabs. Dan always paid. Gregor was famously 'careful' with money. Besides, as show creator, producer and chief writer, Dan earned more. They had a corner table in the green, foresty room, well away from the other diners. It was the first day of March, officially springtime in a couple of weeks, but outside, through the stained-glass windows onto Buchanan Street, the Glasgow weather went on doing its terrible winter business – slush the colour of ash and urine.

They'd got swiftly through the pleasantries, Dan and Gregor. *'And Grace is up and about? Good. How's the wee one sleeping? Oh, good.'* And then quickly down to the real business: how Gregor was going to convince Dan to keep McCallister alive.

Dan had purposefully positioned himself with his back to the room so that he wouldn't have to see the parade of middle-aged women finding excuses to detour past their table to bat their eyelashes coyly at Gregor, which he returned with a slight smile and an incline of the head, the warmth of the smile and the depth of the incline directly related to their attractiveness. Now and then one of these women would interrupt their conversation, usually saying 'sorry' or 'excuse me' to Dan before turning their back on him to address Gregor.

'I just had to tell you how much I love your show.'

'I'm your biggest fan.'

'Och, see that episode where you . . .'

'I've been watching you since I was a wee girl.'

This last, with its implication of age, of the incredible amount of time the show had been on air, was obviously less pleasing to Gregor. His smile would become a bit strained on that one, his 'that's very kind, thank you' a shade curter. The restaurant was quiet this afternoon. Only three fans had attempted conversation in the two hours they'd been here. Their finished entrées lay between them, the dessert menus unread. Oops, make that four, another woman was breaking towards them now. 'Excuse me,' she said to Dan before turning to Gregor and unleashing her full smile, flattening a palm against her breast to stress the sincerity of whatever she was saying.

Dan felt sorry for Gregor now. Being forced into the position of suggesting McCallister's long-lost twin brother rocks up? The poor old fucker. All the women. All the kids. It was time to play his trump card. Gregor was thanking the woman and saying goodbye to her with a lingering handshake. 'Gregor, listen,' Dan said, leaning forward, lowering his voice, moving his wine glass towards Gregor like a chess piece. 'I've been waiting to tell you. There are conversations going on with the powers that be. Nothing's certain yet, but they want to keep going, after this series.' Gregor, instantly brightening. 'But they want to recast. Younger.' The face falling. 'They'll keep the brand – *McCallister* – but it'll be a new McCallister. I've told them I'm not going to be involved creatively, but the good news is, under our contracts, they'd have to make us both exec producers.' Dan raised his glass, smiling. 'Eh?'

Gregor did not reach for his. 'Great,' he said flatly.

'Come on. Nice fat fee every episode for doing absolutely hee-haw? What's not to like? Plus, you'll still get paid on all the re-runs, *plus*, now you can go off and do whatever you like.' Dan was thinking panto here. Gregor was probably thinking Lear. Aye, dream on, pal.

'And whom is to replace me?'

You mean *who*, you pompous, illiterate old wank, Dan thought. But he said, 'Replace you? It's not like—'

'Who will be the new McCallister?'

'Well, there won't *be* a new McCallister. It's not *Doctor Who* – you're not fucking regenerating. It'll be a new character.'

Gregor's eyes narrowed. 'An existing character?'

'Well . . .'

'Dan, please.'

'OK . . .' He took a deep breath. Fucker would be finding

out soon enough anyway. 'Nothing's set, but, uh, they're talking about bringing Toby forward.'

A pause. Lengthening into a glacial silence. Gregor staring at him. Dan fiddling with the stem of his wine glass.

And now, stage three: *anger.*

'*Toby???!!*' Gregor hissed, eyes popping, voice all italics, with three question marks and a couple of exclamation points. Toby Liddle had played McCallister's handsome, hapless, yet dogged, assistant DC Angus Kerr for the last four seasons. The viewers, young women especially, loved him. He was also – and this opinion would go unvoiced at this lunch – not a bad wee actor, Dan thought. 'Fucking Toby? That wee shite! That fucking hack! He couldnae act his way oot o' a paper fucking ba–' Dan had heard this before – Gregor's silky, manufactured RADA brogue collapsing under duress, giving way to his real Glasgow accent.

'Easy,' Dan said.

'Come on, Dan! Jesus fuck!'

And now we were fast moving into stage four: *fear.* Gregor looked desperate. Like he was going to burst into tears. Dan finally got it. It wasn't about the money at all. It was about this – the parade of women, the good table in the nice restaurant – all of *this* ending. Gregor was insane, yes, of course he was, he was an actor for fuck's sake, but somewhere in his heart, in the dark night of the soul, he knew himself that within a few years he wouldn't be giving it '*O reason not the need!*' No, he'd be giving it 'HE'S BEHIND YOU!' to a few hundred schoolchildren, flicking the Vs and throwing boiled sweets at him. Every fucking year from late November through to the end of January. Gregor at sixty-five, seventy, struggling into the tights and the pointy felt shoes in the cold, tiled Victorian dressing room. The 'GOOD LUCK!' card from wife number six on the ledge behind him, next to the envelopes containing the final demands for school fees, university tuition, whatever. Christ. Once again, Dan almost found himself feeling sorry for the poor old bastard.

'Dan, one more season. Please. Let's find a way to—'

'Sorry, Gregor. We're done.' Dan signalled for the bill.

Across from him Gregor's shoulders dropped. He reached for his wine glass, drained the lot, and, with a sigh as heavy as the Pomerol, said, 'When do we start shooting?'

'End of June as always. Monday after Solstice.'

Dan's heart danced at the thought of the end being in sight. Granted, with Gregor fuming and death-staring and one-upping Toby at every turn, it wasn't destined to be a fun shoot. And he was dreading — dreading — being away from Grace and Tom so much. He'd go up on the Tuesday morning and back on the Friday afternoon. They were interviewing nannies next week, and the grandparents would be around, but, even so, it would be tough on Grace. Still, this would be the very last time. And Tom would only be six months old. He wouldn't even remember him being away when he grew up.

'Come on, pal,' he said now to Gregor. 'You knew this was coming. Nearly twenty years. We had a good run, eh?'

Gregor just stared at the tablecloth, fingering a breadcrumb. As the waitress approached with the bill, he sighed, 'Oh well.' And then he sombrely made with the Shakespeare. '*Glory is like a circle in the water, which never ceaseth to enlarge itself, till by broad spreading it disperse to nought.*' He finished and smiled at the waitress. The girl — early twenties, very good-looking, East European — smiled gently back at Gregor, in the way young people do at the old and the mad.

Beaming, Dan slipped his credit card into the leather folder, not even bothering to look at the total. It took everything in him not to scream, 'HE'S BEHIND YOU!'

Here it was, finally steaming into view.

The good ship Acceptance.

PART TWO

SIX MONTHS LATER

TWELVE

Through the window, Jada watched the Scottish late summer rain falling soft and vertical, so very different from the Scottish winter rain, which came at you diagonally, horizontally, from below sometimes. The early September sky this morning the colour of a tea-soaked J cloth. The bleakness of the estate below: the overflowing bins and abandoned white goods.

'Aye, haud oan a minute, cannae hear ye in here,' Jada said, jamming a finger in his ear, struggling to keep the excitement out of his voice as he crossed the living room. In order to ford the tiny space, Jada had to take three steps over a drift of Duplo bricks, a plastic train track, half a dozen plates with toast rinds on them, the tinfoil containers the Chinese food had arrived in (some still half-full), a pizza box or two, a brimming ashtray and a pile of laundry. Fucking Nicola. Lazy cow. He was jamming that finger in his ear to counter several sources of noise: the television blaring some demented kids' programme, Nicola banging around in the galley kitchen off the living room and eight-month-old Jayden (the definitive name change had occurred some months back) in his crib in the corner, flat on his back and singing a mindless series of 'ba-ba-ba-ba's as he clattered his plastic beaker off the bars like a guy in the drunk tank on a Friday night.

'That's better,' Jada said as he closed the UPVC door behind him and stepped out onto the balcony – a narrow ledge with waist-high railings that overlooked the other 60s block opposite, with its colourful ornamentation of kids' bikes, satellite dishes and drying washing. Jada completed the action he always performed upon contact with fresh air – he jammed a cigarette into his mouth and lit it – before saying, 'Whit ye saying?'

'We're on. Next week,' the Shite said.

'Aye?' Jada said. Finally.

'Aye. Meet us up the Flaps and Ah'll fill ye in.'

Yesss, Jada wanted to say. Or, *fucking magic.* But he kept his game face on, just said, 'Aye. Awright.' He looked at his watch, the new TAG Heuer. 'Gies hauf an hour.'

Jada hung up smiling – a rare enough event these days. He fucking needed this tae come aff. Full disclosure: the wee windfall from that Tesla back at the start of the year hadn't gone quite as far as he had hoped. And the fucking wean was costing him a fortune, wi' aw the shite it needed. And he'd treated him and Nicola to some stuff: the watches, some new clothes, a wee bit o' Stone Island. Old school. Shite was dearer now than it had been back in the early 90s, when Jada first started buying it. And, aye, there'd been a couple of ill-advised rushes of blood on the betting front that had had to be settled. And, sure, there had been a few big nights out in the weeks after the windfall, some large bar tabs – in the Flaps, up the Hun, down the Saltire – that he'd airily picked up. Well, that was a business expense in a way, eh? A man in his position. Ye hud tae project success in order tae get it an aw that pish. He had also made what turned out to be a spectacularly poor investment . . .

Shuggie Rankine knew a boy down Ayrshire way who was

selling knock-off vodka – Romanian or something – for twenty quid a case. One pound sixty-odd a bottle. Sell it tae aw the wee offies he knew around Partick and Whiteinch for three shitters a pop. They'd knock it out tae aw the mad alkies for six or seven notes – everyone doubled their money. Got tae speculate tae accumulate an aw that. Shuggie just wanted a finder's fee for hooking them up and Jada did the deal in the car park down Irvine beach, handing over five hundred nicker for twenty-five cases to two unsmiling Eastern European guys.

To be fair, 20/20 hindsight an aw that, the alarm bells should have started ringing right away. Jada should have picked up on the label, on the fact that something called 'Flaming Cozzak Voddka' was not going to be a top-shelf product. And so it proved when he got the first angry phone call from Mr Mukherjee who ran PriceBeaster on Dumbarton Road, followed by similar calls from Mr Patel and Mrs Khan. Speculate tae accumulate? It transpired that most of the speculation had been done somewhere in Bulgaria, where some cunt had speculated wildly on the chemical question of what exactly constituted vodka. For Flaming Cozzak had turned out to be more of a potato liqueur. And a weak one at that: you'd have had to drink three bottles of it to get the mildest buzz. (As one of Mr Patel's more tenacious clients had attempted to do.) Jada had had to wearily point out his terms of sale to his customers – if you don't like it, get tae fuck. This including tanning the jaw of Mr Mukherjee's very insistent elder son. But the damage was done. Word got round and the orders dried up. Over twenty cases of the undrinkable pishwater were now languishing in Jada's lock-up and the mobile number he had for the Eastern Europeans was no longer in service. Jada had taken what satisfaction he could from kicking Shuggie's

117

balls to tatters while the Shite and Mad Toby held him down, but it had been cold comfort. And the fifty-odd quid Shuggie had on him at the time of the beating wasn't going to recoup Jada's investment by a long shot.

Anyway, whatever, it was all gone. He fucking needed this tae come off. Greatly cheered, he stepped back into the living room and planted his bare right foot straight into a foil carton of congealed chicken Chow Mein.

'AH, YA DIRTY FUCKEN HOOR'S BASTARD!'

Nicola appeared in the doorway to the kitchen, Jayden wedged into one armpit now and sucking happily on his plastic beaker of Rush! energy drink. Most of his wee pals just got Irn-Bru or Coca-Cola in theirs, but the wee man had really developed a taste for the Rush! Maybe it was hereditary – it was Nicola and Jada's favourite soft drink too.

'DADA!' Jayden suddenly said, delightedly. He'd only started doing it in the last couple of weeks, but it was constant now. Not quite nine months old. 'A prodigy!' that doctor had said. Whatever the fuck that was. A prodigy at bursting your coupon. 'DADADADADADADADADADA!' following him around the flat like a machine gun. The boy was smiling, beaming, showing his new bottom front teeth. And was it Jada's imagination or were those new teeth already showing faint signs of discolouration?

'Dae ye have tae talk like that in front o' the wean?' Nicola said. 'Can ye no just say "fuck" or "shite" like a normal person for fuck's sake?'

Wearily, his foot dangling in mid-air, a long, lone noodle suspended from his big toe, Jada took her in – the grey, shapeless sweats hiding her increasingly grey and shapeless form, the top dotted with a kaleidoscopic range of stains. The red, pouched eyes. The hair that hadn't been cut in months, all straggling and split and greasy. What a fucking midden. 'And can you no tidy this fucking cowp up now and then, ya manky cow?' came Jada's rejoinder.

'DADADADA!' Jayden gurgled happily as he threw his now empty beaker across the room, where it cracked off the door frame and rolled to a halt next to a tea towel Jada had used to wipe up some Buckfast the other night.

'And ye said ye wouldnae smoke in the flat!'

'Eh?' Jada looked down and was surprised to see the lit Belgravia still smouldering between his fingers. 'Ah didnae . . . fuck sake!' He took a big drag before hurriedly stubbing it out in the overflowing ashtray on the shelf by the door to the balcony and stepping, more carefully this time, across the room towards the two of them.

'Listen–' Jada began.

'DADADADA!'

'Aye, Ah hear ye, Jayden. Gies peace. Ah–'

'DADADADADADA!'

'Here, he just wants to see ye,' Nicola said, passing the baby to Jada.

Jayden delightedly buried his face into his dad's neck, unbothered by the cloud of tobacco reeking from him.

'Aye, aye, aw right. Fuck sake.' Jada patted the boy's back. 'Look, Ah've got tae go oot. Bit o' business.'

'Eh? It's Saturday, but! Ah thought we were going shopping!'

'Whit dae ye think Ah um, Nicola? A fucking . . .' He thought for a moment. 'A . . . *teacher* or something? Ah've got a meeting.'

Nicola snorted. 'Meeting, ma erse.'

'Gies peace, Nicola.'

'Where?'

'Whit?' Jada juggled Jayden around to his other shoulder; he'd felt the boy gumming his neck, looking for purchase with those two tiny wee teeth. Tiny wee, aye, but the fucker could still inflict some serious damage wi' them.

'Where's this meeting?'

'In the Flaps.'

Another snort.

'Hey, some cun–' he remembered the baby, 'some bastard's goat tae pay fur aw this!' Jada flung his arm out to indicate the tiny flat as though he were gesturing to the Palace of Versailles at the very peak of its glory.

'And ye said ye'd take him oot fur a walk! Let me huv a wee nap.'

'Walk? Fucking pishing doon!'

'It's no that bad.'

Jada looked at her, at the exhaustion sand-blasted into her face. Only nineteen and she looked like fucking whit's-his-name. Methuselah. But, on this occasion – and perhaps this had something to do with the proximity of his son, with his baby flesh, his warmth and innocence – Jada was able to feel more pity than disgust when he looked at the boy's mother. He felt his anger recede and he cupped Nicola's cheek gently. 'Look, Ah'll just huv a couple o' pints, right? Ah'll be back by five and Ah'll take him oot fur a walk then. Bring us back something fae the Indian fur dinner, eh? Smash a big fucking ruby down us, get an early night an that.'

Nicola hesitated, then allowed herself to be pulled roughly into him. 'Aye, awright, then.'

Jada nodded tolerantly, as though his kindness and decency were drawn from a very deep well, one whose reserves were finite and would one day run dry. This rare and tender moment was broken as he felt Jayden stiffening in his arms. And then the short, angry report as the baby squirted a hot blast of liquid hell into his nappy just inches from Jada's nostrils. Even Jada – a connoisseur, an afficionado, of farts – was stunned by the instantaneousness of the stench. No warm-up, no gradual release. Just there, immediately filling the room, the reek of, say, a month-old badger's corpse marinated in sulphur. 'Fuck sake,' Jada said, dry heaving. 'Pick the change oot o' that, doll.' He handed him back to Nicola and went off to find his keys.

Half an hour later, having succeeded in changing the baby and then herself (it had turned into a dirty protest when Jayden pulled his leg free of her grasp halfway through getting the nappy off), Nicola lay slumped and exhausted in her dressing gown on the sofa while Jayden stared at a cartoon on the TV. She contemplated the rest of the day. Too early to roll a joint. Maybe get dressed in a bit. Go tae the shops and then the playground. Come back and put the wee man down for his afternoon sleep and *then* smoke a big bifta. Ye had tae take some responsibility. Still, Nicola could see how things got out of hand, for some o' her pals, for her mum back in the day, back on the estate. Ye hud wee weans and nothing to do and the whole day just yawning ahead o' ye and then yer doorbell goes and it's wee Rab from up the road, or Big Malky fae across the street, and they've got a couple o' bottles o' Bucky and some ectoids, maybe a bit o' the brown, and before ye know it the afternoon's turned into a mad party and yer getting double-ended on the living-room floor while the wean's having his nap. Wiz easy enough tae get intae that kinda life, especially when the kids were too wee tae tell any tales. Nicola didnae want that for Jayden. She had some dim and distant memories herself of . . .

In these memories she was looking through bars, so still in her cot, still dead wee, and there was music and dancing and her mum and a couple o' guys and . . .

Aye, they were dim and distant, these memories.

THIRTEEN

Dan checked the fridge again: the four small bottles lined up in the top shelf of the right-hand door, teated and capped and ready to go. The stock of extra dummies – already sterilised and floating in their tub. One of his favourite cuddly toys – the wee kangaroo – was on the stairs. Just in case he . . . Wait, what was that? Dan crossed the kitchen to the island in the centre and picked up the monitor. No, nothing. He'd just rolled over. Was the temperature a bit too . . . no, it was fine. Acceptable. He turned the volume on the monitor up to the absolute max.

'Relax, he's fast asleep.'

'I know. I was just–'

He looked up from the screen to see Grace coming in and setting her overnight bag down. 'Wow,' Dan said. She was wearing her black jumpsuit with the long black boots, and she'd had her hair done that afternoon and was in full make-up. She looked like Saturday night personified. 'You. Look. Gorgeous.'

'Thank you. Have you seen my phone?'

'Listen, are you sure that's enough milk?'

'Dan,' she began, the weary warning tone in her voice. They'd already been over this. 'He'll want a feed around midnight and then likely another around two or three, then there's one for first thing and an extra one just in case. I'll be back by ten tomorrow morning at the very latest.'

It was a kind of hen night, for her pal Becky, over on the Southside. Dinner and a sleepover. It was the first time Grace had gone out overnight in eight months – since Tom arrived. 'You know, I thought he was going to say it earlier,' Dan said.

'Really?' Grace said, still searching for her phone.

'Yeah. He was going *d-d-d-*, I swear. It was so close.'

'It'll come. Where the fuck did I–'

Dan, an avid reader of all the literature, had heard that some babies started saying 'dada' around the eight- or nine-month mark and he was desperate for Tom to join this pantheon of wunderkids. But so far, nothing.

'Can you just call my phone?' Grace asked.

This was a thrice-daily process. He dialled the number and her phone started ringing. In her handbag on the side, the red Birkin. 'Ah,' Grace said. 'My bad. Right! I'm offski.' She came around the island and gave him a quick hug and a peck on the cheek, smelling of that customised perfume she had – sandalwood and spice and pine. Dan felt the enormity of the occasion demanded something more than a peck. It wanted a full embrace, tears. A lock of hair exchanged. The kind of farewell due to a soldier going off on a five-year campaign. He pulled her in, hugging her again. 'Oh, for God's sake, Dan,' Grace said, laughing. 'You'd think I was going off around the world. The worst thing that can happen is that he wakes up and cries for a wee while. So calm down and I'll see you in the morning, OK?'

'OK. Have a good time. Say hi to everyone from me.' They were walking down the long hallway now, her boots clacking on the grey slate flagstones.

124

'Will do.'

Grace turned back from the open front door, their new black Tesla gleaming on the kerb behind her (insurance had taken a while, but they'd come through) to say, 'And don't go in there checking on him every ten minutes. You'll just wake him up.'

'I won't!'

'Hmm,' she said, meaning 'we both know what you're like.'

'Have a good time. We'll be fine.'

'Night, darling.' Grace closed the door behind her. Dan stood in the hallway for a minute, listening to the creaks and gurgles of the great house around him. He checked his watch – a few minutes after seven. What to do? He wanted to rewrite a couple of the scenes they'd be shooting next week. (The train back up to Inverness on Monday night.) But he didn't want to go down to his study in the basement. Even though you got a signal, he didn't trust the baby monitor to function properly through two floors. Watch a movie? Mmm, what if he couldn't hear the monitor over the TV? Maybe reading a book was the safest bet. Could he risk a glass of wine? No, best not. Just in case something happ–

A noise, from the monitor in the kitchen, like a click. Dan *ran* through and picked it up. He'd rolled over again, the sound had been the dummy clamped in his fist – one of five Dan had scattered around his sleeping form, just in case – hitting the wooden bars of the cot. But there was still one in his mouth; he was still asleep.

And the whole question of whether he should have dummies at all had been vexed. Dan had obviously spent days online doing the research: the case studies, the debates on Mumsnet, the unpublished PhD thesis he'd found from – where else? – America that

125

traced early school performance of groups of babies who'd had dummies against those who hadn't. And, if they went the dummy path, what kind of dummy? Dan had found some high-end silicone ones online. Custom-shaped for different palates. Not cheap. As he read about all of this, over breakfast, or in bed at night, agonising and fretting, Grace would turn the pages of her newspaper, or her book, and murmur the odd 'mmm' or 'really?' or 'interesting'. And then, one night around the three-month mark, back in April, while the discussion was still very much live (in Dan's mind at any rate) Tom had his worst-ever crying jag, one that started at the outer edge of hysteria and escalated from there. Finally, after an hour, Grace said 'fuck this' and drove to the 24-hour Tesco, where she swept a shelfful of dummies into her basket. She stuck one in Tom's mouth and peace and silence descended immediately. And that was the end of the dummy debate. Dan quietly dropped his phonebook of research into the wastepaper basket beside his desk.

He opened the fridge again. The four bottles still there. Good. He hadn't eaten. But no point in cooking just for himself. Phone a takeaway? Hmm. Despite any instructions to the contrary, they were bound to ring the bloody doorbell. He took out a tub of posh soup – Thai green curry – loosened the plastic lid and placed it in the microwave. In the three and a half minutes it took to cook his supper, Dan ran downstairs, with the monitor in his hand, to get his laptop. He could work in the kitchen. His study took up the basement. Bookshelves ran the length of one wall, nearly thirty feet, the entire depth of the house. At the other end of the room from his work area was a kind of den. Two low brown leather sofas faced each other across a glass and driftwood coffee table. The big flatscreen set on the wall. The tasteful

126

framed movie posters: *Rushmore*, Godard's *A Bout de Souffle*, *The Conversation*, *The King of Comedy*. (Languishing in the cupboard along the hall, dust gathering on their frames: *Manhattan* and *Annie Hall*. Well, you couldn't any more, could you? Not after the documentary and everything.)

He got back upstairs well before the 'ping', settled himself at the island and opened the Final Draft document he'd been working on.

INT. POLICE STATION - DAY

McCallister walks briskly through...

Just as he went to start typing he heard a mewl from the monitor. Dan pulled it towards him and looked at the screen. Hmm. Tom had rolled over and got his cashmere blanket tangled across him, over his sleeping bag. Could he . . .? I mean, it's unlikely, Dan thought, but he had read a couple of studies where babies had . . . Christ. Well, it was warm enough. Best just take it out.

He crept into the nursery and stood over the cot. The chest rising and falling rhythmically, the mouth slightly open, the arms raised each side of the head, as though in a gesture of supplication, of surrender. The thumbs clenched around the fingers, no bigger than shrimps. Gently, ever so gently, not wanting to wake Tom, but very much wanting to indulge in the sweetest pleasure, Dan leaned down and got his nostrils close to the crown of the skull, to the fine, silky dark hair, and sucked in a lungful of the incredible scent: talcum powder and green fields and open skies with a faintly warm, hamsterish note just beneath it. Above all – like a just-painted house, or just-laid carpeting, or the car straight off the production line – the baby smell delivered one thing: freshness. *I am brand new*, it said. If you could bottle this scent, Dan reflected, not for the first time, you'd be a billionaire. Every other fragrance in the world demoted overnight to fish heads and manure. All the perfumiers of Florence, begging in the streets. He held as still as he could, trying to get his breathing in tempo with Tom's, every rise in his son's chest timed with the flaring of his own nostrils and the deep filling of his lungs with the baby waft. He finally got it, the way old ladies went on, the way the grannies went on. *'Ah'm gaunnae eat you up!'* He thought it was just a cliché before. Of course, like all clichés, it had its roots in an essential human truth: he wanted to possess the boy completely. To consume him. To have him be part of his organs in the same way he had once been part of Grace's. Dan stood there, crouched over the warm bundle, and, for a moment, he was conscious in a way that we so rarely are that he was as happy as it was possible to be.

'Oh my God,' Grace was saying. 'He was not!'

Yvonne just screamed.

'He fucking well was!' said Sarah. Sarah was short, blonde, freckled and the last one of them to be resolutely, unapologetically single. She worked in music PR.

'What did you do?' Grace and Becky in unison.

They were in a restaurant called Big Counter, on the northern end of Victoria Road, Sarah's choice, as she was the 'sort of' bridesmaid and it was close to her flat where they'd be staying the night. It was an unusually warm night for this wet summer and the door was open onto the street.

This was a part of the city, Grace reflected, that once upon a time you only drove through to get to other places, a strip of arterial road studded with wasteland and old man pubs. Now it was Moscow mules served in battered copper mugs with fresh lime and mint and sharing plates all over the place. When Sarah moved here, ten years ago, they'd all thought she was off her bloody head. Now the huge three-bedroom flat she'd bought for a song looked like a very smart investment. It was a 'sort of' hen night, and Sarah a 'sort of' bridesmaid, because Becky didn't want any fuss. She was in her late thirties, like the rest of them, and had been with her partner Alan for fifteen years. They had two small kids and were finally 'just getting round to it', in her words.

'Well, I had two choices, right?' Sarah went on. 'Either hang up right away or . . .'

'Oh. My. God.' This was Yvonne, the most easily shocked of the group. Matronly – her brown hair already greying – Yvonne was what Sarah called a 'total Phase Eight/6 Music mum' and she'd pretty much presented as middle-aged since they'd all been at university together. She'd worked as a teacher for a wee while before the kids. Now a self-styled 'homemaker'. 'Didn't you just bang the laptop shut?'

'No!' Sarah laughed. 'So,' she looked around and lowered her voice – the restaurant was very small, but there was only one other table left at this point, a couple in the window across the room – before resuming her story, 'he's totally naked, and it is *not* impressive. Like a wee chipolata poking out a bird's nest.'

'Eww!' Yvonne. The others shushed her.

'At least he wasn't erect,' Becky said. Grace saw that Becky's starter lay untouched – her last-minute push to shift a few pounds before the wedding photographs. And Becky, by her own admission, had piled it on in the last few years, a by-product of the boys being small and at home all day. Snacks and biscuits and cakes and finishing their food off and what have you.

They'd known each other since they were eighteen, and Grace could still see the cheeky chipmunk features of the old Becky submerged in the fleshy puddle of the new Becky's face. Becky worked in social care, in Glasgow's outer burghs and, dear God, the stories she had, alternating between hysterical and heartbreaking.

'More to come on that, my friend,' Sarah said.

'Hang on – and this was the first date?' Grace asked.

'It wasn't even a date!' Sarah said. 'We'd matched on Tinder, and this was the quick Zoom to see how we got on before we met up IRL! You know – the old "here's what I look like, I'm not a serial killer" chat.' The others – all married – did not know. They nodded anyway. 'So I'd been getting ready for bed, I'm wearing my old Nirvana T-shirt, and he says, all husky like, "Take that fucking thing off."'

'Oh, gross.' Yvonne.

'What a keeper.' Becky.

'So I look down at the T-shirt, and then back at him, all innocent, and I say, "So you were more of a Pearl Jam guy then?"'

A beat – and then they all exploded into laughter. Except one. 'I don't get it,' Yvonne said, frowning.

'And *then* you hung up?' Rose said. Rose was the real beauty of the group. Tall and gamine. 'A racehorse', the others would say. 'Bloody carthorse more like,' Rose would say. She'd been married to Will for nine years and they had three kids, two boys and a girl. It had seemed to take Rose fifteen minutes each time to get her figure back. 'The fucking bitch,' as Becky had it. She was a commercial litigation lawyer and had only just gone back to work last year, after their youngest started nursery.

130

'Well . . .' Sarah said, holding up the empty wine bottle and making a pleading face at the waiter, who smiled and nodded.

'Oh, you dirty bitch,' Grace said, through tears of laughter. How she'd missed this. Looking around the table at her friends' faces, it was hard to miss the differences in the intensity of their expressions: Sarah – single, childless – looked normal. Like this was just another night out. Which it was. The other three all had a gleam in their eyes, a glint that said, *we are going to take the absolute maximum out of this*. They radiated the almost hysterical shine of those who didn't get out very often. Sarah only looked around the restaurant when she wanted something. The others did it regularly in an I-can't-quite-believe-I'm-here-without-the-kids manner. And now Grace, until very recently a Sarah herself, had joined the other side. She was one of them, one of the mums. It occurred to her that she wasn't entirely sure how she felt about this yet.

'So how . . .' Becky said, her own laughing fit finally subsiding now. 'How did this all end?'

A beat of comic timing, then: 'Seeing him Friday.'

Another torrent of screams and laughter. The tiny 'O' of Yvonne's mouth, her utterly scandalised face.

The waiter arrived with the fresh bottle of Pinot amid their cries of 'you skank', 'you slag' and – from Grace – a delighted 'you utter bike!'

'Nice to see old friends getting along,' the waiter said, pouring. Grace placed a hand primly over her glass. 'Better not,' she said. Off the looks of the others she said, 'What? I'm still breast-feeding!'

'God, newbie,' Becky said. 'You express enough for the next day too and freeze it.'

'My bloody tits nearly fell off expressing enough to leave

Dan for tonight! Anyway, how do you cope in the morning, with a hangover and a baby?'

'Ah,' Rose cut in. 'Once again inexperience betrays you, young Padawan. You don't negotiate for the night out. You negotiate for the next day off.'

'Do you?' Grace said, genuinely interested in the lawyer's take here.

'Fuck aye,' Rose went on. 'Listen to me, this is the good stuff I'm telling you here.' She sat back and folded her arms. 'What do they do when you go out for the night?'

'Uh . . .' Grace thought.

'They think it's fucking Christmas. Think about it. *You* get the wee ones down before you go out and then what do they do? Eh? They phone Domino's and sit around stuffing an American Hot into their faces and having a Tarantino triple bill or whatever on the big-screen telly and then the next morning you're meant to act like they did you a favour?'

'Mmm-hmm,' Becky nodded in agreement.

'Fuck all that. I tell Will, "It's not about tonight. It's about *tomorrow*. I am going to wallow in bed, feed my hangover, and you and the wee shites can crack on, my son."'

'Really?' Grace said. 'Well, this *is* the good stuff. I'm not getting any of this from the books.'

'Stick wi' yer aunt Rose, hen,' Rose said, topping her up.

An hour later, and they were all back at Sarah's, busting extreme moves to Wyclef Jean's 'Perfect Gentleman'. After Sarah had performed with such ferocity that she almost broke her own coffee table when delivering Hope's rap – testifying about being born with the body of a goddess and did they, in fact, have any idea how hard this is? – Grace staggered through to the kitchen for a glass of water, checking her phone as she went. She was stunned to see it was only half ten. Her body was telling her it was four in the morning. Three texts from Dan. Becky was in the kitchen, having a rare cigarette out of the window. 'Did she do the rap?'

'Oh, yes,' Grace replied. 'Hey, listen to this. *All good here. Are you having a nice time? x*, at 8.32. *Still all fine. x*, at 9.28. And then, at 10.01, *Off to bed. All good. Speak in the morning. Love you darling. Night xx.*'

'Why's he going to bed at ten o'clock?'

'Because he'll be scared to do anything except very quietly read his book with one eye glued to the monitor.' She filled a pint glass from the tap and took a deep draught of what Sarah called 'council juice'. 'You know Dan.'

'Aww,' Becky said. 'He's so sweet.'

'I know . . .' Grace said, sitting down at the kitchen table. Dan *was* sweet.

When Grace ran through the things that vexed her about her husband, she found that, sweetly, they were mostly small and rooted in his desire to please, to try and make life nicer for them. They were so small in fact that she filed them under 'SDAs': Small Daily Annoyances.

One: over-communication. Like the three texts she'd received in a ninety-minute period tonight. Dan was incapable of doing anything – going to the supermarket, downstairs to his study or out for a walk – without at least half a dozen texts and/or a phone call or two informing her of his progress. Related to this were his over-elaborate goodbyes and hellos, often saying farewell to Grace as she went off on a quick trip to the shops as though she was going away on a journey of Phileas Fogg proportions. His greeting upon her return would be commensurately excessive.

Two: obsessive tidying. Dan valued neatness over convenience and ease. For instance, all cables and plug leads had to be hidden from view, as though it was a disgrace to admit that electrical goods had to be plugged in. Consequently, it was a pain in the arse when you had to plug something in or take the plug out. When it came to the kitchen, he hated appliances being scattered randomly around the work surfaces. He had a corner he liked to keep stuff in. It was an awkward corner, slightly hidden away, and Grace would regularly find that Dan had tucked the rice cooker, the toaster, the food processor, the water filter *and* the kitchen-roll holder all in there. Seeing as these were things they used on a near daily basis, Grace would regularly find herself having to reach around into this corner to take one or other of them out.

Three: fastidiousness. Dan was a very good cook. But, God, he was methodical. Every ingredient had to be weighed and measured and prepared beforehand. Finely chopped and then placed in little bowls beside the hob, like he was on *Saturday* bloody *Kitchen* or something, and then the recipe was followed with chilling precision – even for something he'd made many times before. He was a good cook, yes, but you wouldn't want Dan in your corner if you had to knock together a meal for four in thirty minutes. Grace reckoned Dan's average time from peeling the first clove of garlic to plating the food was around two hours. His cookbook might well be called *Dan's One-Hundred-and-Twenty-Minute Meals*. His speed in the kitchen was also hindered by another SDA . . .

Four: inability to task focus. If Grace asked Dan to go into the living room to retrieve, say, a newspaper for her, or a sweater, it might well be twenty minutes before he reappeared. Because, on the way, he would notice five or six other small tasks that urgently needed his attention: a cable that was insufficiently hidden perhaps. Or some laundry that needed folding. Or a picture that was hanging slightly skew-whiff. If Dan was tasked with making a pot of tea, Grace would steel herself for the half-hour wait. Because other jobs would intervene. Sometimes to the degree that the original tea would have gone cold and have to be remade. Sometimes Dan would come whistling back into the room and she would look at him and say, 'Uh, Dan, the tea?' (or the paper/sweater/whatever) and he'd say, 'Oh shit!' He'd have become so involved in the subsidiary tasks that the primary mission had been forgotten. In Grace's mind this was possibly connected to . . .

Five: the non-sequiturs. Maybe it was the writer in him – not always fully present, forever working on a plot – but Dan would often start or resume conversations in a completely ad hoc fashion. They'd be talking about, say, interest rates and Dan would suddenly say, 'I mean, I didn't even want to go in the first place.' Grace would say, '*What?*' It would transpire that Dan was continuing a conversation Grace thought they'd finished fifteen minutes ago, having long moved onto the fresh topic.

But then Grace considered some of the things that had gone on with the girls and their relationships. The sexting affair Rose had busted Will having a few years back. The couples counselling Yvonne and Barry had been through. Sarah's ongoing campaign to find the Very Worst Man on Tinder. And then she took a breath and counted herself incredibly lucky that this handful of Small Daily Annoyances were all she could come up with after a decade together.

So she texted back: *Love you too darling. Night x.*

Becky flicked the butt out into the night – a tiny firework of orange cinders arcing off into the dark sky – closed the window and took a fresh bottle of white wine from the fridge. She sat down across from Grace. 'And how's you?' she asked, going to pour. Grace held the thumb and index finger of her right hand a centimetre apart as she yawned. Then laughed. 'There's my answer!' Becky said, pouring just a finger of wine into Grace's glass then dousing her own.

'Well, yeah. He doesn't seem to be able to sleep for longer than two hours without clamping onto my tits, the greedy wee bugger.'

'Enough about Dan,' Becky said. 'How's the wean?'

'Barrumph-tisch!' Grace said, doing the snare and cymbal.

Becky raised her brimming glass and said, 'You did it, pal.' And Grace saw now that there were tears in her eyes.

'Och, Becks, come on.' Grace, setting her inch of wine back down and taking her hand. 'It's all good. We got there, eh?'

'I know. I'm just that happy for you.'

'I know you are.' She squeezed her hand. Nothing else to be said. Because, of course, from the first attempts to get pregnant, through every round of IVF, through to the meetings with the adoption agencies, Grace had told her friends *everything*. Especially Becky. She had wept with sorrow in front of her – panting tears, a lake of salt in her throat – after the third failed attempt, after she'd got a false positive reading and her hopes had briefly soared like a drunkard's. She'd wept with frustration after rounds four and five. She'd even wept with anxiety after the sixth round and the definite positive with Tom, when it felt like she was carrying a crystal bulb around in her stomach for the first few months. *What if something goes wrong?* Becky understood everything. Grace knew Dan had been less forthcoming with his friends, the group dynamics of men being what they were. *Just crack on. Mustn't grumble. Och, fine. Fine.* She suspected he might have told Jack *something*. (The timbre of Jack's voice when he'd called round to see the baby a few weeks in, something about the depth of his sincerity when he told her how pleased he was for them, when Dan was out of the room making the tea — taking forever, of course.) But a round table discussion with the lot of them? No chance. Sometimes Grace wondered if it was as simple and idiotic as Dan not wanting them to think his spunk was all fucked up or something. Becky wiped her tears away with her thumb as, with the bang of the kitchen door being shouldered open, Sarah appeared, swaying, a cigarette clamped in her mouth, a bottle of champagne in one hand and a tumbler full of the stuff in the other. 'Come to fuck, you pair of—' She stopped, frowning, taking in Becky's smeared mascara. Becky laughed and Sarah knew without asking what they were talking about and that they were happy tears. 'Aye, OK. Come to fuck, you pair of fucking lezzers. Time to get real.' Behind her, from the lounge, the opening scratching and drum clatter of 'Fuck Tha Police' rang out.

'Woo!' Sarah said, heading back through, punching the air. They laughed. Fuck it. Grace topped up her wine and took a long swallow. Then she looked at Becky before saying, with great seriousness, 'Then, why won't you tell everybody what the fuck you gotta say?' The beat dropped as they both leapt up and ran shrieking through to the living room.

FOURTEEN

Jada lit a fresh Belgravia with the stub of the last one and crushed the old butt out in the ashtray of the Audi. The car clock was telling him it was 7.12am, the autumn morning chilly. Where the fuck were they? At this rate they were going to get stuck in the rush hour over the Kingston Bridge. He was parked up on the access road that led to a far corner of Prestwick Airport, having got here over an hour ago, well ahead of the appointed 6.30 rendezvous time, and he was tired, hungry and hungover. The boyish thrill of watching the fat jets haul themselves skywards every few minutes – like watching an obese man struggling to get out of an armchair, you always thought they weren't quite going to make it – had long worn off. The perimeter lights were switching off now as the sun got stronger. Fuck. What if – he took a hard pull on the fresh cigarette, running a trembling hand through his hair – what if they'd been busted? Captured. Huckled. Right this minute they might be in some cell, somewhere in the bowels of the airport, being sweated, about to give up Jada's name. Should he call Billy or Fat Boab? Naw, emergencies only they'd agreed. Nae contact except in an emergency. And this wasn't that. Yet. In a way Jada's escort was perfunctory – this was the second run, Boab and Chas knew the way – but him and Billy had agreed it was worth it in case the underlings got the idea to stop off on the way and do some deals of their own.

The first run, a month back, had gone smoothly but less profitably than hoped. Chas and Boab, who weren't the brightest pair o' bulbs in the box, and who were likely panicking at this first attempt, had grabbed crates from the back of the Hercules transport aircraft seemingly at random – some of them weren't clearly marked, they'd said – and at the unloading they'd discovered that all they'd wound up with was some mess kits and a lot of crates of parachutes. 'Fucking *parachutes*?' the Gypsy had said to Jada. In the end, after Boab and Chas and Dom had all got their bungs, after Billy's two grand, and his petrol money to Carlisle and back, Jada had walked away with a few hundred quid. Hardly worth the fucking bother. But, Jada reasoned, there were bound to be teething problems in any operation. (And thinking of this phrase made Jada think of Jayden and the tiny top fangs that had recently joined their bottom counterparts. A powerful combo, as Jada had found out at breakfast the other day, when the boy leaned over from his bowl of ChoccoTastics in chocolate milk and sank his new fangs into Jada's thumb. Jada near hooked the wee shite.) What they were after, Jada explained to Chas and Boab at the debrief, was stuff like the more desirable NATO army-grade sleeping bags. They went fast, the Gypsy said. Tents and combat boots were good. Uniforms and blank dog tags too. Basically, the kind of stuff that the Gypsy's contacts in the military-surplus world would be able to sell to their customers, the lumbering psychos who liked dressing up and playing soldiers. *Parachutes?* Fuck sake. Most o' those fat bastards would need a parachute the size of fucking Ibrox.

But, encouragingly, the *system* had worked. They'd just loaded up the extra van, which was then simply waved through onto the distant exit road by the senior man on deck: Billy. Then on to Dom's garage and then Carlisle. Hopefully the pair of them would be more relaxed and discerning this time, after they'd seen how easily it had gone. But where the fuck were the useless pair of fucking Laurel and Hardy bastards? It was nearly half-seven now an–

Thank God. Here it came, finally, the 2.5-tonne white Luton van, trundling slowly towards the sentry box at the perimeter, about half a kilometre from where Jada was parked. He flicked his fag out of the window, turned the engine on and drove slowly towards them. As he got closer, he could see they'd pulled up and were bantering away with the boy in the sentry box. Fat Boab – in his mid-twenties, the senior of the two – was at the steering wheel. Wee Chas in the passenger seat. Jada drove past them, went a few hundred metres along the road and pulled over again. He watched in the rear-view as the barrier went up and the van came onto the road. He pulled out and led the way, following the signs for the M8 towards the city. His mobile rang. 'Aye?'

'Jada, it's Boab.' Jada could see him in the rear-view, the phone pressed to his ear. The daft fat cunt. 'Sorry about the hold-up. Plane was late in and–'

Jada hung up on him and took the turning. Up to Glasgow and onto the Kingston Bridge, the Clyde glittering each way beneath them as they sat in bumper-to-bumper traffic. All in all it took them just over an hour to make the forty-minute drive to Royston.

'Aye. Sorry about that . . .' Boab began, climbing down from the cab of the van and walking towards Jada as Dom closed the garage doors behind them. 'Must have got cut aff. Ah wiz saying–'

Jada booted him in the balls. He gave it a moment, allowing Boab to writhe and whinny. 'What are ye, fucking daft? Oan the phone while driving a load o' stolen gear? Are ye looking tae get pulled over? Don't ever fucking call me oan a mobile phone during a job again.' He said all of this to the crown of Boab's head, Boab now being crumpled on his knees on the oil-stained cement floor, retching and panting and, pathetically, holding onto Jada's calf. Chas stood back uncertainly, watching.

'Ye awright, son?' Jada said to Boab, helping him up now. He'd only used half-force. Didnae want tae hurt the boy. Just had to make the point. Boab was coughing and shaking as he steadied himself against the van, but he managed a nod. 'Yer awright, Boab,' Jada said, patting his back. 'Jist use yer heid in future, aye? Right, Chas, come on then, wee man.'

They rolled the door of the van up, and Jada, Chas and two of Dom's young apprentices started a chain, getting the packing crates down onto the floor before they were reloaded into the other Luton hired by Jada, this one tomato-red. After a moment Boab silently and shamefacedly joined them. Jada worked a crowbar into the top of the first crate down and moved the Styrofoam packing chips aside to reveal the label on a bundle inside. He held it up to Chas, who read hesitantly: 'Wan . . . one dozen . . . Dutch Army . . . Mil-military 3 Season Mod-mod-modular Warm Weather Sleeping Bag Grade 1.'

'These aw the same this time?' Jada said, gesturing to the crates stacked on the floor and in the van.

'Aye, Jada, honest,' Chas said. 'We took our time this time. Thirty crates, aw the same so they ur. Ah swear oan ma maw's fucking life, man.'

Jada checked the load, doing quick calculations: thirty crates, twelve sleeping bags in each one was three hundred and sixty bags at thirty nicker each tae Jada was . . . near eleven thousand pounds. A tenner a bag tae Billy was three and a half grand, a grand for Dom, another grand between Chas and Boab here plus petrol and van hire. Clear five k, easy. No bad fur a day's work. Fucking lawyers didnae earn that. And victimless too. Well . . . Jada briefly pictured some Ukrainian soldier freezing his chanks aff, but so fuck. Don't sign up if ye cannae handle it an aw that. Jada peeled four fifty-pound notes off his roll. The boys were Billy's cost, aye, but it was a good idea to keep them sweet. Wiz always nice tae be nice. 'Here, boys,' he said, handing two of the pink notes to each of them. 'Good job. Have a couple o' pints oan me, eh?'

'Aye, fuck. Thanks, Jada,' Chas said, grinning like the proverbial two-penised dog. Boy was only a wean. A ton was like a grand at that age.

'Cheers, Jada,' Boab said, still scared to meet his eye. 'And Ah'm sorry, like. Didnae think. Gaunnae no tell Billy, eh?'

'Yer awright, son. Between us. Just use the heid in future.' He tapped Boab's temple. 'Go oan now, GTF back tae the airport. Ah'll see youse next month.'

Jada watched Boab waddle off towards the driver's side, walking gingerly to spare his aching plums. 'Right,' Jada turned back to Dom's two wee apprentices. 'Let's load this shite up.'

The motorway sizzled past, Glasgow growing distant in the rear-view mirror and Jada gradually relaxing as he grew used to driving the heavy Luton and digested his delayed breakfast of three sausage and egg McMuffins. The long trip – a little over four hours there and back – was a chance for Jada to contemplate, to take stock, unwind and think. Naturally he did this with the aid of his *Gluebuzzer Live at Fantazia 1993* mix

CD at blood-stunning volume. One of the few upsides of renting vans from Rab's Wrecks in Govanhill was that the vehicles were so old they still came with that increasing rarity: a CD player. And Jada was a devotee of the dying format. He turned it up now as the gabba flowed: The BumBangers' 'Acid-K-Speed-Acid' giving way to Scott Brown, then into Charly Lownoise and Mental Theo, then into the Rotterdam Terror Corporation as the tempos increased, hurtling towards the 200bpm hell zone that characterised the frenzied climax of a classic Gluebuzzer set. As the M8 became the M74, the Scottish fields gradually becoming English, Jada bathed himself in warm memories. For Jada was old school – Original Hardcore Crew – and he'd been at this gig, the Big Bang, back in '93. Seventeen years old. Him and Fanny Douglas and wee Panda (short for the Pandemonium he created) and Stevie Walker and Mad Malky and the Beast. The outfit Panda had created for that night: the white boiler suit with 'MR E' emblazoned on the back in black lettering. Mr E. Mr Ectoids, ya bass. All set off with a gas mask, like some mad rave terrorist from a nuclear future. All of them pissing themselves as Panda paraded up and down outside the SECC while they finished washing down their pills – big fucking Doves, man – with Bucky. The sheer scale of the venue: the *doof* deafening, drifting up to the roof miles above them, 10,000 ravers, every cunt wired to the moon on speed and Es and jellies. It was all innocent back then; they were just weans, they hadn't got into smack or even coke yet. At one point in the night Jada and Malky had climbed up one of the scaffolding towers – hardly any security – and sat there, maybe a hundred feet in the air, looking down on the whole thing, at the surging black mass below, at the thousands of Day-Glo sticks waving green, lemon and strawberry in the

143

darkness, like fireflies in some ancient, hidden jungle. It was as though they were in a treetop far above the forest canopy, the whistles and air horns echoing up to them faintly, like the screeching and cawing of distant beasts, crying out for their mates or for their children. Jada had stared down, speechless. It had been Malky who'd found the words equal to the beauty of the moment. Malky who had exhaled deeply, blowing his cheeks out as he turned to Jada and said, 'Jada, Ah'm cunted aff ma fucken boax, so Ah um.'

Jada smiled at the memory, then frowned as he followed it all the way through to its conclusion, sometime around lunchtime the following day. He'd finally arrived home, staggering into the hallway of the flat to see his dad coming out of the living room, steaming drunk and ready, one fist bunched by his side, the other already drawing back as he growled, 'Whit fucken time dae ye call this?' He hadn't felt anything as the fists descended. Too fucked. But then his maw was screaming, 'Stop, Wullie! Stop! Yer gaunnae kill the boy!' Worth it, but, Jada thought, thirty years on. Still worth it. *Or was it? His front teeth, lying on the hall floor.* He turned the music all the way up – The Berserkers feat. MC Forced Entry, doing 'Bitches Regard Bass' – and put his foot down, heading south, heading away from Scotland, from the past, the acceleration and the hardcore drowning it all out, obliterating it, and soon enough he was taking the exit off the motorway just past Carlisle, following the country lane east and then he was pulling up the long, muddy gravel driveway of the Gypsy.

How it had stunned him, the first time he came here, maybe four years back, looking to sell a few dozen cases of Bacardi he'd got from a cash-and-carry break-in. He'd come up the driveway expecting to find, what exactly? A collection of

144

decrepit auld caravans. The burned-out hulks of cars used for shotgun practice. A buck-toothed inbred in dungarees plunking at a banjo on the porch of a shack. Not *this*. Not the Tudor mansion Jada was now parking up in front of. There were leaded, diamond-pattern windows, ivy growing up the white walls, old oak beams coming through here and there like exposed ribs and those mad metal 'S' and 'X' things dotted on the walls, something that had always puzzled Jada – he thought it might be linked to some cult or something. Or maybe it was a sex thing: swingers letting other swingers know there was good pumping to be had here – until he found out they were a structural device, used to fix bowing on very old houses, where the weight of the building causes the walls to bend outwards. The vast garden stretched off in all directions, just beginning to show the creeping brown of autumn. The apple trees were full and heavy. And here, coming down the steps to greet him, munching on one of those apples, was the man himself, dressed, as ever, in his ragged, olive-green army jumper, filthy, oil-stained jeans and heavy black steel toecap boots, the leather worn away at the front, exposing the glinting metal. Seeing him coming down the steps of this place was always a little disconcerting. Like seeing, well, like seeing a gypsy striding out of the home of a very successful barrister.

''ow do?' the Gypsy said as Jada got out.

'Awright man, aye,' Jada said, climbing down from the cab. He saw now that the Gypsy wasn't crunching on an apple. It was a raw onion.

'Right.' He took a last bite of the onion, threw it away into some bushes and wiped his hands on his jeans. 'Let's see what ye got for the old Gyp-Gyp . . .' He rolled the concertina door of the Luton up and clambered into the back, producing a small crowbar – seemingly from the crack of his arse, as if he carried one as casually as most folk might carry a cigarette lighter or a pen – as he went, eager to get into one of the crates. You had to say this – the man *loved* his work. Pruch, knock-off, fell-off-the-back-of-a-lorry, whatever, he took great joy in the valuation and redistribution of stolen goods. It was said, in the pubs of Clydebank, the nightclubs of Manchester and the drinking dens of Birmingham, that the Gypsy could fence anything from forks to fighter planes. His head was like a Parker's Guide to used car prices but solely tuned to an illegal channel. Jada watched as he levered the lid off one of the wooden crates, the wide nostrils flaring even wider with excitement as he took a sleeping bag out of the Styrofoam chips, hefted it up and examined the label with the same relish a wine collector might contemplate a dusty bottle of rare vintage.

'Arr. The Dutch 'uns. That's good, Jada. That's quality. Better than that last load o' old tin ye brought. Aye, I reckon me boy down south'll go a bomb on these.' The Gypsy's West Country accent, still comedic to Jada. That cunt off *Crossroads*, wi' the bunnet. 'How many cases ye got here?'

'Bang on thirty.'

'Ten grand,' the Gypsy said instantly, his hand shooting out to shake, each nail a little black crescent, the oil and dirt crusted beneath.

Jada hesitated. 'Come oan. Goat tae be worth thirty nicker a bag. Ye'll double yer money. So will yer boy down south. Seems tae me that makes a fair price mair like elev–'

'Ten thousand eight hundred it would be at thirty a bag, aye,' the Gypsy said. 'But you're gonna give the Gypsy a little discount on account of the bulk buy. And all the future business we gonna be doin' with your new set-up. And ten thousand is a nice round number, ain't she?' The Gypsy held his gaze. His hand was still floating in front of Jada, and there was still a smile on his face, but it was trembling a little at the corners, the suggestion being that it might vanish at any moment. And the dark eyes, deep, deep brown, the colour of wet earth, staring into him. Suddenly it was very warm in the box of the van. It was very warm, and it smelled faintly of onions. Jada had to be mindful of the central fact here: the Gypsy knew many Jadas. Jada only knew one Gypsy. And, anyway, there was only 800 quid in it. What did it matter? So it was easy enough, really.

'Ach, fuck it,' Jada said, clasping the warm, powerful hand. 'Deal.'

'Grand,' said the Gypsy, instantly brightening. 'Come and we'll 'ave ourselves a cuppa an get you sorted with the folding stuff while I gets the boys to check through it all. No offence.'

'Nane taken.'

The business taken care of, they could relax while the Gypsy's boys – some of them his sons, some not – climbed into the van and swarmed over the crates like Jawas, checking the contents of the lot before unloading them and wheeling them off towards one of the many outbuildings dotted around the property. Jada and the Gypsy took their tea in the afternoon sunshine, sitting out back at a little wrought-iron table, Jada hiding his fridge-white Glasgow skin in the shade, the Gypsy happily taking the full force of the sun on his leathery face, as they watched some of the Gypsy's younger children playing further down the garden. Ten thousand pounds in two banded blocks of fifty-pound notes sat by Jada's mug. The tea had been brought out by the Gypsy's wife Anna-Marie – a dowdy figure of indeterminate age (and, possibly, gender) – who seemed to materialise magically whenever the Gypsy wanted something and who never addressed Jada directly, always saying 'do he want biscuits too?' or whatever to the Gypsy, who would ask Jada and then pass on the answer. Possibly some old Romany thing, Jada thought. A superstition that the woman of the house directly addressing a male visitor would mean that the first daughter born to the family would be miscarried or have a fucking boaby or something. He imagined the ancient rhyme: *'If thy wife do speak to he, thy firstborn maid with cock shall be.'*

'I've got tae say,' Jada said, surveying the bucolic scene, 'ye've got some life doon here, pal.'

'Aye, 't'aint bad at that,' the Gypsy said. He turned to look at Jada. 'You be tiring of the big city life? Fancy some o' this, do you?'

'Aye, maybe . . .' Jada said, smiling. Images flashed through his head: wee Nicola in a big country kitchen, cooking (cooking fucking what? Nicola couldnae boil water) while wee Jayden ran through the grass, chasing butterflies or some shite. Jada was off camera in this dreamscape. Doing what? Working on the motor maybe. But the fantasy film quickly caught in the wheel of the projector and burned out. He could no more see himself in the countryside than he could see himself in New York, Paris or Bangkok. The Gypsy, in his turn, smiled as he looked over at Jada, seeing him for what he was: a no-mark chancer. He would never make it all the way to somewhere like this. The Gypsy never gambled, he never drank anything stronger than tea or cola and he drove a fifteen-year-old estate car. Because, whereas Jada treated money like shit, something to be thrown at the wall, flushed away, wasted, the Gypsy treated it like sperm, or blood. Something sacred. The source of creation, of life. To be revered and nourished. When he was thirteen, the Gypsy had wanted to buy an electric guitar, like his heroes in the mid-seventies, Status Quo. He'd saved up the money, over fifty pounds, and he was going to go into Gloucester the next morning to buy it. Then his dad said, 'Look, it's your money, son. But if you buys the guitar, you won't have any money left. If you keep it, you'll haves the money and you can still buy the guitar later.'

The Gypsy didn't buy the guitar.

Pot-and-pan man his dad might have been, but he'd died with near sixty grand under the mattress and hidden in the walls of the caravan. He'd loved his son, and when he'd got a little older, he'd shown the Gypsy how to turn his fifty pounds into a hundred. Then two hundred. The Gypsy smiled, hands clasped behind his head, surveying his property, wishing his dad had lived long enough to see him make it this far. God rest his soul. But guys like Jada? Like that negotiation in the van a minute ago. *'Ach, fuck it. Deal.'* Jada had probably thought something like *'What's the difference? It's only eight hundred quid.'* The Gypsy knew no 'only'. What was the difference? The difference was *eight hundred quid*. Ten Gs Jada had just been handed, and the Gypsy knew he'd be flat broke soon enough. Down the bookies. Down the boozer. Down the garage, buying some newer, flashier motor. *Down, down, deeper and down*. Still, there was no harm in the boy. And, for the moment, it looked like he might have something half-decent and regular going on with this connection of his at the airport. So the Gypsy just nodded and smiled at Jada's quiet 'aye, maybe . . .' and raised his mug of tea and said, 'Well, good luck to you then, sir!'

Nicola added two tinned steak pies to her basket, dropping them on top of the tinned potatoes, the loaf of sliced white

Scotland's Pride (she found it the best bread – it literally stayed fresh and edible for over a month) and the jumbo multi-bag of crisps. Here in PriceBeaster they had the wee plastic baskets that had a handle on them that you pulled up and then it trundled along behind you like a wee trolley. She found she was able to push Jayden's buggy with one hand and pull the trolley behind her. Oh, they needed more soups. She'd get the packet stuff. They were lighter and smaller than the tinned soup and there was a limit to how much shopping she could get shoved under the buggy. As well as being lighter, the packet soups were cheaper. Because that was the other thing about PriceBeaster – it was dead expensive. But it was right here on the corner. The Aldi, where they sometimes did the big shop, was miles away. She always needed to talk Jada into taking her in the car for that. Nicola paused at the fruit and veg rack – four potatoes, a couple of blackening bananas and a single orange.

Queuing up for the tills, she idly flipped through the new *Time For You!* (*'My husband was killed by a bee then I was trolled for finding happiness . . . I fell pregnant TWICE in one week . . . my parents moved my rapist into our home. If only they had known the truth . . .'*) and wondered about how late home Jada would be tonight. She also wondered about the twenty-odd pounds she had in her purse and hoped it would be enough to cover the contents of her basket. Here was the thing . . .

Jada was forever working, out all hours of the day and night, but she never seemed to see the fruits of all this industry. If indeed there were any fruits. He'd pay for the big shop, and he'd give her the odd ten or twenty here and there, but if she ever wanted a larger sum for any reason – maybe clothes for the wean – it always ended with Jada throwing his hands up and shouting something like 'Dae ye think Ah'm made o' fucking money?' before storming out. She looked around at her fellow shoppers, their baskets like hers, their skin yellow and their teeth brown under the harsh fluorescent tubes. There was that Katrina from down the hall over at the fizzy drinks. *Dirty cow*, Nicola automatically thought. According to Jada, she was a proper slag. The Partick bike. No one in here looked like they were made of anything but tinned and frozen food. Certainly not money.

'We've a good deal on this vodka at the moment,' the Indian boy serving her said, gesturing as he rang up her purchases. Nicola looked at the stack of bottles next to the till. Flaming Cozzak. A hand-written felt-tip sign told her that the price had been marked down from £6.99 a bottle to just £4.99. That really did seem like a good deal. But still.

'Naw, Ah'm awright,' Nicola said, noticing now that the boy was about her age and had the fading remnants of a nasty black eye. Probably a rough line o' work this, right enough. Wi' aw the shoplifters and that. Ye got some proper bams in here.

The guy just nodded as he took her twenty and gave her the change. 'Next,' he sighed.

FIFTEEN

Dan sank gratefully into his hot bath.

No fool he, he'd slipped away from location early and got one of the runners to drive him back to the Gables. The production unit had been staying at this hotel for over a decade now, and all the old hands knew what happened when everyone returned from the day's filming and started to bathe and shower at the same time: you soon found yourself under an arctic spray or stepping into a few inches of tepid water. The Gables was great value otherwise: lovely rooms and beds, acceptable food and a walnut-panelled whisky bar with over 200 malts. It was just outside Elgin – their major location – and a short drive from all their secondary locations: Findhorn beach, scene of many a ruminative stroll for McCallister, Loch Spynie, the stunning backdrop to many a drive, and the old gravel quarry to the south at Cloddach, where many a fictional body had been fished out over the years. (*'Sir! Over here!'*) Best of all, it was just a forty-minute drive from Inverness, with its airport and rail links.

There was, of course, one major drawback to filming in the Highlands. Dan lifted his legs out of the steaming water and looked at them, at the dozens of tiny red pinpricks, where the midges had somehow got through his chinos and the long socks he wore pulled up to his knees to sink their probosces gratefully into his pale flesh.

It wasn't as bad as it had been early on, when they filmed in the high summer. When they were near water in July and August it was not unusual to see the camera crew dressed head to foot in beekeepers' outfits. Of course, the actors could have no such protection, and they had entire outtake reels of Gregor just managing to finish a scene (usually where he stood on a bank overlooking a shimmering stretch of loch and said something like *'It's a damn long time to be gone fishing . . .'*) before, as soon as 'CUT!' had been yelled, he was running around clawing at his face and screaming, 'YA DIRTY WEE BASTARRRDDDS!' Whenever the cast and crew saw the words 'EXT. LOCHSIDE – DAY' on the call sheet there was a collective groan and cursing of Dan. But it was something Dan had always suspected would be key to the show's success: Tourist Board Scotland. The sheer number of viewers googling 'where is McCallister filmed?' On Airbnb, the lochside cottage McCallister lived in (obviously, with its floor-to-ceiling windows and acreage of parquet flooring, it would only have been affordable to the most corrupt police officer Scotland had ever seen) was solidly booked two to three years in advance. In his grander moments, back in the early days, Dan thought the midges also helped add a patina of verisimilitude to the show: just as the Glaswegian McCallister initially hated being in the Highlands, so the viewer sensed Gregor's physical rage at being there, at being served up as a human feast for the midges. But, after the midge apocalypse of season two, they'd decided to shoot the Highland exteriors in late September and early October. The nights were still (just) long enough this far north and you had as much chance at decent weather as you had at any other time of year in Scotland, but the midge population was way, way down.

The bath having soothed his bites, he got out and wrapped a towel around himself. He crossed the junior suite and poured himself a senior whisky – a 16-year-old Old Tom's Crankshaft – from the bottle on the dresser. He screwed the cork top back in and stood at the window, taking a long swallow as he watched the first people carriers coming up the driveway, cast and crew returning, doubtless having noticed and much discussed his early departure. Ah, fuck it. Rank has its privileges and all that. Besides, who cared? This was his last rodeo. His mobile started ringing from the bed. Grace.

'Hey, baby. Wha–'

'Are you on wi-fi? Can you do Facetime?' Her voice, urgent.

'Er, aye. What's wro–'

'Facetime! Now!'

Jesus. He clicked it over. A moment – *connecting* . . . – and then the screen was flooded with light, light that gradually assumed the shape of their kitchen. Grace was holding Tom in one arm, the phone in the other, focused on Tom. 'Again, darling. Do it again,' Grace said. Nothing. Tom just looked blankly at the screen, then at Grace. 'Come on,' she said. A beat, and then Tom, looking at the screen again, at Dan, suddenly pointed and delightedly shouted, 'DADA!'

Dan had to sit down.

'DADA! DADA! DADA!' Tom yelled, a floodgate seemingly having been opened.

'Yes, son! Dada! Dada!' For a second, the whisky and the emotion hitting him together, Dan thought he might cry. Grace put the camera back on herself; she was laughing, her eyes wide with wonder. 'Wha . . . when . . .?' was all Dan could manage.

'Just this minute!' Grace said. 'We were upstairs in the hall. I was on the phone to Sarah, carrying him, and we were standing next to that wedding photo of us, and he just pointed at you and blurted it out!' All the while Grace was saying this, in the background, the excited 'DADADADADA!' was still going on.

'Oh God,' Dan said, joy and sorrow roiling within him, slugging it out. He'd missed it. The first time, and he'd missed it. Grace swung the camera back onto Tom, which had the effect of momentarily shutting him up. Then he looked at Grace and said, softly, querulously, 'Dada?'

'Yes, Tom! Dada!' she said.

'Unbelievable,' Dan said.

'Ten months!' Grace said.

Knocking on Dan's door.

'What's that?' Grace asked.

'Someone at the door.'

'OK, call me later then? What time you back tomorrow?'

'About lunchtime. I–' More knocking. Angrier knocking. 'Jesus. OK, darling. Speak soon. Bye, son! Bye, bye!' Now Tom hid his face in Grace's neck, suddenly shy. 'See you tomorrow, pal!'

Dan hung up, secured his towel and headed for the door, which was even now being knocked again. 'Jesus fu–' He pulled it open and Gregor strode into the room unasked, still in costume, in McCallister's shabby grey suit and tie.

'That wee fucking turd!'

'Gregor, come in,' Dan said, closing the door.

'Pompous wee shite!' Gregor threw himself into the armchair in the corner, folding his arms tightly across his chest and crossing his legs, the right foot tapping away, a pose Gregor

155

had seen often and which he thought would make a good sculpture – *Artist in State of High Dudgeon*.

'Drink? And could you narrow it down a bit?' Though Dan knew where this was headed.

'Who do you fucking think?'

Dan poured Gregor three fingers of malt.

'Liddle!'

'Right.'

'We're in the middle of the last scene – *my* scene – and I'm saying the line, "Well, sooner or later, he's going to have to go to the police." And he says' – and here Gregor modulated into a prissy camp voice, a sort of Truman Capote on helium – '"Sorry, Amanda,"' – the director – '"could we cut?" We all look at him and he says, "Gregor, would you mind changing that line to 'he's going to have to go to the police, sooner or later'." And I say, "Why?" And he says, get this, "To give me time to register the word 'police' before I respond." I mean, for fuck's sake!'

Dan went gently. 'Well, to be fair to Toby, it's not really a big change.'

'*Not a big change?*' Here Gregor went up two octaves. 'I just walked off, Dan. That wee fucking Olivier-De Niro-Gielgud-give-me-time-to-register fucking *WANK*!'

Dan handed Gregor the drink. He drained it in one and exhaled deeply, seeming to calm down a notch. He sighed, then went on, 'I mean, it's your material, Dan . . .' Ah, Gregor as Friend of the Writer. OK, this'll be good, Dan thought, settling into the armchair opposite. 'It's *your* words he's taking liberties with. You know, perhaps it's coming from the theatre, but I always regard the text as a sacred . . .' Apart from all the times you don't, Dan thought. But, OK, play on pal. 'When I was doing *The Birthday Party* at the Citz in '88 . . .' Dan sipped his drink and listened politely as this mad old dog barked and yelped on, and it suddenly occurred to him how much of a fuck he didn't give any more. *Dada.* That was all there was to it. He'd missed those first words, but that would be it. When this was over, never again would he have to be away from home for huge chunks of time: the first steps, the first sentence, feeding himself for the first time, he'd see it all. With many a soothing 'I understand' and a placating 'I'll have a word' and countless 'right, right's', he let Gregor say his piece before pointing out that he was still naked and the dining room would be closing soon and could they continue this later, please, and then he was ushering the soon-to-be-former McCallister out into the corridor, where he walked off, still gibbering on about Pinter and fuck knows what.

Fresh hell awaited Dan on his way down to the dining room. 'Have you got a minute?' Amanda the director said, magically appearing as he reached the bottom of the stairs.

'Sure, Amanda.'

'Mind if I have a quick fag?'

'No bother.' They headed for the back door, for the stone steps that led down to the garden. Dan liked Amanda – early thirties, tiny, elfin, serious and hardworking – even though she was prone to banging on about 'visual fabrics' and the like but, hey, she was a director.

'He's driving me mad,' she said as they went into the garden. 'Join the club,' Dan said.

'He wants me to re-block tomorrow's scene to "play more off his reaction shots".' She sighed heavily, surprising Dan by pulling a pack of red Marlboro from one of the pockets of her leather biker's jacket, rather than the tobacco and rolling papers seemingly favoured these days by anyone much under forty. Like tattoos, back in Dan's day roll-ups were solely the province of convicts and sailors.

'Gregor?'

'No, *Toby*.'

'Ah. Fucking hell.' Amanda offered the pack to Dan. After a moment's hesitation he took a very rare cigarette and accepted a light off her Zippo as he thought about the problem. *Ah. God, that was good.* The problem, part of the problem, was that they were dealing with two stars in very different stages of their evolution here: one just beginning to coalesce, to assume form out of a swirling vortex of vapours, the other beginning to come apart with terrible energy, breaking up, heading towards its final stage – a black hole. 'Have you got time to shoot it both ways? Make them both happy, then we can just do what we want in the edit?'

'Come on, Dan, you know the budget.' This was undoubtedly true, as Dan's company also produced the show. They sat down on the bottom step, on the warm, worn stone. 'And I know this must all be hard on Gregor ATM.' She said the letters, the acronym, out loud. 'The thing is, with Toby–'

'Yeah, I get it, Amanda.' And he did. Directing *McCallister* was a nice, fat gig. Amanda's future lay with the coalescing star, not with the erupting ball of gases headed for matinees at the Gaiety. Dan was also mindful of his new mantra – *fuck it.* 'Look, I'll talk to Toby. See if I can get him to go easy on the old bastard.'

As luck would have it, Dan entered the dining room to see it was practically empty apart from, at a table in the bay window, frowning into a paperback, Toby.

Jean, the young, dour waitress, was approaching him, menu

in hand, the usual snarl on her face. At this point, the very presentation of the menu was an act of aggression on her part: after nearly two months, she knew that Dan knew it off by heart.

'Hey, Jean, I'll have a bottle of the Chenin Blanc and the Cullen skink.'

'The special tonight is—' She seemed determined to get this out, as though not doing so would somehow constitute a failing on her part.

'Doesn't matter,' Dan said, trying to get past her.

'Sea trout with samphire and—'

'Great.'

'New potatoes and horseradish mayonnaise.'

'Brilliant, cheers.'

They walked off in opposite directions, Jean towards the kitchen and Dan across the expanse of blue tartan carpeting towards Toby's table, where Toby, seeing his approach, closed his book and put it underneath his napkin. Autodidacts, Dan thought, always embarrassed about being busted in the catching up. 'Toby!' he said, arriving at the table.

'Maestro!' Toby said.

'Mind if I . . .' Dan gestured to the empty chair.

'Of course, of course.'

'You ordered yet?'

'Just finished.' Dan took in Toby's terrifyingly unspoiled side of the tablecloth, the core of an apple on his side plate the only sign that eating had taken place. Then Dan remembered that Toby didn't really eat in the evenings, just some fruit and mineral water. Some mad diet he'd heard Daniel Day-Lewis followed when he was shooting, one of the wardrobe girls had told Dan. And Toby's person was always as pristine as the tablecloth: clean-shaven, his blond hair perfectly combed, his dress shirts always crisply ironed and neatly tucked into his slender waist and his eyes the clear blue of someone who lived on fruit and mineral water. He favoured cufflinks and – whenever the occasion would allow it – a tie fastened with a silver clip.

'You mind if I eat?' Dan said.

'No, no. Go for it.'

'So how's things?'

'Good. Good. Tricky wee moment this afternoon, you know?'

Feign ignorance? No, Gregor storming off set was something Dan would have heard about quickly. 'Yeah, I heard,' Dan said, smiling.

'It's . . .' Toby looked around the empty dining room, lowering his voice anyway. 'He seems to think I'm his enemy, Dan. I just . . . I'm just trying to be that bit better. To help us *all* be that bit better.'

Dan nodded, looked at him, thinking, was I this confident at twenty-seven? Probably. It was about the same age he'd sold the *McCallister* pitch. 'You're nuts if you don't want to do this,' he remembered telling one forty-something commissioning editor. 'Just nuts.' Dan thought it would always be that easy – you sell the first show you come up with. What's the big deal? And he had to be mindful that this was all new to Toby. Of where the kid had been just a handful of years ago – on a Kilmarnock council estate. Toby talked all right now, in his carefully modulated Scottish actor's accent – that Morningside/ Kelvinbridge/RADA hybrid – but you could tell it was still a bit like riding a bucking bronco for him. Here and there, you heard the real accent trying to slip out. Like the way he'd had to lasso the word 'better' just then, almost breaking it into two

words as he fought to pronounce it 'bett-*err*' and not 'beh-*urr*.'
Dan often felt that talking to Toby was like talking to someone
with two faces: the one visible to the world and the real one
hidden behind it, the nervous, working-class schoolkid. He
pictured Toby's life to this point. Always a little bit different at
school. Bullied. Ideas above their station and all that. And then
the discovery of the drama club when he was fourteen or
fifteen, the joyous sense of finally finding his tribe. The school
plays and musicals. Then the acceptance into the Royal
Conservatoire in Glasgow. The failed auditions for commercials
and theatre. The couple of bit parts in other Scottish soaps and
then – finally – the successful *McCallister* audition that saved
him from the fate of so many of his peers: handing out leaflets
at car and boat shows in the SEC, doing the entertainment at
children's parties, permanently stunned and enraged that you're
not giving it *'To be or not to be . . .'* with the RSC.

Jean arrived with the wine and began her nightly struggle
with the corkscrew, a performance Dan thought of as 'Small
Woman Trying to Wrench the Head Off Tiny Robot'. As usual,
Dan allowed it to continue for a moment before saying, 'Here,
Jean, let me do that.' Again, something in Jean recoiled at the
dereliction of duty this was asking of her, but, ultimately, she
acquiesced, placing the corkscrew and the (only slightly mangled)
bottle on the table and retreating towards the kitchen again.

As Dan got to work, he said, 'The thing is, Toby, Gregor's
been doing this for nearly twenty years . . .'

'I appreciate that, but–'

'So he's probably got a fair idea of what he thinks works.'

'Of course,' Toby said, leaning forward. 'But the character of
McCallister, as written, historically, he's been this outsider, the
classic Camus figure, a man who has . . .'

161

Toby pronounced 'Camus' to rhyme with 'famous', so it took Dan a moment to work out what the fuck he was talking about. But he didn't hold this against the boy, mispronunciation being a hallmark of the autodidact and all that. Dan took the long swallow of wine necessary to maintain a neutral expression and keep listening, nodding seriously as the young actor talked on about how the detective he was going to play would be different, would reflect a new world. *Dada!* Dan thought. How sweet the sound. When Toby had finished, Dan saw that his Cullen skink had been placed in front of him and that a response was now required. He went standard issue. 'I hear you, Toby. Let me think about all that.'

'Of course. Enjoy your dinner, Dan.' Toby was getting up, sweeping his paperback up from beneath the napkin and folding it by his side, but not quickly enough to prevent Dan from catching the title page – *An Actor Prepares*.

'Stanislavski, eh?' Dan said.

'Oh . . .' Toby looked down at the book in his hand, as if surprised to see it there. 'Yeah. Re-reading.'

'Emotional memory and all that?'

'Mmm.'

'Well, think about this, eh?' Dan spread his napkin in his lap, then tore off a piece of his bread roll. 'This is it for Gregor. It's the last trip around the bay. After this he's the guy who *used* to be McCallister. It's ads and voiceovers and panto and the odd walk-on if he's lucky. And then age. And then the only end of age.' Would the kid get the Larkin reference? Unlikely. 'You're talking about emotional memory, Toby? All Gregor's got now are emotional memories.'

Toby stood there, nodding. 'I understand, Dan. Enjoy your dinner.'

'Night, Toby.'

'See you tomorrow.'

No, you won't, pal, Dan thought, dipping bread into soup. DADA!

'Ooh, thanks, Keith!' Grace took her flat white, cupping it in both hands for the warmth.

'No bother. And how are you this morning, wee man?' This was directed to Tom, chewing on his plastic rocket.

'DADADADA!' Tom said.

'Aww, is he missing his daddy?'

'That's all he bloody says!' Grace said.

'Och, he knows where his bread's buttered, believe you me. Are ye wanting anything to eat?' Keith – all tattoos and piercings, and maybe twenty-eight – was wiping his hands on his apron.

'God, no. I'm fine, thanks, Keith.' He nodded and went back into the deli. Grace sipped her coffee and watched the traffic rattle past on Great Western Road. About that 'God, no'. She'd noticed lately the extra flab gathering around her midriff. And no wonder. Her routine with Tom while Dan had been away filming seemed to have become well established. The two of them would get up nice and early and stroll down Highburgh Road and into Tinderbox for her morning coffee, usually with a croissant or a cinnamon bun. Then north along Byres Road, looking into a few shops here and there and usually bumping into someone she knew which would often lead to another coffee and maybe a piece of cake. Then up to Great Western Road, heading towards Roots & Fruits or Mellis the cheesemongers, where she'd pick up a few bits and pieces of groceries they needed. (Some celeriac today; she was going to make a nice dinner for Dan's return tonight.) It'd normally be around lunchtime by this point, and she'd find herself at one or other of the many cafés that had flourished towards the eastern end of Great Western Road. Indeed, she was now on first-name terms with many of the waiters. Like Keith. It was an area that had pretty much been a dead zone back when they were students: the Azad video shop, a few ancient grocers and a couple of stalwart old-school pubs: Wintersgills, the Captain's Rest. Nowadays you couldn't move for macchiatos, pastel de natas and designer knitwear. So Grace would find herself tucking into, say, a jackfruit curry while giving Tom a feed, or spooning him the baby rice he'd started on. A few weeks of this, and she was becoming afeared of the bathroom scales. But she told herself not to worry about it. The idea had always been that she'd take the first year off completely and then ease herself back into work part-time until Tom was around three and went to nursery. But Grace did wonder. A few of the girls who'd decided that was it with work – at least until the kids were off to school – were looking at, what, five years of strolls and playgrounds and cafés and multiple coffee-and-cake stops? With the days stretching out before you. Tom was mewling now and kicking his heels. She picked him up and put him over her shoulder, gently rubbing his back. I mean, you got your baby, you had everything you wanted and all that, and they had plenty of help, but she could see how some of them wound up opening that wine a little earlier every day. Tom vibrated as he expelled a huge burp. She laughed and held him up, looking into his delighted face. 'Is that better, wee one?'

'DADADADA!'

'Sod,' Grace said. Well, he'd be home soon.

★ ★ ★

And here he was — after the car from Elgin to Inverness, a train to Glasgow Queen Street, then a cab to the West End — hearing it himself for real for the first time.

'DaDaDaDaDaDa!'

'It hasn't bloody stopped!' Grace said.

Tom was struggling fiercely and reaching out to him as he dropped his bags in the hall and took him from her. 'Hello, son! Hello, wee man! Daddy missed you! Daddy missed you! Yes, he did!' He buried his face in the boy's neck and nuzzled him fiercely, drinking in his billion-dollar scent. Tom laughed, throwing his head back.

'Hi, darling,' he said, managing to get his free arm around Grace and kiss her cheek. 'Oh, come here, you,' he said to Tom as he ran into the living room and threw him down onto the sofa, getting on top and burying his face in the boy's tummy, play-biting and growling.

'MOW!' Tom yelled when he stopped. 'MOW!' He did it again.

'Easy,' Grace said, from the doorway. 'Don't get him too worked up. Time for his nap in a minute.'

'MOW DADDY!'

'Do you fancy a cuppa?' Grace asked.

'Oh, please.'

Grace went off down the hall and Dan changed tack, gripping the meat of Tom's thighs and digging his thumbs in, sending him into paroxysms of laughter so fierce that Dan started laughing too. He buried his face into his neck again, nuzzling and kissing, growling and play-biting. Dan stopped, frozen, crouched over his son, his clawed fingers hovering in mid-air, twinned birds of prey about to strike. Tom lay there, panting, on the verge of giggling, watching Dan intently, waiting for his next move. They were looking right into each other's eyes. Dan stopped and held his breath – the incredible clarity of the whites, the detailing of the irises, the vastness of the pupils. The boy's expression simply said trust. *I trust you.* Then Tom reached out and touched Dan's face, gently tracing his chin, his stubble, and said again, but softly and very seriously this time, just a whispered declaration, 'Dada.' *Jesus Christ.* All at once Dan felt his heart jemmying its way out of his chest and climbing up into his throat, where it acted as a stopper, damming up the powerful spring that was threatening to become a geyser, exploding upwards. And once again Dan Chambers murmured something like a vow: *I will always love you and protect you.* As he made his vow he found himself thinking of all the fathers in history who would have made the same promise, some of them ending up (and *why* does the Dad Mind do this stuff? Seriously, what does it want? What's it after?) huddled with their children screaming as the plane comes apart around them. Or shivering in the selection line, weeping with impotent rage as the guards take their babies away towards the reeking smokestacks. Or . . .

'Here you go. Wha . . .?' Grace, in the doorway with the mugs. 'Are you *crying*?'

Dan blinked back the tears, fanning himself. He managed a laugh. 'Just had a wee bit of a moment, didn't we, son?' he said, turning back to Tom. Who took the opportunity to jab his index finger into Dan's left eye socket.

SIXTEEN

A very frosty Saturday morning, the second week of December, and the first true signs of winter in the wind gusting up University Avenue, shaking the bare branches of the trees around the McMillan Reading Room, where Dan remembered madly cramming for his finals nearly a quarter of a century ago. Dan was pushing Tom – snugly wrapped – in his buggy, the compact and manoeuvrable Yo Yo Zen that folded up to come on the plane with you. With accessories it had cost more than Dan's first car. Father and son were both wearing thick wool overcoats, scarves and gloves. 'Who's my little genius, eh? Who's my little genius?' Dan cooed at Tom. For it had been a momentous morning.

It had happened just after breakfast when, as he'd been doing for a while, Tom had pulled himself up onto his feet using the leg of one of the chairs around the kitchen table. He'd been looking across the room to where his cuddly kangaroo lay and Grace had picked up on the thought process in Tom's brain: 'I want that.' Dan had been reading the paper and drinking his tea when she tapped his thigh, not saying anything, just urging him to watch. Sure enough, after a moment of steadying himself against the chair leg, like a drunken man about to step out of a doorway into a gale, Tom had tremblingly placed one foot in front of the other, and then another. This time, the twanging knees held, locked in place and, rather than going straight down onto his bum, he shuffled another step forward. Then another. And then Grace – unable to help herself and even with her fist stuffed in her mouth – had uttered such a high-pitched squeak of joy that Tom looked over as he went to take his fifth step (he was halfway towards his target now), which had made him lose his balance and go toppling over sideways. Dan rushed to pick him up and staunch his tears while both of them yelled, 'TOM! YOU DID IT!' The hero himself was caught somewhere between laughter and tears and was utterly oblivious to the scale of his triumph. But the moment also filled Dan with an ominous sense of the work ahead of him in the coming weeks: he needed to finish completely Tom-proofing the house.

Grace's arm was threaded through his as they headed downhill towards Byres Road. They were talking about the month ahead – always a hectic time of year. They had their annual Christmas party at the house on Saturday. Then there was the *McCallister* Christmas party – the *last McCallister* Christmas party, Dan heh-heh-ed to himself – at some bar in town. Then Christmas itself would be upon them, the in-laws would descend and then you were into January and Tom's first birthday party and, for Dan, the final stretch of post-production. Grace was ticking off food items they still had to get for Saturday.

'Could Brigit not help with some of that?' Dan said.

'Well, it's not technically her job.'

'Yeah, I know, but everyone else says their nannies help with shopping and stuff. We did put her on the insurance for the cars. She can have my credit card.' Brigit, twenty-three, from Dublin, was the nanny they'd both finally agreed on after a flurry of interviews last month. They were still learning the

168

boundaries, but she'd proved a great asset so far. Very can-do. And Tom loved her.

'OK. I'll ask her,' Grace said.

'Have we got your mum and dad anything yet?' Dan asked.

'Voucher for two nights at the Caledonian in Edinburgh.'

'Experiential gift. Good. Like it.'

They reached the lights at the junction of Byres Road, where they waited to cross and head into Tinderbox for some coffee. Dan looked along towards Hillhead tube station and saw him coming towards them, walking beside a girl, a teenager, who was pushing a baby buggy. They drew level.

'Hi, Jada,' Dan said, causing Grace to turn around, shielding her eyes against the sun as she took the trio in. The guy was about Dan's age and for a second she thought it was some friend of his who'd been out for a run – the jogging trousers, trainers and thin sweatshirt – and had bumped into their nanny, the frail, waif-like young girl beside him with a baby boy in the pushchair. But something told her no. These were not people from their world. For one thing, the infant appeared to be aggressively masticating a full-size Mars Bar, its proportions in his tiny hands approaching those of a Yule log.

'Er, aye. Awright . . .' Jada sniffed and looked around, apparently already bored of them.

'Ah, this is my wife Grace,' Dan said.

'Hi!' Grace said brightly.

'Awright?' Jada said, not looking at her. The teenage girl said nothing, just stared into the middle distance. Like Jada, Grace noticed, she was woefully underdressed for December.

'Grace,' Dan went on, 'this is Jada and . . .' He paused expectantly, feeling increasingly like a character from a nineteenth-century novel for indulging in the archaic pomposity

169

of introductions. *Good morrow to thee, sir. I do not believe I have yet had the pleasure of meeting thy lovely wife. Will she please accept my most bountiful felicitations.*

Jada looked down, as if noticing Nicola standing there for the first time. 'Nicola,' Jada shrugged.

'Pleased to meet you, Nicola,' Grace said. Nicola just nodded.

'Ah, so Jada and Nicola's son was born the same day as Tom,' Dan went on by way of explanation. 'We met outside the hospital.'

'Oh,' Grace said. And now she remembered Dan telling her something about this guy. Months back. A fight somewhere. 'Congratulations.' She beamed down at the pram. Jayden had now broken the Mars Bar in half and was attempting to shove both pieces into his mouth at the same time. He was so covered in chocolate that it was borderline blackface at this point. 'What's his name?'

'Jayden,' Nicola said.

'Hi, Jayden,' Grace said. 'This is Tom.' The two babies regarded one another. Well, truer to say that Tom regarded Jayden, for Jayden was fully engaged in regurgitating a miasma of chocolate mud down his front.

Dan couldn't help himself. 'Tom took his first steps this morning!'

'Aye?' Jada said. 'The wee man's been doing that a while.'

'Oh.' *You lying bastard*, Dan thought.

And then Nicola made her only contribution to the conversation. Nodding towards Tom, she said, 'Does the wee man want a bit o' his chocolate?'

'Ah, no, no. He's fine, thanks,' Grace said hurriedly. It was 11am.

From behind them came the *beep-beep-beep* of the green man.

170

'Right, nice to see you again,' Dan said.

'Aye, see ye,' Jada said.

Dan and Grace crossed towards Tinderbox, Jada and Nicola staying on their side of Byres Road and continuing down towards Dumbarton Road. As soon as they were out of earshot Grace said, 'What. The. Actual. Fuck?'

'I know.'

'Is that the guy from the—'

'Yep. He kicked that guy in the balls. In the Chip.'

'Jesus. And how old is she? Seventeen?'

'I know.'

'And a *Mars Bar*?'

'I know.'

'I mean, the sugar . . .'

Dan and Grace ordered their flat whites and their croissants, Grace talking on about low-quality parenting while Dan wondered about how many stair gates they would have to install. They handed over Tom's bottle to be filled with fresh, pure water and gave him one of his tiny sugarless sweets.

Further along the street, Jada and Nicola were crossing the road towards the University Café.

'Who wiz that then?' Nicola asked.

'Jist some fanny,' Jada said equably.

'Right snobby cow she wiz,' Nicola agreed.

Jada remembered something. 'He does something oan that programme yer maw likes.'

'Whit programme?'

'Ach, wan o' they detective pish things.'

'*Criminal Minds*?'

'Naw, fuck sake. Scottish wan.'

'*Taggart*?'

'Eh, naw, the other wan. Wi' the cunt that's up wi' aw the fucking sheep shaggers an aw that.'

'Aw, *McCallister*?'

'That's it. Aye. He's a . . .' Jada tried to remember, to think of what folk did on TV programmes. 'Like . . . a fucking cameraman or something.'

'Aye?' Nicola said, impressed. 'Is he now?'

They entered the busy café, the windows all steamed up, the usual crowd of hungover students and starving pensioners crammed around the narrow Formica tabletops: all drawn by the cheap, chip-heavy menu. They crammed themselves onto the end of a window table, Jada airily waving away the proffered menus like a movie star. 'Three egg, chips and beans, hen,' he said to the waitress. 'Two teas and an Irn-Bru fur the wee man.' Jada fidgeted, trying to think of something to talk to Nicola about as she got busy with the wet wipes, trying to get the chocolate off the protesting Jayden's cheeks and forehead.

In truth, a working man, a grafter by nature, he found weekends and holidays difficult. The wean couldn't do anything yet except crawl around shouting and trying to fucking top himself at any given opportunity – sticking his tongue in an electrical socket, his head down the bog. Nicola was always moaning away about whatever and Jada often found himself longing for Monday. Nose back to the grindstone an aw that. White man's burden, eh? Their drinks arrived and Nicola started to fill the wee man's bottle with Irn-Bru.

As ever, Jada was distracted by financial considerations. While the several thousand pounds he was clearing on the monthly airport runs had looked, in theory, like very comfortable amounts to tide them over, it hadn't quite worked out like that. Costs seemed to expand to fit means. Last month, once he'd settled the usual accounts (the bookies, the Flaps, the dealers, the various parking tickets and fines he was forever paying off at thirty pence a week or whatever the minimum was) he'd found he barely had enough money to cover the basics: food, weed, booze and gambling. The fucking vodka fiasco hadn't helped. Oh, and there was the two grand he'd lost up the casino the other night. Bad run at the blackjack table with Malky, Big Tam Ferguson and Tonto McIntyre.

As if reading his thoughts, Nicola suddenly piped up. 'Ah need some money, Jada,' she said quietly, her dark-ringed eyes downcast as their food arrived.

Fuck sake! It never ended. 'Whit? Whit fur *now*?' The 'now' implying that Nicola's financial demands were endless and complex.

'For the wee man,' Nicola said, nodding to Jayden, who was beginning the process of licking all the ketchup from the chips Nicola handed him before throwing the worthless, hated vegetable itself to the floor. 'He's grown out o' aw his onesies.'

'He's fine,' Jada said, making generously with the vinegar, though even he could see that Jayden's toes were being bent down at an alarming degree by the tightness of the off-white romper suit he wore, while the shoulder straps were digging into his flesh like a stripper's thong.

'They're no that dear,' Nicola said.

'Fuck sake.' Jada sighed. 'How much?'

'Like, a tenner fur a pack o' three in Asda?'

'*Asda?*' Jada shrieked, doing a good job of making it sound like 'Fortnum and Mason?' or 'Harrods?' 'Do they no dae them in Poundland?' Incredibly, he was *still* spraying vinegar onto his food, oblivious to the customers at the next table who were now coughing and wiping their streaming eyes.

'Naw, Ah looked.'

'Fuck sake,' Jada said again. He smacked the (now empty) vinegar bottle down onto the table and, with a world-weary air, reached into his trouser pocket for the warm, furled roll of notes. 'Bring us the change, aye?' he said as he tossed a couple down onto her plate.

'We need nappies an aw', but.'

'Fuck sake.' He signalled the waitress for fresh vinegar.

'And Ah wanted tae get some stuff fur the party the night.'

This fucking daft Christmas party she was having. She'd end up bankrupting him yet. It was just a wee do at the flat, nothing major, just a few o' Nicola's pals – Big Margo, Alison, Vicky, that wee ride Stacey – and Malky and Stevie. Oh, and Malky's pal, some mate from Belfast he had staying with him who he'd asked if he could bring along. Mixing business with pleasure, Jada had also invited Billy Campbell. The Shite would probably swing by too. Nine or ten in total. Max.

'Eh? Whit stuff? Ah've already got aw the bevvy in.'

There were three slabs of lagers in the boot of the Audi along with a few bottles of Turning Leaves Chardonnay (PriceBeaster: £3.50 a pop) for the birds. Fucking expensive, this entertaining. However, once everyone was pished enough, Jada figured he could cut down on his booze costs by slipping a couple of bottles of Flaming Cozzak into the mix, heavily qualified with Red Bull or Irn-Bru to kill the taste, of course.

'Nibbles an that,' Nicola said.

'Fucking *nibbles*? Tell the cunts tae nibble ma fucken baws. Jist get a few fucking bags o' crisps or whatever.'

'Aww, please, Jada. Ah've no been oot fur ages.'

This was true. Nicola hadn't really been to a social event since Jayden's birth. She'd envisaged something a little more elegant for her Christmas party than crisps and lager. Some wee vols-au-vent. Cocktail sausages and, what were they chicken things Stacey had at her birthday party a while back? Satay? Aye, them.

She found herself wondering about the couple they had just met, the camera guy and the snobby cow, in their big coats and scarves. What kind of food did they serve at their parties? Probably stuff like you saw Jamie and Nigella an aw that cooking on the telly. Nicola had caught a bit o' that Nigella's programme the other day, on one o' those food channels when she was hopping through the many options available to them through Jada's bewildering combination of dodgy Firesticks and illegal cable hook-ups. (The reason he'd throw himself down onto the carpet and near have a heart attack whenever he saw a Sky van in the car park at the foot of the block.) Nigella was having a roast chicken with this guy and they'd made it wi' hunners o' garlic and they were just eating it with a loaf of bread. No tatties or anything. Just pulling chunks off the chicken and pounding it with the bread. Mental. And the noises the pair o' them were making eating the fucking thing. Aw *mmmmmm* this and *ohhhhh* that. Like they were getting pumped or gobbled aff or something. Nicola had wondered about the response she might get if Jada came in the door shrieking for his dinner an aw he got was a massive chicken wi' garlic and bread. He'd hit the fucking roof, so he would. Maybe this is what that posh pair had at their parties – every cunt standing about tearing whole chickens apart wi' their bare hands. Or maybe they just got their vol-au-vents and their wee spring rolls and samosas and stuff at a better place than Aldi or PriceBeaster. M&S. Waitrose even. Nicola sensed there was a better life out there somewhere, but how to get to it? She remembered Miss Kinross,

175

that total cow, saying to her once, 'You'll never amount to anything, Nicola McGovern.' Aye, well, she could get tae fuck. Look at her – a man and a wean and a flat and they didnae have a bad life, really. No like they were mad junkies or anything. A wee dig now and then, aye, fine, but they weren't total mentals.

'Ah just wanted tae get some nice food in,' she said quietly.

'Look,' Jada began, growling through gritted teeth, 'Ah'm no fucking made o' mon–' But, before he could finish the sentence, an image came back to him from the casino last week: of himself, laughing, steaming, as he pushed the teetering stack of twenty-quid chips into the middle. The stack that, a few seconds later, the dealer swept unsmilingly into the bank. Something rarely experienced flickered through him, softening the heart of Jada Hamilton: guilt. 'Ach, here,' he said, tossing down another pair of twenty-quid notes. 'Go on. You get yer nibbles in, doll.' Ach, well, easy come, easy go. Nae pockets in a shroud. Share the wealth. White man's burden an aw that. Roll on next Thursday. The slip road near the airport. The drive to Royston. Then Carlisle and the Gypsy and payday.

'Thanks, Jada,' Nicola said, collecting up the money. 'Yer a good dad.'

Jada nodded, accepting this. The deep well of his sweet, sweet patience. Surely one day it would run dry.

SEVENTEEN

It really was going resoundingly well, Nicola thought later that night as she looked around the flat. The girls were all dancing in the living room to the old classics – Beyoncé, Little Mix, Nicki Minaj. Jada had finally been persuaded to give up control of the stereo – the charms of his happy hardcore compilation *Bonkers Vol. 4* having been pushed to their very limit – so the boys were packed into the kitchen, talking business or whatever. She'd managed to stretch Jada's forty pounds a long way in Iceland, adding some wee mini samosas that everyone loved. After the nibbles, Malky had produced a wrap of coke. Even though Nicola had sworn to indulge only when the wee man was over at her mum's, after another tumbler of white wine, she'd relented. Come on, first time she'd had a party in ages. Just a tiny line. And the coke made it easier for her to relent further a couple of hours later, when Malky produced the bag of Es. Just a cheeky half. She'd also relented on the smoking ban, with the result that the living room was now very smoky indeed, while the tight galley kitchen, where the men were all smoking, resembled a trench that had just taken a direct hit from some sort of chemical weapon. 'JADA,' she shouted through, over the music, 'keep the window open in there for fuck sake!'

'Aye, aye,' Jada muttered, reaching over and cracking the window a few more inches. 'Fucking freezing.' He and Malky were at the wee breakfast nook by the window with Jimmy – Malky's Belfast mate. A right moody cunt. Had hardly said a word all night. Aw that preoccupied way. Looked like he could handle himself, right enough, Jada thought, Jada's responses to humanity being binary: if it's a woman, will I fuck it? A man, will I fight it? Stevie and the Shite were sitting up on the counter while Billy had the floor, telling an endless anecdote about a huge shipment of sex toys that were stolen from the airport a few years back. Jada had heard the story before. Still, buzzed from the coke and with his own pill just starting to kick in – and mindful of their business relationship – he indulged Billy by laughing along at the right moments and pitching in with many a good-natured 'no way' and a 'get tae fuck'.

'Swear tae God,' Billy was saying. 'They call him the Dildo King o' Maryhill. They say there's no a bird oan that estate disnae huv wan o' his joyboys in their bedroom drawer. Anyway . . .' Laughter as Billy went on, mostly directing the story to Stevie and the Shite, who hadn't heard it before, while Malky started shaping more lines on the back of the *Bonkers* CD cover. Jada leaned over to Jimmy, trying to be sociable, and shouted over the music coming in from the living room, 'So whit line o' work are ye in over in Belfast, Jimmy?'

Jimmy was watching the girls dancing. He turned slowly to look at Jada. He was in his early thirties, a good-looking boy, fair-haired and well dressed in jeans and a smart shirt, the sleeves rolled up to mid forearm, the bottom of a tattoo, something like a horse's legs, just visible below the cuff. Nice trainers. Not a big lad by any means, but, aye, there was something

178

about him, about the way he carried himself, that made Jada instinctively take him seriously. And Jimmy really was looking at Jada now, a slight smile on his lips as he scanned him up and down, as if trying to decide whether Jada was worthy of an answer or not. This went on for a few seconds, becoming unnerving, finally forcing Jada to add, 'If ye don't mind me asking an aw that.' Something in Jimmy relaxed, as though he had just won a very subtle battle. 'I'm in the taxi business now, Jada,' he said in his thick Northern Irish accent.

'Aye? Good. Good,' Jada said, lifting his can of Viking and nervously draining half of it in one long swallow. But he had to keep going with something. The fucking coke, making him jabber on. 'And whit, uh, whit brings ye over tae Glasgow?'

Another pause. The heavy-lidded stare, then a sly grin as he said, 'Just keeping my head down, pal.' Jimmy took a long pull on his lager as he turned back to continue watching the girls dancing. Jada reached out for the CD Malky was passing to him, grateful for the distraction. As he leaned in to snort his line, Jada saw that Jimmy – in profile to him now, saying something across the room to Billy – had pulled his shirt sleeves up to the elbow, fully revealing that tattoo: Good King Billy, sat atop his white charger, with the date 1690 in cursive script above his raised sword.

Later, everyone dancing now, the boys all finally fucked enough to join in, even fat Billy strutting like a fanny, trying to move in on Big Margo, Jada found himself out on the balcony, smoking with Malky, both of their jaws going from the coke, in the cool night. 'So yer pal Jimmy,' Jada said experimentally, 'how long's he staying wi' ye fur?'

'Couple o' weeks,' Malky said. He looked around. 'Wee bit o' bother back home.'

'Aye?' Jada said. 'Whit kind o' bother?'

Malky took a long draw on the massive joint he was smoking. 'The kind ye don't ask about, Jada.'

'Fair enough,' Jada said, flicking his fag end off into the night and staggering back inside. He threaded his way through the dancing bodies in the living room, then into the hall, heading to the bog for a piss, or maybe a shite, that pill really kicking in now, and stopped to examine himself in the hall mirror: the massive pupils, the set jaw and mad chin, the ectoid mask. Then he became aware of a sound, muffled, rhythmic and urgent. He stepped across the hall, pushed the door to the small bedroom open and went in to see Jayden standing up in his cot – he'd started doing this recently, grabbing furniture and stuff and pulling himself up – and crying hard, his face soaked with tears. How long for? Whit fucking time wiz it? Middle o' the fucking night. Shite, the wee bastard would be waking up in a few hours anyway. Everybody aff their fucking boaxes. Whit was she thinking? Getting oot her nut. Well, she'd just have tae call her maw. Pap him aff tae her fur the day. Jada hesitated in the doorway. His first instinct would normally have been to call Nicola and let her deal, after abusing her for not hearing the wean sooner in the first place, but the (relatively high-quality) MDMA now coursing through him gave him pause. He approached the cot, cautiously, softly, as though approaching a caged beast of uncertain temper. As he got closer the boy's crying slowed and he reached out for Jada, the fingers opening and closing frantically, pleading. 'Aye, awright. Fuck,' Jada said, picking him up. Jayden immediately started pointing at the floor and trying to say something through his sobs. 'Doh . . . doh . . .' Jada's eyes adjusted to the darkness of the room – the only light coming from the streetlight outside and the yellow bar on the wall, from the quarter-open door to the hallway – and he saw the blue dummy on the floor next to the cot. What Nicola called his 'Dodi'. Fumbling, Jada got down on his knees, got hold of it and jammed it back into the wet mouth. The crying stopped immediately, his son sighing gratefully as he flattened his warm cheek against Jada's chest, nestling the warm crown of his head under his chin.

Jada leaned back against the wall and sat there, rhythmically rubbing the soft cotton of the new Babygro, utterly flummoxed with ecstasy and . . . *something else*. It occurred to him that this was the first time he'd settled the wean himself. Nearly a year now, and, on the rare occasions he was home at night and they were sitting watching the telly, it was always Nicola who responded to the cries when they came. Jada assumed she used some form of witchcraft, some maw voodoo to settle the boy. Was it really this easy? He'd just lost his dummy and needed to be held? It seemed impossible to comprehend, but Jada now found himself wondering if his dad had ever done this for him, in the time before memory, in the ocean of gloop before consciousness is formed. Had the fists that later (and often) came swooping in from sharp, unexpected angles to glance off his arms, his backside, his jaw, his nose . . . had they once stroked his back? Smoothed his hair? Had the lips that spat, '*Ya stupid wee bastard*' and '*Get yerself tae fuck*' and '*You're nae son o' mine*', once said 'shh' and 'there, there'? Had they even formed 'I lo–' Nah . . . nae chance. But still, Jada rode the fantasy along on a fresh wave of the pill, seeing himself as Jayden, nestled into his da on the floor of the bedroom in the cold, damp flat in Whiteinch. He could feel the wee rabbit heart against his, slowing down now, the breathing deepening as Jayden swam into the current of sleep once again.

181

Simultaneously, the gouch from the heavy, smacky E was over-taking Jada, drowning the coke high, slowing his own heartbeat so that, for a moment, it felt like their twinned pumps were flexing softly and precisely together, that their blood was traversing their bodies at the same exact rate. It felt like the boy was inside him, like Nicola must have felt. Fuck me, he was *pilled*. The light from the streetlamp outside the flat was coming in through a crack in the curtains, glinting on the silver dreamcatcher thing Nicola had put up above the cot and then spangling off onto the walls, sending Lucozade-coloured shards flying around the room. Jada watched in wonder with the sleeping infant splayed on his chest, a bunched fist on each of his shoulders. Jayden stretched, looking for a better position, chasing sleep down its burrow, and his left fist reached out, opening, to rest on Jada's bare neck, like the wean was trying to hug him, to cuddle him. The infant sighed again, the tiny ribcage filling out, pressing against Jada, and he felt it coming, *knew* it was coming, and that he was powerless to stop it. His lips were already doing it, forming the phrase, the words he had never heard himself and that he sometimes thought might have made all the difference. 'Ah . . . Ah . . .' Like he was going to sneeze, and then his tongue was pressing up behind his top teeth, searching, looking for that little bump on the roof of the mouth, for the alveolar ridge, as Jada tried to make what he did not know was called the lateral approximant. And it *is* difficult, one of the hardest sounds for our palates to learn, one of the last things children get, somewhere around the age of thirty-six months, after many a *'wook!'* and a *'wemon!'* and Mary having a *'wittle wamb'*. Small wonder it is a struggle to get it out – it takes us *three years* to learn how to say it. And, even now, it was something Jada only dared to whisper, lying there in the swirling sodium half-light, with his baby warm on his chest, with the bass thudding distantly down the hall, the treble of the shrieks and laughter and glasses clinking over it all, and then the four words coming out all mad and uncertain on his lips, like a slippery foreign language, like something that really had no business being in his larynx. So quiet and soft as he leaned into the ear like a tiny pasta shell.

'Ah *love* you, son.'

They reached the corners of his mouth a few seconds later, having made their way down the runnels of his face, through the channels gouged by hard living, across the stubble and the pockmarked ridges. The curious, alkaline taste. Here were the very rarest of creatures, something only spotted in the dead of night by the edge of the watering hole, something half-glimpsed, sparkling and monstrous, in the depths of the Mariana Trench, before vanishing into the murk with a flick of a prehistoric tail.

The tears of Jada Hamilton.

EIGHTEEN

'Where is the bloody knife sharpener?' Dan sighed, rooting through the four-foot-wide top drawer beneath the hob, the one where they kept all the random kitchen stuff.

'Eees in beeg drawer?' Anna shouted back from the sink across the room, where she was rinsing glasses and dishes as fast as they were used.

'Nope,' Dan said. 'Grace? *Grace?*'

The Saturday before Christmas. Their party. Through the sliding doors that formed the back wall of the kitchen, Dan could see that a fair few of their guests – mostly the smokers and the vapers – had drifted out into the garden. It was a bright, clear afternoon, very cold but dry, and they were all wrapped up well, standing around the flames dancing in the firepit, the big pot of mulled wine steaming on the quartz shelf next to the pizza oven. All the age groups were represented here today: from the gang of toddlers being followed by Tom – who was alternating crawling with a few tremulous steps here and there, all under the watchful eye of Brigit – to the five-and-six-year-olds forming their own snootily superior enclave in the Wendy house, to Jack and Marianne's and Ally and Sinéad's four teenagers – two girls and two boys – encamped at the end of the big outside dining table, all thumbing away at their phones, now and then showing each other some clip and laughing or saying 'no way!' according to the content.

A dozen or so adults stood around in knots and groups in the kitchen, holding frosted Heinekens, or beaded flutes of champagne, or San Pellegrino coolers – grapefruit, blood-orange, peach – for the drivers. Phil Spector's Christmas album came burbling from the speakers. Dan had made five-bean chilli for the vegetarians. For the meat-eaters, there was a four-kilo piece of brisket that had been in the smoker since yesterday morning. A huge pot of chocolate-coloured gravy was bubbling on the stove. He'd pop the brioche rolls in the oven to warm in a bit. A raft of extras was laid out in bowls and platters on the long kitchen table: leafy green salads, lemon rice, arancini, prosciutto, little bell peppers stuffed with mozzarella, padron peppers and fat, glistening olives.

'Grace?' he shouted hopefully again. He hated working with a less than sharp knife. He was making fresh fruit salad, slicing grapes and strawberries, pears and kiwifruits, dicing melon, taking great care with the bigger pieces of fruit to cut them up properly. Get this all done, pop it in the fridge, then he could put his feet up for a bit.

'I think she's upstairs showing Sarah a dress or something, Dan,' said Rose, passing him on her way to the wine cooler. 'Is it OK if I open some white? A bit champagned out.'

'Of course, help yourself. Nice Montrachet in there.'

'DADADADA!' A tug at his trouser leg.

He looked down to see Tom, leading two of his crawling mates, beaming up at him, out of his mind with excitement, thoroughly refreshed from his nap and ready to party hard. 'GRRR!' Dan said, pretending to launch at him with clawed hands.

'HAHAHAHAHAHAHA!' Tom erupted into laughter and crawled off shrieking, Pied Piper-style, the others following him down the hall towards the living room. The Dad Mind instantly – anything dangerous lying about in there? No. Any adults present? Yes, he could hear Frazer their neighbour droning on about something or other. Oh well, goodwill to all men and that.

Jack came in from the garden, reeking of cigar smoke. 'Anything I can do?'

'Wash your bloody hands. Then top me up, eh?' Dan nodded to his flute as he peeled a kiwifruit. Jack picked up a half-full bottle of champagne and poured. 'Oh, and have a look through that right-hand drawer in the dresser over there and see if you can find the knife sharpener.'

'Hey,' Jack said. 'Have you spoken to Fintan yet?'

'Ah, no. He's been going on about it too. I will.'

'Fuck sake, Dan. You've got responsibilities now.' Fintan was Dan's lawyer, and Jack had been going on at Dan about getting his will in order, drawing up a power of attorney and stuff. 'Just in case anything happens to you. You've got the wee man to think about now. It's just filling in a form. I'll do it if you like.'

'No, no. I'll speak to Fintan. Promise.' In truth, Dan didn't like thinking about this stuff. Bloody lawyers, with their worst-case scenarios.

Upstairs, Grace was saying 'Holy. *Shitballs.*' Although, in truth, she'd got there just a second before Sarah had said the two words. For Grace had noticed the can of Pellegrino she was sipping. Then there was her VW Golf parked outside, the incredible fact that she – Sarah – had driven to a party, and the lush, healthy sheen to her hair and skin. Then Grace

186

remembered she'd thought she was looking well at the restaurant last weekend. And she hadn't noticed a drink in her hand then either, come to think of it. And the fact that she'd asked to come up to the bedroom to see some neither-here-nor-there dress. And then the way she'd said 'Sooo . . .' as soon as she sat down on the bed. So Grace had *just* managed to put it all together a split second before Sarah said it.

'How long?' Grace asked now.

'Twelve weeks,' Sarah said.

Grace was in the doorway to the dressing room off their bedroom, the dress she'd taken out over her shoulder, the sounds of the party drifting up from downstairs. 'Twelve? Shit, so you've–'

'Yep. Had the old scan.'

'I . . .' How best to phrase it? Was there ever an elegant way to ask 'who's the dad?'

'Who's the dad?'

'Rob.'

'Ah . . .' *Who the fuck is Rob?* was obviously on the tip of Grace's tongue, but she modulated it to 'Remind me?'

'You know,' Sarah sighed. 'He of . . . online . . .'

It took Grace a second. 'Wait. You don't mean he of "chipolata poking out a bird's nest" fame?'

'Yep!' Sarah said.

A beat, and then they both fell about laughing. 'What can I say?' Sarah said. 'His name's Rob. He just kind of . . . grew on me.'

'Holy shitballs,' Grace said once she'd recovered enough. She went across to Sarah and hugged her. 'How old is he?'

'Ah, twenty-eight, twenty-nine? Look, I had to tell someone. But don't say anything to the others, OK?'

187

'Of course not. But, what, I mean–'

'What am I going to do?' Sarah said.

'Yeah.'

There was a long pause. 'Santa Claus Is Coming To Town' drifting up from downstairs. Laughter. Finally, Sarah smiled and said, 'I'm nearly forty, babe.'

Downstairs, Jack had the floor. 'Oh, wee Danny McLean, I mean, this guy is a belter. So he's up in front of Callaghan, literally the most hardcore magistrate in Glasgow . . .' Jack had joined Dan and Ally at the kitchen island, all three of them a few glasses in now, the mountain of fruit in the big glass bowl growing as Dan chopped and sliced and laughed. 'I mean, Callaghan, if we still had hanging, he'd be permanently wearing a black fu–' lowering his voice as the toddlers ran by – 'a black fucking cap. Right? So after Danny says, "Ah cannae remember," for about the twentieth time–'

'DADADADADA!' Tom was pulling at his leg again, laughter already all over his face, hoping to once again produce the clawed-hands-and-GRRR! monster reaction. Dan obliged, with perhaps less commitment than he had shown the last five times. Disappointed by this (tiny children being the most finely tuned critics, instinctively sensing when a performance is underdone), Tom crawled off in search of better amusement, his nappy bulging out of his beige 'CALIFORNIA' body suit as he found his wee red toy car and started playing with it.

'Sorry, Jack, go on . . .' Dan said, slicing the last few grapes in half.

'So Callaghan interrupts the brief and says,' and here Jack adopted a pompous, Morningside accent, '"It seems there is much you cannot remember about the evening in question, Mr McLean."'

'"Er, aye," wee Danny says. "Ah wiz jellied aff ma fucking nut, so Ah wiz."' Dan and Ally buckled with laughter. 'Callaghan just looks at him. There's a pause and then Danny adds, "Er, sorry, Ah wiz jellied aff ma nut, *your honour*."' Jack doubled up, slapping his thigh. Dan sliced his last grape in half, tears of laughter in his eyes. Except he didn't quite slice it in half. For this grape was slightly larger than the others. And the knife was a little blunter than it should have been. Which meant that, rather than cutting sharply through the middle, the knife slid over a little before breaking the skin of the grape, going through the flesh at an angle, so that, rather than producing two exact halves, it was more like a 70/30 split. Being a little drunk and distracted, Dan didn't notice this. And then, still laughing at Jack's punchline – 'fucker gave him two years' – he didn't notice the 70 per cent segment of grape falling off the side of the heavy maple chopping board as he scooped the rest of them into the glass bowl. It bounced once on the polished oak floor and came to rest against the kicker board of the island.

'Do you think he, this Rob, will want to be involved?' Grace was asking, upstairs.

'He says he does,' Sarah said.

Grace thought for a moment. What else was there to say? 'Well, then, congratulations!'

'But?'

'But what?'

'Come on, Grace – there's "but" written all over your face!'

'No, no.' Then, 'But . . .' Sarah laughed. 'It's just . . . it's harder work than you can ever imagine, this first year. Even when both of you are . . . you know . . .' How best to put it? Fully grown up? Have known each other for years? Are totally committed to each other. Grace settled for 'pretty settled'.

'Well,' Sarah said, 'I know he's young-ish, but I think he'll–'

Don't say 'change', don't say 'change' . . .

'Change,' Sarah said.

Downstairs, Dan was shouting, 'Right, guys!' as he clamped clingfilm across the top of the bowl of fruit salad, tighter than a snare drum, and slid it into the fridge. 'Lunch in ten min–' He felt Tom's hand grabbing at his trouser leg again. The kitchen was packed and noisy now, the others having drifted back in from the garden. The clatter of plates as a couple of the girls got them out of the dresser across the room, the clack of the fresh bottles of wine and champagne that Ally was unloading from the cooler. 'Not now, wee man,' Dan said. Then a noise, a kind of spluttering, coughing sound. And then the little fist wasn't grabbing at his leg – it was banging it. Dan looked down and saw Tom was sitting on the floor, next to his foot. One hand was flapping at Dan's leg while the other was grabbing at his own throat as he tried to speak, but no sound was coming out, just a hellish gurgle.

Fear tore through Dan – brushfire through dry forest.

He dropped to his knees beside the boy. 'Tom! Tom! What is it?' Tom was panicking now, his eyes casting wildly about as he tried to speak, nothing coming out of his mouth but saliva. Dan realised. 'Out, Tom!' And now he was shouting, *'SPIT IT OUT!'* Silence fell behind him in the room, everyone stopping what they were doing and turning to look. Dan was trying to hook his fingers into Tom's mouth, but Tom was shaking his head, his face going bright red. 'TOM!' Dan flipped him around and started doing what he thought was the Heimlich manoeuvre – jabbing his twinned thumbs into the centre of his son's stomach, just below the joining point of the ribcage. Marianne came running in from the hall and screamed, for she could see what Dan now could not – that the child's lips were turning blue. 'OH MY GOD! TURN HIM UPSIDE DOWN!' And now real terror kicked in, Dan shaking as he got Tom by the sides, then the ankles. Behind him he heard Jack saying, 'Ambulance, *please*! It's an emergency!'

And it was the tone of this, the quality of panic that Dan had never heard in Jack's voice before, that scared him most of all.

'I mean, he'll be thirty this year so–' Sarah was saying this when Grace heard Marianne scream. And she knew, immediately, that it had to be one of the children. She leapt up from the bed and sprinted along the hallway, taking the wide stairs two at a time. She came hurtling along the downstairs hallway, elbowing Frazer out of the way like a scrum half, and burst through the doorway into the kitchen. What she saw would stay with her forever: Dan, holding Tom upside down by his ankles, moving him up and down, Dan crying, Tom's face, wild and beseeching. 'TOM!' Grace screamed. She ran in as Dan flipped him back up. Tom's whole face was turning blue and he was grabbing at both of them wildly, his eyes darting everywhere. And soundless. There was no sound. Like a landed fish, gasping for air. From a thousand miles away, underwater, she heard Jack saying something about an ambulance being on its way, and something about the uselessness of this, about the insanely relaxed attitude that *waiting* for an ambulance to arrive implied, brought Grace back into herself. '*Car! Now! Come on!*' she was saying to Dan as she took her flailing baby from him and started sprinting down the hall. 'THE FUCKING DOOR!' she screamed.

Frazer got it open just as she reached it, and Dan was behind her as they reached the car. She got into the back with Tom as Dan got into the driver's seat. 'QUEEN ELIZABETH!' Grace shouted as Dan, panicking, mis-keyed the code. 'COME ON!'

'SHUT UP! I'M TRY–'

Grace was already dialling 999 on her mobile. It was hooked up to the Bluetooth so the voice came loud through the car's speakers: 'Police, Fire, Amb–'

'My son's choking! I need to know what to do! Now!'

'Please hold–'

'NOW!'

Dan got the code in and floored it, hurtling out onto Hyndland Road and turning left as Grace pulled the seatbelt around her and Tom. The car was fully charged and just a tap of the accelerator took them from twenty to sixty miles an hour in a couple of seconds. Dan drove straight through the first red light, his palm mashed onto the horn, drowning out the enraged horn of the driver in the process of pulling out in front of him, Dan swerving, just missing. 'Grace! Is he still conscious? GRACE!'

Tom's eyes, his perfect blue eyes, were wide, the pupils flipping upwards, vibrating, the whites of the corneas beginning to pattern now with the crimson spiderwebbing of breaking blood vessels. The flapping of his limbs was slowing, just little twitches and kicks.

Jesus fucking Christ.

Grace flipped him over, putting him on his stomach across her knees as she started punching him in the back as hard as she dared. She flipped him back. Nothing. He was going limp. And suddenly, amid the chaos and speed, of Dan's shouting and screaming and the mechanical voice bleating 'please continue to hold' and the houses and the shops blurring past, Grace knew. She just knew.

Oh, you tried, little one. You tried so hard.

She turned him back over and tenderly stroked his face. And then – and it was the oddest thing, something she would spend the rest of her life pondering – all the terror and panic were being driven out of her and the strangest sense of calm was descending, the calm she felt she owed him in this moment. She cupped her son's face with her right hand, her left arm supporting his limp neck, and she leaned down close to his ear, not wanting Dan to hear, for fear of what it might do to him, because they were travelling so fast now, so very fast. And yet, it all felt like it was slowing down at the same time, like her body, her spirit, was telling her she had to be here, she had to be in this moment with the full force of her being. She felt nothing less than the presence of God as she cupped his gorgeous soft cheeks and smelled his fine sandy hair. The words came back to her. It had been so very long, but here they were, unbidden and intact from her youth, from the days with her parents, with the school, on the hated hard pews with the onion-skinned Bible pages in her hands and the amethyst-coloured light streaming through stained-glass windows. Grace was crying softly as she whispered it, but she got it all out, a good Catholic girl pulling dignity around them. She would not know it until she died too, many years from now, but this was to be the finest moment of her life, here in this moment from hell, on the backseat of a car speeding through the West End of Glasgow as she whispered, '*In the name of the Father, and of the Son and of the Holy Spirit, I commend you, my dearest son, to Almighty God, and I entrust you to your Creator,*' her tears falling on his face now, '*May you return to Him who formed you from the dust of this earth. May holy Mary, the angels and all the saints come to meet you as you go forth from this life . . .*' In this moment, she became her name.

193

And then the child was utterly still with his eyes open and staring, and she closed his eyelids and kissed them and Dan was shouting and screaming and then the car was tilting crazily to the right with the sound of tyres screeching and rubber melting and she tried to lift her head up against the incredible G-force of the braking that was pulling her forward and she closed her eyes too and clutched the little body to her as she said her *'Amen'* and then the sound of metal rending apart and a deafening bang and then there was nothing at all.

PART THREE

SIX MONTHS LATER

NINETEEN

Another day, another dollar, Chas thought, as he and Big Boab watched the ground crew, waiting to begin their unloading. Late June, summer in full stride, the grass shimmering green between the concrete runways stretching off into the distance around them. There was the buzz of the light aircraft, Cessnas and Pipers taking off and landing from the flying club away in the northern corner, the little planes like gnats, midges, compared to the monster they were parked in the shadow of. Billy was talking with a uniformed soldier over by the Hercules transport, nodding away as he looked over a form on a clipboard. By Christ, they'd had a good run at this one. Nearly a year now, and not a whimper from anyone. It seemed like NATO had an endless supply of military equipment that no one minded them siphoning a wee bit from every month. Now Billy was walking away towards them as the tailgate of the aircraft started to come down, the size of the front of a council house. Billy walked past their van, heading to his own car, and gave them a tight nod. Boab reversed the van into position, next to the other, identical one, they'd already parked. Chas opened his door and started heaving himself down onto the ground. Across the hot tarmac, up the ramp and into the cool of the vast Hercules belly with the trolleys.

He hadn't lost his sense of wonder at being in the cargo bay of a big military airplane like this. The long metal tube with its iron ribbing stretching off ahead of them, the webbing hanging down at the sides, that they used to lash down Jeeps and tanks and stuff when they carried them. The wee canvas seats the soldiers sat in when they carried them. Fucking nightmare, Chas thought. Worse than fucking Ryanair, man. They got to work, most of the load going into the right-hand van that would go over to the warehouse. The odd crate going into the left-hand van destined for Royston. Chas was sweating, having wiggled a crate of socks out of the way (too low value, no worth the hassle) to get to a couple of crates of sleeping bags he could see in the middle. There was another, unmarked, crate still in his way. He went to move it, only to discover it weighed a fucking ton. No labels or anything on it. Take it? Aye, fuck it. Heavy. Might be worth a few bob. Show initiative an aw that.

Two hours later, they were unloading in the oil-scented garage in Royston. 'The fuck's this?' Jada said, standing in the back of the van with the crowbar, breathing heavily, sweating as he tried to move one of the crates.

Chas had manoeuvred it well towards the back. And now he affected innocence. 'What?'

'This,' Jada said again. Chas squinted at it, as if noticing it for the first time. 'Fucked if Ah know. Did you load that wan, Boab?'

'Did Ah fuck,' Boab said.

Jada worked the crowbar under the lid and started jemmying it up, wood squeaking and cracking as it came loose and then off. 'Are ye trying tae fucking tell me,' Jada said over his shoulder, 'that ye didnae notice the weight o' this fucking thing whe . . .'

He stopped mid-sentence as his hand brushed away the top layer of packing chips.

Silence.

'Fuck sake,' Jada said quietly. They'd heard these words before, often, but this was a tone of voice completely new to all of them. Close to wonder. Or horror. 'Whit the fuck . . .'

A few hours later, Jada was listening to the musical quality of the Gypsy's sigh. It wasn't disapproval. The Gypsy didn't really do disapproval. The way another man chose to make money, or to enjoy himself, was none of his business, and over the years he had trafficked in goods as varied as amphetamines, Nazi memorabilia and rubber phalluses. No, the sigh contained more sorrow than disapproval. The sorrow was twofold. He gave Jada the most obvious reason first: 'Don't get me wrong now. I'd like to be making the money.' They were sat with their tea at the little wrought-iron table in the back garden, as was usual in the summer months, though after the panicked, hectic nature of his morning, Jada had been hoping for something stronger. 'But this type of stuff' – the Gypsy pushed the oilcloth-wrapped bundle a little further away from him – 'you're entering a whole world of pain here, old friend.'

Jada had only heard the word 'money' in the whole statement. 'Aye, but how much dae ye reckon they're worth?'

'Jada, you're not just talking about the old bill here. You're talking anti-terrorism and all sorts. You're talking ten bloody year for having *one* of these things. How many did you say you've got?'

'About two fucking hundred.'

'Jesus God. You're talking about life, mate. Walk away.'

Jada thought for a moment. 'FUCK!' He got up and walked

around in a little circle while the Gypsy watched him: a man caught between greed and sanity.

The thought of just dumping them all. Jada realised that before he could decide, he had to at least know the value of what he was dumping. His instinct was something like a hundred quid a pop, maybe more. So that could be twenty to forty fucking grand going straight down the shitter. 'Ah, look, if, in theory, like, say Ah could get rid of them on ma own,' he said, 'how much dae ye reckon a fair price would be?'

The Gypsy leaned back in his chair, hands clasped behind his head. The man wasn't going to let this go. 'Specialised field, Jada.'

'Come tae fuck, man.'

'But I reckons I know a fella who might know.' The Gypsy tipped forward, bringing his chair back down. He looked around to make sure none of his many children were approaching and unwrapped the package again. He took a stubby bookies' pen from behind his ear and jotted on the back of his hand – make, model and serial number – before covering it up again. 'Gimme a minute. More tea in that pot.' He disappeared into the house. Jada waited till he was gone and pulled back the oilcloth once more. There it lay, glinting, lethal. And in the bright sunlight you could see now that it wasn't the total black you initially thought it was. There was a tinge of blue to it, almost violet here and there. He picked it up, the surprising weight of it in his hand still giving that same childish thrill of playing soldiers.

A handgun.

'Fuck me,' he'd said, and then just stood there, saying nothing as the boys crept up behind him in the van. 'Oh Jesus,' Chas had said. 'Ya daft wee cunt,' Boab had said to Chas as the

recriminations and panic broke out. Jada, after his initial aston-
ishment, calmed down. He was seeing problems here, for sure,
but he was also seeing dollar signs. The pistols were packed in
rows of ten, fitted snugly into wooden racks. Two rows of ten
in each layer. The crate was ten layers deep. No wonder it was
so fucking heavy.

He tried to think things through, shouting, 'RIGHT!
EVERYBODY! SHUT THE FUCK UP! First things first. You
two pricks' – he'd turned to Chas and Boab – 'we need to
wait and see if these are going tae be missed, right?'

'Aye, Jada.'

'So that means we need to store them somewhere for a bit.'

Dominic was already shaking his head. 'Not a chance, pal,'
he said. Yes, Dom was crazy, but he wasn't crazy enough to
keep an arsenal of unlicensed firearms on his premises.

'Come tae fuck,' Jada tried.

'Get tae fuck,' Dom replied.

So the rest of the morning had involved Jada in moving the
guns to his storage unit, at that place off the M8 as you came
into the town. He'd slipped one of Dom's boys a ton to help
him, impressing upon the lad the severity of the consequences
of breathing a word of what he'd seen to anyone. A ton to a
young boy was one thing. Chas and Boab were another. He'd
taken them aside before they left to head back to the airport
and said, 'Listen, boys, this is some new shite we're dealing with
here.'

'Yer no fucking joking,' Boab said, glaring at Chas.

'Hey, boy was showing initiative, Boab,' Jada said, patting
Chas on the shoulder.

'Aye. Fucking initiative,' Chas said, tapping his temple.

'But these aren't gaunnae be easy tae shift,' Jada went on.

'Ah'll talk tae ma contacts and that. Make enquiries. But, seeing as this is, like, a special case, Ah don't think Billy needs to know about this one, does he?'

'Naw, Jada,' Boab said.

'Aye, maybe no,' Chas said.

'Maybe?' Jada repeated. 'Fucking *maybe*?'

'Hey, Ah'm the wan took the risk and nicked it in the first place,' Chas said. 'If yer cutting Billy oot, then who's tae say ye'll no–'

'Awright, awright,' Jada said, palms up, appealing for calm. Reason. 'Ah'll tell ye what. Nae bung this time. Proper profit share. Ah'll cut you boys in for ten per cent.'

'Us?' Chas said, nodding at Boab.

'Away tae fuck, ya greedy wee–' Boab began.

'Fifteen,' Chas said. 'Ten for me, five for Boab.'

'Listen,' Jada hissed. 'Ah don't give a fuck how ye split it up, but ten per cent is aw yer getting. Ye got it out, well done. That's you finished now. It's me taking aw the risk from here.'

'How about–' Boab began.

'How about ye shut the fuck up, take yer ten per cent, get in that fucking truck and back tae work before yer missed?' Jada held his hand out in seal-the-deal style.

A moment's hesitation before Chas took it and shook. Then Boab. 'Remember, as far as Billy's concerned, it was the usual type o' load.'

'Aye,' Boab said. 'Crystal, Jada.'

'How much dae ye think ye'll get for them?' Chas said.

'Dae Ah look like a fucking arms dealer tae you, son?' Jada said. 'Fuck knows if Ah'll even get anyone tae take them. But as soon as Ah know, you'll know. Awright? Now get tae fuck.'

Jada could hear them already arguing in the cab as they

pulled away, trundling out of the cool dark of the garage and into the light. End of the day, what did their percentage matter? It would be a fuck sight less than Billy's. And they had no way of knowing how much Jada would get for the guns. Tell them anything.

Jada heard footsteps from the house and managed to cover the pistol back up before the Gypsy emerged with a small piece of paper in his hand, the wee pen tucked back behind his ear. 'Bloody hell,' he said, settling back down. 'He don't half go on, that boy. Always the same when you get a man going on his passion, eh? Right, what you got here is a MAC 50 9mm pistol. Used to be standard issue to the French army. Been phased out in recent years though. Replaced with summat newer.'

'Is that right?' Jada said.

'Arr. Anyway, he says they're a decent little handgun and black-market value for an automatic o' that type is about five hundred pound.'

A pause. Jada blinked once, like a lizard. 'Each?'

'That's what the man said.' The Gypsy nodded. 'Maybe even a bit more depending on the, ah, motivation of your buyer, like.'

Jada was sitting on two hundred of them.

100k.

One hundred thou.

A hundred large.

'Jesus fuck,' Jada whispered.

The Gypsy nodded, thinking of how very difficult it was going to be for Jada to ever shift these things, knowing that a couple of missteps were all that stood between him and the rest of his life in an 8x10 cell. But he could see the greed in the eyes, so he knew that anything he said was going to fall on deaf ears. Still, he had one last try. 'I wouldn't go calling the Big Man that, Jaydarr.' He drained his cold tea. 'You might be needing his help soon enough . . .' Because the Gypsy knew it before Jada did. Knew that a potential windfall this large was not something Jada was going to pass up, whatever the risks. The Gypsy knew it as soon as he saw Jada doing the mental arithmetic. Jada didn't know it for sure until a couple of hours later, when he was halfway back to Glasgow. His hands were drumming on the steering wheel, his mind was in that loose, free-connecting state it sometimes got into when he'd cranked the hardcore loud and long enough. So, as his DJ Chobble mix CD reached its demented climax with the classic 'Rave Armageddon' by Maximus and Chanks featuring MC Shitter, Jada had an idea about how he was going to sell the guns.

TWENTY

'Sorry, pal, what were ye after again?' Sandy said, taking in his customer. He was rough-looking, this boy – dirty fingernails, three-day stubble and bloodshot drinker's eyes, with some faint bruising on his forehead and what looked like a recently broken nose – and he was pished enough as well. But, even so, he still didn't look like he quite belonged in here. The clothes, though grubby, were expensive. And that was some watch he had on. He wanted to be careful with a watch like that in a place like this. And you could see he'd had a decent haircut sometime in living memory. He'd been coming in more and more the past couple of weeks.

'*Anothapineannaubblejin,*' the guy repeated.

In most pubs – even in Glasgow – this kind of attempt to order another pint and a double gin would have resulted in ejection from the premises. But this was the Flaps. Sandy placed a glass beneath the optic, pumped in two shots and started pouring the lager. It was overcast and hot, the door to the main bar open to Dumbarton Road, the diesel fumes and roar of traffic negating the scant breeze the open door afforded. Dan shifted on his bar stool and drifted off again, back into the Calculations. Some days he worked on the Grapes. Some days he worked on the Route. Some days on the Closures. Today he was working on the Knife Sharpener.

The knife sharpener, it turned out a few days later, had been put in the *second* drawer down in the dresser, a place where it *never* lived. As much as he felt strongly about anything any more, Dan strongly suspected the reorganising principles of his mother-in-law here. He'd asked Ally – or was it Jack? One of them – to look in the *top* drawer of the dresser, he remembered that. It was a regular secondary location for the sharpener and one much favoured by Anna, while he and Grace usually used the wide drawer immediately below the hob. It was an issue of categorisation, of course. Anna, and certainly Grace's mother, viewed it as a posh frippery, a dilettante's plaything that could be relegated to the 'more rarely used' second drawer down, where things like the potato ricer lived. Whereas Dan, and to a lesser extent Grace, viewed the sharpener as a necessary and regularly used kitchen appliance. And certainly not for the Siberian exile of the very bottom drawer, where the likes of the ice-cream maker lived, or the appliance gulag of the top shelf of the pantry where the truly wretched – the George Foreman Grill and the air fryer, both gifts from family members – dustily awaited execution by charity shop. An *air fryer*? Who thought that was a good idea? Grace's sister? Hang on, where was he? Focus. But was a knife sharpener an appliance? No. A tool, surely, he mused as he dumped his fresh large gin into the remains of the last large gin and knocked back half of it. Tool, appliance, whatever – focus, FOCUS. Or perhaps the sharpener problem – he was tracing a finger down the cold, beaded side of the fresh pint he'd just been handed now – wasn't one of location so much as *provenance*.

He kept circling back to this. If he'd just spent *more money* on it. You see, when he bought the knife sharpener, about five years ago, he'd gone middle market. John Lewis. About forty quid. £42.99 to be precise. It had taken Dan a long time to confirm this exact figure. He'd ransacked his study looking in vain for the receipt until he'd hit on the idea of going through his credit card statements. This had involved going online and printing off a lot of PDFs. But he'd recognised it straight away – £42.99 at John Lewis in the first week of December 2019. *'FOUND IT! I FOUND IT!'* he kept yelling. He'd been lying on his back on the floor of the study at this point, surrounded by an upended drawer of receipts and screeds of printouts, the half-empty bottle of Macallan beside him at eleven o'clock in the morning. Grace had appeared in the doorway, drawn by his shouting. And then she was asking him something, but it was all underwater. Then she was crying, and he was shouting at her, and then she went away. He remembered the purchase well because they had both sets of parents *and* her sisters coming for Christmas lunch that year and he'd wanted to buy a new carving knife and Grace had said something like 'For God's sake, we bought a new carving knife a couple of years ago – just buy a sharpener'. And he did. But he hadn't thought it worth spending the £159.99 they wanted for the HORL 2, with its two interchangeable wheels, diamond and ceramic grinding discs and built-in ball bearings that ensured versatility, flexibility and guaranteed impressive results. No, he hadn't done that. He hadn't bought the cheapest, at £14.99 either. No. Went mid-range. Fucked it. Shit the bed. Because, *if* he'd spent the money on the HORL 2, then maybe the knife would have stayed sharper longer, would have had that bit more of an edge. Maybe it would have gone cleanly through the centre of the grape, creating two exact half-segments, either of which might just have been able to slip down the pinkie-sized aperture of an infant's airway. Maybe then Tom would still be alive. He flashed on it again now, the murder instrument, that monstrous three-quarter grape, still near intact. He'd asked to see it and it had been borne to him on a silver, kidney-shaped bowl by a trembling junior doctor. Ach. He sank the rest of his gin and signalled for another. Dan touched his nose, still a bit sore and wonky. Everyone – his friends that is, back when he still saw them – had assumed it had been broken in the accident. But no. The airbag had smashed into his face – like being punched hard with a soft pillow – after he'd tugged the steering wheel to the right at the last second, the empty passenger seat taking all the impact from the parked bin lorry he hadn't seen. (Grace had got it worse. And Tom, of course. But, as Grace told him later, he was already dead, so that was good, eh? That was something.) But the airbag hadn't broken his nose. That happened a few weeks later, when he fell down the stairs to the basement at home, having drunk a bottle and a half of whisky.

The signs that he was losing it.

There had been the afternoon on the park bench, in Kelvingrove. He'd been drunk, of course, sipping gin from a hip flask, when he became aware of an old guy nearby, feeding the pigeons. Dan had peered closer at the pecking birds – the petrol-in-a-puddle splash around their necks – and seen that they were eating seeds. He remembered putting seeds in her lunchbox, back when they were trying. The next thing he knew he was curled up on the grass and two policemen were talking to him, trying to calm him. Apparently he'd been 'wailing'.

There had been the *McCallister* meeting he'd attended at the office, sometime in spring he guessed, a few months after the funeral anyway. He'd sat there, stupefied, while they all talked around him. The meeting had run into lunchtime – Dan contributing very little – and one of the juniors started bringing in platters of food: smoked salmon sandwiches. Egg salad sandwiches. A cheese platter. A fruit bowl, a bunch of green grapes prominent within it. Dan had stared at the grapes for a long time before he vomited all over the conference table. Meeting over.

The time he'd woken up beneath a tree in the Botanical Gardens (it must have been summer now), with his jeans ripped and blood all over his left leg (from climbing over the spiked railings?) and a bagful of baby toys – rattles, teethers, a rubber frog – he could not remember buying in an Early Learning Centre carrier bag next to him.

The time he tried to punch Jack.

The time he told his mother to fuck off.

The time he tried to smash all the crockery.

The time, the time, the time . . .

If 'losing it' was a process, it was, Dan felt, surely now complete. Here he was in Fanny Bryce's at lunchtime. He had lost it. He took a deep draught of his lager and looked around at his fellow drinkers, at the vagrants and semi-vagrants and the just plain psychotic. He didn't much mind it here, in this terrible, blasted pub on the very western edge of Partick. He really didn't. And there were few options left available to him east of here. It had been a slow process over the last six months, the process of getting himself banned from almost every pub in Hillhead. People had come and gone during this period, appearing to him at odd hours, as though in a dream. Then again, all hours were odd. He'd taken to drinking as soon as he woke up – which was increasingly in the middle of the afternoon – and usually passing out in the small hours. Ally, Jack and Bob all came and went with variations of the same speech. Phrases like 'come on, mate' and 'snap out of it' and 'need to get help' and whatever. He seemed to remember Gregor being at the foot of his bed at one point, blathering away. And his mum, his poor mum, crying, asking him to stop, to think about Grace and their life together. Well, he thought about all that and reached for the bottle again. After a few months of this, they all stopped coming. Sometimes, when he'd been out drinking hard, touring increasingly far afield pubs, he'd find himself waking up in random hotel bedrooms: a Premier Inn in the city centre, the Ramada down by the Hydro, a Leonardo Inn out in Anniesland. On several occasions he'd favoured the Hilton at the junction of Byres and Great Western Road, the hotel anyone his age still thought of as the Grosvenor. Wherever it was, the tableau upon waking was always the same: the empty whisky bottle close to hand and Dan fully clothed athwart the twisted sheets or face down on the carpet. 'You . . . you're disintegrating,' Grace said to him once, coughing the words out through tears. And this sounded good. Ideal. From the thick red dictionary that bore his surname – *'to separate into parts, to break up, to crumble'*. If only it could be achieved. Several times upon waking, ruined again, he really thought about attempting this fabled 'snapping out of it'. And then two thoughts, thoughts that had occurred almost a year apart, would come at him, ambushing him, unmanning him.

'I will always protect you.'

Followed closely by, *'I have killed you.'*

And 'crack' would go the ring pull. 'Pop!' went the cork.

Go on, *you* stay sober with that in your head every morning.

So it had been a slow process, yes, but he'd doggedly stuck to his guns until, after many a 'fuck you' and a 'get fucked' and a 'just fuck off then' and a couple of glasses hurled at the optics – and once, in the Chip, urinating against the bar – he'd finally washed up here, in the Flaps, for the first time a couple of weeks ago. It was fine. Fine. No complaints. You really had to wonder what you'd have to do to get barred from this place. Fuck a dog on the bar? And even then, Dan could hear the barman wearily saying something like 'Fuck sake, son, there's a bathroom fur that kind o' thing.'

He drained his pint, signalled for another.

Bloody hell, Sandy thought.

A little over two miles due east from where Dan sat, Dr Bonniker was reaching for the tissues and passing them across. Grace dried her eyes, blew her nose and said, 'Thank you.'

Outside the big bay window, across Park Circus, Kelvingrove Park fell away below them. 'Anyway,' Grace said, shrugging, moving on, 'I went back to work.'

'Good. I'm glad. How has that been?'

Bonniker's voice was soft, here in this large, well-appointed room on the ground floor of the fine sandstone tenement tucked in among the offices of architects and solicitors and private doctors, the professional elite servicing Glasgow's upper-middle class. The tasteful, antique furniture, the lush, well-tended plants in huge ceramic pots. (The new, teal-coloured one that Grace had paid for.) The oak shelves filled with hardback books. The big aquarium glowing blue-green in the corner. The relaxing, just audible, hiss of its filter. She considered Bonniker's face, awaiting her answer, expressionless as always. Grace sometimes tried to picture him on the brink of orgasm. Or upon being informed he had pancreatic cancer. She came up with the same expression.

'Oh, difficult.' She winced as she crossed her left leg over her right, the fractured femur, from the crash, still capable of sending the odd sharp jolt of pain a full six months on. 'The whole post-production on *McCallister* just . . . stopped.' It had, of course, stopped when Dan went insane and stopped coming in, or answering emails, or having anything to do with the show at all. Everyone was sympathetic, naturally, and Grace had eventually got Dan to agree to let them resume work without him. Well, he didn't agree so much as look up from his whisky glass and say, 'I don't give a fuck, Grace.' She sighed and went on. 'We're back into it now. But it's meant pushing the broadcast back until the late autumn. We . . .' As she droned on about all this, Grace suddenly felt sympathy for Dan. Who cared, really? 'We've, uh, we've got a couple of new things in development. Early stages. It's kind of nice being around the kids, the young ones. They're just out of uni, full of ideas, hope. They don't know the numbers yet, you know? That out of maybe a hundred scripts you develop, one might actually get made and become a TV show. Well, they do know the numbers, but they're idealistic enough to think they won't apply to them. That their show, their idea, their pitch – this book they want to option, this director they want to work with – will be the one idea that gets through. That then it'll be them and Leo in the VIP area at the BAFTAs after-party.' It was, Grace thought, the same mad impulse that led young men to fly Spitfires or jump onto Omaha beach on D-Day. *I'll be the one who gets through.* 'It's . . . sweet. They haven't been, you know . . .'

Bonniker let it hang there until he saw she wasn't going to finish the sentence. 'Beaten down by life yet?'

'Yeah, I suppose so.'

Bonniker nodded. He looked at the empty club chair across the coffee table from the one Grace was sitting in and decided to address the elephant in the room. He crossed his legs, coughed, smoothed down his tie and said, 'And how has Dan been these past few weeks?' Meaning: *since he stopped coming.*

'Oh, about the same? Worse? I don't know. We don't really see each other any more. He's been sleeping down in the basement, on the couch in his study. He's still asleep whe

n I leave for work. He's out when I get home. I'm asleep when he gets back and . . . and on we go.'

'And the drinking?'

'He's either drunk or hungover all the time.'

Bonniker nodded, clicked his pen and made a note. 'This is very serious, Grace. A very unhealthy situation.'

Grace gave a short, mirthless bark. 'No shit.'

'It's important Dan knows that I want him to come back. That I bear no ill-will towards him for what happened the last time he was here . . .'

The last time Dan was here. Three weeks ago. Grace suspected he'd already been drinking before they came in: he was smoking (he'd started again, furiously so) *and* chewing gum on the pavement out front as he waited for her to arrive so they could go in together. He'd flicked the butt into the gutter and sighed, 'Right then.' Spoiling for a fight from the off. It had duly arrived, when Bonniker used the phrase 'abnormal and enduring grief reaction'. He hadn't even been talking about Dan and Grace; he'd been quoting a case study, to answer a question Grace had asked, but, as usual, Dan hadn't been listening. Unknown to either the psychiatrist or his wife, he had been miles away, deep in the Calculations, pondering a fascinating new aspect of the Grapes he'd recently discovered. According to the internet, it had been an unusually warm spring in Almeria, where the pack of black grapes he'd bought in Waitrose for the fruit salad had come from. The heat had likely contributed to the grapes being larger and riper than usual when they were harvested and shipped to the UK, where, after a spell in cold storage, they eventually ended up at Waitrose on Byres Road, where Dan's murdering hand had alighted on the pack, having nearly taken the smaller Chilean green grapes from right next to the Spanish ones, before deciding to go with the black because they'd make a pleasant colour contrast in the fruit salad, what with it already having a lot of green in it: kiwifruit and melon and so on. Anyway, what Dan was thinking was: maybe it was climate change that had done it. Perhaps global warming, in a roundabout way, had killed Tom? If the weather had been poorer, colder, then maybe the grape would have been just a few millimetres smaller, maybe then Tom could have swallowed it, worked it down? Maybe then . . .

Suddenly Dan had snapped out of his reverie and barked, 'Say that again?'

'I'm sorry, Dan?' Bonniker said.

'What did you just say about grief reactions?'

'Ah, I was talking about abnormal and enduring grief reactions.'

'*Abnormal and enduring . . . abnormal and enduring . . .*' Dan repeated it over and over, his voice a parody of sheer fascination.

Grace thought something like, *Oh boy. Here we go . . .*

'So you guys,' Dan went on, meaning psychiatrists, 'have a *normal*?' There's a *normal* grief reaction? Oh, that's good. Oh, most good! What is this *normal*? When will I *normally* stop grieving for my dead son? Because, I have to tell you, I'm dying to fucking know.'

'No, no,' Bonniker said softly, 'that's not my point.' He took off his glasses, polishing them on his tie. Staying cool.

'Because I've gotta say, doc, from where I'm sitting, it . . . it feels pretty enduring, you know?' Dan was raising his voice now. 'Proper fucking *enduring*.'

'Dan,' Grace tried, 'he's–'

'I mean, *GET FUCKED*.'

Bonniker was utterly calm and still.

'Dan!' Grace was crying now. 'Stop it!'

'FUCK THIS!' Dan screamed. He was on his feet by this point, and, lashing out a kick, his brown leather brogue connected with a massive, glazed ceramic pot that contained a tall fern, the kick cracking the pot and toppling the whole thing over, the pot then smashing open completely when it fell on its side, earth spilling out across the wood floor like blood and viscera from a wound. Dan stood there panting for a moment, fists clenched by his sides, like a stunned prizefighter who has just unexpectedly dealt his opponent a knockout blow.

Bonniker didn't move. Didn't even blink. The only sound was Grace's sobbing.

'Is that *abnormal*?' Dan said, panting, before he turned and walked out.

In a way, terrible though it had been, Grace missed this version of Dan. At least this version spoke. Well, he mostly shouted and raged, but it was human communication of a sort. The rant Dan had spewed in this room three weeks ago constituted, by some distance, the longest speech she had heard him make in recent memory.

'It's all a normal part of the process,' Bonniker was saying now. 'I've tried to talk to him about it, but he won't answer my calls or emails.'

'Join the club.' Grace sighed. She felt the tears coming. *Not again.* She'd found herself wondering about this recently. About the human body's incredible capacity for weeping. She kept imagining a meeting going on, somewhere down in her tear ducts, the little guys with their clipboards stood in front of a big panel that controlled pumps and reservoirs, with its dials and levers, taking their hard hats off, hands on hips, scratching their heads and muttering darkly about 'usage' and 'remaining levels'. I mean, was this kind of crying sustainable? 'I just . . .' She blew her cheeks out, got hold of herself. 'I keep thinking about the coffin.'

A long pause. 'That's understandable.'

'It was so *small*. It was, you know . . . it was almost funny. Comedy small. Do you know what I kept thinking about? At the funeral?'

'Tell me.'

'When our goldfish died, Pamela wanted to bury it. I was maybe nine or ten, her and Maria a bit younger? And she got this matchbox, and mum helped her colour it in black, and she was so . . . serious. Putting it in the wee grave in the garden. She was *so* serious that I was just trying not to laugh, you know? It just seemed so . . . out of proportion.'

'I understand.'

'And that's how I felt at the funeral. It just felt . . . nuts. Fucking insane. Sorry. Unreal. I just wanted to laugh. Is that . . . I mean is that *normal*? Have you ever heard a patient say anything like that in your life?'

'Yes. Many times.'

'Oh boy.'

216

Grace cried softly for a little while. She thought of her mum, what felt like a lifetime ago, saying to her, 'God was listening.' *Was he listening now?* She took a deep breath and blew her nose. 'Anyway. Fuck it. Where were we? Oh yeah. I went back to work.'

TWENTY-ONE

Jada Hamilton, enjoying the late afternoon sunshine in the beer garden of the Flaps. And there were, it had to be admitted, three serious misnomers in that fourteen-word sentence. For 'garden' was a grandiose term for the forty-foot-square prison-exercise yard of cement, with its cheap wooden picnic tables bolted into place, with its overflowing ashtrays and fag butts crammed into every crack of the broken paving and its crates of empties and steel beer barrels taking up much of one corner and the two ancient, broken washing machines occupying the other. Yes, 'garden' was doing a lot of work here. As was 'sunshine', for, while certainly warm, the overcast August afternoon wasn't giving out much in that department, the sky bruised and dark, heavy with unspent rain. And as for 'enjoying', well, as ever, there was much on Jada's mind. There were his many mouths to feed. (Well. Nicola and Jayden, really. The other weans were all fine, he guessed.) There was his ever-expanding tab behind the bar in here. (Had tae cut down on that. Stop being the big man, buying every fucker a drink. Pay cash and don't run it up.) There was the phenomenal amount of dollar he seemed to spend on fags and takeaway food. (Needed to cut back on aw that shite: for his health as well as the money.) There were his ongoing monstrous monthly payments to bookies and loan

218

sharks. (Things in that last department were certainly starting to heat up: Big Simack and Ranta Campbell were both moving out of the 'polite reminder' stage.) There were his many court-ordered fines. For all his rage about the unfairness of all of this, Jada was capable of the odd moment of self-awareness, of insight. He knew he was the kind of guy who thought gravy trains never ran dry, that rainy days never came and that golden geese went on cranking out their gleaming eggs forever. He'd probably made something like thirty grand out of the Prestwick Airport scam to date. Yet here he was a year down the line: gravy-less and sat in a downpour with a massive hunk of dead poultry in his lap. But, in terms of assets, there was still that crate, squatting in his storage unit, with 200 pistols in it. Of course, the Gypsy had been right. He always was. Jada had spent the past few weeks making enquiries and trying to shift the things. Nightmare. The criminals Jada knew were small-time. Amateurs. If they wanted a gun, they were prepared to pay a couple of ton at the most for a Saturday Night Special: a shonky wee .32 calibre revolver. Or maybe an ancient sawn-off. Not the 500 quid Jada had set his stall at for his primo 9mm French automatics. What Jada needed was *professionals*. True connoisseurs who would appreciate a quality product. There just didn't seem to be many of these knocking about in Partick and Whiteinch. Which led to his brainwave, and the reason he was sitting here waiting for Malky, lighting another Eaton Square and pointing to his pint glass to Wee Sandy, who'd just come out the back door with a crate of empties.

Just as Sandy went back in, here came Malky. 'Make that two, Sandy,' Jada shouted at the barman's back as Malky came over and sat down.

'Awright, wee sacks?' Jada said.

'Getting some fresh air?' Malky grinned, nodding at the smouldering cancer stick in Jada's paw, at the crematoria of ashtrays surrounding him.

'How's tricks, pal?'

'Ach, ye see it aw, J.'

'How did yer boy get on?' Malky's grandson, wee Danny, had been up in court a wee while back.

'Fuck sake.' Malky shook his head. 'Two years for aggravated assault?'

'Who'd he get?' Jada asked.

'Callaghan.'

Jada sucked air in through his teeth.

'Aye. He cheeked the auld bastard an aw.'

'No smart.' Jada lit a fresh fag with the stub of the last one.

'Naw. Ye know oor Danny, but. Boy's daft as a brush.' Malky sighed. 'Ah'm still helping tae pay aff his bloody fine from the last time he was up.'

'Ah know how that goes, pal.'

'When does your Rory get oot?'

'Another year if he keeps his head down.'

Sandy arrived with the pints. 'Cheers, Sandy, stick it oan ma tab. And bring us a couple o' bags o' pork scratchings when you've got a minute, eh?' Sandy nodded and retreated, sighing to himself.

'Well,' Malky said, raising his pint, 'here's hoping.'

They clinked glasses.

'Weans, eh?' Jada said.

There began a discussion of the joys and pitfalls of parenting, of the happiness of those first grandchildren arriving, when you were in your late twenties or early thirties and still young enough to enjoy them. And then the inevitable corollary of that experience, around a decade and a half later: their first court appearances. The curve of life. The continuation of the blood. Drug addictions and school expulsions and incarcerations. After many a 'fuck sake' and a 'whit can ye dae?' and a 'ye try yer best' they were well into their second pints before Jada got around to it. 'Malky, mind yer pal Ah met a while back, at the wee Christmas party we had?'

'Whit pal?' Malky said, taking a draught of lager.

'Mind. The Belfast boy that was staying wi' ye?'

'Oh. Jimmy?'

'Aye. Jimmy. Look . . .' Jada glanced around the empty beer garden and leaned in closer, lowering his voice. 'Ah got the impression he was kinda . . . connected. Over there. Said he was in the "taxi business", if you get ma drift.'

Malky chose not to play dumb. 'Well, aye. Maybe a wee bit o' truth in that. But don't go shouting it about, like.'

'Naw, naw. Course not. Ye know me. But, listen, if he is, like, connected, there's a wee bit o' business Ah might be able tae dae wi' him.'

'Aye? Whit kind o' business?'

'The kind it's better ye don't know about, Malky.'

'Come tae fuck, big man. Ah need to know *something* if ye want hooking up wi' Jimmy. He's a serious boy.'

Jada thought for a moment. 'Right,' he said, leaning even further in. 'Listen, if it aw plays out, it's worth two grand tae ye. A wee finder's fee, like.'

Malky sat back. 'Is that right?'

'Fucking aye it is.'

Now it was Malky's turn to think for a moment. In truth, he didn't really know Jimmy that well. He was his brother Wullie's pal really. But, as Wullie was currently doing a three-year stretch for handling stolen goods, and Wullie's wife wasn't really a fan of anything relating to his Belfast connections, Wullie had asked Malky to do him a favour and put Jimmy up for a wee while when he'd been over some months back. The boy had been all right, and had certainly dropped some heavy hints that he was connected to – how had he put it? – 'the ongoing resistance to the Fenians'. Malky weighed it up. He'd heard through the grapevine that Jada had got his hands on some stolen shooters and was obviously trying to offload them. All he'd have to do was to call Jimmy and say Jada wanted to speak to him and then tell Jada it was either on or off. If it was on, and it all worked out, two grand. Not to be sniffed at. If not, who cared?

'Awright, then,' Malky said. 'Ah'll gie him a phone. But, listen, Jada, like I say, these are serious fucking boys. Know what I'm saying?'

'Ho,' Jada said, spreading his arms, as if to display his kingdom stretched out behind him, the battered, creosoted fence and the rusting washing machines. 'Whit am Ah? Some fanny?'

'Fair enough,' Malky said, extending his hand. They shook.

'Right,' Jada said. 'Ah'm away for a single fish. Ye fancy another and mibbe a wee whisky?'

'Don't mind if Ah do,' Malky said.

Jada marched inside, smiling as he headed for the gents', phase one accomplished. Shite, the time. How did it get tae be five o'clock? Better phone Nicola. He dialled as he pushed the door open and stepped into the tangy air of the gents' toilets.

Nicola hung up. Fuck sake. The usual pish. *Sorry, doll. Bit o' business. Just stick it in the oven then.* She looked at the roast chicken, surrounded by Aunt Bessie's roast potatoes. The bag was lying on the side, Aunt Bessie oan there, daft cow smiling away, stirring a bowl o' some pish. She widnae be smiling if she could see what had happened here. Nicola had given the chicken a good three hours. Thought it was best to double the cooking time from what the Nigella recipe she'd found on her phone said. Ye couldnae be too careful wi' poultry, could ye? But Nigella had talked about tucking tatties in around the chicken and she'd done that but maybe the tatties hadn't quite needed the three hours. They looked like lumps o' coal. Maybe they'd taste awright. Nicola sat down at the small kitchen table and looked through the doorway to the living room where Jayden was teetering around, banging a couple of pieces of Lego together. Nearly eighteen months old now and a wee terror. She looked at the time on her phone, the screen smeared with vegetable oil from where she'd picked it up while she was cooking. The recipe had said tae use 'good quality' olive oil but they didnae have any o' that of whatever fucking quality and oil wiz oil for fuck sake. It was just after five. She'd a good mind to put the wee man in his buggy and stride down there into the Flaps and just hand him over tae Jada and say 'your turn' and head to the bar and get herself a drink. Something occurred to her . . .

Nicola crossed over to the fridge, took out a can of lager, cracked it open defiantly, then sat back down at the table and took a long swallow. On top of the half-Temazepam she'd taken earlier, it might create a decent wee buzz. See, she'd thought, after ye had a wean, things would be . . . that ye'd just get better at stuff. But ye didnae. She should have known that. Look at her own maw. Letting ye . . . putting ye in a situation where . . . Ach, fuck it, nae sense in . . . Spilt milk an aw that. She reached over and took one of the potatoes out of the roasting tray. This involved a fair bit of prising it loose, the blackened tattie finally coming off the tin with a crack. She bit in. Fuck sake. Tasted like a lump o' fucking coal an aw. Nicola dropped it on the table, put her head down in her hands and started to cry softly. Couldnae do fucking anything right.

'Mammy?' She looked up. Jayden was standing there in chocolate-stained vest and bulging nappy, looking up at her, puzzled. 'Mammy sad.' She wiped her face with her sleeve and picked him up. 'Mammy's awright, wee man,' she sniffed, hugging him and settling him on her lap. Jayden reached out and picked up the blackened potato. 'Naw, son,' she said, taking it from him. 'No nice.' There was half a loaf of Scotland's Pride in the cupboard. 'Come on. We'll have a wee piece and chicken for our tea, eh?'

'Wee man!' Jada shouted along the bar to Sandy, who was in the middle of serving some guy at the far end, some right steamer by the looks of it. 'Two mair pints and two double Pipers oot the back when you've got a minute. And have one yerself. And—'

'Stick it on yer tab?' Sandy muttered.

'Stick it on ma ta—' Jada looked again at the guy Sandy was serving. A right alky-looking cunt, but something familiar about him an aw. Jada walked over.

At the last moment, Dan saw someone approaching and, sensing danger, swivelled around on his bar stool. This somehow necessitated a second manoeuvre — that of picking himself up off the floor.

'Fuck sake,' Sandy said. 'He's had about twelve gins and six fucking pints.'

'Dan? It's Jada,' Jada said, helping him up.

'Jada?' Dan croaked. Oh yeah — from that fight in the . . . from the hospital. The same day that Tom was . . . a fresh wave

224

of pain tried to surf up through him, but the firewall of booze held it in place. 'Ah, Jada,' Dan said. 'How ye doing, mate?'

'Fuck sake,' Jada said. 'Start early the day?' There was no judgement or affront in Jada's twinkling eyes, just vague amusement, and perhaps respect for this fellow lover of life.

'Aye, maybe, aye . . .' Dan said, swaying, Jada holding him up by the shoulders now.

'Whit ye daeing in here? Didnae think this wid be your kinda place. Are you no mair aw that Ubiquitous Chip wey?' The word 'ubiquitous' sounded crazily unexpected in Jada's mouth, like hearing a dog suddenly say 'algorithm' or 'Flaubert'.

Dan looked around the hellish interior of the pub. The acreage of cheap wood panelling. The handful of red-faced, aged alcoholics. The group of young bams in the corner. What was he doing in here? 'Ach, y'know,' Dan said, his accent as roughed up as he could make it. 'Fancied a wee change.'

'Been in the wars, have ye?' Jada said, nodding at Dan's forehead. Oh yeah. The coppery bruising.

'Aye, something like that,' Dan said, touching his hairline. Then, before he knew it was coming, he was adding, 'I had a bit of a . . . y'know . . . ma . . . see, the thing is, my wee boy died.' He shrugged. He had not uttered these words to anyone in months, no matter how much drink he had in him. But there was something about where he was, who he was with, that was kind of . . . freeing. You sensed that, here in the Flaps – perhaps like at Sobibor or Treblinka – the value systems were different. Nothing was shocking. Everything was permitted.

There was silence. Jada looked down at the worn linoleum floor. Finally, he shook his head slowly as he found the words equal to Dan's news.

'Fuck sake.'

225

TWENTY-TWO

'HAHAHAHA! WHIT A FANNY! Whit a total fucking waste o' space! Whit did Ah tell ye, Dan?' Nudging him hard in the ribs. 'Boy's no got two brain cells tae rub thegither!' The laughter of Jada Hamilton: a merciless powerhouse of uproar. And Dan was laughing hard too now, at the latest misfortune of the hapless Sammy, sitting across from him at the wooden table in the beer garden, fuming, his face heavily bruised. Much worse than Dan's. 'Boy's no real,' Jada concluded.

'Mental,' Dan agreed, wiping a tear of laughter away. He took a cigarette from his pack and lit it, placing the pack on the table and indicating that the boys should help themselves, which several did. It was a Scottish working–class custom Dan had forgotten about, not having smoked since the early days of Tony Blair's government. The first time he'd smoked in front of the boys he'd lit one and then slid the pack back into his pocket. There had been a moment of silence, then Jada had growled, 'Are ye a fucking dentist then, Dan?' Dan had frowned, confused. 'Cause you're pulling them oot one by one, ya cunt,' Jada clarified. It was a big no–no. You had to offer your fags around. Given the prodigious rate Dan was now smoking at, this was proving expensive. And, about the smoking, what a rediscovery! What a fool he'd been! Surely man or nature had never designed anything finer? All those years he'd wasted *not* smoking. Of course, he wasn't insane. Every time he crushed one out he thought something like 'God, what am I doing?' And then, twenty to thirty minutes later, there he was, fumbling with the lighter and a Marlboro. It was like sex in that respect – urgent need immediately quenched and guaranteed to return. So Dan smoked on and listened to Sammy being abused as he stared down at the crazy paving of the Flaps beer garden, greased and slick with the earlier rainfall. (And surely calling anything in the Flaps 'crazy' was superfluous? The décor. The drinks. The clientele. The food. It was *all* fucking crazy.) Dan drained his pint and said, 'Same again, boys?' He counted their nods and ayes and headed for the bar.

It had been quite the few weeks.

Dan's new routine had firmly established itself. He'd wake up on the sofa bed in his office in the early afternoon, rarely before twelve, and have a light breakfast at his desk – usually just a bowl of cereal or a slice of toast – while he worked on whichever aspect of the Calculations he was currently making the most headway with. As he worked, the great house lay silent above him. No more Tom so, of course, no more Brigit. It had taken him a while to notice there was no more Anna either. Well, in truth, he hadn't noticed. The curt note on the kitchen table had simply read: *Anna quit. Please clean up after yourself until I find a new cleaner. G.*

He'd missed the whole tearful scene in the hallway, Grace hugging Anna as she said, 'I so sorry, Miss Grace, I so sorry. I cannot. Is too sad for me here now. Anna no come any more.' Around lunchtime, which was two or three o'clock in the afternoon these days, he'd have a large, bracing whisky (he was buying Macallan by the case now, 700 quid a pop, delivered from Oddbins on Hyndland Road, a case of twelve bottles seeming to last him a fortnight on average, sometimes not quite that long) before getting dressed (in whatever was lying on the floor by the sofa bed) and then wandering off, heading south down Byres Road, then turning right and heading west on Dumbarton. He'd grab something for dinner en route, usually a bag of chips – sometimes something more nutritious, a cheese slice or a couple of steak bakes from Greggs – that he'd munch on the hoof, finishing eating just before he arrived at the Flaps around four. None of the boys in the Flaps seemed to eat much. If you suggested going out for dinner, you were treated as a cross between Oscar Wilde and RuPaul. Dan knew this because once, early on, around half seven one evening, he really had suggested going somewhere for dinner. The uproar was instant and insane. One of the younger lads got up and capered around, mincing and holding his Stone Island top out to make tiny breasts while repeating the words, 'Ooh. Let's go for dinner! Ah'm Dan! Pump me up the erse!'

So, yeah, he'd learned his lesson on that one. And you really didn't want to mess with the food in the Flaps, with those ancient pies and sausages in the glass case at the end of the bar. As the renowned restaurant critic Jada Hamilton had it, 'Ye'd be better aff chewing oan a dosser's fucken bawbag. Ah widnae gie that shite tae the fucken dug, so Ah widnae.' It was a review that even the proprietor, Big Sandy, had not seen fit to question. Big Sandy, who was even now saying to Dan, 'Same again, Dan, son?'

'Aye, cheers, Sandy,' Dan pronouncing the name like the others did, in his new voice, his Flaps voice: 'Saw-nay. And have one yerself.'

'Cheers. Good o' ye.'

'Wee Sandy no in the day?' Dan, leaning on the bar now.

'Working the night, so he is.'

'Seventeen pound eighty, please, Dan.'

Flattening a twenty down. 'Keep the change, Sandy.'

'Thanking you. Go on, Ah'll bring the other two over.'

Dan returned to the table with two pints and sat down amid fresh peals of laughter and 'NO WAY!'s as Sammy pulled his shirt up to show the others something, some mark, on his flank. Respectful of the pub hierarchy, Dan handed one of the fresh lagers to Jada. Sammy and the Shite could wait for Big Sandy. It had taken Dan a little while to feel comfortable with some of the nicknames Jada's friends went by, to understand that the Shite, for instance, bore you no ill-will if you said, 'Same again, Shite?' Or, 'Ho, Shitey, get us a packet o' crisps an aw.' He would also respond cheerfully enough to 'Skitter', 'Shiteos', 'Wee Shiteos', 'The Keech' and 'Turd'. When exploring the etymology of the name, as he did early on, Dan discovered that, when he was fourteen, the Shite had been denied entry to the school Christmas disco and had responded by going around the back of the building and excreting into a Kwenchy Kup (before Dan's time – it was explained to him that this was a type of soft drink available in the 70s that came in a fluted, plastic cup with a foil lid), which he then attempted to throw at his entry-denier, Mr Travers, head of the maths department. Alas, as he drew his throwing arm back, the projectile had slipped from its protective casing and detonated upon the assailant himself. 'So,' Dan had asked after Jada told him the story, 'the Shite's shite shited the Shite?' Jada had sprayed lager across the table before collapsing in the golden sound of his own laughter, saying, 'Ho! Listen tae whit Dan said!'

Everyone thought Dan was extremely witty for that one.

So, more than four decades on, this fifty-something man was still called the Shite. There were similarly involved origin stories behind several of the others' nicknames. Although 'Panda' was simply a diminutive of the 'pandemonium' he caused, and the Sex Pest was as basic as it sounded, a few of the guys had nicknames they didn't know about, including, daringly, Jada, who was occasionally, and discreetly, referred to as 'Mr Positions' when he was out of earshot. Dan hadn't yet enquired as to the provenance of that one.

'Fuck sake, look at this, Dan!' Jada was saying.

Dan peered at Sammy's pale flank, at the large crimson bruise stamped into the quivering flesh Sammy was holding. 'What did that?' he asked.

'Cunt leathered me wi' a fucking golf club, Dan!'

'Ya daft bastard,' Jada said. 'Tell ye whit – the cunt was fucking lucky he didnae come doon the stairs tae meet me.'

'What cunt?' Dan went on, having missed the beginning of this. 'What happened?'

What had happened was that a guy had walked in on Sammy while Sammy was burgling his home. It was a downside to the way Sammy did business, he freely admitted as much. He was an opportunistic burglar whose MO was to roam the streets of Hyndland, Dowanhill and Hillhead in the middle of the night in the hope that someone had left a window open somewhere. Sammy was a wee guy, mouse-like in his ability to squeeze into a place through the smallest opening. He'd quickly and stealthily move through the basement or kitchen of one of the big Victorian homes (homes like Dan's), grabbing any easily portable fast-cash items – laptops, iPhones, purses or wallets – before legging it. The downside was that Sammy was sometimes caught, which occasionally (well, more than occasionally) meant taking a beating or being arrested. Or beaten and then arrested. 'Look at the state o' me!' Sammy lamented. 'Ah was already running oot the fucking place when Ah tripped and fell doon. Ah'm oan the flair and he wires intae me with a seven-iron!' There was a pause as they all shook their heads and sipped their pints and pondered this injustice.

'Well, same time, Sammy,' Dan said slowly, 'the boy hud tae play it as it lies . . .'

A pause, and then the table erupted in laughter again. Jada clapped Dan on the back, well pleased with his prodigy. Look at him, Jada thought fondly. Wee Dan. Dan the man. Fan Dan. Fanny Danski. If you'd told Jada when he'd picked the boy up off the floor in here a few weeks back that he'd be sat here, mixing it up with the boys, knocking out the patter, smoking and drinking it up a storm, well, Jada would have told you to get bent. Similarly, if you'd told Dan that he'd be sitting here, pissed at five o'clock in the afternoon in one of the worst pubs in Glasgow (putting it in the running for one of the worst pubs in the world, of course) and howling at the story of a failed attempt to burgle a home very much like the one he lived in, well, he would not have believed you. But, then again, a lot of things Dan wouldn't have believed had gone ahead and happened recently anyway. The conversation quickly moved on, from Sammy's beating to the other night's appalling performance by Glasgow Rangers, to an acquaintance of the Shite's who had recently had sexual relations with a teenage girl whom he now had reason to believe he might be related to. Dan sometimes tried to imagine this kind of stuff going down in his old life. The drink in the golf club bar where it was casually revealed that Ally – say – might have accidentally committed incest. Or that Jack had been arrested the night before for aggravated assault. All while Dan sat there covered in bruises from his latest beating. It was all unbelievable, of course, but no more unbelievable than some of the other language Dan had heard in recent memory. *Occlusion at the level of the laryngeal inlet . . . direct laryngoscopy . . . cerebral and pulmonary oedema . . . cardiac arrest.*

Jada's phone lit up on the wet table. Jada looked at the number and felt an almost electrical charge shoot through him when he recognised the Belfast area code. *Finally.* He picked it up and stood up, saying, 'Back in a minute, boys,' his face assuming the stern mask Dan had come to know as meaning serious business was afoot.

'Ho, Dan,' Sammy said as Jada left. 'Who wiz the wee bird that wiz his assistant, back early on? Wee ginger. Stonking, so she wiz.'

'Er . . .' Dan tried to think.

Once it had been made clear he was under Jada's patronage and that he wasn't shy about getting the drinks in — often chucking in a wee round of shots on the side — they had all quickly accepted Dan. He was, as they sometimes said when calling on his learning to settle a rare non–football argument, 'an educated man'. Less reverentially, he had once been accused of having eaten 'dictionary fucking cornflakes' when, early on, in a move that astonished him now, he'd used the word 'superfluous'. He was also 'the professor', a title handed to him one afternoon when they were all playing The Knowledge quiz machine in the corner. Dan had confidently punched in '1962' in response to the question 'When was the Cuban Missile Crisis?' The other two options had been '1862' and '1992'. 'How the fuck,' one or other of the boys had asked, 'did ye know that, Dan?'

'Well,' Dan had said, 'I don't think they had nuclear missiles in 1862 and we were all alive in 1992. Don't you think we'd remember it?'

A beat. And then the reply – 'Aye, right enough, professor.'

But, really, the only tax exerted for their friendship was the odd request for *McCallister* trivia. And it was something they tended only to indulge in when Jada was out of earshot, Jada having discouraged it a couple of times with a growled 'gie the fucking boy a fucking break wi' aw that shite fur fuck's sake'.

'Oh,' Dan said. 'You mean DC Helen Winton?'

'Aye. What was she like?'

'Well . . .'

It was *bliss* to be here. Where the conversations were easy, consisting entirely of anecdote and remember-when and set-pieces, or about something someone had seen on TV or read in a tabloid newspaper. They never, ever strayed into anything difficult, anything abstract or theoretical. They could get philosophical now and again, these guys, but only lightly so. A sighed 'aye, son, whit's fur ye willnae go by ye'. A ruminative 'it's a long road wi' no turning'. That was about the extent of it.

And no one ever, *ever*, mentioned his dead baby son.

As Dan was setting about inventing a couple of salacious anecdotes about Shirley Meikle, the actor who had played DC Winton in seasons three to seven, Jada was pacing the exercise yard of the beer garden, phone pressed to his ear. 'So I took this up the line,' Jimmy was saying (and Jada still pictured a big cable running under the Irish Sea, even though he knew it was all wireless now), 'and there might be a bit of business we could do together here. With these . . . hand blenders you're talking about.'

'Aye?' Jada said, sucking nervously on a Marble Arch.

233

'We might, Jada. We just might. I'll need to come over. For verification, you understand?'

'Aye. Nae bother. When?'

'I'll be in touch. And, Jada? If I were you, I'd keep this very, very quiet.'

'Course. Whit dae ye think Ah fucking am?'

Click. Jimmy hung up.

Fucking magic, Jada was thinking.

Jimmy, in his turn, was sitting in his car outside another bleak pub, the Belfast rain lashing down the windscreen. What was he thinking? He was thinking that this Jada was a fucking chancer who was in way over his head and no mistake. Which meant that there might be a bargain to be had here . . .

If Jimmy could pull this off, if he was the guy to secure *two hundred* 9mm pistols for the cause at a rock-bottom price, his ascension in the Free Ulster Division would be assured. But, even if he did negotiate a phenomenal deal, you were still talking about a lot of money here. Way above his pay grade to authorise that kind of expenditure. Time to talk to the man who could. He got out and hurried through the rain and into the boozer.

Carruthers drummed his fingers on the table, thinking.

Jimmy sat across from him, his pint untouched. Stevie Carruthers was a big man, in every sense. Sixty years old and tipping the scales at twenty stone, he didn't do field work any more. But he'd done plenty back in the day. No stranger to the roadside IED, the muzzle to the kneecap and the car-battery-to-the-bollocks interrogation was Stevie. Yes, a serious man. An Ulsterman who could trace his lineage back to the blood and mud of the Boyne and a legendary destroyer of

Fenians. They were in the backroom, just the two of them, the distant murmur of conversation from the public bar, the muted roars from the TV, Rangers v. Hibs.

'Mmm,' Carruthers said. 'Ye know what they say now, son. If something's too good to be true . . .'

'From what I hear, this guy got lucky.'

Carruthers regarded Jimmy Gemmill. Wee Danny's boy. He was a comer. No faulting the boy's ambition. Still a few question marks over his ability though. Mind you, what he was saying, if it was true, was music to Stevie Carruthers' ears. For these were difficult times. Back fifteen-odd years ago, when the whole peace craze was really getting going, Carruthers had been one of the few senior men of the FUD arguing against fully decommissioning their stock of weapons. What if all this blows over? What if we find ourselves once again in need of harsh words backed up by big guns? And here they were. The Ultra IRA had been making their presence felt for months now: shooting that journalist lad. Then the copper. They had AK-47s and Uzis and whatnot and what did we have left? The odd cache of ancient weapons hidden around the Londonderry countryside. Half of them rusted and fucked from decades lying dormant. So what young Jimmy here was proposing would certainly be attractive to some of the powers that be who were less than happy about slowly becoming the powers that had been. Might all be a crock of utter shite and bollocks though. 'How are you thinking about proceeding then?'

'Gonna go over there and put my eyes on it first.'

'OK. Well, let me know what you find, son.' A mammoth roar came through from the bar – Rangers scoring. 'If it's all simpatico, then, yeah, I believe we could find the money. Make the necessary arrangements for transportation and so forth.'

'How high can I go?'

Carruthers calculated. 'Two hundred 9mms? I'd say fifty, maybe sixty grand depending on age, condition and all that? Tell me this, Jimmy – how well do ye know your handguns, son?'

'They're MAC 50s. Ex-French army. Reliable. Decent wee pistol.' He had spent some time on Wikipedia.

'Mmm. And this fella, your contact, is he reliable?'

'He's a chancer, Stevie. He had a wee thing going stealing army stuff from Prestwick Airport – mess kits and sleeping bags and shite. Got hold of these by accident and shit his fucking drawers. And put it this way – I know where he lives.' Jimmy grinned.

Carruthers smiled too. 'All right, then. I'll make some enquiries up the chain. Let me know how you get on over there.'

Jimmy nodded, shook hands and stood up. Walked out, whistling. *Up the FUD*, he thought to himself.

TWENTY-THREE

Dan woke up as usual on the sofa bed in his basement study, his eyes crackling open, the fuzz of whisky still coating his mouth. He found that, again as usual, he had fallen asleep cradling the framed photograph of Tom, the one taken on the morning of his first steps, a couple of weeks before he died. The boy had a huge grin on his face as he stood there. You could just see Dan's ankles in the background of the shot. Dan's arms had been raised in cheering triumph. He remembered the week afterwards, as he had frantically Tom-proofed the entire house. There were still stair gates on every landing. The custom-cut foam was still taped around the edges of the low-lying, sharp-edged coffee table in his study, just across the room from him and covered now in empty whisky bottles and beer cans. There were still child-proof locks on the doors of every conceivably Tom-reachable cupboard. And a few inconceivable ones: 'Do we really need a child lock on the bathroom cabinet?' Grace had said. 'It's five feet up the fucking wall!' But the Dad Mind had foreseen an eventuality where an increasingly mobile and ingenious Tom might just use the pedal bin as a stepping stone onto the sink and from there into the cabinet filled with toxic medication. Better safe than sorry. Then there had been Dan's daily, hourly, patrols, where he scoured all four floors of the townhouse finding death traps set for his boy: the pair of earrings his own mother had left dangling from the edge of her vanity table in the bedroom, just begging to be gulped down. There, in the hallway, the loose change bowl that, during her dusting, Anna had left in a terrifyingly reachable position. Or how about the TV remotes that his father-in-law, in a fit of insanity, had simply left lying on the sofa, where they lay like a pair of hand grenades, begging Tom to prise them open and gobble down their life-ending batteries. The remotes had been one thing, but Dan had never been fully satisfied on the question of electrical cables. Tom would increasingly use his sharp, healthy little teeth (brushed thoroughly by Dan twice daily, a fraught process not unlike trying to draw a moustache on a live eel with a felt-tip pen) to chew and nibble on anything he got his hands on. It was far from inconceivable to Dan that he might gnaw through one of the lamp cables, or the one for the Sky box, or the stereo, or . . . well, the list was endless. But, short of going fully Amish, he'd never devised a solution he felt he could present to Grace. And then there was Brigit. He'd noticed she was sometimes prone to having a hot cup of tea or coffee within arm's reach when she was reading to the boy and the Dad Mind could only see Tom knocking *That's My Pig!* out of her hands and scrambling over her in a flash to upend the steaming mug over his own dome. He'd had a word with her. 'Uh . . . OK,' Brigit had said, in the gentle tone someone uses when dealing with a madman. She should have heard what Dan *wanted* to do – the idea he'd got from an American website, from idahomom1979, after a few hours spent googling 'toddler hot drink accidents' – the policy of allowing only sealed, *lidded* hot drinks within a metre of Tom. He'd floated it by Grace, reading next to him in bed. She'd laughed for quite a long time. He shook his head at the memory of it all. How useless it had all been. *One grape.* Dan yawned. What time was it? Early afternoon surely? His mouth was desiccated, and he badly needed a cold Coke from the fridge upstairs. And he wanted to get back to work. A page of his handwritten (well, drunkenly scrawled) notes from late last night lay on the floor near him. He'd been working on the Closures. *Restructuring of hospital provision in Glasgow . . . Western Infirmary closed in autumn 2015 . . . expansion of services at Gartnavel and building of Queen Elizabeth on site of Southern General . . .* If they hadn't closed the Western, it would have been a six-minute drive from their house, as opposed to the thirteen minutes (without traffic) to the Queen Elizabeth. They might even have made it to the Western in three or four minutes. If they had . . .

Grace was sipping her tea at the kitchen table. She put her cup down in the saucer and brushed a strand of hair back from her face, trying for a sitting position of 'neutral'. She wanted to avoid sitting too upright, too cocked, or with her hands clasped or arms folded. Anything that might be considered 'confrontational' or 'interventional'. Bonniker had said it was important to appear calm and matter-of-fact. Try to avoid ultimatums. She could hear him coughing downstairs now as he got out of bed and started moving around. The clock on the wall read 2.37. They'd bought the clock in John Lewis, way back when. Not long after they first moved in together. She remembered that afternoon. Just before Christmas. They'd gone for a drink at the bar in Rogano and ended up staying there for hours, snuggled in one of the wee walnut booths, drinking Black Velvets. Where did that life go? What happened to it? All the stuff that seemed like it would come so easily, that would just happen. Marriage, pregnancy, a child, and then more children. A family. '*Hey!*' Grace wanted to say. Or '*Oi!*' This wasn't the fucking deal. How had she seen their life unfolding when she was in her early twenties? She'd never have counted on them being as rich as this, but, in cinematic terms, some kind of rom-com surely featured. Not anything as daft as the two of them twirling laughingly through a park connected by one very long fucking scarf or anything like that, but jokes and autumnal walks and eating ice-cream from a shared carton and spoon on the sofa and shit like that – yeah, why not? Romance and comedy were definitely the pictured genres. Instead of what they found themselves in now. Which was what? Kitchen-sink drama? Social realism? Slice-of-life? No, no – it was *horror*, of course. But here they were. This was the deal. And you either came to terms with it or you didn't. She heard his footsteps on the stairs up from the basement and took a deep breath. *Calm. Matter-of-fact.*

Dan appeared in the doorway and stopped, surprised to see her sitting there. *Holy Mother of God*, Grace thought.

He hadn't shaved in days, the eyes were just crimson slits, the hair matted and straggly, and he was panting slightly from the exertion of climbing a single flight of stairs. His recent paunch hung over his pyjama bottoms, pushing out the front of the (filthy) NEW JERSEY T-shirt he sometimes wore in bed.

'Hi,' Grace said.

'What's wrong?' His voice was cracked and husky.

'Can you sit down, please?'

'Look, Grace' – he was already moving towards the fridge – 'I don't feel great. Whatever this is, can't it wait?'

'I'm afraid it can't.'

'Fuck sake.' He took out a Coke, cracked it open and guzzled

240

it, standing at the fridge with his back to her. Grace flashed on him standing in the same spot a couple of summers back, sweating, fresh in from his morning run, getting apples and celery and spinach out to take over to the juicer. *This man is a stranger to me now,* Grace thought. She waited. Silence. 'Well, go on then,' he said, turning, burping.

'How long are we going to go on like this?'

'Like *what?*'

'Please don't make this harder than it is.'

'I don't fucking know.'

'Do you want me to just watch you drink yourself to death?'

'I don't care, Grace.'

'What are you going to do with yourself? I mean, eventually. With work?'

A long pause. Dan gazed off out of the kitchen windows, for a moment looking like he was really thinking. 'I was thinking . . .' Grace waited. 'I might drive a van. Like, a delivery van. You know? Like . . . long-distance deliveries.'

Grace looked at him for a full ten seconds. *Try to avoid ultimatums.* Then she found herself saying, 'I don't think I can do this any more, Dan. I think you should move out.' She sucked back her tears. This was hard, but she was ready for it. Ready for the fight.

Dan drained the Coke, crushed the can and burped again. 'Fine. That it?'

Grace was digging her right thumbnail into the cuticle of her left thumb very hard. Trying to focus on the pain, trying not to cry. Dan was walking past her now, heading back downstairs. Then he stopped beside her, in profile. 'I just wish . . .' he said in a new, softer tone as he searched for the right words, steadying himself with one hand on the back of her chair, like

241

a pensioner. Grace looked up at him, his voice, his posture of defeat, his hand was so close to hers, closer than it had been for months, all leading her face to form itself into an expression resembling hope. She had known this man for fifteen years, since she was twenty-three-years old. She had loved him for fourteen of those.

Go on, Grace was thinking. *Wish it. Whatever you wish for I will help you do. We can somehow get out of this.*

Out of this hole that felt like they were falling down a tunnel through the centre of the earth, blackness all around them, blackness ahead of them, the only light the one that they had come from, already so far gone that it was just a pinprick a thousand miles behind them. The tunnel was endless and tight, their fingertips scraping the sides, catching dirt beneath their clawing nails, brushing the heads of blind worms, and neither of them could hear the other's screams. And in this image, Dan was always falling ahead of her. She could make out his outline in the blackness, his soundless, flailing limbs. She realised he still hadn't completed his thought.

'Dan?' She was almost whispering. 'You wish what?'

'. . . that I could kill myself.'

He patted her arm, then shuffled off down the hall. It occurred to her to shout after him, to say, 'Do you think that's what he would have wanted?' Something like that. But Tom had only been a little baby. No one knew what he wanted. So Grace didn't say that. She started to cry instead. After a moment she heard him turn the downstairs shower on.

The following day Dan went into an estate agent on Byres Road and rented the first available thing he saw in the West End: a Victorian flat just along the road on leafy Huntly Gardens. One bedroom, living room, bathroom, kitchen. £1,350 a month.

Two months' deposit down. 'When would you like to view it?' the estate agent girl asked.

'Nah,' Dan said, tossing down a credit card.

It was that easy.

Why was he here? Jada hated this fucking place and had sworn he'd never darken its doors again. Maybe it was to do with spending more time with Dan . . .

Maybe what had happened to his wee boy had made Jada more aware of, not just Jayden, but of all his children. And when Nicola had pointed out it was Rory's birthday this week, well, it just seemed like the decent thing to do. So here they were, having dinner together. Well, it was brunch really, the caged clock on the breeze-blocked wall telling him it was just after 11.30 in the morning. The brown paper bag, having already been thoroughly searched, had been torn open to form a platter for four portions of large fries. Arranged around this centrepiece were the starters (twenty chicken nuggets with various dips), the entrées (one Big Mac, no lettuce, and one Quarter Pounder with Cheese) and the dessert course: an Oreo McFlurry and an apple pie. An extravagant meal, but then it wasn't every day your eldest son turned twenty-one. Jada sucked on his Coke and watched Rory tucking in like he hadn't seen such a feast for a long time. Which he hadn't, McDonald's not featuring on HMP Barlinnie's regular bill of fare. 'Happy birthday, son,' Jada said. One of the screws patrolling the visiting lounge came by the table and feinted towards their food, making as if he was going to take a fry before smiling and moving away. The rotting visiting room, with its ancient furniture and strip-lighting. 'Fucking wank,' Jada growled softly.

'He's awright that wan, da,' Rory said.

'Aye, son, some o' them are better than others, true enough. But they're aw fucking wanks at the end o' the day. You mind that.'

Rory shrugged, letting it go, and moved onto his burger, which he was pleased to see his father had remembered to excise any hateful traces of green from. Too soft, the boy, Jada thought. That was part of the whole problem. It was how Rory got roped into doing the job that landed him here in the first place. Fucking half-arsed armed robbery that he'd only gone on because he was too fucking soft to say naw to his pal Davy. Took doon the bookies over in Maryhill, couple of years back, Cheltenham weekend. Three o' them: Davy Bryson, Big Lee Chanks and Rory as the door man. Two shotguns and a high-powered air pistol they'd borrowed fae Davy's dad Mikey. Jada knew fuck all about it till after. They'd got away with a tidy wee score and all – over fifteen grand. Well, they got away with it for a day, until Lee had a massive barney with some daft boot he was pumping, some wee lassie who thought she was his fiancée who walked in and caught him celebrating wi' a couple o' local hoors and a big bag o' chang. Raging, so she was. Phoned in an anonymous tip-off. Boy was still partying when the polis kicked in the door to find Lee baws deep, with a pile of cocaine on the table and a shotgun and four and a half grand in a William Hill bag in the wardrobe. Took Lee about thirty minutes to roll over on Rory and Davy. Lee got six months, and Davy and Rory got four years each. Mikey Bryson caught in the crossfire an aw. He was doing a stretch along the corridor from Rory, for illegal possession of firearms. Third offence. On the upside, this had meant Jada didn't have to deal with Lee. Mikey's firm had. Ye still saw the boy about, in his wheelchair. Mad twitch and everything. Couldnae talk right any more.

'Whit's yer brief saying about yer parole hearing, then?' Jada said, opening the damp cardboard box containing his Quarter Pounder. It was cold. After a bite he set it aside.

'Usual pish,' Rory said, wolfing his Big Mac, already close to finishing it, not seeming to mind that it was lukewarm at best.

'Ye keeping yer head doon, but?'

'Aye, da.'

'Same time, don't take any pish.'

'Naw, da.'

The same words had been handed down to Jada from his father, on his first incarceration here. Not that his dad had come to visit him. He'd passed this wisdom on before the trial, sensing, rightly, that the odds of Jada escaping a custodial sentence were low; the plastic bag with 500 Es in it, tucked into the lining of Jada's jacket when the polis pulled him over. Summer of 1999. He'd have been about the same age as the boy here. *'Keep yer heed doon and ye'll be fine. Same time, don't take any fucking pish.'* Jada's dad had gone on to say that, from what he heard, the Bar-L was luxury these days anyway compared to when he'd last been in, back in the late 70s, for breaking and entering. Jada vaguely remembered it, remembered being told his dad had got a job on the rigs and would be away for a while. Something else he remembered about that time. What was it?

'How's the wee man getting oan?' Rory asked.

'Magic. Proper wee lunatic, so he is.'

'Got any photos?'

'Er—' Jada didn't think so. He never took photos of the wean. Nicola's fucking phone was full o' them. Nothing but photos o' Jayden. Hang on though, she'd texted him a couple. 'Aye . . .

haud oan.' Jada found Nicola's texts – none of which he'd replied to – and thumbed down until he hit the pictures. He enlarged one: Jayden, laughing on a swing.

'Magic,' Rory smiled, getting in close to the photo. 'Cannae wait to meet him.'

'Aye, well, no long now, son,' Jada said. Another twelve to eighteen months, depending on good behaviour to be exact.

'Ye heard fae Rhiannon?' Rory suddenly asked him.

'Huv Ah fuck,' Jada said, pulling his phone back as though from the maw of a serpent. The abrupt ferocity of his response surprised even him, a man whose very speciality was abrupt ferocity. But then his feelings were always complicated when it came to Rory's big sister, his eldest daughter and the black sheep of the family.

'Ah huv,' Rory went on, digging into his McFlurry now.

'Oh aye?' Jada said, slipping his phone back into his pocket. 'How's she getting oan?'

'Good, she says. Working away.'

'Is that right? Well, she knows where tae fucking find me, doesn't she?' Jada said this with finality, signalling that the subject was closed, and underscored it by biting savagely into his apple pie. '*Theesus!*' he screeched, banging a clenched fist on the scarred wooden table.

'Ye awright there?'

How did they do it? Jada wondered through the pain. The boffins over at the McDonald's corporation. Within five minutes of taking the bag, all the food inside was cold as marble, with the singular exception of the apple pie, whose power to retain heat seemed to be on a par with the fission rod. '*Theesus 'ucking Christh!*' That pastry casing, they should sell it to insulate houses. Houses? Baws. The reactor cores of nuclear subs. Jada slaked

246

his mouth with flat, watery Coke before he managed to finally reply. 'Too fucking hoat!'

It was later – as he was checking his fat, blistered tongue in the car mirror, sat in the vast Barlinnie car park – that it came back to Jada, the other thing from 1979, when his dad had 'gone away to the rigs'. It was the silence. How quiet it had been for a time. The unholy peace that had settled on the flat. And not just silence, there had been *music*. How happy his maw had been, with Radio 1 always on in the kitchen, on the wee tranny, and her dancing about, singing that song she liked that was a big hit that summer, during the school holidays. What was it? Something about it was sad, but his maw had always sounded happy when she sang it, something about how it was in fact funny that the couple in the song did not talk any more.

Thinking about this sentiment reminded Jada of Rhiannon again. Be near four years since he spoke to her, since she started wi' aw that pish. Getting aw they daft ideas intae her head. Aw the shite she started talking. What was it she'd said about him, in that last row they'd had? *Limited emotional intelligence.* Something like that. The brass fucking flaps on her. Good job she was a bird. If she'd been a boy, she'd huv been playing wi' her fucking teeth and no mistake. Fucking weans, his weans, they didnae understand how lucky they were. He'd never hit them in any serious way. The odd bare erse spanking when they were wee, fair enough. The odd boot up the erse. Normal. But nothing like . . . Ah mean if they'd been old enough to remember their grandda, Jada's dad. He was old school. He'd been born, when? Jada tried to work it out. He'd been a good age when he died, maybe sixty-odd? Decent enough innings round their way. They'd let Jada out for the funeral. Two screws flanking him and that mad tag on his ankle. Sixty-odd meant he'd have been born in, what, the 40s? And *his* dad had been born during the First World War. Nineteen fucking canteen. Aw that olden days way. Mad wi' the fucking horse and carts and the bowler hats an aw that pish. He'd been proper old school. Jada had never met him. The auld bastard had missed the first war right enough, but he'd signed up for the second one, probably to get away from the wife and weans for a bit. Infantry. Killed in action. Well, kind of. The story went that a mate of his had thrown a turnip at him when he was driving a big 2-ton truck during basic. Just for a laugh, like. But it had gone through the windscreen and he'd crashed intae a ditch and broken his neck. Aw got hushed up. Official secrets an aw that. Anyway, Jada's da used tae show him and his brothers and sisters this wee round scar he had oan his side, about the size o' a ten-pence piece, from where his dad, their grandfather, had stabbed him with a metal peashooter. Jada's dad – just a wee boy – had fired a pea aff his dome for a laugh and he'd grabbed it and stabbed it right into him. Just missed puncturing his liver, so it did. A few inches lower, and he'd have been pan breid oan the spot. They told the doctor he'd been running and fell on it. (Not that anyone asked any questions back then, mind you. No like today when ye give yer wean a skelp and there's fifteen social workers up your fucking erse wi' piles o' forms before you're oot the hospital.) Jada's dad used tae tell him all this after a battering sometimes – *'ma ain da near killed me wi' a rusty peashooter, so stop yer fucking crying.'* And they'd try, him and his brothers and sisters. Try tae stop crying as they lay on the floor, or flattened themselves under their bed, or trembled against a wall, tasting blood in their mouths, feeling loose teeth with their cut tongues, clinging by jelly to the sockets of the gums, with their maw somewhere in the background,

248

bent over the kitchen sink, cleaning her own face with the crimson-stained dishtowel. Now there was a man of limited fucking emotional intelligence.

Fucking Rhiannon. Fuck sake. She hadn't crossed his mind in ages. What did the wee dick have to go and bring her up for? She'd disgraced the family. What the fuck did she have to go and do it for? *University*, no less. Jada cranked his tunes up, 'Thundercore' by The Waffen-SS drowning out these vexing thoughts about character and destiny and nature and nurture, the crunching jackboots mixing in with the 180bpm stomp of the kick drum, deafening as he accelerated downhill through Riddrie, heading southwest, away from the hulking prison, away from his past and towards his future, towards Glasgow, the mad twists and coils of the motorways surrounding the city glittering in the midday heat haze like a sci-fi set.

TWENTY-FOUR

'Careful, Jayden!' Nicola shouted from the bench, looking up from her copy of *Time For You!* (*'Help me, doc! I told friends I was dead!'*) She watched as he edged closer to the roundabout on which two older toddlers were being burled around by their dad. It was quieter here now. September, the schools all back in. Just toddlers like Jayden, staggering and stumbling like the town drunks. She watched her son fall again, turned to one of the mums sitting on the next bench along from her and said pleasantly, 'He's a mad wee bastard sometimes, so he is.' The woman looked confused for a moment, then smiled tightly, Starbucks cup in hand, and turned back to her pal. *Snobby auld cow*, Nicola thought. When she'd first come across this playground a few months back, up here on the fringes of Hyndland, she'd thought it was populated solely by grandparents. This wasn't unusual round her way, the grandparents being the primary caregivers for the few kids whose parents had jobs. But, after several visits she'd realised that these old wrecks, most of them in their late thirties (some of them even looked to be in their forties!) *were* the parents. It seemed like a thing around here, having an ancient maw and da. It did make her a bit uncomfortable, this place, and it was a long, uphill walk, but it was so much nicer than the playground near the flat, a concrete wasteland of broken glass, dogshit and fag ends. With its graffiti and used syringes and the swings that you had to uncoil because they were always wrapped around the top bar. And the Partick Young Team boys standing around, dressed in black from head to toe, swilling Bucky and swearing their fucking heids aff. Thinking of the Young Team, Nicola once again found herself drifting off into her own lost, distant youth, the morning once again slipping away in a Temazepam haze. The thing no one had told her was how very long the days were with a toddler. Up at the crack of dawn with the whole morning stretching ahead of you like a long, featureless road. There was the free playgroup in Partick three mornings a week, in the freezing community centre. She'd looked into getting Jayden into a private nursery for a couple of mornings, but the *cost* of it . . . not even worth mentioning to Jada. Besides, as he said, 'Whit the fuck else have ye got to dae wi' yer time? Ah'm oot there fucking grafting while you're just sitting around on yer fucking erse. Ah wish Ah had the time to just fanny aboot playing wi' the wean.' Still, the Temazepam helped. She'd mostly stuck to her pledge to lay off the class A. A bit of puff was fine. She'd had the odd tiny line of brown. Just snorting. Hadn't really done the other since the wee man was born. Missed it sometimes. That *whumf* when the plunger went in . . .

Jayden was yelling joyfully now as he ran around in circles chasing the swirling roundabout. Nicola was watching, half-smiling, lost in the rhythms of her own lightly medicated thoughts, as though there was a filter between her and reality – a stocking, or Vaseline, over the lens – when she became aware of a voice nearby.

'Excuse me. Uh, hi. It's Nicola, isn't it?'

She turned, startled, bringing her hand up to shield her eyes from the multi-million-pound glare of the sun glittering off the massive sash windows of the townhouses that surrounded the playground. A woman was standing there in a flowery summer dress and a denim jacket. She was wearing big mad sunglasses. Couldnae see her eyes.

'Aye?' Nicola eventually said with some caution, as though addressing a bailiff or a polis.

'It's Grace. We met a while back, I think? On Byres Road?' No response. 'Your wee boy was born the same day as ours?'

'Aye?' Nicola repeated, not remembering. She was posh as fuck this woman, aw that Nigella way, standing there, smiling down at her. Suddenly fear gripped Nicola. This place, it had to be private or something. Had never felt quite right that she could just walk in here. As it tended to, her fear morphed quickly into a bristling, defensive anger, something along the lines of, *if this fucking daft cow is gaunnae try and huckle us out of here, she'd better have fucking hauners oan the firm.*

'Ah . . . yeah. Lovely day, isn't it?' the woman said as Nicola continued to stare at her. A long pause. Then this Grace sat down on the end of the bench, hands in the pockets of her denim jacket. 'Your wee boy's certainly having a good time,' she said, nodding towards where Jayden was trying to climb onto the centre of the seesaw. In the last few minutes Jayden had: 1) almost run into the feet of a boy on the swing, 2) tried to eat the chewing gum he found on the bottom of the seesaw, 3) fallen off the little piggy bouncing thing and 4) almost got his head stuck in the railings. All unseen – or unremarked upon at any rate – by Nicola.

'Aye,' Nicola said. A further awkward pause. 'Where's your wee–'

'Tom,' Grace said.

'Aye. Tom.'

'He's . . . at home. Having his nap,' Grace said.

Nicola nodded, thinking, but not adding, *then whit the fuck are ye doing here then, ya fucking weirdo?* Nicola no longer felt threatened; she sensed she wasn't going to get bounced, but she decided to end this awkward encounter on her own terms, getting slowly to her feet and saying, 'Right. Ah better get up the road. Ah've ma man's dinner tae get oan.' This was obviously a lie. She was just letting this snobby auld boot know that – whatever she was thinking – Nicola wisnae a single maw or anything like that. She had a man and a home and a life.

'Oh, right. Well, nice to see you again,' Grace said.

'Aye. See ye.'

Grace watched her walking off towards her son, pushing a battered McLaren stroller through all the Yo Yo Zens, Bugaboos and Silver Crosses. She was so thin and pale. Grace had to fight the urge to call her back, to offer to take her home for the afternoon, to give her a good meal and let her have a nap for two or three hours. Or two or three days. Heavily, Grace realised this maternal urge was partly generational: she was old enough to be Nicola's mother. She sat back and watched the children play. Somewhere inside Grace a voice was saying, 'You need to stop doing this. You need to stop coming here.' But there were times when she just couldn't stand it in the house any longer. There used to be so much life, so much noise. Anna and Brigit coming and going. Their parents. Dan. Tom. The sound of the vacuum cleaner and dishes clanking and various TVs going on and off and feet on the stairs and shouts from distant rooms. Now there was only silence. Her things – clothes, books, papers – stayed in the same sad little piles until she moved them. It was big. A textbook 'family home'. Now neither was true. No family. No home. Just a great, silent folly. She'd have to talk to Dan about putting it on the market. She leaned back on the bench. When she watched the young children, she often thought of the battery recharger Dan had bought once, that you stuck your AAAs in and plugged into the socket. Another one of his crusades. 'We must reduce the number of batteries we buy.' When they were fully charged there would be four glowing green bars up the side of the device. These were the toddlers – fully charged batteries. Then there were the old people – blinking on one red bar. Here she was – somewhere in the middle. She watched the toddlers running and shrieking and spinning, and the voice went on gently saying to her, 'You need to stop doing this. You need to stop coming here.' But she wasn't listening to that voice. She was just crying softly behind her big sunglasses.

TWENTY-FIVE

'The caaa . . . the caaa . . .' Jada said, pointing at the picture of the ginger tabby, his wild tongue searching for the consonant.

It wasn't all drinking it up with the lads. As summer gave way to autumn, an unexpected avenue in Dan's relationship with Jada had developed. Which was why they were sitting side-by-side on the sofa at Jada's place on a Tuesday morning, one of the days Nicola took Jayden to playgroup. In the last couple of months, since Dan had moved into the flat, his freedom now limitless, he had taken to driving Jada around during the day as he went about his 'business'. It wasn't a formal arrangement. 'What you up to tomorrow?' Dan would ask, late afternoon in the tea-stained light of the Flaps. 'Usual. Running about. Wee bit o' business,' Jada would reply. 'Need a lift?' Dan would say. 'Aye, awright.' In truth, most of the stops were brief, and having someone at the wheel saved Jada from accumulating the vast number of parking tickets that he seemed to regard as a normal business expense. Dan would pick him up around lunchtime, waiting parked at the bottom of the flats until Jada came shouldering his way around the corner towards the car.

It was good to stay busy, Dan reasoned, and it enforced a little sobriety between the hours of noon and four, which seemed to be the man's peak working hours. The exact nature of Jada's businesses remained somewhat obscure to Dan but seemed to involve popping into various flats and council houses to either receive or, more frequently, drop off money. There were men seen 'about dugs'. There were 'wee bits o' how's yer father'. There was a fair bit of 'ask me no questions, Ah'll tell you no lies'. It had taken a couple of weeks of this routine before Dan picked up on a certain problem. Or, rather, before he put it all together. They had been ordering lunch in some terrible pub and Jada had once again declined to even look at the menu (burger and chips, he'd said automatically) when several moments came together in Dan's head. Jada's blank face as he quickly scanned his tabloids. The way he'd chuckled mirthlessly when Dan had pointed out an amusing headline in one of them. His curt 'just take a fucking left up here' when Dan had asked him to read an address off the satnav. The way, when visiting one of the three commercial bookmakers Jada favoured (as opposed to the unlicensed types who handled his heavier action), he always talked to the person at the till and watched as they wrote his bet down for him. It all came together as they sat there, Dan sipping his Coke, Jada his midday lager top. Jada had been in an especially good mood that morning as some complex bit of business – something that he couldn't discuss but that had been long in the negotiation and seemed to involve frequent phone calls to Belfast – seemed to be about to come to fruition. Before he'd had a chance to think about it too much, after the barman had drifted off along the bar with their food order, Dan had leaned in and said quietly, 'Jada . . . can you not read?'

Jada's breeziness had evaporated instantly, and an awful silence fell. Dan watched as Jada inhaled deeply, his grip tightening on the pint tumbler. For a second, Dan thought he'd made an awful mistake. That he was about to get glassed or take ten rapid to the dome. Then, in a whisper, head down, not making eye contact, Jada said, 'Jist . . . jist didnae happen.' He looked quickly around the pub. 'If you tell any cunt–'

'No, no. Of course not.'

'Seriously . . .'

Dan decided to proceed with caution. He let it hang there for a moment before he said, 'Have you thought about–'

'Whit, sitting in some community centre wi' aw the other fucking dafties, reading *Spot the Dug*? No happening.' He took a long drink.

'Well, listen, I, y'know, I could help you. Nobody needs to know.'

'Ach, Ah'm a bit long in the tooth now, Dan. It is whit it is.'

'We could just give it a go. See how you get on. If you don't want to keep going with it, fine by me.'

A beat, Jada in profile to him, staring at the row of optics. Finally, he'd shrugged. It was as close to an official green light as Dan was going to get. So he went to Waterstones and trawled the shelves in the children's section: some basic phonics books, some Early Years stories, a couple of Julia Donaldsons. Halfway through this shopping spree he'd glanced across the shop to see a woman browsing titles with her three-year-old boy, who was excitedly arguing for a book about sea creatures, and Dan had had to go to the bathroom and throw up, and then remain there foetal and sobbing for a good ten minutes. But he took this as a sign of positive progress: his mega-grief seemed to require specific triggers now, seemed to have moved out of its omnipotent and omnipresent stage.

'The caaat?' Jada said uncertainly.

'Very good,' Dan said, turning the page, where the cat was now pictured sitting upon its traditional destination.

'Sss . . .' Jada began making the sound of a snake hissing.

'Mmm,' Dan encouraged. He waited patiently, glancing around the room. Not so very long ago, Dan would have found this a strange place to be in the middle of the day, the tiny lounge of a high-rise in Partick, with its overflowing ashtrays, its abandoned takeaway food cartons, the cigarette burns on much of the furniture and its gigantic, permanently on, TV set.

'Aah, aah . . .'

'Good.'

'Tih . . . tih . . .'

'Just put it all together . . .'

A beat, then Jada said 'SAT!'

'Excellent!'

Jada stared at the drawing for a moment and then, with all the force of revelation, with the kind of lightning flash appropriate to the finger of Michelangelo's God touching Adam's, he yelled, '*THE CAT SAT OAN THE MAT!*'

'Brilliant, Jada. Really well done.'

Jada was basking in the approval, his nostrils flaring from the mental exertion, when they heard a key in the lock. In one swift motion Jada was on his feet and had swept the children's books up into their carrier bag and dumped it all in Dan's lap before crossing the room in a single stride to stand in front of the TV, where he started saying, 'Aye, so Ah says tae him, "Ho, bawjaws, if ye want to come fucking wide, then–"' just as Nicola and Jayden came in. Jada's pantomime of normality might have been appropriate, Dan thought, if his partner and son had walked in to discover Jada lowering his testicles into Dan's ocular cavities.

'Awright, hen?' Jada said.

'UNKY DAN!' Jayden screeched, running over and throwing his arms around Dan's legs.

'Hiya. Hiya, Nicola,' Dan said, ruffling Jayden's hair, tickling him.

'How come yer back early?' Jada asked.

'They hud tae close. Nae staff. Budget cuts and that.'

'Playground!' Jayden yelled hopefully.

'Ach, Ah told ye, mummy's tired, son,' Nicola said, slumping onto the worn, black pleather sofa. 'Whit you two up tae?'

Jada and Dan exchanged a look. Dan got there first, hefting up the carrier bag. 'Ah . . . I had some books in the house I thought you might like for the wee man. We, y'know, we bought them . . . before.' As he'd intended, this oblique reference to Tom's death had the effect of shutting down any further enquiry from Nicola.

'Aww, thanks, Dan,' she said.

It had taken Nicola a little while to put it together. Jada had mentioned Dan a few times before he started appearing at the flat. Some posh guy whose wean had died who'd started hanging out in the Flaps. Jada had met him at the hospital the morning Jayden was born. And then Nicola remembered. *Your wee boy was born the same day as ours.* That woman in the park a few weeks back. *He's at home having his nap.* A pure lie. But Nicola got it. She just didnae want tae talk about it. Nae wonder. Of course, Nicola had been suspicious of Dan at first, as she would be of anyone who talked the way he did suddenly hanging about with them. She could tell he roughed his accent up a bit for their benefit, but now and again he couldn't help but betray himself – 'bathroom' instead of 'toilet' or 'bog'. Or 'sofa' instead of 'couch'. 'House' instead of 'hoose'. But she got why this Dan liked hanging about with them, getting to hang out with Jayden, the same age as his own boy would have been. And the truth was he was nice enough. He loved hanging out and doing stuff with the wean, and, in all honesty, it gave her a break now and then.

'Aye, cheers,' Jada said, taking the bag of books from him. 'Keep it till he's a wee bit bigger, like.'

'PLAYGROUND!' Jayden shouted again.

'Jada, dae ye fancy taking him tae—' Nicola began.

'Ah've got that thing tae get tae, doll.' Jada stepped over to the window and cracked it open an inch or two as he lit a cigarette.

'I'll take him,' Dan said quietly.

'Fuck sake, Jada, gaunnae no smoke in front o' the wean?' Nicola said this more in deference to Dan's presence than in a spirit of actual outrage.

'Ah've opened the fucking window!' Jada said.

'I'll take him,' Dan said again.

'Ach, thanks, Dan, but—'

They began a dialogue they'd already enacted several times before: Nicola saying no, it was fine, she was sure Dan was busy, she'd take him, Dan reassuring her that he wasn't and it was no bother, then Nicola conceding that she was quite tired and a wee lie-down would be great, but just for an hour or so if Dan was sure. And again, today, like all the other times, before he knew it Dan was bundling the wee man into his buggy and they were tremblingly descending in the stainless-steel box of the ancient, urine-reeking lift.

'Peek-a-boo!' Dan yelled.

He stuck his face through the triangular hole cut in the plastic tunnel, just inches away from Jayden's face, causing the boy to shriek with delight and start backing away as Dan sought another one of the holes to effect another surprise appearance. Nicola, he was certain, intuited that these stolen moments with her son were a substitute for playtime with his dead boy. But Dan figured that, from where Nicola was sitting, any reason for her to get a little peace and quiet was good by her. As for Jada . . . Well, as with much in Jada's life, Dan wasn't sure how closely examined anything was. (*The unexamined life is not worth living* . . . Socrates? Dan couldn't quite remember.) To Jada, Dan probably seemed like a typical 'new man'. A product of middle-class conditioning who thought there was nothing odd, weird, or – let's face it – downright *bent* about a grown man not only choosing to spend time one-on-one with a toddler, but actually enjoying it.

'Peek-a-boo!'

Dan picked Jayden up at the end of the yellow plastic tunnel and lifted him down onto the spongy safety matting. He ran into interference as the boy staggered over towards the seesaw, keeping himself between Jayden and the broken glass and dogshit that circled the playground. He'd have dearly loved to have taken him up the hill and into the Hyndland playpark that he knew Nicola sometimes took him to, but that was out of the question. The hushed whispers from the mums: *'Isn't that Dan Chambers with that wee boy? Did you hear what happened? Yeah, I heard he's moved out . . .'* So they made do with the Partick playground, where the other occupants were the odd single mum and the gang of youths smoking joints, all of whom looked at Dan and thought something like 'grandad looking after the wee boy while his maw's at work'.

Dan lifted Jayden onto one end of the seesaw, making sure he was gripping tightly, and then got on the other end himself.

He very gently pushed with his toes, raising and lowering the boy, who grinned with delight at this rare treat. Dan had been to the playground before with Nicola, who had just slumped on the bench and scrolled on her phone. And Jada was as likely to take the boy to New York as to the playground.

Some plants grow taller with less water.

Christ, son, Dan thought, watching Jayden, you're going to be seven foot five.

He checked his watch – almost time to go. And his heart gave a heavy, downward tug as he thought about handing back this precious thing, about the sorrowful 'bye, bye, Unky Dan'. Christ, he suddenly needed a drink very, very badly. A thought occurred to him. After he'd strapped the protesting Jayden safely back into his buggy, he wandered over to the climbing frame in the corner, now, in the late afternoon, festooned with teenage boys, one of whom was sitting on the top of the slide, drinking from a half-full bottle of Buckfast.

'Here, son,' Dan said. 'How much for that?'

'Eh?' the kid said.

'The wine.'

The boy looked at the bottle. Those innocent monks. 'Ye want tae buy ma fucking Bucky? Away and get tae fuck, ya mad paedo.'

Dan held out a twenty-pound note.

'Ye fucking serious, man?'

Dan nodded. The kid took the note in disbelief and handed over the bottle. Dan wiped the neck clean with his sleeve as he walked back over towards Jayden, already hearing the boy behind him shouting to his pals, 'Ho, the mad fanny gie'd us twenty bar fur a half-bottle o' Bucky, man!'

'Cheers, son,' Dan said to Jayden as he raised the bottle. He

262

drained most of it in two long swallows, the foul, sticky-sweet, caffeine-laced wine bursting through his bloodstream, the day suddenly booming into bright Technicolor around him. 'Here, Jayden, come on and we'll have a seat and read ye a wee story.' Dan had stuck the copy of *The Tiger Who Came to Tea* into the bottom of the buggy as they left the flat. He got the book and settled the boy on his lap on the chewing-gum-festooned bench.

'The tiger didn't take just one sandwich. He took all the sandwiches on the plate! GULP!' Dan mimed taking a great big bite. 'ULP!' Jayden said, laughing, delighted. They did it again, the boy laughing harder this time. You could see it clearly now, sparkling in the eyes, around the corners of the mouth, the way the dark hair was growing in sworls and waves – the baby giving way to an actual person. He would be two on his next birthday and so, of course, would Tom. Dan had found himself increasingly picturing his son's body, in the small wooden box under the cemetery turf for all these months. When he did this, he always imagined the skeleton laying on its side, curled, foetal, looking for warmth. *Mummy, daddy, where are you?* But would there even be a skeleton after a year? Wondering about this had inevitably led him to Google, where he was grateful to one Dr Donald Westlake, head of forensic anthropology at Missouri State University, for his article in which he stated that 'on average', a body buried in a standard coffin 'usually starts to break down within a year, but takes up to a decade to fully decompose, leaving only a skeleton'. A decade! His face still his own, even now, as Dan sat here. And that 'break down' was good. Yes, very good! It was what Dan did every night as he sat hunched over the whisky bottle, his mind doing its thing, picturing decomposition, collapse, entropy. The weeds, worms and maggots looking for a way in. The whole time he'd been off on this train of thought he'd still been reading, knowing the story by rote now, but he became aware that Jayden was trying to tell him something, was poking his finger into his mouth and saying something.

'What is it?' Dan said.

'Ouch,' the child said. 'Jayden ouch.'

'Here, let me see . . .'

Jayden struggled a little, his heels kicking in the grubby playsuit, but Dan managed to hold his lips open and angle his mouth towards the weak sunshine. He could see it clearly, as he pulled the bottom lip down a little – the beginnings of a black hole in the bottom left premolar, the tooth itself not more than a few weeks old and already . . . Dan felt a tremor of pure anger. The beakers of fizzy drinks. The chocolates and ice-lollies and the sugar tossed over the already mind-bendingly sweet cereals.

Why would you? Who the fuck gives . . .

Later, much later, Dan realised that the rudiments of his plan started to come to him around now, as writing ideas sometimes would in the early evenings, when the mind was enlivened by a couple of drinks. It was just the first thoughts, really, the merest outline, nothing detailed. That would all come later. But, yes, the first strands came to him there in the ruined playground, with the cheap wine charging through his veins and the dun skies darkening over Partick. A way to restore balance. For justice to be done. To fix everything.

He had the *what*. The *how* would take a little time. He knew this from writing. He'd let his subconscious go to work on it. Dan drained the bottle and crammed it into the overflowing bin. 'Let's get you home, wee man.'

TWENTY-SIX

Jada led the way down the corridor. It was a bleak space that never failed to slightly unsettle him: a long concrete hallway dimly lit by caged bulbs every couple of metres. Both sides of the corridor were lined with metal doors that were starkly stamped with black numbers – 041, 042, 043. Prison. It reminded him of prison. And, adjacent to that thought, the potential lifetime in prison that awaited him behind the door to 045, the padlock to which he was now fitting his key into while Jimmy stood behind him, saying nothing. Jada was aware that his heart was beating faster than it should have been. What was it about this guy that bothered him? The silences were no fun, true enough. Two hours in the motor up from Stranraer, the entire length of the A77, and he'd got exactly eleven words out of him: a yawned 'fine', after being asked how his crossing was, an 'ate on the ferry', in response to Jada's suggestion that they hit the services for a wee bit of breakfast, and a positively expansive 'on the six o'clock boat tonight' upon being asked when he was heading back home. It wasn't even like he fell asleep. Just sat staring out the window. Jada wasn't looking for a stand-up routine or anything, but fuck sake, a few words. Pass the time o' day like a fucking normal person.

This fucking padlock, come tae fuck . . .

Jimmy checked up and down the corridor while the clown fumbled with the padlock. It had briefly crossed his mind that the whole thing might be a set-up. All his nervous gibbering in the car. An undercover police way out of his depth on his first job? No, he was just out of his depth full stop. Finally, with a grunted 'fucking thing', the padlock was snapping open and Jada was stepping into the lock-up and turning on the light. With a last glance down the hallway, Jimmy followed him in, closing the door behind him.

'There we go . . .' Jada gestured to the wooden crate that squatted in the middle of the 10-foot-square unit. There were other crates stacked around. Some vodka. Flaming Cozzack. Jada bent down and picked up a crowbar. Jimmy stood there waiting as he got the tip in and edged the wooden lid off with a squeak. He stepped back, holding the lid with one hand, the other hand extended towards the crate in *voilá!* fashion. There they were: two rows of black handguns, ten in each row, all held in wooden stocks, like bottles of wine might be, the grips towards you, inviting you to pick them up. Which Jimmy now did. He held the pistol up to the bare bulb overhead, turning it over in the light, examining the blue gunmetal, the MAC logo on the side. Then he pulled the slide back, cocking the weapon, checked the chamber was empty, then let the slide snap back into place with a loud *clack*. Jimmy dry-fired it, producing a metallic *snick*. Then, with his thumb, he pressed in a little stud behind the trigger and the magazine fell out of the butt of the gun and into the waiting palm of the left hand Jimmy had already cupped below it. He examined the magazine briefly then slid it back into place. He cocked the hammer with his thumb this time and pulled the trigger again. *Snick*. Jada watched the whole display, impressed. Jimmy held the gun

266

back up to the light, re-examining it. In truth, he was now out of moves, for this was as far as his YouTube research had taken him. He stood there for a second until Jada finally spoke . . .

'So?'

Jimmy let it hang for a moment. 'How much are ye asking?'

Jada was ready. 'Five hundred a piece.'

Jimmy smiled, shook his head. 'Not a chance.'

'Fair fucking price, that,' Jada countered.

'Maybe if you were selling one gun to a highly motivated buyer. We'd be looking for more of a bulk discount here.'

Jada took a few steps around the room, pretending to think, scratching his cheek. 'Well, seeing as yer taking the lot, I might come down to four hundred.'

'Nah.'

This fucking prick. 'Awright, then,' Jada said. 'How fucking much were ye thinking?'

Jimmy leaned against the crate and folded his arms, the pistol still in his right hand. 'I might be able to go as high as twenty grand. For the lot.'

Jada did the mental arithmetic. 'That's only a hundred quid a pop! Away tae fuck. Ah'm needing double that at least. Costs an that.'

'Fair enough.' Jimmy put the gun back in the rack. 'Come on, then. Long drive back.' He started for the door.

'Haud oan, haud oan, for fuck sake.' Jada lit a cigarette. 'Listen, final offer, right? Thirty grand for the lot. That's a hunner and fifty a gun. Fucking bargain.'

'Twenty-five,' Jimmy said, making eye contact for the first time in the entire negotiation and holding it. The silent close. The next person to speak would lose.

'Fuck it,' Jada said. It was aw found money anyway. Take the win. 'Aye, awright.'

Jimmy extended his hand across the crate and the two men shook. Jada suddenly became aware of the fact that Jimmy had no luggage of any sort. 'Have ye, like . . . where's the cash?'

Jimmy laughed. 'That's gonna take a while. There's things we need to figure out, y'know? In terms of getting a crate of fucking guns across the water. You don't just roll onto the old Stena Line.'

'Aye, but, how long are we talking about?'

'Early December.' This was what Carruthers reckoned was feasible.

'Fuck sake!'

'If that's a problem, Jada, we can take our business elsewhere.'

'Naw, naw, but don't, like, hang aboot too long, eh? Plenty o' other buyers interested.'

Jimmy laughed again at this. 'Yeah, sure.' What a result. Carruthers had authorised him to go as high as sixty grand. He'd be a hero. 'I'll be in touch.'

TWENTY-SEVEN

'He'll be back,' Becky said.

'Of course he will,' said Rose.

'I think Dan just needs . . .' Becky began theorising.

Grace dunked a dumpling in soy. The four of them were in the Hanoi Bike Shop, down Ruthven Lane, opposite Hillhead tube station. Outside, the October wind blew leaves along the alley, the cobbles wet from the rain, shining bright as jewels. Autumn in the West End always reminded Grace of the first term of first year, when she'd arrived here for the first time, eighteen years old and everything – Dan, TV, Tom – ahead of her. And now, seemingly, behind her. This was a late lunch, half-two, so the place was quiet, as Grace had intended. She could just about cope with the girls, who knew everything, who nothing had to be explained to or recapped. Who had moved out of the extreme sympathy stage. But she didn't want to risk running into more casual acquaintances if she could help it. The head tilts. The eyes crinkling in sorrow. A couple of women – other nursery mums she barely knew – had simply burst into tears in front of her, one of them just running away, saying, 'I'm sorry, I'm sorry.' *Well, fuck you*, Grace thought.

'How's Sarah?' Grace said, changing the subject, sick of talking about bloody Dan. There was a pause. Sarah had, pointedly, not

269

been invited to any of these recent lunches. Grace hadn't seen her since that awful day. There'd been the odd text. The odd WhatsApp. Grace smiled into the pause. 'Come on. We might as well address the elephant in the room.'

'Oh, she's doing fine,' Rose said.

'Yeah,' Yvonne joined in, 'but, you know, it's tough. No question. You know, with father of the bloody year on the team . . .'

Incredibly, against the odds, Rob and Sarah were still together. Sarah had had the baby – a wee girl, Joni – back in July. Grace and Sarah had exchanged a few texts, and Grace had sent a cashmere blanket for the child, but there had been no phone calls. As for seeing Sarah and the baby, no. She just couldn't go there yet. But it had obviously been noted. Joni was coming up to three months old now and Grace was the only one of the old gang not to visit. 'I'm sure she understands,' Becky said.

'She's not getting much sleep, obviously,' Rose said, 'but . . .' And then her expression changed as she remembered something, 'Oh my God! That fucking guy. So, the other week, Sarah says to me, "Oh, Rob's renting a studio in town." I said, "What for?" She says – get this – because he *needs peace to work on his music*. I mean . . .'

'His *music*?' Grace said.

'Yep. Didn't you know?' Rose said. 'He makes techno tracks.'

'And who's paying for all that?' Grace asked.

'He is,' Rose said.

'How?'

'Oh, you haven't heard. Apparently, Rob's minted,' Becky said. 'Well, his family are minted.'

'Are they?' Grace said.

'You know Late Reservations dot com?' Rose said.

'I am familiar with the household-name website, yes, Rose.'

'Rob's dad set it up.'

'Jesus.'

'Oh, lots of things have come to light over the last year or so. Let's just say our Sarah's not so daft as she first might have appeared . . .' Rose said, signalling the waiter over. Against Becky's protests she began ordering more dim sum and another flask of sake.

Grace's mind drifted. She looked out of the window at the gusting wind blowing the leaves along. October. Then November. Then Christmas on the horizon. It would have been his first Christmas Day. She'd already bought . . . 'Sorry, can I say something?' she said.

Becky and Rose fell silent.

'Here's the difference between me and Dan. Just there, right now, I started thinking about Christmas. And that led me straight onto Tom and the wee things I'd already bought for him last year, for his first Christmas, and what I'm learning in Cognitive is that you need to shut that road down. That it only leads to the past and what could have been. And that serves no purpose except to feed sorrow.' She took a gulp of sake. She wasn't crying. She was angry. 'But Dan – fucking Dan – not only is he *not* shutting that road down, he's *living* on it. *Gorging* on it. He's . . .' She stopped, wondering whether to tell them.

'He's what?' Rose asked.

'Do you know what I found in his desk?' They were both looking at her, watching her turn the empty sake cup over in her fingers. 'All these files. Pages and pages of them. All these meteorological charts. About the weather in Almeria this past year.'

'Almeria?' Rose said, taking Grace's cup, refilling it.

271

'Apparently, it was a very dry spring and a very warm start to the summer over there. So the grapes were very abundant and *in some cases plumper.*' Grace put the emphasis into her voice, but they both continued to look at her, not quite getting it.

'I don't underst–' Yvonne began.

'Dan's thinking that if it had been colder, then the grapes might have been just slightly smaller and then Tom might have been able to swallow it.' They both looked at her. Grace laughed. 'He's also got files full of research on fucking *knife sharpeners.* Files on different traffic routes from our house to the hospital. Files on how the closure of the Western came about. I mean, right down to PDFs of the minutes of Health Board meetings about it.'

'Eh?' said Yvonne.

'He's thinking that if the Western hadn't been shut down and we didn't have to go all the way to the Southside for an A&E, then Tom might have made it.'

'Jesus Christ,' Rose said.

'I still don't–' Yvonne began.

Rose looked at her and said, 'All work and no play makes Jack a dull boy . . .'

'Exactly,' Grace said, smiling. 'He's gone mad, bonkers, and I am become Shelley fucking Duvall.'

'But . . . but what does Dan think he's going to–' Becky persisted.

'Becks, let me spell it out for you.' Grace leaned forward. 'Dan thinks he can *fix* this. That, if he works out exactly what went wrong, then somehow, magically, Tom is going to come back to us.'

The four of them sat there for a moment, the steam rising from the last wicker basket of dumplings.

Becky spoke first. 'Why do they always think it's about fixing everything?'

Rose shook her head. 'Fucking men.'

'The thing is,' Grace went on, 'I keep hoping that all of this is going to pass. That it'll eventually break like some mad fever. That he'll come out of it and things can . . . I don't know . . . get better. I mean' – she looked up, sheepishly, twisting her napkin in her lap – 'I miss him. I still love him.' A single tear rolled down her cheek as she felt Rose's arm pulling her close.

TWENTY-EIGHT

Friday, 12 December

In the end, Dan's *how* got nudged along by an accidental discovery.

The invitation had been casual. 'Jist a few folk coming by Friday night. Pop yer heid in if ye've got nothing oan, Dan.' But Dan sensed from Jada's subtle hints – 'bit o' business coming aff this week, Danski, cannae really talk about it, but' – that a big celebration was in the offing. He wondered about what to bring. Wine? Mmm. An area fraught with difficulty. Dan had seen the empties left lying on the side in Jada's kitchen, the stuff Nicola drank. Ocean Cove and Turning Leaves and the like. Shirazes like clotted, sweetened blood. Chardonnays the dark, chemically oaked, unnatural yellow you'd normally only see on a renal unit, flowing from catheters into milky plastic pouches as the kidneys of aged alcoholics packed up. To take something decent might be to imply insult. And then what if your bottles were just plonked on the side and you were handed a glass of the already open Sunset Bay Chenin Blanc? (£3.99 from PriceBeaster on Dumbarton Road.) Nightmare. Dan was quite far gone, he knew that, but he wasn't far gone enough to be drinking that. In the end he decided whisky was a safer bet and he took along a nice bottle of Glenfarclas. He handed it to Jada as he came in the door to the tiny, packed, noisy flat and saw that it was promptly placed on the side as he was handed a brimming tumbler of Highland Warrior. (£8.99 a bottle from PriceBeaster.) What the hell, Dan thought, downing it in two gulps, tasting engine oil and burned rubber and formaldehyde. No matter – he was off. He accepted another. And, boy, was his drinking accelerating this week, what with the anniversary looming. A year this Saturday since . . .

A few hours later, he'd found himself sharing a few lines of very rough cocaine at the kitchen table with some of the regular faces from the Flaps – Malky, the Shite and the Sex Pest – and a couple of Jada's neighbours. It was unlike the parties Dan and Grace (ah, Grace. God. When had he last seen her? Last week? Shit, maybe it was last month? Glimpsed across the road as he stood smoking in the doorway of Curlers) used to have, in his old life, where couples were split up boy–girl around the long cherrywood dining table and then everyone decamped to the living room together for charades or the name game. No, here the girls gravitated towards the living room, where they were dancing around the big Bluetooth speaker with the flashing lights while all the men gathered in the galley kitchen to discuss the issues of the day. As always, and no matter that he was now quite far into the life of an alcoholic and frequent drug user, it took Dan a little while to fully dial into the conversational pitch of Jada and his lads. Having analysed at length the current form of Glasgow Rangers, they were now onto the recent coming-out of some celebrity, some guy from a reality show Dan had vaguely heard of.

'It wiz fucking obvious that cunt was as queer as a bottle o' chips,' Malky offered.

'Fine by me,' countered the Pest. 'Mair fanny for the boys.'

'Ah don't know why he bothered hiding it,' Jada reasoned, topping up everyone's glasses with Highland Warrior. 'Every cunt oan the telly's bent these days. It's no even like it's a . . . whit dae ye call it?'

'Handicap?' Dan offered.

'Aye, exactly, Dan,' Jada said. 'It's nae handicap. Being bent disnae make ye a mongo!' Everyone roared with laughter at this, Dan joining in gratefully, having teed the big man up. Jada looked around at his friends enjoying his party. The largesse of Jada Hamilton – the crates of lager, the towers of empty Iceland food boxes, the small pile of cocaine, the bag of Es. That very morning, in the lock-up, Jimmy had handed over twenty-five grand in cash, and then he and his two muscle lads had loaded the crate into their transit van and headed back down to Stranraer. It had taken nearly six months, but what a score! Jada had spent the rest of the day clearing tabs across town – the bookies, the Flaps, various pawnbrokers and dealers – and then he popped into the Car Krazy showroom in Whiteinch where he paid cash to treat himself to a new motor – the black, five-year-old Audi A4 now parked proudly downstairs.

'Here, Dan,' Malky said. 'You're aw that TV way. Who's bent that we don't know about?'

'God,' Dan thought. 'Like Jada said, it's all pretty out in the open now.'

'Don't be telling us McCallister's a fucking bum bandit,' said the Shite.

'Noo. Far from it.'

'Aye, don't talk shite, Shite,' the Pest said. 'He's been married about five times. Weans aw over the shop. He'd shag a hot loaf, am I right, Dan?'

'Pretty much.' McCallister. Gregor. Toby. He wondered how all those guys were. But it was like trying to remember kids you were at primary school with. Just the vaguest faces. The odd Christian name.

'Aye, like being married stops them!' Malky said. 'Elton John was fucking married. That cunt's pure bent fur the rent, man!' They embarked on a long discussion of the phenomenon of what they didn't know were called 'beards'.

Much later, the party had thinned out a little and Dan noticed a definite gear change had taken place; the tunes had got more lugubrious, and of the dozen or so people left they had split into smaller groups, a couple of the girls chatting on the sofa and stroking each other's faces, Malky and the Shite hunkered down at the far end of the kitchen, engaged in earnest, hushed conversation. Dan checked the clock – nearly three in the morning – and thought he'd call it a night. He wandered off in search of his host, to thank him for the lovely party. He could hear Nicola laughing through the bedroom door at the end of the short hallway. He knocked twice, softly, heard Jada cough, then, 'Who is it?'

'It's Dan. I'm just heading off.'

A whispered exchange, another laugh from Nicola, and then Jada was saying. 'C'mon in, Dan . . .'

He hesitated, then pushed the door open, with the words 'thanks for the party' forming on his lips. But there they died. He saw that Nicola was flat on her back on the mattress, with one leg raised up, being held by the ankle by Jada, who was crouching on the floor by the bed with a syringe clamped between his teeth. 'Shut the door, wee man,' Jada said.

'Er,' Dan said, edging into the room. 'What are–'

'Real party's in here, Dan,' Nicola said, giggling.

Dan pressed his back to the door, feeling it shut behind him, and watched as Jada took the syringe out of his mouth and placed the needle between Nicola's big toe and the one next to it. Jada pressed the plunger down with his thumb. Nicola's back arched up off the bed and then she gasped and sank back down, writhing with pleasure.

Jada looked up at him. 'This aw a bit too heavy for ye, Dan?'

'Eh? No. No.'

'Here, come and sit doon,' Jada said. Dan walked over and took a seat on the chair that served as a nightstand. Jada put the needle down on the floor, opened a bedside drawer and took out a charred piece of tinfoil. 'Jist try a wee bang on this. Ah'm no gaunnae be the cunt that shoots ye up for the first time, but smoking it isnae a big deal. Bit o' a waste, mind . . .'

Dan looked at Nicola, who was still moaning gently on the duvet, seemingly in the throes of a mild orgasm. Jada said, 'We hardly ever dae it these days, but the wee man's away fur the weekend wi' his gran, so we thought we'd jist have a wee dig. Let oor hair doon . . .'

'Right,' Dan said. He was blind drunk and high on cocaine, but a part of him, the tiny, sane fragment that still floated around somewhere in his skull, knew that this was a very odd situation.

'Here.' Jada handed him a straw and started moving a purple disposable lighter back and forth beneath the tinfoil onto which he'd poured a few grains of the light brown powder. 'Come on!' Jada said. 'Get in there!' Before he quite knew he was doing it, Dan was hovering the straw over the acrid smoke and sucking. He coughed, retched, not really getting it. 'Again! Quick!' Jada said. Dan did it again, and this time he felt himself taking a long draw of the hot smoke right down into his lungs.

'Hold it,' Jada instructed. Dan was going red. 'Fucking hold it.' Eyes watering. 'And slow oot yer nose,' Jada said. Dan exhaled as slowly as he could and then . . . *whummmmfffff.*

It could have been five minutes later, it could have been fifty, when Dan found himself stumbling along the hallway of the flat. He didn't feel like he was stumbling, however. No, it felt much more confident, much grander, than that. He felt like he was floating, with the soles of his feet just brushing the carpet. He'd never known such peace. Well, after the vomiting at any rate, the memory of which was already vague. He had a trace memory of Nicola stroking his back, saying, as if to a child, 'That's it, that's it, get it aw up,' while he heaved into a bucket at the foot of the bed, Jada lying splayed on his back on the floor across the room, the belt still around his right arm, the syringe in his left fist. Dan was heading back to the living room, where voices and soft music could still be heard, pushing himself along using the wall as support when he suddenly felt the wall falling away under the weight of his outstretched palm and then he too was falling sideways and landing with a thump on the carpet. He laughed. No pain, no pain. He found he was lying on his back, looking up at the Artex ceiling. Something dangling from it – three gently bobbing shapes, one red, one yellow and one blue. It took a moment before Dan realised: they were elephants. It was a mobile. Jayden's room. He refocused on the ceiling above the trembling elephants and saw that what he thought was plain white paint was in fact patterned, speckled with dark spots. A few minutes later, he came to a further understanding about what they were: mould. Black spores of mould. He turned his head and looked under the cot: dustballs and discarded toys and a carrier bag containing the kids' books Dan had given

Jada sometime ago. On the bookshelf above the cot were a few more cuddly toys and a framed photo: of Jayden smiling on his mum's knee, with Jada beside them, scowling his habitual scowl into the camera. There were no books on the bookshelf, no books in the house apart from the ones stuffed in the bag that had been kicked (hidden?) beneath the cot.

Dan performed this inventory dispassionately, with a smile on his face and the warmth of the heroin coursing through him. Still, the thought occurred: how did they – well, how did Nicola – read to the boy? And the answer soon followed: they didn't. It all started coming together in his mind. There was no anger, not even any judgement, really, just the slow accumulation of facts enabled (or encouraged at any rate) by the heroin, by the creamy, spangled free association it made possible. The mouldy room. The absence of any kind of input or encouragement. The terrible diet. The exposure to racism and the homophobia. The drug-fuelled parties and the comedowns. The neglect. And then, maybe fifteen years from now, the teenage Jayden. Dan saw him clearly, the sweet boy, the eager vessel, replaced by the swaggering bam in black trackie bottoms and hoodie, taking his place beside his fellows on the climbing frame and raising the glittering green Buckfast bottle to his lips. No more '*Unky Dan!*' That delighted cry would be replaced by the snarl of '*whit you looking at, ya auld fucking bender?*' And then Jayden taking his place at his father's side, learning the ways of cheating and swindling and ducking and diving and skanking and mugging off and fucking up. Then, as he further fulfilled his destiny, taking his place in the Bar-L. Dan's heroin mind kept going with it. The ejaculation up an alleyway – or behind the bins at the Flaps, or in the woodchip-papered bedroom of a council house – and then the continuation of the line, a line of Jadas stretching away into eternity. And here was Dan – the last living Chambers. Lying flat on his back in the small, damp bedroom, these various strands of thought being massaged by the heroin until they were coming together into something like an epiphany. Dan had read about this phenomenon. That heroin, in the early stages of its use, can awaken great creativity in people, that one can suddenly have tremendous ideas, see great vistas of possibility blossoming before you. It was the heroin that finally led to it all crystallising in his mind.

Once you have the *what*, you need the *how*.

TWENTY-NINE

Monday, 15 December

Jimmy strolled through the public bar towards the backroom, feeling tired but very pleased with himself. Everything had gone smoothly: the mug Jada gratefully accepting his pittance, the blocks of used twenties in the cheap sports bag, then the drive back down to Stranraer and the boy on their payroll from the ferry company directing them to the right lane, where the copper on their payroll waved them straight onto the boat. And then the delivery of the crate in the early hours of Saturday morning to the armoury – a farmhouse on the northern edge of Belfast. He'd got it all done fast and without any fuss and at a rock-bottom price. Now he would reap the rewards. Jimmy was smiling to himself, humming 'The Sash', as he entered the backroom.

And then he saw Carruthers' face.

The big man was sat at his usual table, next to someone Jimmy had never seen before, a granite-faced fella in his forties, arms folded and no hint of a smile either. As he crossed the room towards them (and this walk suddenly felt like it was taking a very long time, feeling less like a victory parade and increasingly like a funeral march) Jimmy became aware of another presence – Archie, the bigger of his two boys who'd gone to Glasgow for the collection, who he'd last seen in the early hours of this very morning. Archie, leaning against the wall, looking at the floor, very much not making eye contact with Jimmy. What the fuck was *Archie* doing here?

'Sit down, Jimmy,' Carruthers said.

As he sat, feeling his legs weakening, Jimmy noticed Archie moving across the room to stand guard at the curtained door to the main pub. On the table in front of Carruthers was a piece of oilcloth.

'Tommy,' Jimmy began. 'What's the prob–'

'Shut up,' Carruthers said, in a tone Jimmy had never heard him use before. The other man leaned over and picked up the oilcloth to reveal what lay beneath it: a handgun. MAC 50. One of the guns Jimmy had just brought back. The guy looked at Jimmy with cold, cold eyes. It was Carruthers who spoke. 'You shit the fucking bed, son.' Before Jimmy could reply, the 'what?' framing itself on his lips, the other guy abruptly stood up, picked up the gun, put it to Jimmy's head and pulled the hammer back with his thumb.

Given his line of work, and long given to thinking of himself as a hardman, Jimmy had sometimes wondered what he would do if someone ever pulled a gun on him. A connoisseur of action movies, he'd fondly imagined that if it happened at close quarters – like now – he would smoothly disarm his opponent, grabbing the gun and turning it upon them, just like Bruce Willis or Van Damme or Arnie would have done. That he'd at least remain composed, just looking at them unblinkingly and saying something cool like 'take it easy' or whatever. The reality was very different. As soon as the cold metal was put to his forehead and he heard the pistol being cocked, he did something none of these action heroes ever did.

He squirted a hot jet of liquid excrement into his pants.

Then – and again this was unlike Bruce or Arnie or Jean-Claude – Jimmy found himself crumpling to the floor, where he curled up into a little ball, trying to turn his head away as little high-pitched mewls escaped him. He was trying to say 'please' or 'no', but his mouth had dried up and he couldn't breathe properly. All he could imagine was how much it was going to hurt: the force of ten baseball bats off the cranium and then, hopefully, nothing.

The man pulled the trigger.

Click.

'THE FUCKING THINGS ARE DECOMMISSIONED!' the man screamed, banging the gun back down on the table.

'Wh-wh-what?' Jimmy squeaked.

Carruthers picked the gun up and professionally ejected the magazine, then pulled the slide back while the other man walked in circles, hands on hips. 'Look, ya fucking eejit.'

Jimmy peered into the chamber and then down the barrel. He didn't even know what he was looking for. 'What? I can't see anything!'

'Exactly! The fucking barrel's been filled in! ON THE FUCKING LOT OF THEM!'

'But . . . but . . .'

The other man came back over and planted his fists on the table, towering over Jimmy. He had moved from apoplectic fury into simply being very, very angry. Jimmy could now smell his own stench. And the horrible sensation of that miasma in his underwear, already cooling. 'Listen to me, ya fucking imbecile. These have been decommissioned by filling in the barrels.

Probably being shipped to fucking America or somewhere to sell to collectors. Great if you want a talking piece on the wall of your den, not so good if you *actually need to shoot some bastard*.'

'I didn't know! I thought–'

Carruthers held up a hand. 'Jimmy, please, for your own sake, son, shut your mouth. Here's what's going to happen. You're going to get our money back. Do you understand? Otherwise, it's over to Mr Thompson.'

Jimmy now risked a proper look at the granite-faced man who was staring down at him, looking like he'd enjoy nothing better than to beat Jimmy to death with the useless weapon lying on the table.

Mr Thompson leaned forward. 'Get this sorted, ya fucking eejit, or I'll be coming to see you. And I'll be bringing my own gun. And trust me, son – it works just fine, so it does.'

'I'll get it. I'll get the fucking money back.'

'Archie?' Mr Thompson said.

And the name was no sooner out of his mouth than Jimmy heard footsteps behind him, then massive hands were upon him, pulling him to his feet, pulling his own arms around behind his back and pinning them tight as Mr Thompson stepped around the table. *Wham-wham-wham* – he drove three fast, hard punches into Jimmy's stomach, driving all the breath out of him. Jimmy felt his legs buckling, only Archie's muscle holding him up, as Mr Thompson took a step back, placed his hands on Jimmy's shoulders to steady himself, drew his right leg back and kicked Jimmy in the balls with everything he had. Game over. Archie let go and Jimmy hit the worn linoleum, his head a galaxy of swirling stars, nausea rising within him as he teetered on the brink of passing out. And then Mr Thompson's face appeared, very close to Jimmy's, as he knelt and picked Jimmy's head up by the hair. Jimmy could smell his breath – whisky and cigarettes and maybe a tinned vegetable? – as he hissed right into his face, 'No one – *no one* – makes a cunt of the FUD!'

Jimmy nodded and then fainted. When he came round, he was alone on the floor in the backroom. He clambered slowly to his feet, trying very hard not to disturb his throbbing testicles, and shambled into the bathroom in a wide-legged John Wayne stride. As he stood there in bare feet on the cold stone floor (it had even got into his *socks*) with his trousers off, mucking out as best as he could with toilet paper, one thought offered Jimmy some comfort . . .

He was going to get their money back and then he was going to shoot Jada Hamilton in the fucking kneecaps.

When do we finally shift from thinking about something in the abstract – the thought experiment – into it becoming something real? Something we will likely do? For Dan the moment arrived on the third morning after his Friday night heroin debut. The tremendous, smack-inspired idea was roaming around his head all that time, but he had other things to worry about. For the first forty-eight hours following Jada and Nicola's party he had devoted himself solely to coping with the physical symptoms of the comedown from the drugs and the lake of cheap booze. He did this as most men in their forties do: he'd spent much of the first day asleep, crawling from his bed in the rented flat only to perform essential tasks: vomiting, urinating, and gobbling down painkillers. On the second day his range of activities had broadened to include comfort-watching episodes of *Friends* (bar a sudden breakdown into aching sobbing when Phoebe has the babies) and answering

286

the buzzer to receive life-saving deliveries of pizza. By the third morning he found he was able to get out of bed. Indeed, his recovery had proceeded far enough to allow him to sit wrapped in a duvet in the armchair by the window, smoking and sipping Diet Coke as he watched the comings and goings down below on Huntly Gardens. He was doing just this when a group of primary school children in the bright blue blazers of Kelvinside Academy went by, about fifteen of them, boys and girls, being led by two teachers. The tears came again as he recalled the phone call where he'd put Tom down for Kelvinside. It was around £3,500 a term, Dan remembered. Roughly £15,000 a year including lunch. He saw his little son – or, rather, he didn't – raising his hand in class. Excelling on sports day. Graduating . . .

And then, from nowhere, the voice appeared. It didn't sound like the voice of a madman. No. It sounded calm and rational as it whispered, *He can still go.*

No, he can't. Dan's own voice, his internal monologue voice, answered. Then, in a less certain voice, it added, Can he?

They're the same age. Born on the same day.

But . . .

He's only two. You can turn it around. You'd be doing him – the world – a favour.

This voice was very compelling. It sounded a little like the voice of the actor Danny DeVito when he was playing a nice guy. Dan poured himself a midday whisky and gave free rein to Danny. He seemed to know a lot.

Come on, it'd be easy. He's illiterate, for Christ's sake.

Dan got a pad and pen from one of the boxes he hadn't unpacked yet and started making some notes. By the early evening, by the time the streetlamps were coming on and the Christmas trees in the windows of the flats across the gardens were lighting up, he found that he had made quite a lot of progress with his plan. The sensations he felt, the solving of successive difficulties, of edging his way towards a surprising yet convincing and inevitable outcome, of covering his tracks and hiding his workings – they all continued to remind him of the writing he hadn't done in a very long time. As the evening wore on and the whisky went down, he became more and more convinced of the viability – and the rightness – of the whole thing. But a tricksy problem remained. To be sure, to really be sure, he'd need to get Jada to . . . how to initiate the conversation? Propose himself as a godparent? That might look suspicious. And would mean a christening. Unlikely. And even then, certain difficulties might remain. A persistent and devoted grandparent for instance. Again, unlikely, but this had to be watertight. Sign-on-the-dotted-line watertight.

But the fates, of course, were watching. And a few miles to the southwest of Dan's flat, Jada's mobile phone duly started ringing.

'You're a dead man, Jada. Ye hear me? Dead.'

'Jimmy, wait. I . . . whit?'

'Those guns you sold us don't work. They're deactivated.'

'Whit? Fuck off.'

'Say goodbye to the wife and kids.'

'Jimmy, calm down for fuck sake.'

'DEAD!'

'Calm down, man!'

Jada slid the door to the balcony shut behind him, trembling, and lit a Trafalgar Square, still listening to that very angry

Northern Irish accent. Through the glass he could see Nicola in the kitchen, cooking something for the wee man.

'Listen to me, you fucking dickhead, I'm gonna be charitable and assume you didn't mean to fuck us over. That you're just an idiot as opposed to suicidal. So here's what's going to happen: I'm coming over tomorrow and you're going to give me our money back, plus our costs.'

'Eh? Whit? Who says they're deactivated?'

'Jada, you need to believe me here.'

'Naw,' Jada said firmly, trying for authoritative. 'You should've checked them before. Buyer beware, eh? Deal's a deal an aw that.'

He heard Jimmy laughing. 'That what you want on your gravestone? *Buyer beware!* Do you know who you're fucking with here?'

'Eh . . . what fucking costs are we talking about?'

'You think you just take a crate of firearms onto the ferry hoping you won't be stopped? There's people need sorting. Costs.'

'How fucking much like?'

'All in?' Jimmy thought: the two lads, the van, the ferry and polis pay-offs. Fucking *petrol*. 'Another ten grand. Thirty-five thousand.'

'Whit? Get tae fuck!'

'Jada, you're playing with your life here.'

Fuck, fuck, FUCK. Those wankers at the airport. Should have listened to the Gypsy. How much did he have left? Fuck all. Time to bargain. 'I can give you half. Split the difference, like.'

'OK, then you might live. But you'll be spending the rest of your life in a wheelchair with a colostomy bag.'

'Fuck sake, Jimmy! Whit's wrong wi' the guns? Can ye no, uh, fix them?'

'Jada, listen. All the money. Tomorrow. No joke.'

'Ah need proof. And Ah need they guns back.'

'You need the fucking guns back? Do you know what's involved in this? Sure – you arrange a way to get them back over and you can have them.'

This was a nightmare. Jada was leaning against the balcony for support, just a T-shirt on, freezing. Head spinning. He thought he might throw up.

Jimmy's voice softened. 'Look, Jada, this is easy. You just have to say, "I'll get you your money, Jimmy." Because the only other way out of this is in a pine fucking box.'

A long pause, during which Jada accepted the enormity of his situation. He took a deep breath. 'I'll get ye yer money, but Ah . . . Ah need a week, OK? Ah made a couple of . . . investments, like. Ah jist need tae get the money thegither.'

There was a long pause. 'You have one week.'

Click. The line went dead.

Jada stood there, staring out at the estate for a moment, numb, before he stumbled back into the living room. There were shopping bags laid out on the sofa, new clothes for Jayden. Brochures on the table for some winter holiday shite. 'Whit the fuck's aw this?' he said.

Nicola looked up from feeding the wean, Jayden turning around too. 'Eh? Oh aye, I got the holiday brochures we were talking about and–'

'WE CANNAE AFFORD AW THIS SHITE!'

Jayden burst into tears. Nicola just stared at him. 'Wh-whit's happened?'

But she was speaking to Jada's back as he strode out of the

room and down the hallway. And then the bedroom door was slamming. Nicola picked up her son and held him to her. 'Shh, shh, wee man. Daddy didnae mean it, so he didnae. He's just a wee bit upset . . .'

Jada sat down heavily on the bed and started doing mental arithmetic. In truth he had maybe five grand left. Seven days to come up with another thirty. What would he get for the car? Maybe five or six. Pawning his watch again? Another two. Still well short. Fuck. Fucking Jesus. What the fuck did 'deactivated' even mean? How was he going to get out of this? Why hadn't he put some money away this past year when they were coining it in? Rainy day an aw that. Here it was – a fucking monsoon.

Who the fuck did he know who he could call and casually say, 'Hey, can ye lend me thirty-five thousand fucking quid?'

Jada didn't sleep much that night, until finally, around dawn, he realised what he had to do. What had been staring him in the face all along. He waited until it was light, got up, went into the kitchen and dialled the number.

'Aye, it's me. Ye busy? Ah need tae talk tae ye . . . Naw, no the Flaps. Òran Mór . . . Aye, twelve's fine.'

THIRTY

Tuesday, 16 December

'Fucking hell, Jada.'

'Aye, fucking hell is right.'

'Who are these guys?'

'Probably best if ye don't know, Dan. But let's just say they're serious. Very fucking serious.'

'What are you gonna do?'

'Ah don't fucking know . . .' Jada looked flustered, embarrassed even. He wasn't making eye contact, was playing nervously with his pint glass, turning it in his hands.

Dan, in his turn, exhaled and took a long pull on his lager. They were in one of the booths off to the side, the huge pub almost empty at this early hour. Dan was doing his best to keep a poker face on, but, in truth, he was having to stop his foot tapping eagerly on the floor. He was shivering with anticipation, scarcely able to believe his luck, to believe the timing. For he already knew where this was going. Dan knew the routine. When he'd become properly rich, in his mid-thirties, after they started producing *McCallister* themselves, after the show started taking off overseas, and especially after news of his wealth started appearing in the Scottish papers, he'd begun

292

to have his fair share of these conversations with friends and relatives.

The shamefaced, nervous requests. There had been ten grand to Jack, just after his divorce, twenty to Grace's sister when they moved house, the seemingly endless five hundred or a thousand here and there to Bob over the years. Jack had paid him back, but mostly you never saw it again. Dan didn't much care. It was all chump change, really. And, as a token socialist, he kind of believed that part of the responsibility of becoming rich was to help those within your reach. So he sipped his lager and waited until, with many a 'the thing is' and 'Ah'll pay ye back' and even 'Ah wouldn't normally ask', Jada got to it . . .

'Do ye think ye could lend me some money?'

'Well . . .' *Easy, Danny boy. Play hard to get.* 'Exactly how much are we talking about?'

'Right . . .' Jada thought. How deep were Dan's pockets? He had no idea how much ye made from what Dan did. To be honest, Jada was still astonished you got paid at all for making shite up for folk to say on the telly. But he'd seen the house and the cars, the clothes and the watches. He decided to be bold. 'Thir . . . maybe forty grand.' He waited. Anxious.

Dan felt relief surge through his bones. He had to fight to maintain a serious expression, to just nod. In truth, he'd been worried it would be a lot less, some stupid piddling amount that would make what he had to request in return seem over the top. But this, this was enough to justify it.

Dan sucked some air in through his teeth, making it look like he was weighing it up, like this was really going to hurt. Like he had some serious misgivings. Finally, just as Jada was opening his mouth to say, 'Look, just fucking forget Ah mentioned it, awright?' Dan said, 'OK. I think I can do that, mate.'

Grace had time to kill, so she took the longer route, walking down University Avenue, then around the students' union and down Gibson Street – Christmas trees all green behind the winter-frosted windows of the cafés – and then north along the Kelvin towards Great Western Road. She was following the river without thinking when she suddenly realised she was at *that* spot, a few hundred yards south of the big bridge, the car park for Kelvinbridge Underground just across the roaring torrent. In winter, the river could get very fierce and deep here, fast flowing, the icy water breaking and spuming on the rocks twenty feet below her. As it was now. As it had been back in March, when she'd last stood here, nearly three months after it happened. Grace stared into the dark water, remembering. It had been around six, dusk, just starting to get properly dark. She'd been out walking and crying, a daily activity back then. And not one unfraught with difficulty – she'd had the cast off her leg by then, but she'd still been using her stick. Dan had been back at the house, locked down in the basement, drinking and crying, utterly lost, gone.

She'd been staring into the river, but not seeing it, seeing only his face as he died. The eyes, wide and terrified as he fought to breathe, wide and terrified with the full force of life. And then not. No life. The light gone. Anyway, she'd been thinking about all of that, as she did hourly – minutely – back then, when her eyes had settled on some big stones lying on the path near her. They were damp and mossy and a couple of them were around the size of bags of sugar. They had to weigh a kilo each, easily. She had her big overcoat on. She'd looked up and down the riverbank. Not a soul around. The voice came to her – *why not?* Slip one in each pocket, climb over the railings, step off and be gone. The drop, the freezing water, the weight. A few moments of pain and terror and struggle – a minute or two at the very most – and then it would all be over. She wondered, if she thought about Tom hard enough as she died, would she slip into being with him in the next realm? In whatever happened next. Much like how you could will yourself into dreaming about a certain thing if you thought about it long and hard enough just before you fell asleep. She'd picked up two of the stones, cold and slippery to the touch and even heavier than she expected. And she'd thought about how it would have taken these stones millions of years to get to this spot: the crumbling glacier somewhere in the Highlands, then the millennia of drifting, of tides, and when you thought about it in these terms what did our exist-ence matter? How stupid and brief it was anyway. Who really cared? She'd dropped a stone into each pocket – the sudden dramatic tug as they pulled her overcoat towards the ground – and put her right foot onto the ledge of the railings – wincing already from the pain – before she realised that there was no way she could swing her fractured left leg up and over. She'd have to find a spot further along where she could scramble down to the bank. But where? As she'd been edging along in the semi-dark, holding onto the railings, looking for a gap, feeling those heavy stones swinging in her pockets, banging off her thighs, she'd heard barking and then a dog – a big golden Labrador – had appeared out of the darkness. Followed by its owners, an elderly couple in Barbour jackets. They all said their good evenings, and by the time they'd passed, so had the moment. She'd shamefully dumped the stones before she got to the steps that led up onto Great Western Road. And that was it. The closest Grace had come. Pathetic, really. She climbed those same steps again now and turned left on Great Western, a two-minute walk taking her to the café, where, through the steamy window, she saw them. She was talking to the baby in her buggy. Tickling her nose. Grace swallowed and went inside.

And now it was Jada's turn to feel blissful, orgasmic relief flooding through him. 'Really? Fuck sake. Ye've saved ma fucking life, Dan. Honestly, pal. Ah'm no even joking. This was the end o' the fucking road for me. Ah'll pay ye back, Dan, Ah swear tae God . . .'

Dan let Jada ramble on while he composed his thoughts. Then he said, 'The thing is, Jada . . .' and leaned in, lowering his voice, trying to sound conspiratorial, 'with that amount of money, there's tax implications and stuff for me.'

'Aye. The Revenue and that. Cunts.'

'Uh, yeah. So my accountant will probably want you to sign some forms, y'know? Just for keeping the books straight and stuff.'

'Aye, aye. Nae bother.' At this point Jada would have signed his own flesh with a branding iron. 'The thing is, Ah need it fast, Dan. Like this week?'

'OK. I'll make a call. Get the ball rolling. Come on, cheer up. See, one thing I've learned, Jada, since the . . . since the wee man died . . .' Dan got a hold of himself and delivered the line reasonably, managing not to get too carried away. 'It's only money, eh? So don't worry about it. Pay me back when you can. OK? Right, on you go, then – you can at least get a round in, ya tight bastard!'

296

'Fuck, aye. Of course.' As Jada got up, he reached out and took Dan's hand, shaking it. 'Seriously, pal, ye've saved ma life. Ah owe ye. Ah really do.'

'No bother. You get them in and I'll be back in a minute. Just gonna go and phone the accountant.' Dan headed outside to the front steps of the old church and then down into the deserted smoking area, torching a cigarette as he went. He wasn't calling his accountant; there was no need for that. He had way over fifty grand sitting in his current account alone. No, he was calling his lawyer.

'Fintan? Dan Chambers.' They got the pleasantries out of the way quickly (Fintan's concerned voice, his solicitous questions about Dan's welfare, how sorry he was to hear about him and Grace) and then Dan said, 'Yeah, sorry. I need those forms we talked about.' He listened. 'Yeah, just leave them blank. I'll fill them in myself . . . Yeah, tomorrow's fine.'

'Are you OK, Dan? We're all a bit worr—'

Dan hung up. He was hoping Jada had been continuing to neglect his literacy homework. But, even if he hadn't, he couldn't see Jada – with his scant mastery of *Maisie Goes to Nursery* – agonising over the small print of a legal document. Fuck, given the desperation coming off the man, Dan was willing to bet he'd leave burn marks on the paper with the speed at which he scrawled his mad signature. Yep, this stage would be easy enough. The next part would be trickier. He took a long final drag on his cigarette and flicked the butt away before heading back inside, feeling for the first time in many months like he was in control of the narrative. Or *a* narrative, at any rate. Jada was already back at their table with two fresh pints.

'All sorted,' Dan said, sitting down.

'Seriously?' Jada said. Fuck, man, things were easy enough

when ye were loaded. Forty Gs. Even after paying back that Paddy wanker he'd still be five grand up. *Merry fucking Christmas.*

'When can ye get—'

'Day after tomorrow.'

'Aww, Dan, my man — that's amazing. Seriously, Ah'll pay ye back. Every penny. Don't care if it takes me—'

Dan waved all this away. 'Happy to help. Like I said, pay me back when you can, pal. But,' Dan looked around, making sure no one was in earshot, 'there is one thing you could help me with right now.'

'Aye? Whit?'

Dan told him.

Jada sighed. 'Seriously?'

'What can I say, Jada. I liked it. It . . . it was the first time in ages I wasn't thinking about, y'know . . .'

Jada nodded. 'Aye, like they say, if God made anything better, the bastard kept it tae himself. But ye need tae be careful wi' that shite, Dan, Ah'm telling ye.'

'Yeah, I know.' Dan just waited, knowing he couldn't be refused anything at this moment.

'OK, right. Ah'll gie ye his number. And Ah'll phone him first tae vouch for ye.'

'Cheers, pal.'

'But Ah mean it — go easy wi' that shite.'

'Course.'

Their pint glasses came gently together. *Clink.*

'I'm just so, so sorry,' Grace said, again.

'Shh. Stop it. Jesus. After what you've been through. What you're still going through. I mean, since this one was born . . . I can't even imagine.' Sarah's eyes started to fill with tears again. She was cradling her daughter in her lap, rocking her gently.

'It's OK,' Grace said. 'Come on. We've both cried enough.'

Grace's eyes kept falling on the baby. The wonder with which she looked at the ceiling. Nearly six months old now and developing a fuller field of vision. It still seemed so odd. Sarah in charge of a baby. Sarah, who'd broken so many coffee tables by jumping up on them and shaking her butt. Sarah, who invented the 'Posh Jock' – champagne and a shot of tequila. Sarah, who streaked across the Quads for a bet after their finals.

'I just mean, I get it, Grace. We all do.' Sarah exhaled deeply, chasing away the tears, fanning herself that way she did, and then she added, 'OK. Moving on, how's it going with Dan?'

Grace gave a sad little laugh. 'I don't know. He's just . . . lost. Drinking and God knows what else. No one sees him.'

'Do you think he'll come back?'

'Don't know. See, I've been reading the stats on couples getting through this kind of thing. On relationships surviving the death, even the severe illness, of a child. They're not . . . encouraging.'

'What do you want to happen, Grace?'

'How about a button I could press that would just wipe out the past year?'

'Fuck,' Sarah said. 'It's been almost exactly–'

'Yep. This Saturday.'

'Look, maybe you shouldn't be alone. Why don't you come and stay with me for the night?' Grace looked at her. 'Please. For me as much as you. I . . . I'm not gonna lie, this one's a handful. I could use the help, and . . . Rob . . . he's fucking useless.' They both laughed. 'I mean, he's sweet but, fuck me, he's a child.'

'OK,' Grace said. 'I will. Just for the night, OK?'

Suddenly, Joni sneezed. Then her eyes went wide, huge, as if to say 'what the fuck was *that*?' Sarah laughed as Grace sucked back tears. Tom, doing just that for the first time, last summer. After a moment, Sarah said, 'Do you want to hold her?' It took another moment for Grace to nod. Sarah handed the baby over and Grace lay her in her lap, rocking her gently with her right leg, her good leg, soothing her instinctive protests about being separated from her mother.

'There's a good girl. Who's a good girl?' Grace said. She held out her pinkie and a tiny fist clamped around it. Grace held back from dipping her head and nuzzling Joni. To get that close to the new baby smell . . . No, she wasn't sure she could survive that just yet.

THIRTY-ONE

Wednesday, 17 December

'Dan,' Fintan said, shaking his hand, a fixed grin on his face, 'good to, uh, see you again.' They were in Fintan's office, on the third floor of a building on Park Circus, not far from where they'd come to see that therapist back in . . . when? No idea. Felt like a very long time ago to Dan. There were Christmas cards lined up all along Fintan's mantelpiece and bookshelves. It had been warm when they were seeing the therapist guy. Summer. Anyway, that was a long time ago.

'Yeah. In a bit of a hurry, Fin.' Why was his grin so fixed? Oh yeah. What with not having seen anyone he knew in a while, anyone vaguely concerned with appearances, and avoiding mirrors as much as possible these days, Dan had forgotten what he looked like. What you looked like wasn't much of a concern up the Flaps. Dan could disintegrate considerably more and still be considered a prince, a real catch, in the Flaps. But he could imagine what Fintan was taking in: the greasy, wild hair, the teeth that hadn't been brushed in God knows how long, the stained clothes and the scraggy beard. The flask of whisky in his inside pocket and the reek of his morning bracer on his breath.

'Uh, sure, ah . . .' Fintan reached into his desk drawer and handed over an A4 manila envelope. 'Here you go.'

Dan was already rising, but Fintan felt decorum demanded a little more chat be exchanged between lawyer and client. 'You'll need to bring them back to be notarised, of course.'

'Yeah. Thanks again. Cheers.'

'Dan?'

Turning back.

'Are you sure you're OK?'

'I'm fine, Fintan.'

'I just . . . you know. I saw Grace the other day. And she, you know, she's worried about you. Everyone is.'

'Yeah?' There was no edge in Dan's voice. Just a vague curiosity, the kind you might feel when you heard the name of someone slightly notable you went to school or university with, someone who got a first, or a third. 'How is she?'

'She's doing fine. It's you we're—'

'I'm fine, Fintan. Thanks for these.'

'Do you—'

Dan just closed the door on him and made his way back through the outer office, oblivious to the glances of the secretaries and paralegals. At the bottom of the grand, dark wood staircase, he steadied himself with a good slug of malt and then hurried out towards the car. He had a meeting with another professional to get to. Busy, busy, busy!

Jada sat alone in the snug of the Flaps, working his way through his second pint of the morning. Steady the nerves and all that. The Flaps' only Christmas decoration was a gold foil reindeer pinned above the bar. He'd told Big Sandy that he had a meeting this morning and that it was with someone 'serious' – shorthand for 'I want the room'. Sandy would keep all the alky traffic in the public bar. Better to do it here, Jada had thought. Don't want them knowing where you live. Then he remembered – the fucker had already been to where he lived. Through the snug doorway he heard the main door to the pub being shoved open and then a Northern Irish accent was mumbling and Sandy was pointing this way and Jimmy was coming into the snug, followed by two men, one of the guys who'd come with him to collect the crate the previous week – Archie? – and another even bigger, rougher-looking lad.

'Ye got it?' Jimmy said before he'd even sat down.

'Tomorrow,' Jada said.

Now Jimmy sat down. He badly wanted a drink too. The old Jimmy, the Jimmy who came to Glasgow last week, would simply have ordered Archie to go and get them in. Now? Not so much. No, safe to say that what with Archie having seen him crying and begging for his life and smelling the awful stench Jimmy had deposited in his own pants – and that story was already doing the rounds back home – his power was much diminished, their dynamic forever altered. Indeed, it would be fair to say that Archie was on this trip to keep an eye on Jimmy, just in case things went tits up and he decided to cut out and head for parts unknown.

'The full amount?'

Jada nodded.

Jimmy was slightly disappointed. He very much wanted any excuse to beat the shit out of this lowlife, amateur wanker who'd put him through all of this. 'We're in a hotel down the road, Jada. I want to be on the six o'clock boat home. Means leaving this shithole by four at the latest.'

'Should be fine. Youse wanting a drink?'

Jimmy did. He really did. But decorum had to be observed. 'Fuck off.'

Three knocks, then a pause, then two more knocks, just as he'd been instructed. Time passed. Dan looked out of the grimy fourth-floor window of the tenement staircase. It was less than three miles from where he lived, yet he'd never been to Milton before: he could see grimy 80s units standing amid slabs of wasteland where he guessed the original 40s and 50s prefabs had been demolished. Fought in a war, came back to this. Jesus. Finally, there was the sound of someone approaching the door and Dan knew he was being sized up through the spyhole. 'Aye?' a voice growled from the other side.

'Dan. Jada's mate.' A further pause. Dan was going to have to play hard and direct to get what he wanted. Get into character. Come on. He'd seen actors do it often enough before the cameras rolled. 'Open the door for fuck's sake. Freezing out here.'

Silence, and then heavy deadbolts were being pulled back and the door – much heavier than the standard door the council would fit in these type of flats – was being opened and, to his surprise, Dan found he was looking at a tiny, mole-like woman, perhaps in her eighties. 'I'm sorry,' he began, briefly using his own voice by accident before converting back. 'Ah, er, Ah wiz lookin' fur–'

'Ye want ma son,' the woman said. 'Through there . . .' She nodded down the dark hallway.

'Right. Cheers.'

He headed off as she began the laborious rebolting of the door behind him. Dan followed the sound of a television until he came to the open doorway into a living room-cum-kitchen.

The room was basic, but clean and neat, the only unusual thing the size of the television, which had to be eighty inches across. A man of about his own age was sitting on a pleather sofa watching horse racing. He was wearing a purple tracksuit and sunglasses, the dark shades an oddity given the lack of light. He did not look up.

'Kevin?' Dan said.

'So you're Jada's pal?'

'Aye.'

'Huv a seat.'

Dan looked around, took the armchair opposite.

'So what are ye after?'

Dan reached into his inside pocket and took out a thick roll of fifty-pound notes. He placed them neatly on the arm of his chair and watched as Kevin eyed them. 'OK, Kevin, listen . . .' Dan's voice suddenly assumed an authority Kevin was only used to hearing from policemen and magistrates. 'Ah'm going to be paying top fucking dollar, understand? So here's the deal. I need your best and I need your worst . . .'

Kevin sat forward and pulled his sunglasses down the bridge of his nose. He smiled. He had very few teeth and his eyes were bloodshot, the red of Tom's toy car.

THIRTY-TWO

Thursday, 18 December

First thing the following morning, Dan visited the Nationwide on Byres Road, where he kept a personal account. It was a sentimental holdover – he'd been a customer here since he was a student, though his business banking had long been done through Adam & Company over in Edinburgh, now owned by Coutts of London. They'd needed twenty-four hours' notice. He couldn't remember the last time he'd been here, in the actual branch. On the rare occasions he'd needed a large cash sum over the years – once when they went to Cheltenham, once when they'd stayed at the Hôtel du Cap, back when it still famously refused to accept credit cards, and one time when he'd been buying a vintage Stratocaster – he'd simply instructed his accountant and someone had delivered it to the house. But he wanted to keep entanglements to a minimum, so yesterday he'd rung the branch personally to arrange for the cash, using the 'buying a vintage guitar' excuse again. Later, if it ever came up, he could just say he'd sold it, or given it away, or lost it. He didn't really give a fuck. There were a few holes in his plan, but this wasn't the biggest one.

He sat in the small office with his holdall and the manager

brought it in himself. It was disappointingly small: just twenty banded stacks of £2,000 each, in £50 notes. It would have comfortably gone in a much smaller bag. 'Here we are, Mr Chambers,' he said. 'And do be careful out there.' He was around thirty, slightly camp, and Dan noticed now that he was nervous, his hands thrumming in his pockets as he stood there watching Dan pack the cash away. Nervous because the amount of cash was unusual or just because he knew who Dan was? Whatever. 'You know,' he went on, 'with all this cash on you I hope you don't have far to go?'

'No. It's fine. Thanks.' Dan was zipping up and shouldering the bag now. The manager was holding the door open for him, almost bowing.

'I hope you enjoy it!'

'Eh?'

'The guitar?'

'Oh, aye.'

'And, Mr Chambers?'

'Mmm?'

'Can I just say how much we're all looking forward to the finale on Saturday night?'

'Uh . . . yeah. Sure.'

What the fuck was the guy on about?

Unusually, and surely a measure of his anxiety, Jada arrived at Dan's place promptly at the arranged time of 1pm. It was the first time he'd been here, and he looked around the rented living room with his practised burglar's eye. Slim pickings. The laptop was about it. A skyline of empty wine and whisky bottles on the mantelpiece.

'Here you go . . .' Dan said. He had set it up so that the

holdall Jada knew contained the money was on the kitchen counter. In front of that was the small two-person dining table, with the sheaf of forms and a biro resting on top of them. The message was subliminal: *sign these to get to that.* 'Just need these signed. For the accountant and all that.'

'Aye, aye.' Jada was settling at the table in front of the forms. There were two separate documents, each requiring a signature at the end and initialling on each page. Dan was sweating now, his heart pounding. The whole game could be up here and now. What if Jada – now frowning at the first page, Dan having, of course, removed the title pages of each document – had really been putting the hours in with *The Very Hungry Caterpillar*? Dan tried to imagine his reaction. The chair being pushed back as he got to his feet, his hand clamping around Dan's throat as he shoved him into the wall snarling, 'Whit the fuck is aw this, eh?' But, no, he was already reaching for the pen. 'Jist . . . anywhere?'

'Bottom right-hand corner, I think.' Dan's voice, slightly higher than usual. Jada made his 'JH' on one, two, three pages and came to the final page where his signature would go alongside Dan's. 'Yeah, and there,' Dan said, watching, forcing himself to breathe, as Jada painstakingly signed 'J. Hamilton'. Dan hadn't watched him write in several weeks and was impressed with how far he'd come, his script now closer to that of an eight-year-old's than a toddler's scrawl. 'Nice,' Dan said. 'You've been practising . . .'

'Aye, wee bit.' Jada shrugged in the manner of the child prodigy who has just tossed off a note-perfect rendition of Rachmaninov's Third. Dan took the top form and Jada moved quickly onto the next one. Flushed with success, he initialled faster now, his manner becoming that of the bestselling author

308

facing the mile-long signing queue, before coming to the final page and signing his full signature again, almost with a flourish this time. All of Dan's fears had been misplaced: he hadn't bothered to read a word of either document, the allure of the contents of that holdall tantalisingly close. Or perhaps, Dan reflected, for someone like Jada, forms, whether they came in the shape of benefit applications or court papers, were the machinery of the state and not to be questioned or toiled over, just signed. Even if he could, Jada was as likely to read these forms as he was Apple's Terms and Conditions. Jada, in his turn, was now properly regretting not asking for a bit more money, fifty or even sixty thousand.

'Right, then,' Dan said, 'here you go.' He unzipped the bag and sat it in front of Jada, the banded stacks of £50 notes rolling around in there.

'Fuck sake, Dan,' Jada said, looking up at him. 'Cheers, pal. Ye've saved ma fucking life. Ah cannae believe it—'

'Hey,' Dan cut him off, bored of this. 'Don't worry, pal.'

Jada zipped the bag and stood up. They shook hands. 'Right,' he said. 'Ah better go and get these fucking potato-munching bastards paid aff and get them tae fuck. Thanks again, Dan. Ah mean it.'

Dan walked him to the door, having to stop himself from saying, 'No, thank *you*.' As Jada stepped out into the hallway, Dan added, making it sound like an afterthought, 'Hey, let's celebrate, eh? How about a wee party this weekend? Maybe Saturday night? Just me, you and Nicola . . . if y'know what I mean.'

The implication was clear. Besides, Jada could hardly refuse Dan anything at this juncture. He grinned. 'Aye, sure, man. You'd need tae come up tae ours, wi' the wee man an aw.'

'Aye, fine. About eight?'

'Nae bother. See ye later.' Jada started down the stairs, stopped and turned back. 'Ho,' he said. 'Ye sure yer no wanting me tae get a wee bird roon fur ye? That Senga fae upstairs likes ye . . .'

'Mmm . . .'

Jada added seductively, 'She's always up for getting her arse blasted, so she is.'

'Ach, still a bit soon, Jada. Y'know . . . Grace and everything.'

Jada nodded, not understanding. 'Aye, fair enough. But ye've got tae move on at some point, Dan. Got tae get that rusty water oot the baws or it rots yer brain.' He tapped his temple. With this, the life coach left the building.

Dan ran back into the kitchen and checked the time on his phone: not even 1.30. Just time to get to his 2pm in the Saltmarket. He picked up the forms, retrieved the two top sheets from the empty cutlery drawer and stapled them all together.

He poured himself a double, tossed it back, picked up his car keys, thought better of it, and opened Uber. Exec car, four minutes away. Fine. Busy, busy, busy!

The office did not disappoint. The worn beige carpet had a large stain – coffee? Oil? – next to the battered wooden chair Dan sat in. The pot plant in the corner had given up the ghost and the haystack desk in front of him was an example of very early, very 'pre-loved', IKEA. And behind the desk, the florid face of Innes Forbes, Solicitor and Notary, often described by Jack as 'the most bent lawyer in Glasgow'.

In his late fifties, rather than a practising solicitor, Forbes looked more like what you'd imagine a Glaswegian tabloid journalist – or a corrupt policeman – of the 70s to look like:

the nose of broken blood vessels, the clammy sheen of sweat on his face, the few strands of grey hair combed across the gleaming scalp. He was rocking back in his chair, hands folded across his (considerable) gut, and looking at Dan while he considered the proposal just put to him. After a moment, he sat forward, bringing the front two legs of his chair back onto the carpet, cleared his throat and said, 'Let me see if I understand you properly, Mr Chambers. You want to pay me two thousand pounds to simply listen to your proposition and then, if I agree to help, my fee will be ten thousand pounds simply for notarising two documents?' His fruity Kelvinside baritone surprised Dan, who was expecting to hear an accent somewhere between Taggart and Alex Ferguson.

'Correct,' Dan said.

'Hmm. And, if I decide not to proceed, I get to keep the two thousand but I must undertake not to mention our conversation to anyone?'

'Again, correct.'

Forbes picked up a steel Parker pen and clicked it. He talked while writing some numbers on a sheet of A4 paper. 'A couple of things before we proceed. Firstly, this last point is unnecessary. If you pay me two thousand pounds for listening, for what we'll call "legal services", then you become a client of mine and anything you tell me automatically becomes bound by client privilege. I can't tell anyone.' He paused, looked up from his writing, 'Unless, of course, I suspect you are planning on committing a criminal act.'

Dan met his gaze. 'Of course.'

'Secondly, as you can imagine, we get all sorts in here. And, if I may be frank, your appearance does not inspire confidence in the sums being bandied around. No offence.'

'None taken.'

'So I'd need to see that two thousand before we discuss anything.' He slid the sheet of paper across the desk. 'My account details.'

'Great,' Dan said. He took out his phone, opened the banking app and tapped the sort code and account number in. Hit 'move money'. Forbes tapped on his laptop, opening his own account. They waited. 'Care to join me?' Dan said, producing his pewter hip flask and unscrewing the cap. Forbes clicked his pen. 'It's Glenfarclas,' Dan said. 'Twenty-year-old. Rather good.' There came a soft *ping* from Forbes' laptop. 'And there it is,' Forbes said. He picked up his coffee mug, shook the last few drops into his wastepaper basket and pushed the mug towards Dan, who poured a good slug of whisky into it. Forbes took a sip and smiled approvingly. Dan wondered about the chain of events that had led Forbes here, about the many lost cases and failed marriages and unthinkable amounts of child support over the years.

'Mmm. Very good stuff indeed. So shall we proceed, Mr Chambers?'

Room 205 of the Clydeside Premier Inn. Jada standing with his hands in his pockets, watched by Archie, while, on the bed, Jimmy counted the banded bundles. The snooker on the TV in the corner. ' . . . makes thirty-five. I'm impressed. Well fucking impressed, Jada.' He looked at his phone. 'We might even make the five o'clock boat.'

'So we're done then, aye?'

'Just this,' Jimmy said, getting up and coming towards him, his right hand extended for the shake. Jada went to take it, not seeing that Jimmy's left hand was already balled into a fist. As they shook, Jimmy drove that left fist hard into Jada's stomach, smashing the breath out of him. Jada crumpled to his knees, feeling Jimmy grabbing him by the hair on the side of his head and kneeling down close, the ferrety teeth bared, his sour breath on Jada's face. 'Don't ever fuck with me again, you got that?' Jada nodded, trying to catch his breath. Jimmy released his grip and stood over him. 'No one – *no one* – makes a cunt of the FUD.'

Archie helped Jada up with one hand, opened the door with the other and said something like 'You'll be all right, pal' as he pushed him out into the corridor.

Jada steadied himself against the wall for a moment, hand on his stomach, panting. A chambermaid came around the corner by the lifts, a sweet-looking wee thing, dragging a huge vacuum cleaner along behind her. She stopped by Jada and said, 'You are OK?' Polish accent. 'Aye, fine, doll. Something Ah ate. Know whit Ah mean? Cheers.' Jada took a deep breath and tottered off along the hallway. By the time he came out of the lift into the reception area he was smiling again and humming a little tune to himself.

Dan had laid it all out. It only took a couple of minutes.

Forbes drained the Scotch and sat back in his chair again, not looking at Dan this time but looking at the ceiling, considering, before saying quietly, 'What you are asking me to do is completely illegal.'

'It is?'

'Mmm-hmm. But I believe you know that. Both parties must be present at the notarising of the agreement. You might say that is the entire point.'

'Really?'

'I'm assuming you have your reasons for not wanting this to be the case.'

Dan said nothing. Took another draught from the hip flask.

'OK. Well, considering the, ah, perilous nature of the proposed job, I am afraid that the fee involved would be *twenty* thousand pounds. However, this would entitle you to full client confidentiality privileges going forward. In perpetuity, as it were.' Forbes smiled, his bottom teeth the colour of an Inland Revenue envelope.

'Sure,' Dan said.

Another long pause. Forbes clicked the pen again. 'Am I to assume you have these documents with you?'

'Correct.'

'Very well. The fee would be payable now, of course.'

Dan was already reopening the banking app with his thumb. As he made the transfer, Forbes — who, like Jada, was already regretting not asking for more — rooted in a desk drawer and brought out a large piece of heavy iron. The notary stamp.

THIRTY-THREE

Saturday, 20 December

The lift was broken again, so Dan made his way up the sour-smelling stairwell carrying two bottles of champagne and a bottle of malt.

Nicola answered the door with a breezy, 'It's yerself! Come oan in, Dan.'

'Unky Dan!' Jayden was standing behind her, feet splayed apart, naked save for his ever-bulging nappy. He was still up and excited at 8pm, partly, Dan saw, due to the plastic beaker of Irn–Bru the boy was toting. 'Hi, wee man!' Dan said. Jayden ran off down the hall, shrieking.

'Go oan through. Jada's in there,' Nicola said, peering at the bottles. 'That champagne? Fuck sake, Dan.'

'Ach, had some in the house,' he lied.

'Ah'm just trying tae get the wee shite in his bath.'

'Need a hand?'

'Naw, naw, yer awright. Go through and sit down.' Nicola had demurred when Dan had offered to help with Jayden's bath once before when he'd been here around this time. Did she think it was an unseemly task for a man? Jada certainly never did it. Or was it a hardwired council-estate paedo thing?

The suspicion that any man who offered to help bathe a child had to be on a register somewhere? 'Jayden!' she yelled now, marching off down the hall. 'Come here!'

Dan went through into the living room, where Jada was perched on the edge of the sofa very close to the TV, watching Rangers play Hibs. 'Awright, Dan?' Jada said, distracted. 'Nearly fucking done here.' Dan knew that Jada was watching the game on an illegal Sky Sports stream, via his Firestick. The boys in the Flaps had been astounded to learn that Dan paid full whack for his Sky package. He had tried to explain that, certainly when it came to things like movies and TV shows, to stream them illegally was effectively stealing from content creators like himself and that, if everyone did this, soon enough there would be no new films or TV shows to watch. They had all looked at him for a long moment – as though he'd just shouted something like 'BUM BELLYBUTTON FEET!' – before one of them countered his argument with the three-word riposte, 'Away tae fuck.' The score was 1–1 with only a few minutes remaining and Rangers were setting up for a corner into the Hibs box. 'Come tae fuck, come tae fuck, come tae fuck,' Jada muttered to himself.

'Brought some champagne,' Dan said. 'Had it in the house. Ye got any f–' He was about to say 'flutes', like a madman, but modulated just in time to 'fucking wine glasses?'

'Aye, aye – kitchen.' Jada didn't look away from the screen.

Dan went through and started looking in cupboards. Tins of stew. Tinned peas and potatoes. He didn't think you could even get them any more. The odd, ragtag assembly of pint glasses nicked from pubs, petrol station tumblers and goblets. Dan put the malt and one bottle of champagne on the chipped MDF counter, the other in the fridge, next to a jumbo pack of Val-U sliced ham and a half-full bottle of Stormy Valley Chardonnay (£3.99, PriceBeaster). The remains of their dinner lay abandoned on the stovetop: a few breaded chicken bites and some torched oven chips, all encrusted onto a cheap baking tray.

A sudden, agonised cry of 'AWWW, YA FUCKING HOORMASTER, YE!' from next door indicated that Rangers had just failed to make the most of their corner opportunity.

Next to the stove lay a pile of paperwork. Dan had a quick flip through. Mainly bills (overdue . . . final demand . . . bailiffs), parking tickets, letters about court dates and communications regarding Jada's complex system of fine payment. A letter about a missed well-baby check-up for Jayden. Dan started working the cork and it cracked out of the champagne just as the final whistle blew and Jada uttered a low, heartfelt 'bastards'. Dan walked back through with the bottle and the best three glasses he'd managed to find: two opaque frosted glass flutes with jewelled rings around the base and a vast red wine bowl.

'Ah, well,' Jada said, taking the proffered glass, 'easy come, easy go, eh?'

'You have a bet on?'

'Aye, just a couple of ton. Cheers.' Jada took a swig and stood there for a moment, transferring it from cheek to cheek, each alternating in blowing up and deflating, like the mating ritual of a rare Amazonian frog. Something seemed to occur to him. 'Hey, Ah put the bet oan a while back. It's no like, ye know . . .' He glanced down the hallway to make sure Nicola wasn't looming. 'Ah widnae want ye tae think Ah wiz borrowing money aff ye tae gamble wi', Dan.'

'Don't be daft,' Dan said. 'It's fine. Cheers.'

They clinked glasses.

'Honestly, pal, ye saved ma fucking life.'

'Ach, don't mention it.'

'Aye, but, obviously, don't mention it in front o' Nicola, eh?'

'No, no. Course not.'

And here was Nicola coming into the room now, holding the freshly bathed Jayden. 'Ah'm jist gaunnae put him down, fucking knackered so Ah um.'

'FUCK!' Jayden shouted.

'Jayden! Bad!' Nicola shouted back.

Jada laughed and said, 'Wean's mental. Whit can ye dae?'

Dan smiled affectionately, but he was thinking of the long, long list of things that you could do. *Try not swearing constantly in front of him. Try giving him fruit and fresh vegetables now and then. Don't give him a half-pint of full-fat Irn-Bru just before bedtime. Brush his teeth occasionally . . .*

'TIGER!' Jayden said.

'Naw, son,' Nicola said. 'Mummy's too tired for a story the night.'

'Tiger?' Jayden said, tears in his voice now.

'Jayden,' Nicola said warningly, 'Ah said—'

'I'll read to him,' Dan said.

'Ye sure?' Nicola said.

'Aye, aye. No bother. You sit down. Have some of this. Here . . .' He poured her a glass of champagne.

Nicola turned to Jayden. 'Unky Dan read yer wee story?'

Jayden smiled and nodded, reaching out for Dan, his tiny fingers working in a grabbing motion. Dan took him from her, the boy warm and smelling fresh from his bath. 'Right, back in a minute,' Dan said. He carried Jayden down the hall to his bedroom, hearing as he went Nicola saying, 'Ooh, that's pure class, that,' having just taken her first sip of the (decent, vintage) Perrier-Jouët. When Dan was out of earshot, what he didn't hear was Nicola saying, as she watched him carry her son off, 'Ach, it's a sin fur Dan, eh?'

Dan settled down on the floor by the cot with Jayden between his legs and *The Tiger Who Came to Tea* in his hands. Just as he was about to start reading, he spotted something underneath the cot. Dan reached in and pulled out a green felt dinosaur. He stroked it and turned it over, noticing that it was stained with a couple of oily fingerprints, and a memory came back to him, something from his old life, floating up unbidden. He remembered buying a very similar toy for the unborn Tom. An impulse buy, not long before Grace had gone into labour. Oh well. He set it aside and opened the book. 'Right, wee man. Once upon a time . . .'

'Aye,' Jada was agreeing, through in the living room. 'Must still be a sair wan.'

Jada's world was a rougher one than Dan's, he knew that. The Sex Pest once turned up at the pub with his front teeth missing, his fingers splinted, and his broken nose bandaged and taped into place. He'd been rumbled on the job with Tam Ferguson's wife that very morning, Tam coming through the door hours earlier than expected due to a shift mix-up and promptly setting about the Pest with his snooker cue. Dan had remarked how, upon receiving similar injuries, most of his friends would not have been seen for many months, until the expensive dental work and subsequent convalescence had been completed. Not to mention the difficulties of negotiating the social fallout of being caught in the act with your friend's wife. But here was the Pest, drinking it up in the Flaps just hours later and writing off the whole incident as 'fucking mental'.

Thinking of this, Jada – now pouring himself another glass of the dry, fizzy wine (it was all right, but he'd be switching to lager in a minute) – searched his mind for friends of his who had lost children. Sammy Dawes, whose daughter had OD'd when she was fourteen. Gary Sinclair. His son had been stabbed to death outside the KFC on Argyll Street. His cousin Rab's wee girl had been killed in an RTA. Hit and run. Never got the guy. Now that he thought about it, there had been a fair few. How had they handled it? What had been the half-life of their pain? In truth, Jada wasn't sure. It was never talked about. Come to think of it, Gary Sinclair did hang himself a couple of years later, but, then again, he was said to be into Big Ranta Campbell for ten grand or more, so he was probably looking at a wee swim in the fucking Clyde wi' the old concrete Doc Martens oan anyway, so that might have done it, dead wean or no. Jada considered all this. 'Aye,' he sighed to Nicola, 'fucking sair wan, right enough.'

'Ah think the Maldives,' Nicola said. 'Looks nicer, but.'

'Fuck aw tae dae, though,' Jada said. 'Florida's goat water parks an aw that. Disney World fur the wee man.'

'Whit dae you think, Dan?' Nicola said. 'You been there?'

It was getting late, and they had the various brochures Nicola had got from the travel agents (and here were people who still used travel agents) scattered around. Also strewn around were the empty bottles: the two champagnes he'd brought had been joined by one of the Stormy Valleys and Nicola was even now unscrewing the cap on the second one. Dan and Jada were on the whisky, Jada shaping lines from his gram of coke on the smoked-glass coffee table. Nicola and Jada were smashed and wired, Jada's jaw jutting, Nicola's trainer tapping a fast rhythm on the carpet. Nicola was on the sofa, Dan and Jada on the floor. For once, the glaring white of the 'big light' had been turned off; only the lamp in the corner and the screen of the never-turned-off television were on. Every few minutes, either Jada or Nicola would take the remote control and channel-surf for a few minutes in what seemed to be a pointless manner, perhaps settling on something they recognised – a reality show, a quiz programme – for thirty seconds or so before moving on, their coked-up minds unable to alight on anything. Dan was a little pissed and coked up too, the former to keep up appearances, the latter because, well, it was going to be a long night. He needed it.

Down the back way, call box, home on foot.

'Florida?' Dan said.

'Naw. Maldives.'

'Nah, but I know folk who've been to the Maldives. Meant to be lovely.'

'See, Jada!'

'Fuck aw tae dae!' Jada repeated, still channel-hopping, as Nicola leafed through photographs of sugar-coloured beaches fringed by palms, the stilted jetties of the hotels jutting into the transparent blue water. If Jada was at all discomfited by discussing a trip funded by the money that he'd 'borrowed' off Dan that very day, then he was doing a very good job of hiding it, acting throughout as though a luxury winter holiday was no more than his right and due.

Dan noticed something on the TV screen, a brief image, something familiar about it. 'Uh, Jada, hold up. Go back.' Jada flipped back a couple of channels. 'There! Hang on a second.' They all looked at the screen, where McCallister, a streak of blood on his face, lay on his back in the heather. The shot cut to his POV of the sky above, where an eagle (badly CGI'd, Dan would have rejected the shot) was circling high above him. Dan started laughing. So that was what the kid in the bank had been crapping on about yesterday. 'The finale.' The last ever *McCallister*. It seemed insane to Dan that he'd once cared about this stuff.

He drifted off, back to over a year ago, when he'd been working with Christine the editor on this actual scene. 'Oh God, please, Christine, just . . . once more.' Dan had found he was barely able to support himself through his own mirth. He had been kneeling on the floor of the edit suite, his elbows propped up on the leather sofa, his hands covering his face, his cheeks slick with tears of laughter. Behind him, at the console, he heard Christine sigh, though there was laughter in it, amused despite herself. 'You are such a bloody child, Daniel Chambers,' she'd said, twirling her knob, rewinding the footage, her vape stuck in her mouth like a mogul's cigar. They'd been in the edit suite for months, Dan remembered, and the usual bunker mentality had begun to prevail – in-jokes and shorthand and every available surface covered in soft drinks cans, pizza boxes, sandwich wrappers and coffee cups.

As ever, no matter how much time they had at the beginning, here they were: getting closer to the transmission date and still tinkering, especially on this, the final scene of the final episode of the final season of *McCallister*. 'Here you go . . .' Christine had said as she hit 'play' again and a clapperboard briefly appeared on the three huge screens in front of them before you heard the First AD yelling, 'Scene 38, take 12!', the bar was snapped down and Amy was shouting, 'Action!' And then the clapperboard was pulled away to reveal Gregor's face in close-up, that smear of fake blood on his face from the mortal gunshot wound in his chest, his eyes flickering upwards, as though scanning the Highland skies for the doorway to heaven itself. They had shot nineteen takes of this moment back at the end of last summer. Some of them had been demanded by Dan because of a poor line reading, some by the director because of a technical problem, but most had been requested by either Gregor or Toby, both convinced that they could either do it better or, more frequently, that the other had stepped on their line or upstaged them in some small way.

Dan remembered now what had been making him laugh so much. As DI McCallister breathed his last, off camera you heard Toby as DC Angus Kerr, holding his hand and then whispering in a breaking voice, 'Goodbye . . . dad.'

Instantly, Gregor's eyes had snapped wide open, his bottom teeth baring in a snarl and Christine hit 'pause' again at exactly the right moment, catching Gregor in extreme close-up at the very height of fury and loathing.

'AHHHHHAHAHHHAAA!' Dan had collapsed again in hysterics.

'Ooh,' said Christine. 'Gregor is *not* a happy bunny.'

The line had been improvised on the spot by Toby and vetoed – on the spot – by Dan for being way too gauche. It had been a long-running theme over the last five seasons, the father–son dynamic between McCallister and Kerr, the tensions and the arguments and, of course, the underlying love and respect. All unspoken until Toby decided to just go ahead and speak it, causing Gregor to explode in the way any unscripted addition by Toby always did. Christine hit 'play' again just as Gregor hissed, 'Oh, fuck off,' almost in synch with Dan, off camera, yelling 'Cut!' Dan collapsed again, thumping the sofa. 'Oh God, oh God, oh God,' he'd moaned, getting his breath back. 'If only we could leave it in. McCallister's last words . . .'

'*Oh, fuck off,*' Christine had growled in a very decent Gregor impression. 'Right, come on, sunshine, you've had your fun. Back to it . . .' She'd loaded up the scene they were actually working on that morning – an overlong, baggy piece of exposition – and went back to doing what good editors did: making average writing, acting and directing look slick, elegant and masterful.

And Dan remembered, sitting here, coked up on the grimy carpet of the unloved flat, how much he'd loved the editing process. How – with its trimmings and excisions, its solving of difficulties and its mission of structure, of serving the narrative above all else – it was the part of film-making that felt closest to real writing. When the public thought about film-making they thought of people on sets, of cameras zooming in and directors shouting 'Action!' To Dan all of this had been a pain-in-the-arse process, a necessary evil that had to be gone through in order to obtain the raw material you needed to go off and make the show. The real work happened at either end: the writing and the editing. Remembering working with Christine, he thought how much fun it had been sometimes, his old life. Anyway, it was gone. But there was a chance, here, tonight, to get it back.

He became aware that Jada and Nicola were looking at him as he watched the TV. And then Jada said, 'Oh aye. That's . . . that's yer man there, right?'

Dan nodded, still smiling at the memory.

'Aye,' Jada said of the bloodstained detective, 'he's fucking pumped now, eh?'

'He certainly is,' Dan agreed.

'And that's the end of that chapter,' Grace said, turning the TV off, silencing the *McCallister* theme as it played out for the final time. (Barring reruns into eternity on ITVX.) Sarah passed her the plate – cheese, crackers, figs. A nice fire going and a half-drunk bottle of Malbec on the table: a far cry from how a night round at Sarah's place used to go for the pair of them. But she was breastfeeding, and Grace couldn't begin to comprehend dealing with a hangover these days. They sat in silence for a moment, Grace thinking about the *McCallister* theme tune and how Dan had always hated it, how the first time the composer had played it to him Dan – perhaps then still thinking of the show as edgier than it came to be – had spluttered, *'It sounds like a fucking shortbread advert!'* Of course, for a certain generation, the tune was now as much a part of the collective Scottish psyche as Irn-Bru and Old Firm games.

'Does it feel weird?' Sarah asked. 'I mean, I get that in the current context it's not your biggest concern, but, still, it's been part of your lives for so long.'

'Yeah. I was just thinking about that. He was going to . . . ah, well.'

'What?'

'Dan. He was going to write this novel. He was so excited that he was finally free of the show, after twenty-odd bloody years. And now . . .'

Sarah gave it a moment. 'Now you can't see him writing that novel?'

Grace gave a short, mirthless laugh. 'To say the least.'

Sarah reached out and held her hand. They both watched the logs flaming and crackling, the fire reflected gently in the silver balls hanging from the Christmas tree. Then – mewling from the baby monitor. Grace felt herself stiffening, a hardwired reaction. 'Like clockwork,' Sarah said, pushing herself up, groaning. 'Do you want another glass?' she asked Grace, as she passed the bottle on the coffee table.

'Nah,' Grace said. 'Thought I might make herbal tea . . .'

'Ooh, me too,' Sarah said.

'Let the party begin, eh?'

Grace sat there and listened to the cooing and soothing noises coming through the monitor from Joni's bedroom across the hall. '*There, there. S'OK. Mummy's here. Mummy's here. Shh. Back to sleep. Mama's little baby loves shortening, shortening . . .*'

It felt like someone had inserted an enormous key into Grace's stomach and was using it to twist and turn her insides. Exactly one year ago today. Around this time last year, she'd been coming around in a hospital bed, her left leg encased in plaster, her head in a fug of anaesthetic, Dan slumped catatonic on a chair across from her. It had taken her a moment to calibrate where they were, to recall the events that had brought them there. Then she'd started screaming, almost fitting. They'd had to shoot her up with Diazepam. She couldn't remember a thing after that until a couple of days later. Couldn't remember being in hospital, or being discharged, or getting home. Surely her parents would have been there? Maybe Dan's mum too? Her memories only came into focus a few days later – the two of them sitting around the house. Not saying much. Dan disappearing down to his study more and more often. Beginning to smell of drink earlier and earlier in the day. Where was he tonight? What was he doing? Would he ever come back to her? Did she even want him to?

'*Mama's little baby loves shortening bread . . .*'

Enough.

Grace shook her head and blew her cheeks out. She got up and crossed the hallway into the kitchen, where she flicked the kettle on and opened a pack of blackcurrant and vanilla tea.

THIRTY-FOUR

Sunday, 21 December

It was just after midnight as Dan leaned in to snort the huge line Jada had prepared for him. He noticed that the wrap of cocaine was getting low. And he didn't want Jada making the call for more. 'Hey,' Dan said, shifting his weight so he could reach into his pocket. 'I brought a wee gram of the other . . .' He took out the paper wrap

Nicola did a pretend shocked face. 'No way, man. Look, Jada, ye've turned Dan into a right junkie! Buying his ain smack noo an everything!'

Jada looked at the wrap, recognising it as a sommelier would the label of a certain vineyard. 'Oh aye. Made that call, did ye?'

'Well,' Dan said, 'I didn't want to ponce off you guys again . . .'

Jada peered at the coke wrap. 'Wee bit of the auld bugle left. Maybe a wee speedball?' He looked at Nicola.

'Ach, naw, Jada. Ah'm no wanting tae get wired tae the moon. Jist a wee bit o' brown. Bring us doon a bit.'

'Aye, fair enough. Go and get us the works, eh?'

'Whit did yer last slave die of?' Nicola protested. But she was already up and stumbling off down the hall.

'Ye still just smoking it, aye?' Jada said to Dan.

'Aye. That's fine for me.'

'Keep it that way, son,' Jada growled. 'Ye hear me?'

Come two in the morning they had the tunes on, one of Jada's mad rave compilations. Glancing at the digital readout on the Bluetooth speaker, Dan learned that they were listening to a song called 'Life In The K Hole' by The Akai Abusers. Nicola had her head down, rocking back and forth to the beat while Jada, having told Dan there was no way he could talk about it, was finishing up telling him the full story of the guns: a scarcely credible tale of guys on the inside at Glasgow Airport, munitions bound for Ukraine, Loyalist gunmen and God knows what else, the climax of the story getting twisted for Nicola's benefit to present Jada as having triumphed and getting to keep the money. Truthfully, Nicola wasn't really listening anyway, lost as she was in her own private rave. Just like the last time, Jada had shot Nicola up with half a syringe full before giving himself the other half, while Dan had done his own thing with the tinfoil and the lighter, except this time he'd kept the straw a crucial few inches away from the twisting skein of blue-grey smoke. The other two were too far gone in their own rushes to pay him any attention anyway. Except, as hoped for, those rushes weren't quite as powerful as they'd expected.

Dan decided to broach the topic first. Nodding to the open wrap of heroin on the table, he said, 'I don't think that's as good as the stuff you had, Jada.'

'Aye, didnae want to say, Dan, sound fucking ungrateful and all that, but it's weak as fuck, that shite. Ah've hud mair o' a hit aff the steam fae a jakey's pish.'

'It was your guy I bought it off!'

'Aye, your first time, but. And, nae offence, but you're no exactly a hard case. Probably thought he could get away wi' palming ye aff wi' some shite. You've got tae build up, whit dae ye call it . . . customer . . .'

'Loyalty?'

'Aye. Never mind, but. Ah didnae put much in. Always best tae be careful wi' yer first hit, eh? Never know whit ye've got oan yer hands. Just need tae up the dosage. Haud oan tae Ah get another bit o' cotton wool . . .' Jada got up and weaved uncertainly out of the room.

Now or never.

'Ye OK, Nicola?' Dan said, keeping his eyes on Jada's receding back. She kept her head down, bobbing to the music, and raised a thumb aloft. Dan reached across the table for his cigarettes – they were just openly smoking in the living room now – and accidentally on purpose knocked over the remaining half of Nicola's bottle of wine. 'Ah, shite!' he said. 'Sorry . . .'

'Easy, Dan, it's awright . . . Ah'll get a cloth . . .' Nicola was stumbling to her feet and heading for the kitchen. The second she turned her back Dan reached into his pocket and took out the other wrap.

He tipped a little of the powder into his half-full whisky glass, so it roughly matched the amount in the wrap on the table, and then swapped them out, sitting the new wrap open in the same place on the table and balling the old one up and stuffing it into his pocket just as he heard Jada's footsteps coming back down the hallway. There was a slight difference in the colour of the powder, the new one a little darker, but he was betting that, in this light, after six hours of drink and drugs, it wouldn't be noticed. 'Sorry,' he said as Jada came back in. 'Spilt some wine.'

'Ach, ya fucking mutant,' Jada said, settling back down in his place with the bag of cotton-wool balls as Nicola emerged from the kitchen with a filthy tea towel. She got on her knees and started mopping at the stain.

'Let me get it,' Dan said feebly.

'Naw, naw, yer awright, Dan, nae big deal.'

Jada was already getting busy. Dan watched as he tapped what looked to be more than double the previous amount of powder into the teaspoon. Then he filled the syringe from his water glass and squirted a tiny amount onto the powder. He stirred the mixture with a matchstick and held the lighter underneath until it started bubbling. Next, Jada dropped one of the cotton-wool balls into the mixture before drawing the liquid through the cotton and into the syringe. Nicola was already holding her arm out as she tightened the tourniquet, which Dan noticed, with a pang, was the belt from Jayden's dressing gown. *This*, Dan thought, *like everything else, is getting closer to being over.* With the syringe clamped between his teeth, Jada tapped at her thin, pale forearm, the vein coming up, faded blue, the colour of an old tattoo as it appeared through Nicola's flesh, her skin like sun-shot silk. Jada slipped the needle into the crook of her elbow and drew the plunger back a tiny bit, Nicola's blood darkening the plastic chamber. Jada paused, Nicola mumbling, 'C'mon . . . c'mon . . .' before he drove it down with his thumb. Almost instantly, her head snapped back, and she was gasping as she fell back into the sofa, 'Aaahhh . . . fuck . . . fucking hell.'

Jada was already tying off himself, his thicker veins coming quickly to the surface, looking like clothes lines compared to Nicola's electrical wiring. Nicola was still gasping, writhing, trying to speak.

'A bit mair like it, eh, doll?' Jada said. He slipped the needle into his vein.

'Jay . . . Jad . . .'

Jada looked at Dan, who was watching it all, saying nothing, his nerves straining to breaking point. Jada grinned. 'We have lift-off, wee man.' He pushed the plunger down, emptying the syringe into his arm.

'Jada . . .' Nicola's voice was weak, drowning. 'D-d-don't . . .'

She fell forward, smashing her head off the coffee table. Jada plucked the needle from his arm and went to pick her up just as it hit him too. 'Oh,' he said. 'Oh, oh . . . fuck . . . sake . . .' It was all Jada managed before he went over backwards, his head hitting the carpet with a thud. And then it was all very quiet.

'I want your best and I want your worst.'

Dan had cut the worst even further with a little laxative powder, just to be sure. When it came to the best, Kevin the dealer had made a little speech. 'Now listen,' he began. 'You look like a decent cunt. But I'd say yer new tae aw this. This fucker here' – he held up the gram – 'is a true fucking maniac. It's spiked wi' isotonitazene, this new shite the Chinkies are using? Ye know whit that is, son? Synthetic opiate. Like fentanyl. You've heard o' fentanyl, aye? Same kind o' thing. Fucking fifty times stronger than heroin. So, aw ye need, even if yer used tae a fair old fucking dunt, aw ye need is a few grains o' this, right? That's why it's 200 quid a gram, ma man. And mind what I'm telling ye here. *Do not fuck with this stuff.* A few grains, and ye willnae know if ye want a shite or a haircut.'

Dan had peeled off a wad of fifties and handed them over.

A few grains. Jada and Nicola had just shot up about a quarter of a gram between them. Dan got up. They were both breathing, just. Jada was twitching a little, still trying to speak. He pulled Nicola's hair back and lifted her eyelid up. The pupil was gone, pinned, maybe the size of the tip of the needle, just a microdot of black surrounded by green, as though the iris was trying to swallow the pupil whole. But he knew from his research that, while the immediate symptoms can look dramatic, it could take over an hour to die from a heroin overdose. He left them there, walked softly along the hall, and opened the door to Jayden's room.

He was sleeping soundly, his chest rising and falling beneath the blanket. This was the part of the thing he was most dreading, the time that the boy would be left alone, and the complexity of the days that would follow. He'd leave soon, in an hour at most, and call it in. '*Flat 12, Craigend Estate, Partick. Aye, heroin overdose. Looks like they're both deid, man.*' Toss the burner in the Kelvin on the way home. Then the ambulance and cops. They'd find the kid, Nicola's mum would probably be called soon enough, then either someone would find the papers and call him, or he'd give it a couple of days and pretend he'd heard about it – down the Flaps or whatever – and he'd turn up at the police station with his copies. And his explanation.

Yeah, he asked me just a few days ago.
I didn't think anything about it.
Oh God – do you think they did this on purpose?
I know there'd been money troubles.
Criminal activity. Well, junkies, you know.

The papers. Right, that was next. He took the envelope out of the inside pocket of his jacket. Where would Jada and Nicola keep such documents? There was no sideboard or bureau. Nowhere most people filed these things. He walked back through to the kitchen and went through the drawers. There was the usual junk drawer stuffed with bills and pens and pencils and screwdrivers and batteries and whatnot, but not what he was looking for.

Back down the hall and into their bedroom, the carpet barely visible beneath a secondary carpet of discarded clothes, dirty plates and pizza boxes, the full ashtray on Jada's side of the bed and the splayed magazine on Nicola's, one of those supermarket glossies aimed at the barely sentient, with the headline *'Fake daughter stole my £6k dream trip!'* Dan finally found it, in the bottom drawer of their dresser. A box file. The kind of thing people use to keep their important documents in. He tipped the contents onto the bed: Jada's passport (expired), Nicola's birth certificate, a building society passbook in Nicola's name, an account that had peaked with just over £300 in it just over two years ago – accumulated since she was a little girl – but that had now dwindled down to £2.33 (Dan was willing to bet the dwindling coincided with her meeting Jada), and their National Insurance cards. These documents were all that existed to prove these two people had ever lived. There was also Jayden's birth certificate and another bankbook in Jayden's name, with the sum of £86.88 in it. Dan could picture it. The tens and twenties given over by relatives 'for the wee man'. Nicola in the flush of the first months of motherhood. Going to the bank and proudly opening the account in his name. Paying in the slender monies, thinking to herself that it would eventually, if she did it until he was eighteen, add up to a better life for him. Maybe a home of his own. An education. Something like that.

Of course, none of this would ever happen. Jayden's bankbook would come to resemble Nicola's. The pitiful amounts paid in during childhood adding up to a few hundred quid, starting to get withdrawn when he was sixteen or eighteen and all quickly spent. Not that the few hundred quid it had amounted to was ever going to get him a home or an education or any of these things. Nicola and Jada couldn't provide a better life for the boy. Getting off their nuts on coke and smack while their infant son slept next door. Palming him off on his grandmother while they wallowed in two-day hangovers and comedowns. Rotting his teeth and ossifying his bones. Living from one financial disaster to another, with prison always just around the corner. Mum on meds. Dad drinking and robbing and stealing his days away. No, they had nothing to offer society. They couldn't provide a better life for him. But Dan could. He took the papers out of the envelope.

Document 1 gave Dan power of attorney over Jada.

Document 2 named Dan as Jayden's legal guardian in the event of his parents' death.

Both were signed by Jada and had been fully notarised in his presence. He slipped the forms into the folder along with the other crap and took a long drink of whisky from the bottle.

Sitting on the end of the bed – he could see Jada's feet through the living-room door – he pictured the scene as he and Grace were reunited. Dan coming in the front door, with some explaining to do for sure, but with this beautiful little boy toddling in behind him, the same age as Tom would have been. How exactly he would fill their son's place in the universe. And, no, Grace, listen, it's even better than that. Tom was born into privilege. Jayden (and they'd have to do something about that name, of course) was *doomed*. Parents were junkies. Criminals. We've saved a life here. We're going to make it so much better than it could ever have been. Look at him. Look at this sweet, innocent wee boy. He needs us as much as we need him. He won't even remember his mum and dad in a few years. It'll be us. We'll be mum and dad again. And then her tears, hot on his neck, as she wept with gratitude, as she gathered the boy up and the three of them began their lives together. A family. He checked his watch – fifteen minutes had passed. Dan got up, a little unsteady on his feet, and walked back to the dresser. He was tucking the file back where it had been, underneath some old sportswear, when he noticed something else. An A4 workbook. The kind he used to scribble notes in. Dan lifted it out, having to squint to see properly through the whisky and the half-light. There in the top right corner of the front cover were the block capitals 'JaDA HAMILTON'. Well, he'd tried at least. Dan took it over to the bed and opened it.

The first couple of pages were Jada's attempts to copy sentences from his reading books. *The tyGir aT al the sawwiKES.* It was at about the level of a four-year-old, Dan guessed, the letters a crazed mix of upper and lower case, the spelling pure guesswork and phonetics, the words and lines all spaced much too closely together.

ThE caat SAt un th mEt.
MeEEstir bRoan sayD haw aR yew tooDaa.
IT waz CalD. Hee Got hiZ cote.

335

Dan turned the pages. He had to admit there was progress. Hard to believe though it was, Jada had been having a go, gradually improving on spacing and even using full stops, but the spelling still all over the place, the mad letter reversals probably a sign of dyslexia. Then, unexpectedly, after three or four pages of this stuff, there came an abrupt change in genre, into what seemed to be the diary format . . .

Massif Row wit Nicola. Tol her wee cant hav holeady. Pizzed aff wi us. Canna aford it but. Huv too find sum way too pay PADdy cunt. Dont no what dae. Cant sleep. Paddys comin ovver. Shitin myself. Seek too ma stomak

Then another genre shift, this time a lurch into something like memoir . . .

Like when ma da used tae be GetTing oot an ah new hee was cumman hom and ah new ah wood Bee geitn batered stupit

Dan swallowed. He took another drink and turned the page. There was what looked like an attempt at a letter.

Deer Reeannonn,

You were rite what you said about mee. Im sorry but

The missive had been abandoned there. Dan turned another page, stopped and put the bottle down, feeling his own stomak give a sick lurch too. Another letter — more fully realised this time. It went on for almost a page . . .

i cant thank you enuf for what uv don for me. I wAs gon to wat till i can rite beter too rite this but fuck nows how lONg that wood be. Ha ha ha ha. yu hav reilly saved mi ars mait. You dont even no us that long but yo stept up and halped me. Am no much for big words ilke yo but i am tryin. tHank yo fae tha buttom o mi hert. i dnot just meen abut the mony an al that. i havnt haD much skool lik yo hav. Didnnt get much off a sart in lif.

As he laboured over the translation, Dan found that he was really crying quite hard now.

So yo trin to hepl us red anD rite has ben a big thnig. No jus for me but for teh wee man and al. liek yo noo DaN ahm a fuk up haha haa ha. Already had a feu wayans an i fuked them al up gud aN propa. i wnt hings to be beter for Jayden then tha wer for me. its funy how u cant sey stuf lik this in rel lif bit wen u rite it don its beter. Esier if yo no whta I Men. I thkn yo do becos u r a riter. and im sory abot yor wee boy TOM. It mus be sare aw the time. i hOp yo see him agian on day in heven

Yor pal – JadA

Here it was then, the unexamined life.
Examined.
Jada Hamilton. Man of letter.
Oh, what the *fuck* had he done?

★   ★   ★

337

Dan ran full tilt down the hall and burst into the lounge. He fell on Jada first, and his blood lurched when he saw that his lips were the colour of blueberry juice, his face alabaster, marble. The eyelids were open just a crack – the gaze of a slumbering reptile. The microscopic pupils. 'Oh fuck, oh fuck, oh fuck . . .' He slapped the face lightly. 'JADA!' Nothing. Not a flicker. Dan slapped him as hard as he could, the crack of his palm hitting flesh like a rifle shot in the quiet flat. Zero.

He crawled across – 'oh fuck, oh fuck' – onto Nicola.

Oh Jesus. She was dead. She had to be. Slack-jawed, the eyes open but the tiny pupils fixed and staring. Dan felt at her neck, trying to find a pulse, couldn't. Didn't know what he was doing. 'FUCK!' He was shaking all over now. He leaned in, putting his ear close to her mouth. He couldn't hear anything, but he could feel it – just the faintest wind of her breath. It was time for bullet to meet biter. He punched the three digits with his thumb, mouth dry, hands trembling. 'Police, Fire, Ambulance. Which serv–'

'AMBULANCE! NOW!'

'Sir, please calm–'

'They're hardly breathing. It's–'

'Sir, what's the address of the emergency?'

'Just step back a bit further please, sir.'

Dan stumbled back into the battered, ripped armchair and sat down heavily. A man and a woman in their green overalls, both bristling with kit and know-how. The ambulance parked downstairs, its blue lights strobing up to them through the dark. They had got here surprisingly fast, given that it was a Saturday night in Partick. 'You were lucky, we were just heading back from one of these over in Royston,' the woman paramedic had

338

said as they came in and surveyed the living room, snapping on rubber gloves, moving fast. Sober now, and with the big light on, Dan saw it through their eyes – the many stains on the carpet, the two prostrate bodies, the party detritus of empty bottles, full ashtrays and the residue of powder on the glass table. It was a scene the paramedics saw every weekend but that Dan only knew from drama. From films and television. 'Oh boy . . .' The woman hunched over Nicola gave a low whistle through her teeth. The man was examining Jada. 'Is . . . is it bad?' Dan asked. 'Naloxone, Davy,' the woman said, urgency in her voice. The guy reached into the kitbag lying between them. 'Only two left,' he said. He handed her an ampoule, a small, preloaded syringe, taking one for himself. 'What else have they taken?'

'Uhh,' Dan thought. 'Cocaine? A fair bit of drink. Cannabis.' The woman was already pushing the needle into Nicola's bicep. The man rolling Jada's sleeve up to do the same.

'How is he?' she asked.

'Holding on . . . just.'

The woman injected Nicola. Dan watched, half-expecting Nicola to leap up and start running around screeching, his only reference point here being *Pulp Fiction*. No such thing happened, of course. She didn't even stir. 'What's her name?' the woman asked.

'Nic . . . Nicola.'

'Nicola! Come on, love! Nicola!' The woman held her eye open, shining a light into it. 'NICOLA!' Nothing. 'FDP,' the woman said to her colleague, who was preparing to inject Jada. (Dan would later learn that this meant 'fixed, dilated pupil'.) He hesitated and then held his syringe out to her instead. But she shook her head and said, 'Let's go,' then ran into the hall.

339

The guy injected Jada in the bicep just as the woman came back in wheeling the collapsible stretcher they'd brought up. As she started setting it up, Dan became aware of a sound from down the hall. He went to Jayden's room, just stumbling, numb, a zombie, and pushed the door open – Jayden standing up in his cot, crying, reaching out to Dan as he repeated the same word repeatedly. 'Mama, mama, mama,' the boy wailed. Like he knew. Dan picked him up and slid down the wall. 'Let's just stay here. We'll just stay here, son . . .'

Through the open door, Dan saw the woman paramedic wheeling Jada out on the stretcher, saying something into the crackle of her radio, the man following her, carrying Nicola over his shoulder, her long hair dangling to his waist. 'We'll just stay here,' Dan said again, crying now.

He sat on the plastic chair, staring at the vending machines. Just as the paramedics left – the ambulance tearing off with siren whooping – Brenda from next door had come in. Dan gave her a version of events, saying he'd passed out – he'd just been smoking it – and he'd woken up and found them unconscious. Brenda was sad, worried, but utterly unshocked. She had taken Jayden from him and was going to call his grannie, Jayden sobbing and reaching for Dan as she carried him along the passageway to her place. Dan was about to leave, to follow the ambulance to the Queen Elizabeth, when the police arrived. He gave them a second version of events, about how he was just a pal, how he'd come by for a drink quite late and seeing that the door was open had just wandered in and found them. The police were utterly unfazed too, the air they gave off one of not quite believing him while simultaneously not giving a fuck. They'd bagged up the remaining drugs and issued Dan with a caution, saying that in the event of a death he would be questioned further and might be arrested.

He'd finally got here maybe forty minutes after Jada and Nicola had been admitted to A&E. That was over two hours ago. They were still in the ICU. He'd explained to the staff he was their friend who had called it in and begged to see them. He was told to wait here.

The sun was just starting to come up outside. He realised it was almost exactly a year ago when he and Grace had been brought in here on stretchers. Almost two years ago when he'd felt unmitigated joy as all the clichés he'd been told about ran through him: the urge to protect and to nourish, the sense of responsibility and of destiny, as though all his life had been meant to lead here. And, with that, the feeling of total completeness, of not needing anything else. And if you'd told him then that he'd be sitting here again in a very different role? Not in the role of father, of a giver of life, but as he now was – murderer.

He had occasionally experienced the sensation in the universal way, in his nightmares. And how much worse it always was to awaken from the nightmare where you had killed rather than been killed. When you were murdered in your dreams you snapped awake, heart pounding, as you were slowly flooded with the relief that it was just a dream. But the sensation when we awaken having killed in our sleep, the depth of the shame, of the finality of what we have done, the guilt slowly ebbing away as the bedroom comes into focus and we can tell ourselves that it was only a dream – Dan had no such comfort here, on the hard plastic chair in the ICU waiting area of the Queen Elizabeth Hospital at 5am on a cold December morning. He was out of tears now. Just numb. But he knew what he would have to do. He fished in his pocket and took out the caution notice. The phone number of the police station on Dumbarton Road. The names of the attending officers. He was staring at the floor, vaguely wondering how long he would get, when he heard a voice saying, 'Mr Chambers?' A doctor was approaching, about his own age, silver hair, hands deep in the pockets of his white coat and his expression grave.

Dan stood up.

And then he was running.

Out of the hospital and left, north up Govan Road. He hadn't run in so long that his lungs were already bursting. The many months of smoking and drinking and no exercise. He stopped, folded over with his hands on his knees, and threw up booze and bile. Then went on running, the Clyde coming up ahead of him, running over it, along the walkway, the black water beneath him, the tunnel beneath that, sweat pouring down his face, stinging his eyes, salty in his mouth, as he looked to his right, east along the great river towards where the sun was beginning to rise, the first pastels of dawn in the sky, picking out the tall buildings, the blue of the Hilton sign a couple of miles away, the glinting silver of the SEC Armadillo. Over the river with his head down, breathing deeply through his nostrils, trying to oxygenate, the yellow trim of the big Arnold Clark garage flashing past him in the dark, but the darkness getting lighter now as he turned onto Dumbarton Road, running due east, a few Christmas trees still lit from the night before in the windows of the flats above the shops, reds and greens and whites. Cornershops opening, stacks of news-papers being brought inside, light spilling from their doorways, the sound of shutters going up, the smell of fresh rolls from one and a stare from the shopkeeper, an old Asian guy, at the strange sight of a middle-aged man in jeans, sweater and boots half-jogging by in the dawn. Left onto Byres Road, heading north into the wind, his legs like jelly, fighting for every breath on the uphill, his shirt soaked through with sweat, clinging to him, the sweat icy from the wind, and soon enough he was making another left and he could run no more, just stumbling along past the great houses of Hyndland, thighs and calves aching, a muscle torn somewhere, someone at a bus stop saying something to him, asking him if he was OK, but Dan couldn't hear them, could only see their mouth moving, trying to run again, but his body giving up as he came into the square and there, at the end, was the house, still asleep like all the others. He staggered and fell as he came up the broad, smooth stone steps, going down on his right knee and the palms of his hands, getting back up and getting his key in the door, struggling and shaking – crying now – and banging at it before it finally opened, and he came falling into the hallway that he hadn't seen in many months.

Grace was in the bedroom – not long in the door and unpacking her overnight bag – when she heard the noise. Her first thought was that it was the new cleaner letting herself in. Then she remembered it was Sunday morning. And still very early. Maybe her parents? They had keys. She began edging along the upstairs hallway, saying, 'Hello? Hello?' Should she go and get the golf club that Dan kept under the bed? Don't be ridiculous. She was probably hearing things.

She was halfway down the stairs when she saw him, stumbling back up onto his feet near the front door, soaked with sweat, blood on his hand, a streak of it on his face, and he was crying, sobbing. She stopped three steps from the bottom and flattened a hand on the wall to steady herself as he came towards her, trying to speak, getting the words out – 'I'm sorry, I'm so sorry' – as he reached her, collapsing into her, her arms going around him as he wailed and shook, and then his head came up, looking like he hadn't slept in days, hair wild, thick stubble, bloodshot eyes, his breath foul, and despite all of this they were suddenly kissing and then he was pulling her T-shirt off and she was scrabbling at his belt, the morning sun streaming through the stained glass of the front door behind him – navy and gold and ruby – and she didn't understand what was happening but it felt like perhaps a dam had finally burst and Grace just leaned into the flood.

EPILOGUE

EIGHTEEN MONTHS LATER

THIRTY-FIVE

June. Summer in Kelvingrove Park, and the first truly warm weather of the year: everyone in shirtsleeves and a couple of lads, with 'taps aff', laid out on the grass. The sweet smell of cannabis floated over from somewhere. The distant chime of an ice-cream van. It was a Tuesday, almost noon, and a couple of office workers were unwrapping their sandwiches on a bench, groups of students with backpacks and folders were dotted around, sitting in the shade of the leafy trees. Dan had entered from the Gibson Street gate. He pushed on uphill, heading for the top of the park, for the statue of Lord Roberts on horse-back, the sun directly above him, a welcome cool breeze on his face as he got higher. Panting a little, he sat down on a bench in the shadow cast by the mounted Victorian tyrant, pressed the brake on the buggy with his foot, and peered inside. She was still sleeping. He was early.

After all the stuff they'd been through when they were trying to have Tom: the discussions of ovulation problems and poor egg quality. The ruling out of issues with pelvic health, the fallopian tubes or uterus. The testing for polycystic ovary syndrome, for overactive and underactive thyroid glands, for premature ovarian failure. The search for cervical mucus problems and fibroids in and around the womb, for any evidence of endometriosis or pelvic inflammatory disease. And then him: was it poor sperm motility? Poor-quality semen? A low sperm count? Abnormal sperm? Infected or congenitally damaged testicles? And then all of this had been ruled out leaving them with: Unexplained Infertility. Nothing to be done. And then, after six rounds of IVF, the Miracle of Tom. 'We're blessed,' they'd told themselves. And they were. And they knew it would never happen again. Until, of course, it did. That terrible December morning on the stairs.

Once was all it took. *No one knows anything.*

Dan heard a squeak, a gurgle, from the buggy. A tiny fist coming up to rub at a tiny nose. He reached in and lifted his daughter out, her huge brown eyes crinkling shut in the bright sunshine, affronted at the sudden change. 'There we go, sweetheart, there, there . . .' He put Jean over his shoulder and started rhythmically rubbing her back before she started crying, soothing her, letting her wake up as he buried his face in the warm folds of her neck. Just over six months of this, and he still couldn't get enough of it, of the baby smell, of the perfume of God. He blew softly into the pasta shell of the ear, and she wriggled, turning to face him. Yes, he saw him hiding in there, the son that they lost, shimmering in the bones of the daughter they now had, a dimple that came up when she laughed, a gleam that came into her eyes when delighted. He saw Tom encoded in the genes, saying hello from his circuit of eternity. And there was still a sadness that Dan knew now would never go away, that just had to be co-existed with. There was sadness, but it wasn't the only thing now.

'Awright?' He turned to see Jada lumbering into view, coming up the path from Dumbarton Road direction. 'Fuck sake,' he added, puffing, wheezing, folded like a bad hand. 'Could we no just have met doon at the bandstand?'

That had been it for Nicola. The very last time. *Just a wee dig now and then.* Aye, right. Never again. Sure, she'd said that before. But this time she meant it. She'd had to sit down with a doctor at the hospital before they'd let her go home. It was serious, right enough. He was talking like she was a fucking junkie and said she was undernourished and underweight and that her lungs were aw fucked from the puff and the tabs and everything. They were telling her to get eating properly and get healthier, get mair exercise and that. Like maybe go tae a gym or go running or something, this doctor said. *Running?* Away tae fuck, ya fucking footpad. But, 'cause o' the overdose and the polis involved, there was talk of social services and taking Jayden away and everything, and she'd started greeting and they said she had to see a therapist. And Nicola hated her at first. Mrs Haslam. Janet Haslam. Right posh wee cow. Pure up herself. But she had to go because of the wean.

So along she went, and, for the first few sessions, she just sat there no saying anything, and so nothing much got said, but in the end that was just dead boring, so Nicola started talking a wee bit and she was saying how she wiznae a heroin addict, no really, she just had a wee dig here and there, and then one thing led to another and Nicola started telling her about her childhood and about all her uncles and stuff, and finally, one afternoon, this Haslam woman put down her wee notepad and looked at her and said, 'Frankly, I'm amazed you're not a heroin addict.' And she was like, 'Whit ye saying, ya cheeky hoor?' And then she went through it all. How Nicola had never been parented herself. How all these father figures in her life had been abusers, drug addicts and alcoholics and sex cases and everything. How the one person in her life who was meant to provide her with unconditional love and support, her maw – *her own maw!* – had been, at best, indifferent to her and, at worst, had, what was it she said, aye, had *enabled* the abuse she'd suffered from others. How she'd been seduced by Jada when she was still very young and then, before she knew it, she was dealing with motherhood when she was still not much more than a child herself. How Nicola was trapped in a vicious circle of drinking and drugs and that her low self-esteem fed this and then the hangovers fed the low self-esteem and around and around it went.

Getting off drugs wasn't that hard. She'd told Jada she didnae want that stuff around the boy any more. Naw, no puff or anything. If he brought it in the house, she was gaunnae shop him. Shop them both. And then they'd take the boy away. He went mental at this, at the very mention of any cunt shopping any cunt tae the polis. Went fucking scripto, so he did. But he stopped it, right enough. There was no more gear in the house after that. Stopping the drink and the fags was harder. Nicola had smoked since she was ten. Been on the bevvy since twelve. Was hard to sleep at first. She was still pounding the Temazepam at night. But then she ran out and the doctor wouldn't give her more. She gave him dog's abuse and tried getting it aff Haslam an aw, but neither o' them would budge. She thought about getting Jada tae get her some, but she knew where that might lead. So she just stuck it out. Sweating and tossing and turning and awake half the night. But she got through a week of that and then it got easier. She started going to bed just after Jayden went down and soon she was sleeping right through. Mad dreams she'd have. Aw this colour. She wiznae really seeing any of her pals any mair wi' all the nae bevvy and going to bed that early. But she wiznae really bothered. Soon enough, she was waking up dead early, before the wean, even. She was getting the place aw tidied up and hoovered and getting his breakfast ready before he even woke up. Here was the mad thing – she started tae like hanging out wi' Jayden in the morning. Instead of just sticking him front o' *Octonauts* or *Paw Patrol* or whatever while she went back tae sleep oan the couch hungover tae fuck, they'd have a wee laugh together. By the time he was turning three, some of the mad pish he was coming out wi' would crack ye right up, so it would. Her appetite came back an aw and wi' no being half-cut a lot o' the time she found she could follow some o' the recipes. She roasted a chicken and did the tatties herself – no Auntie fucking Bessie involved – and even Jada said it was magic. She started putting on some weight. And wi' aw this sleeping well and eating better food and nae drink or Class As she had aw this new energy and she felt . . . calm. She went and saw her mum and said some of the stuff tae her that Haslam had been saying. Her maw went aw lock-jawed and glassy-eyed and said, 'Away tae fuck wi' aw that pish,' and, 'Ah did ma best wi' ye.' And Nicola said, 'Maybe ye did, but it wiznae very good,' and her maw said, 'Fuck off, then, yer nae daughter o' mine,' and Nicola said, 'Fair enough.' Maybe Ah never was, she thought as she left. And then the most mental thing happened. The thing that amazed her most of all.

Nicola started running.

She felt a right fucking baton the first time she tried it. Felt like everybody was looking at her, so she did. And she didnae get very far. About as far as Dumbarton Road and back before she was coughing and wheezing and sweating like a paedo in a creche. But Haslam – well, it was Janet by this point, and she was awright as it turned out – was pure impressed when she told her about it. Aw that dead encouraging way. So she kept at it and, by the end o' last summer, she was doing three or four miles most days. She'd go from the flat down to the Clyde and along the river as far as the Hydro and back. And see the feeling you got after? When you were in the shower, aw pure mad wi' they endorphins an aw that? Magic, so it wiz. Janet had also said – well, 'suggested' she'd have called it – that Nicola should confront some of her problems with Jada. And she'd done it. She'd got Alison to take Jayden for the day and she'd been sitting waiting at the kitchen table when Jada got up and stumbled out of bed at lunchtime. She'd been dead calm as she said her piece. She wasn't asking for much. They were all to have their tea together most nights and she wanted a decent allowance every week for the big food shop, and he was to drive her there. Every Saturday. And she wanted time to herself every week an aw. Just a few hours a couple of times a week he was to look after Jayden. For the next year or so until he started the school. 'Away tae fuck wi' this pish,' Jada had begun. 'Fine, then,' Nicola said. She told him she was gaunnae leave. She was taking Jayden and they'd go and live wi' Alison until she sorted something out. She'd get herself a wee job or something and get on to the council about a flat and whatever. As aw this was coming out of her mouth, Nicola couldn't quite believe she was saying it, but it was easy. She just sat there with her cup o' tea and her clear skin and clear eyes and she didn't shout or anything, and maybe it was something about this calmness that got to Jada, that scared him even. Because he shat his pants. He backed right down and said, 'Aye, aye, fuck sake, awright, doll.' And, yes, there'd been some slips and a few rows, it wiznae perfect, but it was better. He did take the wean two afternoons a week. And he was home at five for his dinner most nights. And every single Saturday they drove to the Aldi and – while he did moan about the bill and all the fresh fruit and vegetables and could they no just get frozen pizzas – they did the big shop together and then had their lunch in the café.

This morning she'd gone out for her run dead early, just after five, leaving Jayden and Jada both sleeping, and she was coming along the river, pure tearing it up, and then she stopped, panting, hands on her hips. Because the sun was coming up right in front of her, away in the east, on the other side of the city, away over the Kingston Bridge, and it was aw golden and peach and the river was dead flat and calm, and there wiznae a soul around for miles and Nicola laughed. Just laughed out loud because it was amazing. She felt amazing. And she was looking forward to getting back to the flat and seeing the wee man and even him, the big, snoring midden, and having a wee cup o' coffee and a roll and bacon and then they'd maybe go out for a walk. And twenty-three-year-old Nicola McGovern realised something.

She was happy.

What the fuck was all that about?

'No view from the bandstand, Jada!'

And then a shout, a squeal, and Jayden came tearing up behind his dad. He was carrying a long twig and using it to smash the heads off daisies. Three and a half now – a cyclone of mischief and mayhem.

'Hiya, Uncle Dan,' the boy said, slowing as he reached them and peering at the baby. 'Is baby Jean sleepin'?'

'No son, just waking up.'

353

'Oof, yer maw,' Jada said as he eased himself down onto the bench next to Dan.

'That take it out you, auld yin?' Dan said, grinning.

'Away tae f–' Jada stopped, moderated himself to, 'Get it roon ye. Ah had tae carry the boy half the way so Ah did. Should have brought the buggy but he willnae sit in it for mair than five minutes.'

Jean was entranced by Jayden, who had begun running in circles, waving his twig.

'How was your weekend?' Dan asked.

'Ach, ye see it aw, Dan. Working so Ah wiz.'

The salutary effects of the near-death experience . . .

'It was very close,' the doctor had said to Dan, that terrible morning. 'But they're going to make it.' It had taken four times the normal dose of Naloxone to bring Jada back from the brink. But even this hadn't helped Nicola, who had gone into cardiac arrest. 'Ah swear,' Jada had said when Dan visited a few days later, 'Ah thought that was it. Game over.' He explained how he had watched groggily, terrified, across the ICU as the doctors worked with the paddles of the defibrillator, the word 'Clear!' over and over, and then Nicola's tiny feet – about the only part of her that Jada could see – kicking up as the charge went through her one, two, three times. Jada had seen the most terrible sight of all: the lead doctor taking a quick look at the clock on the wall, getting ready to call the time of death, when, on the fourth charge, her heartbeat skittered across the monitor. 'Ah'm no joking, Dan,' Jada said. 'Ah near started greeting.' And then the cry of 'she's breathing' and the surge of relief through the medical team.

As for Dan's culpability, well, it simply never came up. He'd said he'd smoked a wee bit of the brown and drifted off for a while. When he came to, he'd seen Jada and Nicola unconscious and called the ambulance. Reclining in his hospital bed, draining the big bottle of Lucozade Dan had brought, Jada had just said, 'Aye, aw ma fault. It . . . jist felt weak oan that first dunt. Ah upped it too much. Daft bastard so Ah um.' He'd shaken his head, looking across the ward, past the cheerful double amputee opposite, past the chatty terminal cancer guy next to him (Glasgow's poor, who bore neither the universe nor themselves any ill will for washing up here) and out the window into the black night over the city and said, 'Well, that's that done wi'. Never again wi' that shite, Dan.' Jada had asked Dan to bring him some bits from the house and handed over his keys. After filling a carrier bag with pants, bras, T-shirts, toothbrushes and the like, Dan had retrieved the signed documents from the dresser in the bedroom and burned them out on the balcony, the charring, smoking cinders drifting off into the air, floating down over the bins in the back court . . .

'Aye. Anyway. How's Grace?'

'She's fine, Jada. Working away. How's things with you and Nicola?'

'Ach, we're fine. Mad wi' her running.' Aye, she was better than fine. New woman an aw that since the 'accident'. Jada would never have admitted it, of course, but he had properly cranked a log into his fucking pants when she started talking about leaving him. It was like . . . like something had been going on inside him this last couple of years, as he approached fifty. Like, a few months back, him and Jayden were in, Nicola was out for her run, and Big Katrina had knocked on the door, obviously wanting a fucking portion, and there was the time, and fairly recently an aw, when he'd have sat the wee man in front of his cartoons, cranked the volume up, taken her into the other room and fired the message right intae her. Quick hand shandy at the very least. But, naw. He telt her tae get tae fuck. What wiz aw that about? He tried to articulate it for Dan. 'See, Dan, these last few years, Ah don't know, it's mental, but, like, Ah . . . Ah jist don't feel the need tae shovel ma fucking dross into every skank that walks by.' The philosopher cocked an eyebrow. 'Know whit Ah mean?'

Dan smiled and nodded. 'I think it's kind of normal at our age, Jada. The cooling of the blood and all that . . .' Whatever the fuck that meant.

'Here, gie's a wee hold,' Jada said.

Dan passed him Jean, and he bounced her gently on his knee, cooing the usual stuff. 'Who's a wee darling? Eh? Who's the prettiest wee girl? Who's just the belle of the ball?' The baby looked at him with her vast, trusting eyes. Dan smiled. If Grace had been here, such talk would be frowned upon. It wasn't on: praising the girl-child for her physical attributes, the reinforcing of stereotypes. But try explaining that shit to Jada.

Dan tuned into those distant chimes. 'Hey, Jayden,' he called out to the boy, who was running in circles singing some mad song to himself. 'Do you fancy an ice-cream?'

Jayden stopped dead. Looked at Jada. 'Can we, da?'

'Fuck, aye,' Jada said.

'YESSS!'

'Come on, then. My treat,' Dan said.

He took Jean and put her back in her buggy. A little protest, the legs kicking, a whine, until he gave her the blue plastic teething ring and she stuck it in her mouth, working at it with the just-visible tips of the bottom middle incisors, the twinned grains of rice.

The four of them started back down the hill, taking the

path that curved away to their left through the trees towards the middle of the park. Jayden stumble-ran on ahead, whipping at daisies with his stick, Jada following him, the shoulders jutting and pumping like always, as though he was forever walking through a sea of invisible enemies. Dan brought up the rear with the buggy, the sun warm above them now. Ahead of him, Jayden ran faster, his delighted cries carrying back on the clean, spring air.

'Wheeeee!'

He's going to fall, Dan thought. But he didn't. He just kept on running downhill, laughing, his feet a crazy blur, running just for the hell of it, running because he could. Dan walked slowly, taking in the view to the west as they descended. It was all spread out beneath clear skies. From left to right: the art gallery and museum and then the sooty spire of the university, the rooftops of Hillhead, and then, in the distance, the Campsie Fells, not even that far away, so close you could almost touch them, could imagine walking there in a couple of hours.

Like any properly elevated view in Glasgow, it reminded you that it really was a very compact city, a small place where the wildest things happened all the time.